Lover's
Lane

Also by Jill Marie Landis

Summer Moon

Magnolia Creek

Lover's Lane

Jill Marie Landis

BALLANTINE BOOKS • NEW YORK

A Ballantine Book
Published by The Random House Ballantine Publishing Group

www.ballantinebooks.com

Library of Congress Cataloging-in-Publication Data is available upon request from the publisher.

ISBN 0-345-45332-8

Book design by Christine Weathersbee

Manufactured in the United States of America

First Edition: June 2003

1 3 5 7 9 10 8 6 4 2

To Paul Edholm

and

James Schmidt

For answering a whole lot of questions.

Many thanks to you both.

Lover's
Lane

PROLOGUE

March 1997
Borrego Springs,
California

The young woman stared at the well-dressed lawyer across the squalid room. A man in his late forties, he hadn't smiled once since she let him in. Nor had she—not since he'd offered her money for her baby.

Wearing a three-piece suit and monogrammed socks that cost more than she made in tips on a good night, with shoes that dared to shine through a fine layer of Borrego dust, he was as out of place here as filet mignon at a fish fry.

His crisp, spotless business card lay on the arm of the ripped love seat where she waited, mute and terrified, for him to stop talking. Arthur Litton, from the firm of Somebody, Somebody, and Some Other Lawyer, had made the three-hour drive from Long Beach to meet with her—but just now he was brushing at the knee of his suit. A waste of time when a fine coating of sand covered every surface in the room.

Even the mute images of Lucy Ricardo and Ethel Mertz on the television cavorted beneath a dusty haze.

The lawyer's voice was well modulated and cool, betraying no hint of emotion. It made the young woman's skin crawl. She watched his thin lips move, tried to concentrate on the words.

"Now that you've heard the terms, are you willing to accept my clients' offer?"

She opened her mouth, but didn't trust what might come out so she swallowed and tightened her arms around the six-month-old infant in her arms. Her baby boy. Her son.

Her hands shook as she shifted Christopher to her shoulder. That morning she'd dressed him in pale blue sleepers with little brown bears romping over them. She wished it was still early instead of nearly noon—wished she could turn back the clock and start the day over.

"Let me get this straight," she said softly. "You came here to *buy* my baby?"

"That's putting it bluntly. His grandparents want him."

"They expect me to just hand him over and walk away?"

"They're willing to pay a seven-figure settlement for the privilege of raising their only son's child. They want nothing but the best for him and they want things their way."

"You mean they want me out of the way. I'm his *mother*."

"They could file a petition for guardianship."

She didn't know anything about the law but enough to know she didn't want any part of a custody fight—not with her background.

"We're prepared to prove the child will be better off with the Saunders." He paused, pointedly gazed around the room again.

The place looked like a bomb had gone off inside it. Her roommate, Wilt, always said he "wasn't expecting f-ing Martha Stewart, and if people don't like the way I keep house, they can f-ing stop coming over." His old trucking buddies never minded the mess, and since this was Wilt's house, she never insulted him by cleaning.

The living and dining rooms were full of pieces of cast-off furniture. Art supplies were strewn all over—canvases, tubes of paint, rags, and turpentine. A palette of fingerprint smears marred the door frames.

Her own desert landscapes, from her earliest attempts to her latest, were scattered around the room. Smaller pieces hung on one wall in the dining room, just above a battered Early American table.

A moonscape complete with a howling coyote and an eerie silver-blue glow—Wilt's latest passion was painting on black velvet—rested on an easel near the kitchen door.

When the lawyer showed up at the door asking for her, Wilt took cover in the kitchen. Now she heard the sound of ice hitting the bottom of a glass and the freezer door close. She knew that her roommate was close enough to hear every word.

Litton spoke again.

"My clients are certainly in a position to raise the boy the way Richard Saunders would have wanted him raised."

"Rick wanted to marry me. He wanted to raise Christopher *with me*."

"But Richard is dead, isn't he? He's not here to say *what* he did or didn't want."

"I'm Chris' mother. They can't have him, and they can't take him away from me."

"A private investigative firm has started a background search on you." Without even looking at documents, he began listing all the things they'd dug up, reciting them like a litany.

"You were born in Albuquerque, a drug baby whose mother walked out and left you at the hospital. You were raised in a series of foster homes. Social services listed you as a problem child with tendencies to disrupt the environment in every situation in which you were placed. You were charged with shoplifting when you were fourteen and ran away from the last home you were in at seventeen. Six months later, you applied for a California driver's license. You have been openly living with Mr. Walton, a sixty-four-year-old retiree, for four years. . . ."

"We're just *roommates*."

"My clients can make this *extremely* hard on you. The Saunders are very wealthy people with a lot of influence in Southern California. You haven't enough money or connections to fight them."

He leaned forward, as if he had no stake in the outcome of her decision, as if he were speaking from the heart. "If you're smart, you'll take the money."

"But, surely they can't just *buy* my baby. . . ."

Mr. Litton's hand closed around the handle of his briefcase. He paused, then sighed heavily. He stood, looked directly into her eyes. "Take the money and we'll draw up a contract. They will legally adopt the boy. You'll be a very wealthy young woman with your whole life ahead of you."

Anger quickly replaced her initial shock. She shook her head, knowing in her heart that this wasn't right. None of it was what Rick would have wanted for her or for Christopher.

She and Rick Saunders had spent only a month together, but they'd been lovers right from the start. He'd blown into town like a desert dust devil, riding around in a hot, new Porsche, buying up land he planned to develop as soon as he returned from a year in Japan, working for his father's shipping company.

He'd never made her any promises. She'd expected none and never asked for any. It was enough to be with him, to bask in the warmth of a smile that burned bright as a comet in the midnight desert sky.

At the end of a month, Rick left for Japan as planned. She hadn't heard from him again until three weeks ago when he had shown up on the doorstep. That was the day she'd told him that she had given birth to his son.

Once he had laid eyes on Christopher, he shocked her by im-mediately proposing. Deep in her heart, she knew it wasn't out of love, but that Rick wanted to be with his son. He told her that he wanted them to be a family, and she accepted his proposal, hoping that his plans for their son were enough to build a marriage on.

A few days later, Rick drove to Long Beach to break the news about her and Christopher and their plans to his parents. She had been packed and waiting the day Rick was on his way back to Bor-rego to pick them up and take them home, but he never made it.

The Porsche went off the road, and Rick died at the bottom of a ravine amid a twisted tangle of metal and sandstone boulders.

Three days later, while she mourned not only Rick but the end of a dream, the Saunders finally returned her calls, told her they would be holding a private memorial, but that she was not invited. She tried to understand, to make excuses for them. The Saunders didn't know her, they were grieving. Perhaps they blamed her for Rick's death. If he hadn't been on his way to get her . . .

"Rick *wanted* to marry me." She spoke softly, more to reassure herself than anything else. "Just because he's gone, that . . . that doesn't mean I don't want his son. I gave birth to Christopher because I *wanted* him. I intended to raise him by myself before Rick found out our baby even existed. Once he saw Christopher, he wanted us to be a family."

"I'm afraid we only have your word on that." Litton pointedly gazed around the room again. "Do you honestly think he would want his son raised like *this*?" He leveled his cool, emotionless gaze on her. "Perhaps the amount the Saunders are offering isn't enough. If that's the case, I'm sure they'll up the ante."

Christopher stirred. Caroline patted his bottom, juggled him against her shoulder. Fear had crept in to close around her heart, enough fear to give her a burst of courage. She stood and continued to stare up at the lawyer.

"Get out, Mr. Litton."

"If you're smart, you'll reconsider."

"Get *out*."

"You'll be hearing from my clients again. They don't take refusal lightly."

As soon as the door closed on Litton, she sat down, too drained to move. She heard the slap of Wilt's bare feet on the kitchen linoleum before the sound was silenced when he stepped onto the balding shag carpet. His heavy hand, reassuring, solid, soon came to rest on her shoulder.

"Goddamn it to hell." Wilt always had a way of summing things up in as few words as possible.

She couldn't make her mind work. Christopher was fussing, kicking his sturdy legs, tugging at the front of her T-shirt.

"What am I going to do, Wilt?"

"Hell if I know, but whatever you decide, I'm with you."

He cleared the back of the couch, walked around and sat in the lima-bean-green velour chair that Litton had just vacated. A glass of ice water in his hand dripped condensation, forming a moist stain on the arm of the chair. His plaid flannel shirt was rumpled, slept in; his baggy navy-blue sweatpants oozed over the sides of his suntanned bare feet. More gray than blond, a heavy walrus mustache hid his upper lip.

Wilt had been her rock, her savior when he picked her up on the side of Highway 40 in Arizona four years ago. She'd been walking alone, hitching, dazed and confused and too out of it to care what happened to her when he pulled his rig over and offered her a ride. After miles and hours together, he'd opened his home to her, offered to keep her off the streets.

Over the past four years, Wilt had become the grandfather she never knew. One day while he was painting, he gave her a blank canvas, a few hints on blending color and filled a palette with paint for her. He had seen some doodles she'd done on scratch paper and encouraged her to sketch landscapes, recognizing what he called raw talent. Slowly, with his guidance, she learned to paint.

She came to trust him with her life and would trust him with Chris', too. But that afternoon, sitting there amid the dust and the oddly comforting chaos, she had a feeling that even Wilt couldn't help her now.

She waited until late afternoon when he drove down to the fruit stand for grapefruit. She dressed Christopher, packed his diaper bag.

Wilt kept his emergency money in an old Folgers' coffee can in plain sight on a shelf in the kitchen cupboard. He'd shown it to her when she moved in, told her that he was being up front with her and expected the same, even if she was just a kid. He also added that if she ever needed the money for a *real* emergency, she was welcome to it.

As she took the can down off the shelf and pulled off the plastic lid, she figured there probably would never be a bigger emergency in her life and that Wilt would agree.

There was a sizable wad of bills inside the can. She didn't stop to count them, just divided them in two and shoved the rolls deep into the pockets of her jeans.

She grabbed an envelope from some junk mail lying on the cabinet by the phone, found a pencil.

Dear Wilt,

There's nothing I can ever say or do to thank you for what you've done for me. You've treated me better than anyone has in a long time, so it hurts me to repay your kindness by taking your savings stash, but I've thought and thought, and I can't seem to figure out anything else to do but go where the Saunders can't find us.

It'll be easier on you if I don't tell you where I'm going. I'm not real sure where I'll end up, but I can only hope it will be someplace one-tenth as good as what I've had here with you.

Take care of yourself and keep painting. If there ever comes a time in my life when I can pick up a brush to paint again, I'll think of you.

I wish I didn't have to go.

Love,

C.

She set the note beneath the empty coffee can in the middle of the table where he would see it first thing when he walked in.

As she threaded her way through the living room, she purposely avoided looking at all of the paintings she would leave behind. There was a piece of her soul in each and every landscape, a vision in every ghostly shadow figure she'd been inspired to include in all of them.

She'd miss the desert with its ever-changing natural drama as much as she'd miss Wilt, but there was no looking back now.

Holding Christopher close, she took one last glance around the living room before she shut the sliding glass door behind her. She was scared, but she was more frightened of the Saunders than of being alone on the road again.

She had reinvented herself once before. She could do it again.

ONE

Six years later . . .
California Coast

Jake Montgomery left Long Beach before dawn on Thursday morning, leaving town a day early to avoid the weekend traffic headed up the coast. After three hours of driving, the dense population centers thinned and the land unfolded, spread out spring green and inviting. He drove past Santa Maria, cut over to old Highway One and followed the coast through Oceano and Pismo Beach.

As half owner of a private investigative firm he had founded, most of his days were spent not only enduring bumper-to-bumper traffic but L.A. road warriors venting their rage and the crowded, pulsing noise of city life as he gathered minutiae—details that among other things helped solve missing person cases, put an end to lengthy divorce proceedings, helped employers decide whether or not prospective employees had enough integrity to hire or promote.

Today the quiet solitude of the long drive helped ease the coil of tension in his gut, a coil that life in Los Angeles County tended to tighten deftly. This was the kind of getaway that his ex-wife used to talk about taking, but that was eons ago, back when they were still kids and newly married, long before they were consumed with their careers. Before there was no going back and the marriage had ended.

Lost in thought, he missed the turnoff to Twilight Cove. Cursing under his breath, he made a U-turn and followed Alamitos

8

Canyon Road, a two-lane highway that wound down to the ocean alongside a creek of the same name. The gentle slope lined with low-growing chaparral ended abruptly after a sharp curve, and the picturesque town of Twilight Cove appeared suddenly, like a mirage.

The canyon road ended in the heart of a seaside village complete with a central plaza park with an old-fashioned, tiered Spanish fountain in the middle of a wide, grassy bluff overlooking the Pacific.

He slowed, checked out the various shops and stores, noted the location of The Cove Gallery before turning onto Cabrillo Road, which ran parallel to the ocean. Heading north, he found himself winding through residential sections of town, past wooden Craftsman-style houses. Most appeared to have been freshly painted. Many displayed flower boxes overflowing with alyssum, geraniums, and impatiens in delicate hues from white to pink to scarlet.

When he reached the point on the south end of the cove, he pulled into a scenic overlook, killed the engine and set the brake.

The moment he stepped outside his SUV, the onshore breeze kicked up, forcing him to zip his brown leather jacket. He walked to the guardrail. Even with mirrored sunglasses, he had to shield his eyes from the intense sunlight reflecting off the water. He watched distinct lines of swells form peaks offshore and counted six surfers in full wet suits cutting the waves on short boards. Then he turned full circle, taking in the view.

Lazy rolling hills covered in spring green grass and wildflowers tapered down both sides of the canyon to hug the cove. A few homes were scattered here and there on the hillside.

As he looked back toward town with its idyllic Plaza Park and avenue of historic storefronts, he shook his head. The place might look like Mayberry-by-the-Sea, but as long as real people inhabited it, Twilight Cove wasn't as bucolic as it appeared to be. He'd been in the investigative business long enough to know that.

The town still resembled the California dream of a hundred years ago—what so many other beach cities would look like if not for overdevelopment, smog, and too many rats in the maze.

The salt air was tinged with the sea and time. Standing in the cool breeze off the ocean, Jake easily imagined a clipper ship racing under billowing sails, her hold filled with wares to sell to the Spanish dons, Indians, and padres living in the shadow of the missions.

Steep steps and a narrow trail below the bluff led down to the beach. Limited parking and lack of accessibility to the cove kept the town from becoming overrun by seasonal tourists the way Monterey and Carmel were. Twilight Cove's small strand was still pristine. Only the hardy and the surfers didn't mind tackling the steps.

If it hadn't been for obligation and the driving need to see if a hunch would pay off, he would have lingered to inhale the fresh salt air and let the strong breeze whip through his hair and clear his mind. But he wasn't here on vacation. He'd come on what just might prove to be a wild-goose chase, but he was more than willing to risk taking the time if it meant finally winding up a case that had been open far too long.

He'd driven to Twilight Cove because he was a man of detail who hated loose ends, but most of all, he had come because of a personal obligation. He'd come to Twilight out of duty to a friend long gone, a friend as alive as ever in his memory.

The Cove Gallery was exactly as it appeared in the photos he'd seen in the *Budget Traveler* magazine. Uncluttered and open, with glossy golden oak floors and white walls, the interior was the perfect backdrop for the artwork displayed on the walls and free-form sculptures on platforms scattered around the room.

Jake had no sooner cleared the threshold when a slim young man sporting an artfully trimmed, pencil-thin beard along his jawline started across the room to greet him. He wore wire-framed glasses and was dressed entirely in black.

Geoffrey Wilson introduced himself, extended his hand in greeting, his smile both wide and genuine.

Jake shook hands. "My name's Jake Montgomery." He reached into his back pocket, pulled out a folded page carefully torn from a magazine, opened it. "I saw this article on your gallery in *Budget Traveler.*"

The article stated that Geoff Wilson was twenty-nine years old, had moved west from Chicago three years ago after having grown tired of the brutal winters in the Windy City. The gallery had been open for a year and showcased local talent.

"Wonderful! I'm glad you stopped by. Go ahead and have a look around," Wilson invited.

"Actually," Jake pointed to the page that showed a photo of Wilson standing in front of a painting. "I'm interested in the piece on the wall behind you in this photograph. The sunset seascape with the transparent figures in the foreground."

"An excellent choice, but I sold that a month ago."

"Who's the artist?"

"A local. Carly Nolan. Cove Gallery handles her work exclusively. She's one *very* talented lady." He started moving toward the far corner of the room. "Carly brought in a new painting just last weekend. I'm sure you'll find it equally stunning."

"So, she lives around here?"

Wilson paused, as if assessing Jake's character for a second. "She lives nearby, yes."

Jake followed him across the room, their even footsteps echoing in unison on the bare wood floor. The painting on the wall was of good size with a weathered frame that added to the tone of the piece.

The painting showed the huge dark boulders that ringed the cove and hugged the bluffs as violent storm waves crashed over them. The sky was gun-metal gray, dark and forbidding as the ocean. There were no buildings, no town above the cove, just wild grasses and two ragged junipers battered by the wind.

The artist had depicted a ghostly image of a young woman dressed in the style of the early 1800s standing at the edge of the bluff overlooking the water. Entirely painted in a sheer white, as if transposed over the painting, the woman stood with the fingers of one hand clenching the fabric of her long, flowing skirt. In the other hand she held a hat as if she had forgotten it was there. Long ribbons streamed over the brim, rippling just above the ground. Her hair was unbound, in wild disarray.

She was tall and lithe but her features were as subtly depicted as the rest of her, almost as if the artist wanted the viewer to wonder if there was actually a woman in the painting at all.

She could have been beautiful, or perhaps not. The artist left it up to the viewer to decide.

"This oil is of Twilight Cove from a different angle, one of the most dramatic pieces Ms. Nolan has done to date. Any work that showcases the cove tends to sell quickly. Visitors are so impressed by the beauty of this place that they want to take home a memory that will last a lifetime." Wilson rolled up onto his toes, settled back on his heels and smiled. "Not to mention the good investment that original oils become."

The Nolan piece was appealing in a haunting, ethereal way. Staring into the waves on the canvas was almost as hypnotic as watching the ocean. Not only that, but Jake found himself haunted by questions. Why was the young woman alone? Why had she gone to the edge of the bluff during a storm?

Except for a change of weather and time, it was a perfect rendition of the view he'd seen from the scenic viewpoint.

A label on the wall beside the painting listed the title as "Waiting." The price was more than adequate for a local unknown. The name Carly Nolan was printed neatly beneath the title.

"This one's a little dramatic for my taste," Jake said. "Do you have anything else she's done?"

Wilson's smile luffed at the corner like a sail losing wind. "Not at the moment. Are you staying in town or just passing through?"

"I was planning on staying until Monday, if I can find a place."

Geoff leaned forward conspiratorially. "Luckily it's the off-season. I can call a fine B and B right here in town."

"That'd be great."

Jake followed him to the counter to pick up a business card. Wilson picked up the phone and punched in a number. He held his hand over the mouthpiece and whispered, "This is a *wonderful* place. *So romantic.*"

Within two minutes Jake had a room reserved at the Rose Cottage a few blocks away. Geoff Wilson made a sticky note to himself with Jake's name on it with the reference—Nolan painting—and pressed it against the back of the counter.

Jake noticed a couple of tall baskets sitting near the cash register. One was stuffed with Chamber of Commerce maps. The other was filled with five-by-seven-inch cards printed with bios of the gallery's featured artists. Flipping through, he realized that all but Carly Nolan's biocard showed photographs of the artists.

He picked one up and read the scant information.

Carly Nolan is a local artist new upon the scene. Her haunting paintings of Twilight Cove and the surrounding landscape peopled with ghostly figures from California's colorful past are quickly becoming favorites of collectors up and down the coast. Primarily working in oils, she has captured life in the very early days of the area using her own unique vision of color, style, and imagination.

"Please, take one," Geoff urged. "Actually, if you'd like to meet her, Carly may be working here this evening. I'll tell her you might drop by."

"Really?" Jake looked down at the card, at the blank spot where the artist's photo should be, and wondered if he'd hit pay dirt.

It was his partner, Kat Vargas, who'd found the article in *Budget Traveler*, not him. The painting in the background of the photo had reminded her of a small oil hanging on the wall above his desk.

Noting the similarities, Kat tore out the article, brought it in and slapped it on the desk in front of him. Then she had folded her arms, cocked her head, and asked, "Think it could be her? Your Obsession?"

Jake pulled his thoughts back, quickly thanked Geoff, adding that he wasn't certain he'd get by tonight but that he'd be in touch either way.

Before he left, he picked up a map as he turned to go and shoved both the biocard and map into the pocket of his brown leather jacket.

He had justified the drive up here by telling himself that he hadn't had a weekend off in so long that he couldn't remember when. But technically, this wasn't exactly a weekend off.

He was here on the off chance that Caroline Graham had finally slipped up. After six years, the young woman who seemed to have fallen off the face of the earth might have reappeared.

It was a long shot. In fact, it was downright ridiculous to think there might be only one artist using the same technique, but if Caroline Graham *had* surfaced, if she were still painting and now calling herself Carly Nolan, then he might have stumbled onto a woman who had managed to elude one of the top investigative firms in Southern California for years.

TWO

If there was one thing Carly Nolan could do with her eyes closed it was wait tables. She'd been at it off and on since she was fifteen.

"Miss?"

She put a smile on her face and walked over to the booth near the window where a couple of well-dressed tourists stared at the $4.99 breakfast specials she'd set before them two seconds ago.

They weren't happy. She knew the minute they'd parked their sleek new Jaguar out front that they wouldn't be satisfied with anything at Plaza Diner. Their type usually drove straight through on the way to Carmel.

"Do you need something else? Ketchup? Salsa?" Patience was not a virtue. It was a trick of the trade.

The man in his sixties wore a cream-colored sweater draped around his shoulders. He stared at the stack of whole wheat toast triangles oozing butter as if they'd just crawled out of an alien mother ship.

"I *specifically* asked for dry toast," he reminded her.

She reached for the plate of toast. "Sorry about that. I'll get you another order." She hadn't taken two steps before he halted her in her tracks.

"Excuse me? Miss?"

She swung around. Smiled. Again. "Yes?"

"Did the cook use milk in these scrambled eggs? I specifically asked that he use water."

"I wrote it down, so I'm sure he did." Carly continued to smile as she pictured herself turning the stack of toast upside down on the man's carefully styled white hair.

"Just eat it, Frankie." The man's wife barely looked up as she quickly peppered her own scrambled eggs and took a sip of her

15

coffee. She smiled apologetically when her husband lifted the eggs with his fork to peer beneath them.

Carly carried the stack of toast to the wide window behind the counter that separated the kitchen from the main room of the diner. Glasses, the coffee machines, an old mint green malt and shake blender, along with green salad fixings were lined up beneath it. She set the toast down on the ledge beneath the chrome order wheel.

"Dry stack, Joe." She winked at José Caron. In his early sixties, broad shouldered and still devilishly handsome despite the pounds he'd added with age, Joe had been manning the grill at the Plaza Diner since before Carly was born.

"Sure thing." He winked back before he grabbed the stack and daubed each piece of toast with a paper towel and a flourish. Local legend had it that he was once a matador of some renown in Tijuana.

While Carly was waiting, she tallied the couple's check. Before she snapped the vinyl order pad closed, she smiled at the photo of her son taped inside, a shot taken in his new Stingray T-ball T-shirt. The sight of his sunny, innocent smile, the endearing gap where one of his front teeth was missing, and his sparkling blue eyes was enough to remind her why she never missed a day of work. Looking at the photo helped her muster the energy to deal with the monotonous demands of waitressing for $5.25 an hour plus tips. Not that tips were huge in a diner like this.

All things considered, Chris was a happy, well-adjusted little guy, and she was bound and determined to keep him that way. She wanted to raise him right, do things according to the book so that he'd never experience anything like the dark years of her own childhood. The thought of Christopher doing half the things she'd done scared her to death.

While traffic was slow, she busied herself filling the salt and pepper shakers, checking the ketchup and mustard bottles, and readying the salad station before the lunch crowd arrived.

There was nothing fancy about the Plaza Diner. The menu was extensive, the portions plentiful. Fish tacos were Joe's specialty, and on weeknights they sold plenty of take-out meatloaf and baked herb chicken with garlic mashed potatoes to people too tired or too lazy to cook after a hard day's work inland and the drive home through the canyon.

As she wiped down the counter and straightened the plastic-coated menus in their chrome holders, the tourist couple got up to leave.

Carly called out thanks, walked over to the table, picked up the check and the cash they'd left behind.

In a month the town would be packed with hundreds like them, the diner bustling with tourists sightseeing their way up and down the coast. Twilight Cove came alive in the summer when the town rolled out the red carpet for visitors from all over the world for a few weeks. By late October, Twilight settled back into the quiet peacefulness she'd come to cherish.

The phone rang, and Joe waved her over to the window.

"For you." He handed it over, mouthing the word Geoff. She might have known. Unless there had been an emergency at the school, Geoff was the only one besides her next-door neighbor, Etta Schwartz, who would ever call her here.

"Hey. What's up?" She smiled genuinely at the sound of Geoff's voice.

"Can you work this evening from four-thirty to eight-thirty? An old friend of mine just phoned. He's coming through town, and I invited him to stay at my place and *promised* to make my famous *paella*."

"I think so. I'll ask Tracy to take Chris to Etta's after T-ball practice. You have to swear you'll be in by eight-thirty to close up, though."

"Cross my heart."

"Okay. I'll do it."

"Perfect."

"See you at four-fifteen." She handed the phone back to Joe. His liquid dark eyes caught and held hers.

"You keep too much to yourself. You need to get out more, *chica*. I don't mean by just helping out at the gallery, either. It's not good for a young woman to be alone." He leaned close to the window and whispered, "You need a sex life. I watch *Sex and the City*. I know these things."

Her face heated up to her hairline. "I'm hardly alone, Joe."

"A son doesn't count. You need someone *especial*. Someone who stirs the blood and brings the roses to your cheeks and the sparkle to your eyes."

"Are you hitting on me or trying to tell me I need to wear more makeup?"

He laughed, shook his head. "Not only am I too old for you, but you know that I lost my heart years ago." He sighed, shrugged with resignation, and gazed across the room at Selma Gibbs, owner of the diner, as she took an order from a man in a window booth.

Joe sighed. "Ah, Selma. The love of my life. She still refuses to marry me."

"She said you've had more loves of your life than she can count."

"But then, so has she."

Unlike Carly, Selma Gibbs was completely open about her illustrious past. Before she bought the diner in Twilight, she spent her youth managing a truck stop in the middle of the desert—a place she called an oasis between Los Angeles and Arizona. She knew all the truckers by name as well as in a biblical sense and managed to see they were served up anything they ordered, from hot apple pie to a quickie in their cabs.

Carly left Joe, turned around and saw Rand Campbell, resplendent in one of a quiver of Hawaiian print shirts, seated on a stool at the long counter. The local surfer claimed a couple of championship trophies from the eighties and now owned the Wind and Wave Sport Shop down the street. Rand never bothered to grab a menu.

Carly flipped open her order book.

"What'll you have today, Rand?"

"Outside of you agreeing to go into San Luis Obispo for a movie and dinner, not much. But how about a tuna melt?"

"You got it."

"And the movie and dinner?"

"Still no deal."

Behind the window, Joe slammed pots together, his own way of making his opinion known. Carly hid a smile.

"Why is it the prettiest single woman in town is still unavailable?" Elbows on the counter, Rand propped his chin in his hands and stared up at her.

"Let's just say I've got all I can handle right now without adding the complication of a relationship." She'd dated him a handful of times, but there were no sparks.

Sometimes, in low, lonely moments, she had asked herself what would be the harm in a casual relationship with someone like Rand, someone well established in Twilight? Maybe she'd open her heart again when the right man came along.

But dating someone might eventually lead to intimacy, and once a relationship got started, there would come a point where she'd have to be completely open and honest, if it were to last.

As she walked away from the counter, she glanced back at Rand. He certainly was a nice guy. Good looking, too. He wasn't a deep thinker, but his heart was in the right place.

The answer, plain and simple, was that even with his good nature, curly, sun-streaked hair, and perpetual tan, Rand Campbell didn't excite her enough to risk losing everything.

THREE

The lower half of the front window of Potter A#1 Realty was covered with photographs and descriptions of summer rentals, from rooms to cottages to a few larger, secluded homes overlooking the cove.

Standing on the sidewalk out front, Carly spotted Tracy Potter seated inside at her massive desk. Carly waved through the window, opened the door, and walked in. A bell chimed as she crossed the threshold. Soothing New Age Muzak worked its magic as Carly waited while Tracy finished the call.

Wearing a headset and talking into the mouthpiece as she shuffled through a stack of listings, Tracy flashed Carly a wide, perfect smile.

Barely forty, Tracy Potter moved and spoke with efficiency and charm. The petite, quintessential California blonde wore a creamy two-piece linen suit. Her shining hair, drawn back off of her face with a black headband, was cut in a shoulder-length pageboy.

Carly would bet good money that Tracy hadn't changed her hairstyle since high school, but it still worked. The woman had the electric aura of an old cheerleader, the kind of sunny disposition that never seemed to fade. The suit, the posture, the poise and deftness with which Tracy handled the caller on the other end of the line reminded Carly of everything she wasn't and never had been.

Not that she was uncomfortable with who she had become. Her uniform was casual and suited her—a Plaza Diner T-shirt, jeans, and sweatshirts like the pale pink one she'd pulled on when she left work. She hadn't cut her hair in years, nor did she wear much makeup.

When she was a freshman, her high school counselor told her that she had the grades and intelligence to be anything she wanted.

All she had cared about back then was escaping the memories of her bleak childhood, even if it meant using marijuana and alcohol as a way out. Life hadn't always been kind. At eleven, fate had thrust her into the foster care system, forced her to make some tough choices and stick by them.

She wasn't the kind to look back at her life and ask, "What if?" Regret was just a waste of time.

Tracy ended the call, slipped off the headset, and set it on a desk covered in neat stacks of papers, rental flyers and notebooks, a glass vase filled with cobalt-blue marbles and lucky bamboo. She tipped back the seat of her ergonomic chair and stretched before she stood up.

"What a day! The phone hasn't stopped ringing."

"Sounds like it'll be a good summer." Carly tried to stuff an escaped hunk of her ponytail back into the gathered black scrunchie.

"I hope so. How *are* you, Carly?" Tracy came around the desk, greeting her as warmly as she would any important client. To their credit, both the Potters genuinely liked people. There wasn't a phony bone in their bodies.

Glenn and Tracy Potter would have been well known in Twilight Cove even if their photographs weren't plastered on complimentary memo pads and calendars in use all over town. As perfect as Ken and Barbie, they volunteered at Seaweed Week, the annual town festival in July, served on both the PTA board and the Chamber of Commerce. Glenn even coached the boys' T-ball team.

"I'm great. How about you and Glenn?"

"*Wonderful.* What brings you by?"

If anything was wrong, Tracy would never admit it. So life always seemed to be *wonderful* for Glenn and Tracy Potter.

"Geoff needs me at the gallery for a while tonight. I was wondering if you'd drive Christopher home after practice and drop him off at Mrs. Schwartz's?"

"How about if I feed him first?"

"I can ask Etta to warm something up for him." Carly hated owing anyone favors, especially when she always feared she might not be around to pay them back.

Although she hated to do it, she'd had to leave Christopher in someone else's care in order to work, but outside of Etta Schwartz, the elderly woman who had rented them a room in her mobile home when Carly first arrived in town, and occasionally the Potters, she never left Christopher with anyone else.

Tracy's hand went up like a traffic cop's. "It's not an imposition, believe me. Matt would love having him over for dinner. We're just having pizza anyway. I'm not cooking."

Carly thought of all the times the Potters had invited Christopher on outings or to sleepovers, and she had turned them down. She simply wasn't comfortable letting her boy out of her sight.

No matter how safe she and Christopher were now, no matter how carefully she had built a new life for them here in Twilight Cove, she never let go of the fear that he might be taken from her without warning. She'd learned early in life that people could be a part of your life one day and gone forever the next.

She made it a point to tell him how precious he was to her and how she wanted to be with him more than anyone in the whole world.

Words she had longed to hear as a child.

Despite her fears, she knew that she couldn't keep Chris tied to her forever. Carly took a deep breath, looked at the clear blue sky outside the wide front window and the familiar landmarks outside—Plaza Park, the shops and stores lining Cabrillo Road.

Twilight had been their home for three years now. Christopher was happy here. She had finally done what she had set out to do, slipped into quiet anonymity in a safe haven, a place where she was free to raise her son as best she could.

"Carly? How about it? Can Chris stay for pizza?"

Carly turned to Tracy and nodded. "Okay. Thanks. I'll tell Etta that you'll drop him by sometime after dinner."

"That's great!" Tracy clapped her hands. As if cued, her page-boy bounced and her megawatt smile intensified. If she'd leapt into the air and executed perfect splits in the middle of the office, it wouldn't have shocked Carly a bit.

"I owe you one." Carly smiled. It was impossible to resist Tracy's charm.

"Payback is hell. . . ." Tracy laughed, cut off when the phone started ringing. She waved good-bye as she slipped on the headset. "Potter A#1 Realty, Tracy Potter speaking. How may I help you?"

Carly stepped outside, reassured that Christopher would be well taken care of and that he'd be waiting next door at Etta's when she finished at the gallery.

She closed the door, instantly reimmersed in the sound of passing cars and music from a steel drum that floated across from the park where a young man with Rastafarian dreadlocks hammered out a reggae beat.

Without warning, she shivered and slowed down. Her gaze was drawn across the street where she caught sight of a man sitting alone at a table in front of Sweetie's Bakery, the only customer taking advantage of the warm spring sunlight spilling over the sidewalk.

Broad shouldered, with hair that glistened blue-black in a stray shaft of sunlight, he wore jeans and a scuffed leather jacket and sat hunkered down over a map spread across the small table. The corners of the map fluttered in the breeze as he clutched a tall paper coffee cup in one hand.

She didn't recognize him as local. Just then, as if he sensed her stare, he suddenly glanced up. Their eyes met—or maybe not—she couldn't tell from this distance. The usual warning bells that she still experienced at the sight of any interested stranger went off in her head, but this time she couldn't look away and couldn't move on.

He dwarfed the café chair he was seated on. His shoulders were broad, encased in softly worn brown leather.

She watched him for what seemed like an eternity but in reality was only a heartbeat until the man turned his attention back to the map and broke the spell. She watched as he used the cup to anchor one side and then press out the creases with his other hand.

When it appeared he wasn't paying attention to her, her suspicion slowly settled back into the shadowed corner of her heart that it never completely left.

Maybe he hadn't really noticed her at all. Maybe he had just paused to look up, his thoughts elsewhere. Whatever. He was preoccupied with the map again.

There was absolutely nothing to worry about.

She started down the street, breathing easier with every step, convinced there was nothing suspicious about a handsome stranger looking her way.

After all, she was a woman. Men looked at women constantly. They were genetically incapable of *not* looking.

Headed for Christopher's school two blocks away, an old habit born of self-preservation made her pause and look back before she finally turned the corner.

The dark-haired stranger was still at the table sipping coffee, but now he was intently watching Ben, the homeless wino who fed the gulls and pigeons in the park.

FOUR

If a car had jumped the curb and made a drive-thru out of Sweetie's Bakery, Jake wouldn't have taken any harder a hit than he had when he suddenly realized the woman he was searching for was standing right across the street.

At least he *thought* it was her, but since he'd never actually seen Caroline Graham in the flesh, he couldn't be absolutely sure.

Trying to handle a cup of scalding coffee banded with a flimsy corrugated protector, he had stepped out of the small coffee shop with its bright blue awnings and café tables and decided to sit and people watch, to take in the rhythm of the town before he checked into the B and B.

He'd just sat down when he saw her step out of the real estate office across the street. Astounded, he recovered quickly enough to pretend to be absorbed in the Chamber of Commerce map he'd picked up at the gallery.

Just outside the realty office, she paused and looked directly at him. Though he couldn't exactly see into her eyes, he sensed a quick assessment in her stare before she turned and walked off.

Someone who hadn't spent hours memorizing her features might not have recognized her. The one and only photo he had of her was taken almost six years ago. Naturally, she had changed. Now she was calling herself Carly Nolan.

Gone was the close cropped, bleached spiked hair, the line of studs that ringed her earlobe, the heavy liner around her eyes— but the loveliness and promise had blossomed. More than just a hint of what was to be, her natural beauty was now more than apparent.

He almost forgot to breathe when the onshore breeze whipped

her long hair across her eyes and teased the ragged, sun-bleached ponytail hanging past her shoulders.

Denim jeans, an oversized, faded pink sweatshirt and Nike running shoes completed her outfit. The hem of an aqua T-shirt hung below the hem of her sweatshirt.

Though she had changed, he was willing to bet the farm that the woman he was watching was definitely Caroline Graham.

When she turned away, his initial impulse had been to follow at a discreet distance, but lack of cover and fear of panicking her kept him glued to his seat.

This was her town, her home. Unless she suspected something, she wasn't going anywhere.

Jake turned to the map again, kept his eyes lowered and stole surreptitious glances as she continued down the block. He watched her break stride at the corner, knew she was going to stop and look back—exactly what he'd have done in her place.

He sipped his coffee and gazed toward the park as if he had nothing better to do that sunny spring afternoon but enjoy the sound of the waves, the steel-drum reggae music and the warm sun shining down.

He polished off the last thick, dark swill of coffee at the bottom of the cup, not sure if his adrenaline was pumping from too much caffeine or seeing her in the flesh.

He half expected her to step into Cove Gallery as she walked by, but she merely stopped to wave. Noting the time, he scanned the map and assumed that if she *was* Caroline, she might be headed for the grammar school three blocks away.

Jake stood up, deciding to pay a visit to Potter A#1 Realty across the street. Under the guise of being just another tourist interested in a summer rental, he just might find out what Caroline/Carly had been doing there.

He tossed the empty cup into a trash can near the bakery door. The homey, heady scent of cinnamon buns floating on a salt-tinged breeze trailed him across the street.

● ● ●

He stopped to scan two dozen color photos of the rooms and homes available as summer rentals that were evenly spaced and taped inside the window of the real estate office. As soon as he opened the door, a trim blonde with the well-scrubbed look of a Disneyland tour guide and *way* too much perkiness for his taste hurried over to usher him in.

"Hi! I'm Tracy Potter. How can I help you?"

Turn down the wattage. He quickly reminded himself she was only trying to earn a buck and remembered his manners.

"My name's Jake Montgomery. I'm up from the L.A. area and interested in a summer rental."

"Then you've definitely come to the right place. We have the most listings in town."

Since he hadn't seen any other real estate office on the street he figured Potter A#1 had the *only* listings in town, but he didn't call that to her attention.

"What exactly are you looking for?" She wandered behind her desk, picked up a thick three-ringed binder then swiveled her computer monitor in his direction. "I've got a few listings on-line that are still available, and I can give you printed flyers on everything we have open for this summer. Will you be staying a few weeks or a couple of months? I should warn you that this late in the spring, everything's pretty well booked."

He wasn't looking for anything but a connection between the Realtor and Caroline and even wondered if Caroline might be planning to move.

"I'm flexible." He settled into a chair in front of Tracy Potter's wide, well-organized desk.

Flexible. As if. He could just hear his partner, Kat, hooting in his ear. He hadn't been on a real vacation since he'd graduated from college and stopped going on the annual yacht club billfishing tourney to Baja with his granddad. His ex, Marla, had given up nagging about getting out of town after a few years. The amount of time he devoted to his profession had been just one more strike against him in the marriage game.

"Great. I'll pull up the listings we have left. My husband,

Glenn, will be happy to take you around to see them tomorrow morning." She glanced at her Rolex. "I'm afraid I'll be closing up in a few minutes. Our son's T-ball practice is this afternoon."

T-ball. Jake had spent plenty of stolen time sitting on hard park bleachers watching his sister Julie's kids when they played T-ball to know it was for the younger set. Five- and six-year-olds, as far as he could remember.

Kids Caroline Graham's son's age.

"I understand." Jake stood up, checked to make sure the town map was still hanging half out of his pocket, giving him the look of a tourist. "I'm staying at Rose Cottage. Have your husband leave a message, and I'll be ready."

Jake checked into the B and B one street off of the main drag, a comfortable white clapboard cottage surrounded by an English-style garden trimmed with lattice and flooded with roses that his sister would have oohed and ahhed over.

Colin Reynolds, owner and host, greeted him. The silver-haired retiree in a black cable-knit sweater was handsome enough to model for *Modern Maturity.*

Reynolds cheerfully informed him that wine and cheese would be served from five to seven in the living room, so all the guests could meet and chat.

Jake's second-floor corner room had a distant view of the beach, if you stood on your toes and pressed your cheek against the wall. There was enough cabbage rose wallpaper and matching fabric to make his head spin. The spindly legged Victorian furniture scattered around didn't look strong or comfortable enough to suit him, but he figured he wasn't going to waste much time away from L.A. lolling around indoors.

He quickly showered, changed into a pair of slacks and a casual black sweater. Then, to avoid making small talk at happy hour in the living room, he used the time and his cell phone to call Kat at the office.

There was night and day difference between Kat Vargas and

Tracy Potter's phone manners. Kat was clipped and efficient, a no-nonsense, take no prisoners private investigator, five-four in her stocking feet. Born in Hawaii of Hawaiian, Portuguese, and Anglo ancestry, Kat made part of her college tuition dancing the hula and hip-busting Tahitian numbers in a Polynesian review.

In her spare time, Kat had earned a red belt in tae kwon do.

Bright and determined, Kat had convinced him to take her on as his apprentice for the two years experience she needed to qualify for the licensing exam. She'd quickly impressed him with her intuitive investigative skills, so much so that when she passed her test, he asked her to become a partner in his quickly expanding business.

When he lowered himself to the edge of the bed, it melted beneath his weight. A circus of floral pastel pillows threatened to smother him as he tentatively leaned back and tried to stretch out as he listened.

"Your mom called," Kat informed him. "When I told her where you were, she said she forgot that you told her you were leaving. She didn't really need anything, just wanted to say hi."

He could hear Kat rustling through notes on the other end of the line, imagined her in the back office in his two-bedroom condo. He reached for the pen and scratch pad next to the phone on the nightstand, glanced down at the B and B logo. More roses. He jotted the word *Mom*.

Kat moved on. "I got a good lead on the Anderson case today. Haeger and Olson called. They want us to do a background check on a list of candidates they're considering for upper-level positions."

"Great."

"Terry McMahon called. He needs a search and serve on someone in twelve hours. I told him to bite me. He said he might be able to get an extension until Friday, so I told him okay."

"Good."

There was a pause on the end of the line before Kat asked, "So, did you find her?"

"What?"

"You did, didn't you?"

By profession he was a fairly good liar, but Kat's lie detector radar was always on full alert. He didn't want her or anyone else to know he'd found Caroline Graham until he was sure of it himself.

"Sheesh, Jake. If you did, this would put us on the map, you know. This could be *big*. This could be *People* magazine big if we did a press release. Small time investigative firm beats out the big dogs. Wow. You still plan to come back by Monday noon?"

He hesitated a second too long. "Not sure yet."

"Give me a break. You found her, and you're not telling *me*? I'm the one who gave you that gallery article."

"I never said I found her. I may need to hang around until I have something more concrete than a hunch to go on. I'll let you know if and when I'm sure."

"Fine, and if anything important breaks here, I *will* hesitate to call."

"Very funny."

"Is that all?"

"Don't get your panties in a wad, Vargas. When I'm ready to talk, you'll be the first to hear."

FIVE

Carly always found The Cove Gallery a tranquil retreat, especially when traffic was slow and she had the place to herself, like tonight. The cool, austere interior of the gallery was a welcome change from the constant bustle and mingled scents of the diner, like slipping on a warm, comfortable new sweater that fit just right.

Outside the night air was cool and damp but lacked the biting chill of winter. The darkness beyond the wide, uncluttered front windows was comforting. Bathed in the bright light inside the gallery, she felt isolated and alone but not lonely, as if cocooned by the night.

Geoff wanted the lights he'd installed to make the place stand out like a beacon amid the other shops on the street, an art show for locals driving by, as well as an enticement to anyone out strolling.

An artist from Chicago with eclectic tastes and a biting sense of humor, Geoff had begun to eat at the diner nearly every day when he moved to town three years ago.

He saw Selma's Plaza Diner as more than just a local greasy spoon with worn Formica tables and decades-old turquoise, black, and white decor, and he quickly dubbed the place retro, spending hours there before he opened the gallery.

He started sharing his plans with Carly when she showed a genuine interest in his ideas. Geoff Wilson's enthusiasm matched his devotion to art. Familiarizing himself with popular California artists, he pored over design books and other gallery brochures for hours. While Carly refilled his coffee, he coaxed her into sharing her own ideas on style and design.

Whenever the diner was slow, she would sit and chat with him on her break. One day she finally confided in him that she once "dabbled" in art but never admitted to what extent.

She felt safe in establishing a friendship with a man from the other side of the country who had no idea who she was and definitely no interest in her in a sexual way. Their friendship had given her life a boost and allowed her to become part of something she loved and missed.

It was Geoff who had encouraged her to paint again when he showed up one day with a canvas and bag of art supplies and told her to get busy.

Tonight he had left a CD of soft, slow jazz playing. The soothing music filled the room, wrapped around her senses as gently as the night outside hugged the building. It was the kind of night that made her wish she had someone to go home to, made her feel that maybe Joe was right. Sometimes a woman needed more than her kids, needed to feel like a woman and not just a mom.

Carly relaxed on a high barstool behind the counter, leafing through the latest copy of *Architectural Digest* Geoff left out.

A few couples strolled in while walking off dinner, locals she greeted warmly even though they probably had no intention of actually buying anything. They appreciated seeing the new pieces Geoff had acquired, so she let them browse and dream of the day they might somehow be able to invest in a pricey piece of art.

The place was empty again when she smiled over a sticky note tucked into the magazine. In bold marker script Geoff had written, "FABULOUS. FIND FABRIC." He'd even highlighted a headboard upholstered in faux leopard.

She was about to add her opinion on a Post-It and leave it for him to find when the chime over the door signaled another arrival. She set the magazine down, looked up and realized with a jolt that she was staring into the eyes of the very same man she had noticed at Sweetie's that afternoon.

Her heart tripped and then, as it slowly rocked back into place, she chided herself for being ridiculous.

The way he was looking at her made her unconsciously press her palm against the scooped neckline of her wine-colored jersey dress. When she realized her fingers were trembling she dropped her hand and clasped it tight in the other.

She remembered to smile as he walked from the doorway toward Geoff's high, granite sales counter. An embarrassing flush suffused her cheeks as his gaze slowly traveled over her face, down her body and snapped back to her eyes. The distance between them was eaten up by his long, slow stride. He walked like a man who never rushed, but moved with a purpose and a plan. A man on a mission.

His face was tan, with strong features evenly placed. His hair was dark and wavy. Up close, she saw that his eyes were the rich midnight blue of lapis, a color that called to mind ancient jewelry from faraway places with exotic names.

Gone were the casual jeans he'd worn earlier. Tonight he had on pressed khaki slacks and a long-sleeved black sweater shirt that fit him like a glove. His shoulders were wide, his abdomen flat. He was well over six feet tall.

Noticing that he had to be aware of her gaze sliding over him from head to toe, she swallowed, forced herself to meet his eyes. She found them so clear and intense that she was almost convinced that if she looked hard enough she could see the secrets and shadows of his soul.

The truth hit her hard when she realized that she hadn't been this attracted to a man since she had met Christopher's father. Rick Saunders was just as handsome, but he'd been fair with blond hair and blue eyes. Sure of himself and so very charming that he'd swept her off her feet with his first hello. After that it hadn't mattered that what they had between them was only temporary, that they had come from two different worlds or that he would be leaving Borrego in a month.

By now the stranger had reached the desk. His eyes appeared not only deep blue, but also guileless. Everyone had something to hide.

He smiled a slow, easy smile as he held out his hand. She took it automatically and almost closed her eyes. She had expected nothing more than a casual handshake, but the moment her flesh touched his, something akin to lightning jolted her. She nearly jerked her hand away and looked up in shock, but apparently, he hadn't been affected at all.

His touch was warm, reassuring until he said, "Carly Nolan? I'm Jake Montgomery."

The moment he said her name, her radar sounded and she went cold as ice. Shaken, she couldn't pull her hand away or even move.

She swallowed and then asked, "Do I know you?"

"We've never met but I was in earlier and spoke to Geoff. He told me you'd be working tonight. I'm interested in seeing anything you might have done that's comparable to the painting of the sunset over the cove that was pictured in the *Budget Traveler* article."

Slowly, what he said registered. She relaxed, her heart settled down, but she still couldn't respond. He nodded toward the counter.

"There's a Post-It note with my name on it back there. Underneath, by the phone."

She glanced down and sure enough, there it was. Geoff must have been so excited about his intimate soiree that he had forgotten to mention it earlier.

While Jake Montgomery's expression showed nothing more than casual interest, she fought to recover her composure.

"Perhaps I can show you something else," she offered lamely. "We . . . have lots of talented artists on display right now. Once the season starts, things begin to move quickly, and choices become more limited."

"Geoff showed me around a bit earlier, but I'm afraid I had my heart set on one of your sunset seascapes. No one else adds those transparent figures from the past, do they?"

"Not that I know of."

"How did you learn the technique?"

"A friend taught me to paint, but the ghostly images started out as an accident. I didn't know what I was doing when I first used thinned down white paint, but I liked the effect."

For months Geoff had been encouraging her to produce faster, warning her that come summer she would wish she had more pieces to offer. Money was always tight, and on top of rent and utilities, the old, battered Ford station wagon Etta Schwartz had permanently loaned her was going to need a new alternator.

Carly wished she had a sunset piece she could pull out of a hat.

"I'm sorry I don't have any to show you except the piece that's already here." She tried not to sound as disappointed as she felt.

He never took his eyes off her face. "How long have you been painting?"

She paused, glanced at his hands. No wedding ring, but that didn't mean he wasn't married. She tried to avoid his stare, willing herself not to blush. "Not long."

"Your work is quite accomplished for a novice."

She felt herself blush again. "Thank you. Where are you from, Mr. Montgomery?" Uncomfortable with his praise, she attempted to turn the conversation.

"The L.A. area. How about you? Were you born here in Starlight Cove?"

Effortlessly he'd turned the tables back. She hesitated and began straightening the bio cards in the nubby, hand-woven basket on Geoff's desk.

"No. I've only lived here a few years." She sensed his nearness as if he were standing right next to her instead of across the counter, and she turned to fidgeting with the maps beside the cards.

Damn it, Carly, just stand still and smile. Better yet, show him some other paintings. Interest him in a nice, expensive sculpture or something, and make a sale.

It had been centuries since talking to a handsome man had rendered her brain dead, but it almost seemed as if they had some kind of a connection, as if she already knew him. But that was impossible. She found herself wanting to know everything there was to know about him and more, wanted him to linger so that she could spend more time with him.

As an awkward silence stretched, she continued to fidget while he seemed perfectly content to stand and stare.

She hoped it would be a while before Geoff was due in to close up and she glanced down at her watch, a utilitarian waterproof piece with a black polyurethane band. Rand had assured her it was the very latest and yet least expensive of all the rad surf wear time-pieces. She had never been the least worried about style. She bought it for its ability to keep good time and for its durability.

Jake Montgomery shoved his hands in his pockets and walked to the center of the room to get a closer look at a bronze sculpture.

Carly smiled and waited, and in a moment he quickly stepped back from the piece. Most people did, the minute they realized the free-form nude was complete with both female breasts and a penis.

"Interesting." He shook his head. "Not very practical, though." He pointed to the erect penis. "Unless you could use that for a coat hook."

She bit her lips to keep from laughing. "How long will you be in town?"

"I'm not sure. I inquired about a long-term rental today. I guess it will depend on what Glenn Potter shows me tomorrow. I haven't really decided how often I can get away from my business down in the L.A. area."

His mention of the Potters put her somewhat at ease, at least until a slow, uneven smile lit his face and her heart-skipped a beat. She cleared her throat, tried to keep her tone light and even, to find out about him without seeming pushy.

"What kind of business are you in?"

He shifted his stance before he said, "Consulting. I'm growing a client list. Started my own business a few years ago."

"Have you walked down to the cove yet?"

"No, but I saw it from the scenic pullout at the south end of town."

"That's one of my favorite views."

They wandered around the gallery and although he pointed out another painting that he said ran more to his sister's taste, he made no mention of a wife.

Despite the fact that he was a stranger and maybe too charming to be true, Carly found herself settling into an easy exchange of conversation, lured by a growing fascination in Jake Montgomery as much as the honesty in his eyes.

The whole time they talked, Carly remained wary of nurturing her fascination. Getting close to someone meant forging bonds, opening your heart and soul. Secrets could seep out of the cracks of the most carefully constructed fortresses, no matter how securely they had been sealed.

Standing beside Carly, Jake was reminded again of how the old photograph he had always carried hadn't come close to capturing her true essence.

Now, in person, he found her softer, more vulnerable than he ever imagined. Her aura of innocence was so seductive that whenever he looked into her eyes, a gentle warmth suffused him, one akin to summer sunlight, warm spring rains. It was almost impossible to remember that she had been cunning enough to elude the best investigative firm in Southern California, that she was on the run because she no doubt had something to hide. Innocent people didn't run.

Her trail had gone cold six years ago.

He mentioned his sister, Julie, trying to make himself more human, to put her at ease. Mesmerized, he studied Carly's graceful movements, listened to the lilting sound of her voice as she complimented other local artists on display and the merits of their work. He stared as long as he dared—snatches of too-short heartbeats—into her unusual light-green eyes. They were the same fleeting, backlit color of the crest of a wave just before it curled.

She looked younger than twenty-nine. Her hands were smooth, her fingers long and tapered. Her nails evenly trimmed and bare of polish. The dress she had chosen was classic yet plain, a long-sleeved knit that looked soft as an old T-shirt. Her silky hair fell free and golden around her shoulders, tempting him to touch. The only jewelry she wore was a pair of tiny silver shells in her pierced ears.

By the time they completed a tour of the gallery, he knew he should leave, but he was half afraid that if he took his eyes off of her, she would disappear.

They stood awkwardly in the center of the expansive space while the soothing sounds of a jazz saxophone filled the air. Outside a thin layer of fog had wandered up the cliffs from the ocean to bathe the streets in a soft cloud of mist.

"I'll tell Geoff that you stopped by again," she offered.

"Thanks. Maybe he'll persuade you to finish a sunset seascape for me."

There was only a hint of a smile on her lips now, but she was far more relaxed than when he first walked in.

Jake told her good-bye, turned to go and actually made it a few steps before he was compelled to turn around, to look back.

Warning bells went off in his head like heavy-duty home security alarms—the type that sounded worth the money but usually only ended up shattering homeowners' nerves with false alarms. The kind that never stopped hardened criminals.

"Would you have dinner with me Saturday night?"

The light in her marvelous, soft green eyes instantly flared and for a second he thought she was going to accept.

"I'm sorry. I can't." Her response was a swift, no-nonsense refusal, as if she'd repeated it a thousand times.

"Okay. I get the picture." He turned around again, stopped when he heard her say, "I . . . I work Saturday nights. When I'm home, I like to spend my time with my son."

Jake walked back to the counter. "I didn't realize you had a family."

"I don't . . . I mean, I'm not married. I just have my boy. Are you married?"

"What?" He wondered if he really looked like that much of a slimeball to her.

"Lots of men come through town and ask me out. If I did date, it wouldn't be a married man."

"I'm divorced." The minute he'd said the word the light in her eyes shifted. She actually looked sorry for him. He didn't need or want her pity. "What about you?"

"I . . . my son's father died."

"I'm sorry." God forgive him, but in that instant, he found himself wondering what might have happened if Rick had lived and realized he would have met and gotten to know this woman in an entirely different way.

A heavy silence had taken root and was growing. She was watching him with a touch of wariness again.

"How old is your son?"

"He'll be in first grade next year."

Had she smoothly avoided mentioning the boy's exact age on purpose?

"Must be tough raising him alone."

"I'm not the only single mom in the world. We manage." She shrugged, but her eyes continued to search his.

"My sister has three kids," he volunteered, hoping somehow she would see them as kindred spirits. As if mentioning Julie's kids might prove that he was one of the good guys. Someone's uncle. A brother.

"Is she single?"

He hit another pothole. "No, actually, she's happily married."

Carly looked thoughtful. "That's nice to hear for a change."

He warned himself not to push. He needed to shut up and leave.

"Well, I guess I ought to be heading to the B and B. Good-bye, Carly. It was nice meeting you."

She hesitated before offering her hand, reaching out slowly, as if physical contact was difficult for her.

It was hard for him to imagine that she hadn't accepted an invitation to date someone in the last five years. She was too lovely to be ignored by the men in this or any other town for very long. Surely she'd had a relationship since Rick.

Then again, he hadn't exactly been burning up the sheets since his divorce either. He hadn't been that anxious to jump back into the dating pool after his illusions had been shattered. Finally finding Carly, or rather, Caroline, might have revived emotions that had been in a semi-coma for years, but he wasn't about to go there, even though he knew he'd be thinking of her long after he turned out the lights tonight.

Jake took her hand, pressed it with a slight shake. "I'm glad to have met you, Carly," he said carefully.

"Have a nice stay."

He thought of his room in the B and B with its overabundance of roses and nearly groaned.

"Thanks. I'll try."

Warring emotions tugged Jake in every direction as he left the gallery. All he had to do was pick up the phone. One call. *One* phone call, and his life could change overnight. Kat had been right. This was the stuff of *People* magazine articles. This might even be *L.A. Times* front-page news. He'd done what one of the most prestigious private investigative firms in L.A. had failed to do. He had followed a hunch, played a long shot and found Caroline Graham. He was 99.9 percent sure of it.

Now, having met Caroline Graham, a.k.a. Carly Nolan, face to face, he had more questions than answers. For years he had wanted not only to track her down, but to find out why she had disappeared in the first place.

Mr. and Mrs. Charles Saunders, a wealthy Long Beach couple, heartbroken grandparents, had been the darlings of the local media in the first few weeks after their only son's death as they appealed to the public to help them find their missing grandchild and his mother. Not only that, but the Saunders just happened to be the parents of an old friend of Jake's.

They had wanted the best for their late son's love child, wanted to give him all the advantages of their wealth and power, to make all the dreams they once dreamed for their own son come true. But Caroline had taken the boy and disappeared.

Why *not* let them support her and the boy? It was a question no one had been able to answer because no one had ever found Caroline.

He'd been at it since she first disappeared, and not only because back then he had worked for Alexander and Perry, one of the biggest private investigative firms in Southern California, the firm Charles Saunders hired to find Caroline Graham.

He'd asked to be on the case because he'd known Rick since the summer they were both fifteen, the summer they'd met on the beach in Cabo after the billfishing tourney.

It was 1988. Jake had been with his grandfather, Jackson Montgomery; Rick had come along with his dad, Charles. It was the first year ever Jake had been willing to spend the whole summer with his granddad, and he'd convinced himself that even if he and his grandfather sparred the whole time, the trip down the coast to Mexico would be well worth it.

By the time they'd reached Cabo, he was sure he'd made a big mistake. Not only had his grandfather been at his most pompous and belligerent, but all the other young men had grown up in or on the water in exclusive beach communities. Not so, Jake, and from the beginning they'd made him feel like an outsider—until one afternoon when Charles Saunders had come aboard Jackson Montgomery's sixty-foot Hatteras Sportfisher, bringing his son with him.

At first Jake suspected it had been a mercy visit, that maybe his grandfather had asked Charles and Rick over expressly to get the boys together. After Jake got older, he realized his grandfather would never have thought to do anything of the kind and that the visit had been serendipitous.

While the older men talked, drank tequila, told fishing stories, Jake and Rick had eyed each other with carefully postured teenage disinterest, until out of boredom and a need to escape, Rick asked Jake if he wanted to walk into town with him.

Rick had led him straight to a bar on a back street so full of rowdy college students there was barely room to move between the tables. The music was loud, the crowd raucous, and no one appeared to notice that the boys, both lean and tall and obviously *turistas*, were under the drinking age of eighteen.

They bonded on the beach that night as they barfed their guts out not far from a bonfire surrounded by other young people drinking cold long-neck bottles of Mexican *cervezas* and bellowing Jimmy Buffett lyrics at the moon.

That was a lifetime ago. He was good at what he did now. Damn good. That's why it frustrated him to no end not to have been able to find Caroline and Rick's son. Even after he'd left Armstrong and Perry to start his own P.I. firm in Long Beach, he'd continued to devote time to searching for some clue that would lead him to her.

On a professional level, he was curious to know how and why she had been able to hide her identity for so long. On a personal level, duty drove him to find her for Rick, to make certain Rick's son was being well cared for and above all, to get the truth out of her, to find out why she'd run.

The night mist enfolded Jake as he zipped up his leather jacket and started down the street. He wasn't ready to face the rose-infested room yet, so he let the sound of the ocean draw him toward Plaza Park.

He jaywalked across the street, and looking back, saw her through the wide glass window in the gallery. She was behind the counter near the entrance, her chin propped in one hand as she stared out into the night. He could still recall the fresh, floral scent of her hair, the sound of her voice and wished he could get her out of his head.

Jake crossed the park, walked to the edge of the grassy bluff and looked down at the ocean. The city fathers had thought to add spotlights that illuminated the wooden stairs down the face of the cliff and the rolling surf along the shoreline.

Through the light, misty fog he could make out the foaming white shore break. The crashing sound of the surf as it pounded against the rocks was enticing. Its frothy white foam appeared harmless from a distance, reminding him that some things weren't always as innocent as they appeared.

SIX

*Long Beach,
California*

Anna Saunders was growing used to spending nights alone with
her memories. Surrounded by photos of happier days and times, she
made herself a second gin and tonic, squeezed in a splash of lime and
wandered away from the wet bar in her penthouse condominium.

The Portofino Building stood at the corner of Second Street
and Sorrento on the edge of the waterfront community of Naples.
From a bank of windows and balconies she had a panoramic view of
Alamitos Bay and Bayshore Avenue, the gateway to trendy Second
Street with its specialty shops, restaurants, and beach traffic.

Strolling along Second Street to shop wasn't a pastime Anna
ever did partake in. When she went shopping, she *shopped*, Fashion
Island, South Coast Plaza, Pasadena, Rodeo Drive.

She stepped onto her balcony overlooking the city. From the
top of the Portofino Building she could see the lights of downtown Long Beach, various high-rises—hotels, office buildings, and
condos—tucked into a coastline enhanced by landfill.

Across from the marina, the Queen Mary sat with her well-lit
bright red smokestacks thrust against the night sky. For nearly forty
years the once-proud vessel had been docked beside acres of empty
parking lots, a tourist attraction without thrill rides or mouse-eared
hats that only drew visitors who had run out of more exciting things
to see and do in Southern California.

Around and beyond the Queen stretched the Ports of Long Beach and Los Angeles, home to Saunders Shipping since the early nineteen hundreds.

Anna sipped her cocktail at the balcony railing and watched the sunset over the beautiful city she had called home for more than fifty years. Most of her friends had moved away years ago, part of a migration dubbed "white flight" into Orange County. They had mistakenly believed themselves immune to the growing ethnic diversity as natural to Southern California as the morning haze, Santa Ana winds, and earthquakes.

Long ago she had tired of them asking why she stayed in Long Beach when she could live anywhere in the world. Her reply was always the same, an echo of her husband, Charles', opinion.

"This place is home. The Saunders have always lived where they could see the port."

Together, heartbroken and in shock, she and Charles had spread their son Rick's ashes in the waters off the port. Four years later, alone, still grieving, she had done the same for Charles. There was no way she would leave them both now.

When the red-orange, smog-tinted sky finally faded to deepening lilac, she turned her back on the view and wandered inside. Without the television or the stereo playing, the penthouse echoed with silence.

Until Rick died she had always imagined spending her latter years surrounded by her grandchildren who, if not actually fond of her, would at least pretend to be in order to collect on their inheritance.

Now she had no grandchild to pamper and spoil because Caroline Graham had stolen the privilege and broken not only her heart but Charles's as well.

She walked to a low credenza, picked up a silver-framed snapshot of Rick proudly holding his infant son, Christopher, the only photo she had of her grandson. After all these years it was almost impossible to believe she'd lost them both.

Rick had possessed such charisma, such vitality that it was still hard to imagine him gone. Always lighthearted, he'd also inherited a stubborn streak tough as Charles', though he was very much like her own grandfather in looks and temperament. The only difference was that Michael Riley had been an Irish bootlegger who had never made an honest dollar in his life.

She and Charles had spoiled Rick rotten, given him too much money and the freedom to do whatever he wanted. As a result, they thought he would never settle down.

Then out of the blue, one day when he was twenty-eight and had just returned from Japan where he had been overseeing a branch of Saunders Shipping, he shocked them with the announcement that he was going to marry.

Then he proceeded to explain that he'd had an affair with some waitress in the desert, a young woman who had given birth to his child. He had been determined to marry her.

Looking back now, she wished Charles hadn't been so furious with him, wished that she had listened more and objected less, but she couldn't bear the thought of him throwing his life away over some wretched creature who had obviously set out to trap him.

He showed them some snapshots he'd taken of the girl and the baby, insisted she and Charles look at the photos. She'd only taken a fleeting glance at the child's mother. One quick look told her that the girl was nothing more than a cheap slut with short, yellow, spiked hair, made up like a hooker.

Charles had immediately blown his top. Before Rick had stormed out, he demanded they "get with the program" because he was bound and determined to marry the girl no matter what his father said.

Anna rubbed her thumb over the glass in the picture frame. She'd never laid eyes on the baby. All she had was this one fading photo of Rick and the boy that he had tossed on the table the morning he'd left home to drive out to Borrego Springs to pick up Caroline Graham and her baby and bring them home.

After Rick died, Charles offered to pay the girl almost any sum she could name for Christopher, but Caroline disappeared.

Charles became obsessed with getting Christopher back. His determination to find the boy drove him right up to the end of his life, kept him alive months longer than the doctors had predicted when he was first diagnosed with cancer. His anger and frustration ate at him as voraciously as his disease, and even as he lay dying, he made her promise that she would never give up, that she'd find Christopher and bring him home.

When she thought of what might be happening to that poor little boy, her blood ran cold. It was far too easy to imagine Caroline Graham moving from one seedy motel to the next, living hand to mouth. Anna would never understand why a young woman with nothing to lose and everything to gain had turned down their more-than-generous offer in the first place.

For a long time, Charles had hoped Caroline would get hungry and desperate and contact them. Anna suspected the girl had probably snared another wealthy man and was no doubt married and living under another name. That might explain her complete disappearance.

Not even Alexander and Perry, the well-touted and highly regarded investigative firm that Charles had hired, had ever found a solid lead.

Anna looked down at the crystal tumbler in her hand. Slivers of ice cubes floated in half an inch of gin and tonic. She shook the glass, swallowed the last of the cocktail as she headed down the long hall to a master suite bigger than most apartments.

It was nothing compared to the rooms she and Charles shared in their estate overlooking the bluff on Ocean Boulevard. They had set up a nursery there in expectation of finding Christopher. Blue and white, complete with a crib and a rocker, the decorating had been done by one of Long Beach's top designers.

She had scaled down after Charles died, moved into the penthouse and settled into a steady routine of luncheons and meetings and long lonely nights—a routine that required far more cocktails than her doctor thought she needed.

Even now she continued to do what Charles would have wanted. She had set up a room for the boy here, in the penthouse. It wasn't a nursery, for he wasn't a baby anymore. Red, white, and blue highlighted the nautical theme. Some of Rick's sailing trophies and photos adorned the walls and bookshelves.

There were books waiting for Christopher to read, games for him to play, but there were no toys yet. She knew that just like her son, the boy would have his own wishes. They'd shop for toys together.

She shook her head, sighed. After Charles' death, a terrible second blow, the fight had gone out of her. Assuming they would contact her if and when they had any new leads on Caroline and the boy, it had been months since she had spoken to anyone from Alexander and Perry.

Before Charles' death she had never even written a check to pay a bill, but after the deepest bouts of shock and grief left her, she had sat down with the lawyers and personal accountants Charles had trusted for years and learned all she had to know about how to manage for herself.

She was feeling stronger now, no longer so listless and apathetic. In fact, it frustrated her to think that Charles had been denied the one thing he wanted most—to see Rick's son safe.

If Caroline Graham thought she had gotten away, she was wrong. Anna had made a pledge to Charles, and she refused to give up before she found Christopher.

Setting the sweating tumbler on the marble-topped vanity in the master bath, she began to divest herself of diamond earrings, bracelet, the necklace Charles had given her on their final wedding anniversary.

She undressed, hung up her knit sheath and eased a robe over her silk slip. The cocktail had made her slightly woozy, allowing her to take a fuzzy step back from reality. She brushed her teeth and as she carefully removed her makeup, studied the lines around her mouth and eyes.

When had her skin started to dry up and turn brittle as parchment?

Slipping out of her robe and into a long nightgown, she avoided her reflection. She smoothed the lace over the bodice of her nightgown and suddenly recalled something she'd heard at the symphony fund-raiser this afternoon.

Jackson Montgomery was ailing.

He and Charles had been members of the same yacht club, both avid fishermen who cruised to tourneys off of Cabo every summer for years. Montgomery's grandson, Jake, had been a friend of Rick's and had attended Rick's memorial with his grandfather.

Rick and Jake had spent a few weeks together every summer when Jake was living at the beach with his grandfather, but the boys might just as well have lived on different planets during the school year, for Jake lived across town with his mother and stepfather and attended another high school.

After graduation Rick had gone off to USC. She had no idea where or even if Jake Montgomery had gone on to get a degree, or if one needed a degree of any kind to be a private investigator.

One of the reasons Charles had chosen Alexander and Perry was that Jake had worked for them, but Jake had eventually left the agency to start his own private investigative firm. Though Charles had opted to stay with Alexander and Perry because of their resources and reputation, she always felt that Jake might have worked the case much harder because he had known Rick.

Until she heard Jackson's name today, she hadn't thought of nor had she heard from Jake Montgomery in years, but tomorrow she intended to call the elder Montgomery to inquire about his health and ask if his grandson was still doing investigative work. She'd been paying Alexander and Perry's retainer fees of late and decided they were earning a hell of a lot of money for so few results.

She picked up a plastic prescription container of sleeping pills and fumbled with the tamper-proof lid, tipping the vial until the tablets lay nestled in her palm. The ticking of the crystal clock sitting on the marble counter was amplified by shadows. Anna stared at the medication thinking how nice it would be to go to sleep and never again have to awaken to the knowledge that she had outlived her only child.

She tried to bring the words on the container into focus and remembered that she intended to call Jackson Montgomery in the morning. She had a plan. She had a reason to wake up.

She rolled the pills back into the bottle and set the container down on the counter.

Her bed felt wonderful, if not vast and empty. Lying there in the darkness she prayed, "God, bless Charles and Rick."

She tried to picture Christopher's sweet face as it might look now, but instead she saw Rick as a child. She longed to kiss her grandson, to tuck him in, to hold him tight.

"Dear Lord," she whispered, "bless and keep Christopher safe. Help me bring him home."

She didn't think it was too much to ask after everything she'd been through.

SEVEN

Glenn Potter drove his oversized SUV like he had a death wish.

Jake was thankful that he'd belted himself in when they pulled away from the last rental house Glenn had shown him.

"This next place just came on the market. I haven't even seen it myself." Without taking his eyes off the road, Glenn reached into the backseat of his Land Cruiser, rifled through an open briefcase and finally pulled out a manila folder. The car swerved to the left and started to cross the center line.

They were speeding away from a view home in town. Everything Glenn had shown him had been too large, too pricey, too modern for Jake's taste, even if he did have any intention of renting something for the summer.

So far he had wasted an hour and a half with Potter. They'd talked baseball and investments, but Jake hadn't yet broached the subject of Carly Nolan.

Glenn stuffed the folder in the space between his seat and the center console. As the realtor continued to chat amiably, Jake wondered why in the hell Glenn had put their lives in jeopardy to grab the folder if he wasn't even going to look at it.

"This next place is an old house with quite a history. Seems it was built in the twenties by a silent film star. Craftsman style. Wood frame construction with river rock and shiplap siding. Owned by the same family since it was built." He jerked the wheel to the left to avoid a pothole and put the car in four-wheel drive and passed a sign marked Lover's Lane as they started up a winding, narrow gravel road. They crossed the rolling hillside above the scenic overlook Jake had stopped at yesterday.

"It's been years since any of the family has even come to California. They live back in Massachusetts or New Hampshire or one of those cold New England states. The matriarch recently passed on, and the estate is being settled, which they claim will take months. The family is interested in leasing the house with an option to buy, but they can't give any firm time frame yet."

"Sounds interesting." Jake gripped the armrest and concentrated on the view from Lover's Lane as the car wound its way up the hillside. The panorama of the coastline and the cove below went from stunning to spectacular as they climbed higher. Billowing white sails of boats skimming the water contrasted with the deep green ocean. Nothing other than jet contrails marred the azure sky.

They dipped into an arroyo, took the right fork in the road and passed a derelict wooden no trespassing sign.

A horseshoe-shaped, gravel drive curved back on itself in front of the house. Glenn Potter slid to a stop, exciting a cloud of dust. He set the brake. When the dust finally settled, he took one look at the house and shook his head.

"Wow. I've really wasted your time on this one." He pulled the file out of the crack beside his leather upholstered bucket seat, flipped it open, and made some notes on a long listing sheet tucked inside.

Jake caught a glimpse of a smiling Ken and Barbie headshot of Glenn Potter and his wife imprinted on the upper left corner of the page. He turned away to study the house.

No movie star had crossed the threshold in decades. The place was beyond quaint. He couldn't even call it rustic. No doubt it had passed the "fixer-upper" stage ten years ago.

It was a dump. A tear down.

Jake loved it.

He stepped out of the car and headed for the porch. Craftsman in detail, two boxy stone and wood columns framed the sagging top step of the wide porch. Carefully negotiating holes and dry rot in the steps, he turned around. The view down the hillside to the coast almost took his breath away.

A vision of two rocking chairs positioned to take in the view came to mind. When he found it all too easy to imagine Carly Nolan sitting on one of them, he tried to concentrate on what the porch would look like painted a high-gloss shine.

Glenn was out of the car now, climbing the stairs, shaking his head as he sidestepped a loose board.

"I'm really sorry, Jake. I should have checked this out before I brought you here. I had no idea the place was such a mess."

It was a mess. He was wasting his and Potter's time.

Jake continued to stare at the house. "Can we go inside?"

Glenn's expression went from embarrassment to calculation. A smile slowly replaced his mortification. His hand hit the doorknob. There wasn't a key or the need of one.

"Jeezus." Glenn cleared his throat when the door swung open to reveal the squalor inside.

Jake figured Potter wasn't very often speechless. Taking advantage of the moment, he shoved his hands in the pockets of his Levi's, crossed the threshold and took in the living room. A cheap, hideous rust-and-green shag rug from the seventies. He could date it exactly because he'd had one just like it in his room as a kid. The carpet hid what he suspected were original hardwood floors.

Built-in bookcases flanked a river-rock fireplace. The woodwork around every door and window had been painted but was intact. The room felt spacious, the living area connected to the formal dining room with another large built-in sideboard along one wall. Glass was missing from a few of the panes in the doors, but otherwise the trim was in good condition.

The walls were another matter. The plaster was cracked and in some spots, the lath beneath showed through like skeletal ribs. Shredded wallpaper hung like tattered rags around the room.

The ceilings weren't in much better shape, but the wide heavy beams that divided the rooms were exposed to add detail to the overall feel of the place.

He didn't need to walk into the kitchen to know it was a disaster. The glimpse of worn speckled linoleum said enough. An army of field mice as well as an occasional illegal on the way up the coast had probably used the cupboards.

"How many bedrooms?" Jake started toward a long, narrow hallway.

Glenn flipped open the folder. "Three. Two down and one up." He held his breath before opening the door to the first of two back bedrooms. Rotted draperies hung at the windows. The light streamed through the tatters, illuminating dust motes thick in the air. The same hideous carpet ran wall to wall throughout the house. There was a small, old-fashioned walk-in closet complete with an octagonal window—obviously built when movie stars had smaller wardrobes.

Jake walked to a corner, took hold of the shag, and ripped it away from the carpet tacks. Sure enough, there was hardwood floor beneath.

They walked through all three bedrooms. The largest was upstairs with its own bath. Glenn tried to flush the toilet and groaned when the handle fell off.

An open sundeck, a much later addition by the looks of it, was tacked onto the back of the house. It offered a panoramic view of the hillside and low chaparral growing in the streambed running behind the house.

Jake walked back through the house to the front porch and looked up the coast again.

Glenn caught up and fished his car keys out of his pocket.

"Well, at least I can tell Tracy I've seen it. We certainly can't recommend it to any of our clients until the owners do something with it."

"I'll take it." Four hours from Long Beach, from his family and business, Jake realized what he was about to do was either the smartest or the dumbest thing he'd ever done in his life.

"You *want* it?" Glenn Potter's coffee-colored eyes mushroomed to the size of silver-dollar pancakes. "You want to rent it?"

It was exactly the kind of house Jake's stepfather, Manny Olson, had always dreamed of owning but could never afford. Long Beach was full of old Craftsman homes, many in historically designated neighborhoods. Manny had always talked of buying one and restoring it to its original state.

The fact that this house overlooked the ocean, the idea that absentee owners might be willing to sell quickly for less than the place was worth made it too attractive to simply walk away from.

Jake had adored his step-dad as much as he had his real father. A talented carpenter, Manny had been kind and gentle, a man who had to work so hard on other people's homes that he never had time to fix up his own, let alone make his dream come true.

"I want it." Jake shook his head, barely able to believe what he was saying.

"Mind if I ask *why*?"

Jake shrugged. "My step-dad always wanted to renovate a place like this."

He had no idea when or how Manny's dream had become his own. Maybe it had happened the minute he'd laid eyes on this house. He was just as shocked to discover he might have inherited a touch of his Grandpa Montgomery's business savvy. Not everyone could overlook the terrible state the place was in and see it for what it was—a damn good investment.

He figured all he had to do was lease the house until the owners decided whether or not to sell, come up with the down payment, and make the monthly mortgage. He could always turn around, list it with the Potters as a vacation rental when he was in Long Beach, and block out time for his own visits.

That way he would know that it was here waiting for him, and if things didn't work out, he could always resell it for a profit.

Jake mentally tabulated the amount of money he had in savings and figured it was nowhere near enough for a down payment, not for a place with a killer view like this, even a house in such poor condition. Most buyers would consider the place a tear down and build something sprawling and modern that would encompass all the views.

"I'd like to take the lease with an option to buy, but I want it locked up tight so that the house can't be sold out from under me. I may even be in a position to make an offer after I run some numbers."

He couldn't buy the place outright, but a lack of funds had

never stopped him from going after something he really wanted. He had started his own business on a couple of loans that hadn't amounted to a shoestring, yet he'd managed to grow a business and survive.

Staring out at the horizon, at the blue bands of sea and sky, he decided that if he had to, he would do the one thing he always swore he would never do—ask his grandfather for a loan.

He'd never done anything so spur-of-the-moment before. Back when he and Marla had started dating at sixteen, he'd known from the first that she was the only one for him. It had still taken him five years to propose.

The night their marriage imploded she had accused him of being pedantic and predictable. To her, the assets he'd needed in his business—attention to detail, focus, organization—all added up to boring. In her eyes he was single-minded, never spontaneous. He ran his life on a schedule—had to in order to accomplish everything he needed to.

While he'd been building a business, doing surveillance, running all over hell and gone, interviewing clients, tracking down official documents, appearing as an expert witness in court, his childhood sweetheart had taken a liking to banging the doctor she worked for.

No spontaneity? If she could see him now.

"I've got rental applications in the car," Glenn told him. "Fill one out and get it back to me before you leave town. In the meantime, I'll try to contact the owners, though I may not be able to get a hold of them until Monday."

By Monday, Jake was due back in Long Beach. He decided to cross that bridge when he came to it.

"While you're at it, Glenn, tell them I'll have to make some major repairs in order to move in. I'll save all the receipts and deduct the cost from the rent."

He could tell Glenn thought the place was uninhabitable. The realtor wouldn't have to stretch to convince the owners the place should be unloaded immediately.

By the time they headed back to the car, Jake knew he'd waited long enough to mention Carly Nolan. He was careful to snap the seat belt in place and give it a tug first. Glenn had barely closed his door before he started barreling back down Lover's Lane.

"Last night I visited Geoff Wilson's gallery and met an artist whose work I really admire. Maybe you know her? Carly Nolan?"

"Carly? Great gal. In fact, she's a friend of ours. Her son Chris plays on our boy Matt's T-ball team." When they hit a pothole, Glenn was forced to concentrate on the road but kept right on talking. "Carly lives down in Seaside Village. It's an old mobile home park on the beach around the point. She's a pretty private person, keeps to herself, but the boys are best friends. Since they're both only children, Tracy makes sure they have play dates together."

"How old are the kids?"

"My boy's almost six. Chris has to be about the same age."

Suddenly Glenn hollered, "Off road!" and veered into the high weeds. "I never get a chance to put this baby in four-wheel!" They bumped along for a few yards before he turned back onto the gravel road again. "Carly's job keeps her pretty busy. I only see her at PTA meetings and T-ball."

Listening to Glenn, Jake had to hand it to Caroline Graham.

She could have sought out the anonymity of life in the city, but here, her identity was guarded by locals who thought they knew her and regarded her as a friend. Because they knew her so well, they never suspected her of being anything but what she claimed.

The truth was, they didn't really know her at all.

Forty-five minutes later, Jake sat in the park enjoying the sun, watching an old man in a baggy, worn sports coat feed the gulls on the bluff. The birds had begun to gather at the first rustle of a plastic bag filled with stale bread.

Jake took out his cell phone and punched the office memory number, waited for Kat to pick up.

"It's me. What's up?" He imagined her at her desk, unsmiling, leaning back in her chair, feet on the windowsill, tennis shoes wiggling as she stared out the window overlooking the water. He'd watched her do it countless times.

"I did surveillance last night on Penny Burger's husband." She sounded sarcastically gleeful. "She was right. He's having an affair." Kat never tired of exposing adulterers.

"Did you get photos?"

"Does a frog fart in a pond? I'll call her and set up a meeting as soon as I get the prints back."

"Have the Kleenex ready."

"You bet. I got a fresh supply at Costco."

It wasn't just the job that had made them both cynics in regard to fidelity. Jake hadn't just been burned by his significant other, he'd been fried. He guessed Kat had been, too.

Kat was barely twenty-eight and thoroughly convinced happy marriages existed only in romance novels. Suspicious husbands and wives were occasionally proven wrong, but the percentage of mistaken suspicion was low. The only truly happily married couple Jake knew was his sister Julie and her husband, Terry Avery.

He wished he'd been as lucky. He wished things had worked out for him and Marla. He wanted to believe in the dream, but time and delving into other people's heartbreak was slowly disillusioning him.

Suddenly he found himself wondering what Caroline dreamed of and if she ever saw a man in her future.

He liked to think he was a good judge of people. The woman he'd met last night didn't seem capable of hurting a gnat, but something had made her run from the Saunders and keep on running. She had taken Rick's son away from family who cared about him, not to mention a potential fortune in inheritance, without any obvious motive.

He shifted on the hard cement bench as the homeless man across the grassy lawn shook the last crumbs of bread out of the bag.

"Anything else?" Jake asked Kat.

"Your granddad called. Between you and me, he didn't sound very good. He wants you to call him. Said it was important. Something about business."

Perfect. Maybe he'd call Jackson and segue the conversation into the property overlooking the cove. He wasn't about to mention the possibility of renting the house to Kat yet. No sense in getting her Hawaiian-Portuguese temper riled up too soon.

She knew him almost as well as Marla had. She'd think he'd lost his mind.

"I'll give him a call," he promised.

"I'd say don't wait. He didn't sound like himself."

EIGHT

Carly was bent over, trying to wipe sticky maple syrup off a bench seat in a booth, when she had the distinct impression that someone was watching her.

She glanced over her shoulder and froze when she saw Jake Montgomery standing just inside the door, staring at her rear end. Not only that, but he was smiling. The simmering twinkle in his eyes nearly undid her.

She shot up, forgot about the syrup, and tried to pretend her face wasn't on fire.

"This is a surprise," he said.

His smile had widened, but she could almost see the wheels turning in his head as he tried to equate the artist he'd met last night with the disheveled waitress with a wet rag in her hand and a grease-spattered apron tied around her waist.

She wondered how fast his interest would wane. It had become evident to her that professional men often considered waitresses worth no more than a passing flirtation.

"This is my real job." She wiped her hands and brushed an escaped lock of hair behind her ear.

The way he insisted on staring did nothing to help fade her blush. "Have a seat and somebody will be right there."

He chose a vacant stool at the end of the counter, picked up a menu but didn't open it as he watched her finish writing up an order. Finally, still all too aware of his stare, she took a deep breath, walked over to the counter, tossed the rag, and stood over him with her order pad in hand.

Just looking into Jake Montgomery's eyes nudged awake thrilling and terrifying sensations that scared the hell out of her.

She was beginning to think he might be a man who wouldn't take no for an answer.

"What'll it be?" She tried to sound as if it didn't matter that he'd stumbled upon this aspect of her life. "Do you know what you want?"

"I thought I did." He held her stare, ignoring the menu in front of him.

"The . . . um . . . tortilla soup is Joe's specialty. And he makes a mean patty melt, if you're into red meat." She noticed her knees weren't exactly functioning properly.

"I'll try the melt."

Her handwriting came out uneven and shaky as she made a note on the pad. "Anything to drink besides water?"

"Diet Pepsi."

Carly realized that somewhere between the patty melt and the diet Pepsi, Selma had sidled up to her.

"Will that be all?" Carly hardly recognized her own voice.

"For now," he said softly.

As soon as Carly turned away, Selma leaned an elbow on the counter, angling so that Jake got a clear view of her ample cleavage and lowered her rusty voice an octave.

"You in town for long or just passing through?"

Carly shoved the order onto a clip on the chrome wheel and heard Jake explain that he'd originally just driven up for the weekend but that he might end up coming back. Carly reached for a tall glass, filled it with ice and then with Jake's soda.

"Selma, your orders are up!" Joe, who never missed a thing, not even from the kitchen, began pounding the bell on the window ledge.

Carly rotated around the tables, making certain her customers had what they needed. When she returned to the counter, Jake's patty melt was ready. She set it before him and watched him pour a puddle of ketchup on his plate.

"Your boss is quite a character." He glanced over his shoulder at Selma, who was chatting with an elderly woman lingering over a slice of apple pie.

Carly laughed. "You don't know the half of it."

"I'd like to hear all about it sometime." He fell silent for a moment before he added, "You have a beautiful smile, Carly. You should wear it more often."

Jake watched Carly's cheeks bloom at his compliment.

She ignored it but the smile lingered.

"How's the patty melt?"

"Everything you said it would be."

She left him to circulate around her station again, pouring coffee refills, greeting customers, delivering orders. She was definitely a pro, doing ten things at once and smiling the whole time.

Selma was filling a plastic bamboo salad bowl behind the counter when Carly walked back over to check on him. Jake lowered his voice.

"Is working here the reason you can't go to dinner with me tomorrow night? Or will you be at the gallery again?"

"I don't really work there. I only cover for Geoff on occasion. I'm here every Saturday night because the other girls usually have dates."

"You don't date?"

"I told you last night, I prefer to spend time with my son."

He understood what she was saying, but something in her eyes told him that she felt differently, that she wouldn't mind dating if the right man came along. She lingered long enough to ask if he wanted more soda.

No sooner had she left than Selma walked over again.

When the cook started pounding on the order bell, Selma turned around and yelled, "Keep your pants on, José. I hear ya." She leaned over until she was eye to eye with Jake.

"Did I hear you just ask Carly out for dinner tomorrow night?"

"You've got very good ears, Selma."

"That's not the only good thing I've got." She winked. "If Carly suddenly found herself with the night off tomorrow, would you ask her out again?"

"Sure. But maybe she's just using work as an excuse."

Selma glanced across the room. Carly was in deep conversation with a local cop. Jake had to give Carly credit. She was as adept as a chameleon at hiding out in the open.

"Try asking her again tonight." Selma suddenly straightened and gave a slight nod, indicating Carly was on her way back. "If it doesn't work out," Selma winked, "I wouldn't mind spending time with you. I close up at eleven."

NINE

Saturday morning, the metal bleachers at the T-ball diamond were as cold as they were hard.

Chris' team was scattered over the field dressed in matching gray T-shirts emblazoned with sinister black stingrays. Glenn had Chris playing shortstop, but at the moment Chris was busy writing his name in the soft infield dirt with the toe of his shoe.

Carly shoved her hands into the pockets of her hooded sweatshirt and yelled, "Be ready, Chris!"

Her son's face lit up with a smile wide as the Pacific. He beamed and waved just as the batter hit the ball off the T and headed right toward him.

After two attempts, Chris picked up the ball. Thankfully for him, it was a good thirty seconds before the batter realized he was actually supposed to run to first base.

Carly hid a smile behind her hand. The games were little more than comedies of error, the kids never quite sure what was going on.

Tracy Potter, seated two benches below Carly, turned and called, "Aren't they just the cutest things going?"

"I think they're actually improving." Carly watched Chris as his team left the field and headed for the dugout behind a chain-link fence.

Tracy turned around to concentrate on the game again. She was seated with a group of other mothers and always asked Carly to join them, but Carly usually declined, preferring to sit on the upper seat by herself, more comfortable in her self-imposed isolation.

She had her job, Selma and Joe, Etta and Geoff, but that wasn't the same as having family—not that she'd know what having a real family was like. Sometimes she found herself longing for someone close enough to *really* talk to, someone who knew everything about her, who knew about her past and what she had been through. Someone she could share all her doubts and longings, hopes, and dreams with.

She purposely kept her friendship with Geoff Wilson one-sided. He talked and she listened to his dilemmas over the aging parents he left behind in Chicago, his ongoing emotional trauma after splitting with a partner of eight years, his concerns about opening the gallery in a town with an economy that relied on the tourist season.

She knew he would do anything for her, but that wasn't the same as opening her heart to someone as well as being completely honest with him. She hadn't had that kind of relationship since she was fifteen. Not even with Rick, and when she'd finally opened up and told him the truth, it was too late.

Last night, sitting alone in a puddle of moonlight at the kitchen table, sipping warm milk in her flannel robe, she'd actually considered calling the Rose Cottage to tell Jake Montgomery that she had changed her mind.

He was just a weekender. What could be safer? It might have been pleasant being alone with an interesting and undeniably handsome man. No complications. No strings.

But eleven-thirty at night was too late to call anyone. Besides, Jake Montgomery might have already invited someone else, and she *was* supposed to work. If there was one thing Selma hated, it was a last-minute schedule change.

Out on the ball field, the Stingrays were at bat. Glenn was patiently trying to explain that not *all* of them would get a turn *this* inning. His announcement was followed by a collective whine.

"That's probably the way major-league players feel but they don't get to whine out loud."

When a deep, masculine voice wrapped itself around Carly, she quickly turned and found herself face-to-face with Jake. Somehow, she'd been so absorbed that she hadn't even noticed when he climbed the bleachers to sit down beside her.

"Hi." Tongue-tied, she strained to think of something else to say until she realized where they were and wondered how he'd found her. "What are *you* doing here?"

As Jake slid closer, he glanced over both shoulders. "I thought this was a public park."

"Are you stalking me?" She tried to keep her tone light, but she was only half kidding. First he showed up at the gallery, then the diner. And the first time she'd ever seen him, he may or may not have been watching her from the bakery. Now *this*?

She suppressed an urge to grab her purse, head for the dugout, gather up Christopher and his equipment, and make a beeline for Etta's old car, Betty Ford.

But just then Jake held up the papers she'd just noticed in his hand. "Glenn asked me to bring these by. I found a place to lease."

"In Twilight?" So much for no complications. "I didn't realize you were planning to stay around."

"Hey, believe me, I'm just as surprised as you are." He glanced out toward the field, offering her a heart-stopping view of his strong profile. Then he met her eyes again and said, "Clap."

"What?"

"Applaud. One of the Stingrays just hit a homer."

When Carly realized Christopher was rounding first base and headed toward second, she jumped up, forgetting everything but her son and his first-ever home run.

As soon as Chris made it safely across home plate, she became aware that Jake was standing shoulder to shoulder with her, rental forms forgotten and crunched beneath his arm. He was clapping and whistling as if he actually cared about the score.

In his enthusiasm he bumped into her shoulder. Beneath his long-sleeved denim work shirt, he was as solid as a rock, warm, and definitely all male. Carly was tempted to lean against him, hungering for the quiet strength radiating from him, longing to give in to a sudden and unexpected need to be held, to be touched.

It would be so sweet to have someone like Jake to share the joy of the moment with, to appreciate the simple things of life, day-to-day triumphs and sorrows, the quiet hours late at night and just before dawn. Very sweet indeed, but she doubted she could ever completely be able to open up enough and trust anyone. Not with so much at stake.

Beside her, Jake had grown very still. She was almost afraid to meet his eyes, afraid he would glimpse her vulnerability.

"Mom!" Chris was yelling. "Did you see me?"

"I did! Way to go!"

When she sat down again, Jake remained standing, studying Christopher. Her heart stuttered, her protective instincts on high alert. Then suddenly, he sat down and devoted his attention to her.

"He's some boy," he said softly. His gaze swept her face. "You must be proud."

She didn't know him well enough to be certain, but he appeared genuinely impressed with her son.

"He means the world to me." The sun was struggling to break through the marine layer of cloud cover. Carly raised her hand to shield her eyes against the bright haze. Jake pressed the papers in his hand over his thigh and began smoothing out the creases.

He lingered, as if there was something more he wanted to say, but he didn't or couldn't. He suddenly saluted her with the papers.

"Well, I'd better get these to Glenn before I talk myself out of renting the place. Bye, Carly."

"Bye, Jake."

She watched him climb down the bleachers to speak to Tracy, but before he did, he turned and looked over his shoulder at her and smiled, and her heart tripped over itself.

He seemed to be a genuinely nice guy. The kind of guy that Rick had been. The type she thought she would never meet again.

TEN

Chris watched his mom toss her backpack into the backseat before she climbed into the old, dented car Mrs. Schwartz let them use. Mom named it Betty Ford. His friend, Matt Potter, called the faded old station wagon a junker, which kinda made him mad and embarrassed at the same time.

Mom couldn't help it that she didn't have enough money for a new car. Waitresses didn't make a lot of money. She reminded him of that all the time, usually right before she told him that he should be thankful for what he had and that kids were starving in lots of other parts of the world.

He wished that they had a cool new Land Cruiser like Matt's dad. That or a way cool Harley. He'd happily ride on the back, even when it was raining.

Matt Potter was his blood brother. They had a secret ceremony one day, picked scabs then pressed their scraped knees together, but being Matt's blood brother didn't mean he could claim ownership of any of Matt's cool stuff.

He wished for a real brother all the time. He wouldn't even mind sharing his room with one. Sometimes he even thought he'd be willing to take a little sister. That would be better than nothing.

But most of all, he wished he had a dad. Not just so he'd have somebody to go places with like camping or to ball games, or somebody strong enough to ride him around on his shoulders, but 'cause then Mom would have somebody to love besides him.

Usually he felt really special knowing that he was the only one Mom really, truly loved, but sometimes it was kinda hard on him. He didn't want to be the only person she had in the whole world 'cause he was only a little kid. No way could he take very good care of her if she ever really needed it.

Chris sighed and kicked the underside of the glove compartment with the dusty toe of his tennis shoe. He spent a couple of
minutes trying to figure out why it was called a glove compartment
when they didn't ever put any gloves in it.

Mom leaned close, fastened his seat belt and then hers before
she started the car. Most of the time he knew what she was going to
do before she did it, so it was no surprise when she leaned over and
planted a noisy kiss on the top of his head.

"Hey, Mom?"

"Yeah, big guy?"

"Who was that man I saw you talking to?" He snuck a peek at
her as she moved the gear shift to R and the car started backing up.
She was looking over her shoulder, not at him.

"What man?"

He could tell that she *knew* who he was talking about, but she
was trying to act like she didn't. He spotted Matt with his mom and
dad and waved as they pulled away.

"The man in the bleachers wearing the blue shirt."

Mom turned on the radio and started singing a country song
about wide open spaces really loud. Now she usually only did it to
drive him crazy because back in October he made the mistake of
telling her it wasn't cool for moms to sing out loud. He hadn't even
known that it wasn't cool until he overheard some fifth graders
talking behind him in the cafeteria.

"Mom!" he hollered.

"What?" She turned off the radio and rolled down her window.
The air rushed in and mussed up her long hair but she didn't even
care. Matt Potter's mom always yelled, "Close the window!" when
even a tiny bit of air touched her hair.

He didn't think Mom's boss Selma's hair would move either. It
was stiff as cotton candy.

"Who was he, Mom?"

"Are you hungry?"

"Maybe he'll ask you to go out on a date."

He tried to act like he didn't care, but he really, really did. He crossed his heart and hoped like crazy the man would want to take his mom out to a movie or to get something to eat.

His mom *never* went on dates. Matt told him that wasn't a good sign—Chris would never get a dad if his mom didn't start going on dates.

He checked her out from under the bill of his baseball cap. She was biting her lip, watching the road, and worrying. He knew she was worried because funny little lines were folded between her eyebrows.

They turned onto Cabrillo Road and drove past the usual shops and stores. He waved as they went by the diner, even though he didn't see Selma in the window.

Except that she smelled like cigarette smoke, he kinda liked Selma. She had big boobs that stuck out of the top of her Plaza Diner T-shirt. *Amazing* boobs. He always pretended not to look at them even though he did. Once he and Matt even drew pictures of them, but then they tore the papers into little pieces and tossed the scraps in Matt's trash can.

That was one of their blood brother secrets.

"Are you hungry? I can make you peanut butter and jelly sandwiches and cut them out with the star cookie cutter," Mom said.

"If he did ask you to go on a date, would you go?"

She sighed very loudly, probably hoping he would stop asking questions. He saw her hands tighten on the steering wheel as they started down the long hill toward Seaside Village.

She was quiet for so long that he thought she was *never* going to answer his question. Maybe she felt really bad and had started thinking she was really ugly or something because men never asked her to go on dates.

He couldn't figure out why because she was the prettiest mom in the whole world.

"What's all this about going on dates?" She took her eyes off the road for a second and looked down at him.

Chris shrugged and rubbed an itchy spot on his neck. "Matt says that's how I'd get a dad, if you went on dates and then married some guy."

"Lots of kids in your class don't live with their dads."

Mom sounded kinda sad, and he knew it wasn't because she was sad for the other kids. He wished he had kept his mouth shut, but now that he was blabbing away, he couldn't stop.

"Yeah, but they still *have* dads. They might not live with them all the time, but they see them and talk to them and go on overnights to their houses. I don't have a dad *anyplace*. You don't even have any *pictures* of him."

Mom slowed down when they reached the gate to Seaside. She always aimed the car right between the two skinny posts with the gas tiki torches sticking out of them. When she ran over the pothole that was inside the gate, just like always, he pretended to get knocked around in his seat. He did that every time they hit the pothole, but this time Mom didn't laugh.

"You have a dad in Heaven." Her voice sounded soft and full of cotton.

"Yeah. I know. But that's no fun." He didn't have one single cousin or aunt or grandma or anything, which Matt said made for sucky Christmases.

He could tell Mom was still thinking about what he had said as she pulled the car up into the parking space between their mobile home and Mrs. Schwartz's. Betty Ford began to cough and rattle when Mom turned off the motor and the car shook from side to side, twitching like an old, wet dog until it finally died.

Mom didn't move.

"Hey! Maybe we should just get a dog." He tried to make it sound as if he'd just thought of it. As if he hadn't asked her for a dog one hundred thousand million times already. "You wouldn't have to go on a date to get a dog."

"Our place is too small."

"We could get a *tiny* little dog, like Napoleon Bonaparte." Mrs. Schwartz had a mobile home exactly like theirs, and *she* had a dog. It was a little French poodle with kinky white hair and painted toenails to match Mrs. Schwartz's, and a real French name.

"I don't think that would be such a good idea." As Mom unhooked his seat belt, Chris knew exactly what she would say next. And she did.

"We might have to move again."

Mom opened her door and stepped out, reached for her backpack and the duffel bag with his batting helmet and sweatshirt.

He'd lived in lots of places. Mom told him it had been too many for her to count before they had moved here three years ago. He didn't remember any of the other places, he'd been too little to recall them now.

She had been telling him that they might have to move his whole, entire life. It seemed like forever she had been saying the reason they couldn't buy this or that was because they might have to move and they couldn't carry a lot of stuff around. That's why they had no pets. No dog, no bird, cat, or even a fish.

Too hard to move.

He was afraid he would grow up like Mr. Evans, the short, bald man who lived by the bocci ball and shuffleboard courts in the middle of the mobile home park. Mr. Evans swept his walk and front porch three times a day. He didn't want kids or dogs or bikes getting anywhere near his place, and nobody ever came to visit him.

Mr. Evans was such a grump that Mrs. Schwartz never even gave him any of her Christmas jelly, but she gave jars of it away to people she hardly knew.

Chris thought Mr. Evans must be the loneliest man who ever lived, and he was afraid that was what he was headed for since there was no one in the whole world he was related to except his mom.

Mom waited with her hand on the door while he climbed out. He kept his head down, slowly dragged his feet, and kicked the sand at the edge of the pavement just in case she didn't get the picture.

"No dog, Chris," she said softly. "You might as well save the drama for something really important."

He sighed. Loud. The only thing more important than a dog was a dad.

"How about those peanut butter and jelly stars? Want some?" She started across the Astro-Turf that covered the stairs and porch outside their mobile home. The aluminum screen door squealed when she pulled it open. He waited while she turned the key in the front door. One day she said she was tired of looking at all the scratches on it and painted it bright purple.

He wanted to say no to the sandwiches and pout awhile, but his stomach growled. "I guess I could eat a little something."

"I'll make the sandwiches. You wash up."

Mom dumped her backpack on one of the dinette chairs and headed for the kitchen as he walked down the hall to his room.

Star sandwiches were okay. She had made them lots of times. They tasted like ordinary peanut butter sandwiches, but Mom always got excited about recipes and crafts she saw in her magazines, so he pretended they were the best things he ever ate.

He stepped into his room, walked over to the bed, threw himself down on top of his race-car comforter, and stared up at the glow-in-the-dark stars and planets Mom had stuck to the ceiling.

There wasn't any reason to bug her about going on a date with the man who had been talking to her and smiling real big.

She hadn't even told him the guy's name.

ELEVEN

Carly braced both hands against the rim of the kitchen sink and closed her eyes against a sudden wave of guilt and uncertainty.

Chris could probably have everything he ever wanted if he were living with the Saunders. Though she barely made ends meet, she was independent, happy, and safe.

A dog might make him happy now, but what would he say when he was old enough to know the truth? How would he feel about what she'd done, about the privileged life and identity she had kept from him?

His kindergarten teacher claimed he was gifted. He was due to be tested in the fall when school started again.

The Saunders could afford to send him to any of the finest universities in the country. The way things were going, she'd be lucky to scrape together tuition and book money for the local junior college.

Chris was Rick Saunders' son. She looked around a kitchen that was barely large enough to swing a cat in. Was it fair to bring him up this way?

Maybe he would be better off with the Saunders and all the advantages they could give him.

She shuddered at the unthinkable thought and pressed her hand to her mouth. He was her baby. Her heart. She could never give him up. Not for anything.

She knew what he was feeling, though. She had grown up longing for things she'd never have, loving people who weren't there. At eleven she started a life of shuffling from one foster home to another. After that she never had two pieces of clothing that matched, let alone her own room.

She'd worn hand-me-downs and thrift shop specials, worn out

shoes and ragged parkas that failed to keep out the harsh, high desert cold.

At least she was able to give Chris more than she had ever had. Their home here was modest but clean as a new dollar bill. She'd painted the walls, made slipcovers for the used furniture, hand painted race cars in bright primary colors around Christopher's room. He had as many books and toys as she thought he needed and that she could afford.

She read everything she could get her hands on about raising a child and running a home. She tried in every way she could to be a good mom, the kind she wished she'd had.

She'd survived by being a chameleon, watching and imitating the qualities in others that she lacked and admired.

But the one thing she could never be was a dad.

Sighing, she shoved her hair back off her face and looked around her tidy kitchen again. For now, this was enough. It had to be. There was no sense in worrying about how Chris would judge her in the future. For now she could only hope that he would understand that she had let love be her guide.

But was love enough?

She was taking the peanut butter out of the cupboard when Etta Schwartz called through the front screen.

"Woo hoo! Carly?"

"Come on in, Etta."

The screen door screeched and then banged shut. Carly started spreading peanut butter on a slice of whole wheat bread. Etta walked into the kitchen and stood at her elbow.

"Do you ever give that boy any lunch meat?" Etta was losing her hearing, and she had developed a habit of yelling. She also owned an endless wardrobe of spandex leggings that were all bagged out at the knees. She wore them topped with oversized T-shirts hand painted with puffy paint and sequins.

Not only did she also own an abundance of muumuus, some dating back to the forties when her father was stationed at Pearl Harbor, but she had a different wig for every day of the week. They were all too big for her head and made of shiny synthetics in a rainbow of shades with names like Mocha Madness and Chestnut Cherry.

What with the woman's passion for scented candles, Carly's worst fear was that one day Etta was going to set her hair on fire and that one of the wigs would melt onto her head.

Today Etta's faux tresses were a shade close to magenta, set off by a bright chartreuse jumpsuit with a leopard print belt. When she moved, the scent of liniment and peppermint wafted around her.

"The Stingrays won the game today, so this is a special treat." Carly knew that if Etta had any idea of what Carly had grown up eating, it would have curled her toes. She was used to Etta questioning everything she did, but knew Etta did it out of concern, so Carly let it go.

Etta had opened her home to Carly the day Carly and three-year-old Christopher had stepped off of a Greyhound bus with nothing more between them than two backpacks full of essentials. Carly had stopped for a cup of coffee at Selma's after spotting a Help Wanted sign in the diner window.

After a brief, informal interview in a back booth, Selma hired her on the spot and sent her straight to Etta, suggesting Carly ask the widow if she would agree to rent Carly a room in her mobile home. Selma had guessed that Etta could use the extra income and companionship, and she had been right.

It turned out there was a rule at Seaside Village against subletting, so Etta told the manager Carly was a long-lost niece. Etta started baby-sitting Chris while Carly worked, claiming she could always use the extra money for Bunco, her bimonthly dice club.

Etta "loaned" Carly her old Ford. Three years later it was still registered in Etta's name, although it was Carly who paid the registration fees the last two years.

When the mobile home next door to Etta's came up for lease, Carly took it, and the two women remained partners of sorts. It was a symbiotic relationship—Carly needed Etta for childcare, Etta needed the extra money and companionship. Carly drove her into town and into San Luis Obispo to her doctors appointments and to shop.

And they both loved Christopher.

"It's Saturday. You working tonight? Same as usual?" Etta asked.

"Five-thirty." Carly pressed the small cookie cutter into one corner of the peanut butter sandwich and carefully lifted out another star.

"Better warn Christopher it's his turn to come over to my place. It's Bunco night, and all the girls will be there." Etta wriggled her eyebrows like Groucho Marx. "Things get pretty wild."

Carly hid a smile. Not one of the Bunco girls was a day under seventy-seven. "I'll tell him. He'll watch television on your bed and stay out of the way."

"Only if he takes his shoes off. I can't carry that spread to the laundry room. It's too heavy." Etta's mouth puckered into a frown. Carly knew she was already envisioning footprints on the bedspread.

"Want a star, Etta?" Carly offered the plate of peanut butter and jelly stars, but Etta pursed her lips harder and shook her head.

"You really should learn to play Bunco so you could join us. You know, Carly, for a woman your age, your social life is a disaster."

TWELVE

That night at five-fifteen Jake slowed his SUV and turned left off the highway into Seaside Village Mobile Home Park. As soon as he passed the entrance with its flaming gas tiki torches, he knew he'd entered kitsch world.

There was no grass in sight, but yard art was still plentiful. A plastic Bambi watched doe-eyed as Jake navigated a narrow lane that curved between the rows of double-wide mobile homes.

Here, mobile home was an oxymoron. Most of these had never moved. Many were fortified by additions of permanent porches and sundecks, a few even topped by observation platforms with views of the ocean. A wooden sign in the shape of an arrow pointed to a narrow, sandy trail.

Gnomes sprawled on white rock flowerbeds. Plaster squirrels, rabbits, and chipmunks frolicked with tacky pink flamingos amid small evergreens and color pots overflowing with blossoms. Matching markers in front of every home displayed addresses in corroded aluminum numerals.

He kept an eye out for number forty-three and eventually spotted a ceramic burro wearing a sombrero and pulling an empty cart outside of a pea-green mobile home. The place looked as if it might have been one of the park's originals.

Selma had told him that Carly lived right next door.

Jake pulled into a parking stall and killed the motor, then glanced around the interior of the vehicle to make certain he hadn't left anything out that might give him away. Dark, tinted windows hid what he called his office annex. The compact SUV was perfect for surveillance but hell on gas.

He avoided meeting his own eyes in the rearview mirror and tried to convince himself that *not* telling Carly what he was really here for was perfectly justified until he was sure she wasn't a flight risk. He wasn't doing anything he hadn't done before to get information he needed.

It was his duty to learn everything he could about Caroline Graham, a.k.a. Carly Nolan, if not for the Saunders, then for Rick's memory. Besides, he hadn't exactly lied to her. . . . He'd simply avoided the truth.

The minute he stepped out of the car, he heard the sound of the rolling surf, but it was quickly drowned out by wild hoots and hollers. A woman's voice called out, "Bunco!" behind the closed door of the pea-soup green place right next to Carly's.

There were no fake woodland creatures, no impish gnomes adorning the front of Carly's mobile home. Butterflies made of crayon shavings melted between layers of waxed paper floated from a mobile hanging on the porch. He had a sudden flashback of making something like it back in grade school. The strings were tangled, causing the mobile to hang lopsided.

He paused long enough to straighten out the knot and set the butterflies free before he searched for a doorbell. No luck, so he knocked on the frame of the screen door.

Within seconds the bright fuchsia front door opened, and Jake found himself staring down into Carly's son's eyes. Blue eyes, blond hair neatly trimmed. The boy was slight but not overly thin. He looked healthy, well cared for.

"Hi!" A broad smile creased Christopher's face as he stared back at Jake. Then he turned around and yelled, "Hey, Mom! It's that guy! Mom! Hurry up, will ya?"

Christopher looked up at Jake again and shrugged. "She'll be right here. You know how girls are."

"Yeah." Jake nodded. "Yeah. I know."

"What's your name?"

"Jake Montgomery. And yours is Christopher."

"Yeah. I saw you at the game today."

"I saw you hit that homer."

"Where'd you meet my mom? At the diner?"

"The gallery. I like her paintings. I'm trying to get her to paint one for me."

"Oh." Chris' smile dimmed a bit. "Is that *all* you like about her?"

Through the screen, Jake saw Carly hurry out of the narrow hallway between the open kitchen and the living room area and stop dead still. Then she crossed the room, stood behind her son and placed her hands protectively on the boy's shoulders.

She looked tense, even a bit wary, although she was smiling. His sudden, unannounced appearance had obviously rattled her.

"I came to see if you'd like to go out to dinner with me, now that you have the night off," he said.

She failed to smile. If anything, her concern deepened.

"Ow, Mom." Christopher squirmed beneath her hands. "You're squeezin' me."

"How do you know I have the night off?" Carly's eyes never left his, but she released her grip on the boy. "How did you find this place? How did you know where I live?"

"Go, Mom!" Christopher bobbed from foot to foot. "I'll stay at Mrs. Schwartz's. It's Bunco night anyway. They'll need me to write down the score if they drink too much wine."

Carly gently covered Christopher's mouth with her hand.

"What's *really* going on here, Jake?"

Her blunt query startled him. Jake hesitated almost a split second too long before he held out his hands and shrugged. "Selma overheard me ask you to dinner yesterday. When you bowed out because of work, she told me she'd give you the night off, so I came by to ask you out again."

Chris wriggled out from behind his mother's hand. "Wow. Selma *just* called a couple of minutes ago."

Carly remained silent, still watching him somewhat guardedly.

"Listen, Carly," Jake shoved his hands in the pockets of his slacks. "Selma gave me your address. I'm sorry for showing up unannounced like this, but it was her idea. If you don't want to go, just say so, and I'm out of here."

"Aw, Mom." The boy tugged on Carly's hand.

"Chris is invited, too, of course." Though asking her son along was an afterthought, time with them both would give him a chance to see how things really were between them. "He'd probably like to celebrate that home run."

"Really?" Christopher looked up at him with such open admiration that Jake decided he should have "Scum of the Earth" tattooed on his biceps when he got back home.

He met Carly's eyes, marveled again at the stunning deep green in them. "What do you think? Are you both up for some Mexican food? I saw a little hole-in-the-wall where the canyon road hits town."

"Tacos!" Christopher yelled.

Carly took a deep breath, slowly let it out and smiled, finally opening the screen door. "Since it appears I'm outvoted, why not?"

Christopher raised both fists and victoriously cried, "Yes!"

Jake waited in the small living area while Carly went to change and help Chris clean up. The furniture was slipcovered in plain, heavy canvas, maybe painters' drop cloths. A distressed wooden storage chest did double duty as a coffee table. An array of magazines that appealed to women, with headline articles entitled "Flea Market Decorating" and "Get the Most for Your Shopping Dollar," along with recipes, housekeeping and organizational hints, were neatly fanned across the trunk.

A lopsided wicker rocking chair was piled high with so many pillows in bright floral prints that it actually looked inviting.

Toys including Transformer superheroes and Matchbox race cars were tangled up with some deadly looking plastic dinosaurs in a wicker laundry basket in the corner.

From where he stood, he could see most of the small kitchen, too. The appliances were old but clean, the refrigerator covered with magnets displaying kindergarten art and good citizen awards. A closed-in back porch served as her studio. An old, faded floral sheet covered a work in progress on an easel near the wall of windows. A small side table held her paint tubes, jars of brushes, and linseed oil. There was also a long sofa at one end of the room that was draped in a bouquet of tropical print fabrics.

Aside from a television the size of a postage stamp and a portable CD/tape player on a low brick-and-board bookcase, there was nothing of any real value in the living room. Nor were there any photographs on display except for one of Christopher in his T-ball uniform.

Not one of Carly's paintings adorned the plain, faux wood paneling.

Except for the picture of Christopher, there was nothing personal in sight. Not one item that would give any hint as to the identity of the home's occupants. Everything but the photo could easily be left behind at a moment's notice.

He could hear them talking down the hall, mother and son, their voices rising and falling in an easy cadence, but the words were indistinguishable.

Christopher ran back into the living room first, his hair slicked down, his cheeks glowing. Carly had him change into a clean, collared polo shirt tucked into his jeans, and he carried a hooded sweatshirt.

"We're ready!" Chris announced.

When Carly stepped into the room, Jake sensed that she put a lot of time into trying to downplay her striking looks, perhaps attempting to make herself into a woman who wouldn't turn a man's head when she walked into a room, but she had failed miserably. It would be near impossible to disguise her natural, wholesome glow, the grace of her movements, the sparkle in her eyes.

Her long, pale hair gleamed around her shoulders. Glossy pink lipstick echoed the slight tint on her cheeks. She wore the same plain, silver shell earrings as last night. A black turtleneck sweater and jeans completed her outfit. He watched while she scooped up a fleece jacket from a chair near the dining table and the same backpack she'd carried at the ball diamond.

Chris bounded over to him. "How many tacos can you eat, Jake? One time I ate six of 'em."

"Christopher . . ." Carly waited for them by the door. When she smiled over at him, Jake's gut tightened.

She flicked the lock on the doorknob, stepped around him and flashed him an uncertain smile. When she brushed by, he inhaled the floral scent of her hair and the image of summer sunshine immediately came to him. He smiled back, and before he knew it, his hand was riding the small of her back as they walked out the door.

Carly paused and looked up over her shoulder. "Are you sure you want to do this?" she asked him softly.

By the time they had walked down the porch steps, Jake wasn't sure of anything anymore.

THIRTEEN

Casa Grande Restaurant's enchilada combination plate had been Jake's undoing. Thoroughly stuffed, he leaned back in the banquette and wished he'd had the good sense to order a salad and an à la carte entrée as Carly had, but he knew of no better way to ease his conscience than with carbos and plenty of cheese.

Carly sat opposite him, relaxed but quiet, while Christopher slept on the booth bench beside her. She had volunteered nothing about her life before or after she moved to Twilight Cove. Jake filled the silence by telling them about the walking tour of town he'd taken earlier. Both he and Carly had listened to Christopher's tall tales of his adventures at school.

The boy seemed bright, happy, and a well-adjusted six-year-old—squirmy, boisterous at times, pleased whenever he held their attention. His self-esteem was definitely high.

Jake watched the busboy clear the table. "I didn't think he'd be able to eat half that much," Jake commented.

Carly's attention had strayed to a place only she knew. When she turned to him again, Jake found himself staring at her lips.

"He was showing off, but he has a pretty healthy appetite. I can't imagine how much he'll eat when he's a teenager." She brushed Christopher's blond hair off his forehead, watched it fall back into place again. "Thanks for asking him along. You've no idea how much this meant to him."

Jake was afraid that he did, and the knowledge only added to his guilt. He'd been a kid without a dad twice. He'd lost not one, but two beloved fathers, his own and his step-dad.

"Ready?" Jake asked. At Carly's nod, he paid the bill in cash, thanked the waiter and slid out of the booth. When he realized she meant to carry Christopher to the car, he stepped closer.

"Let me do that," he offered.

She hesitated a moment, then allowed him to slip his arms around the boy, who easily drooped like a dead weight over his shoulder. What was nowhere near a burden in his arms only added to the growing weight upon Jake's heart.

Once they were back at Carly's, Jake carried Christopher inside.

"Would you mind?" Carly stood in the hallway, indicating the boy's room.

Earlier Jake had wanted the chance to check out the rest of the place, but not like this. Not this way at all.

Carly turned the blankets back. Jake laid the boy down, then stepped back so Carly could sit on the edge of the bed and take off Chris's shoes and jeans.

"I'll let him sleep in his T-shirt and underwear," she whispered. "If I wake him up he'll have a hard time getting back to sleep."

Christopher's room was as tidy as could be expected for a kindergartner's. The walls were white with detailed race cars painted here and there at random. Homemade valances that matched the comforter trimmed the windows.

There were toys lying around, and near the window, a small student desk covered with crayons, markers, and construction paper. The desk chair sported a bright blue cushion on the seat.

Again Jake was reminded of his own childhood. He'd never had a lot growing up, but there was no shortage of love. After his father died and his mother remarried, Manny and Julie Olson had become his family, too.

Jackson Montgomery, his grandfather, had always been there, always trying to convince Jake that he'd be better off moving in with him full time.

They returned to the living room, and without the boy as a diversion, Carly seemed edgy and uncomfortable alone with him.

"Do I make you uncomfortable? Would you like me to leave?" he asked.

"No!" she protested, then caught herself and laughed nervously.

"It's been a while since I've . . . well, since I've been out on a date with anyone."

He laughed. "You call that a date?"

"Actually, yes. I haven't been on a real date for a long, long time."

"Then I consider myself very lucky."

"Would you like some coffee?"

"Decaf, if you have it, but only if you're having some."

She disappeared into the kitchen. He heard her rustling around, opening drawers, filling a pot with water. When she came back in, she seemed surprised to find him still standing in the middle of the room.

"Please." She indicated the sofa. "Sit down."

"Thanks." He sat on one end. She chose the listing wicker rocker.

"How long have you had this place?" He thought it a safe query, one anyone might ask and not be prying.

"A while."

After a few more attempts and getting nothing but vague answers in return, he stopped asking her questions. She went back into the kitchen to pour the coffee.

"How do you take it?" she called.

"Black is fine." At his place he could never trust the milk not to have turned sour.

She walked back in, set a steaming mug down on the trunk, and sat in the rocker again instead of choosing the space beside him.

"I see Christopher's into race cars," he commented.

"Actually, it's fire trucks now."

"My dad was a race car driver. He died when I was eight."

"You're kidding? Was he famous?"

"He was getting there." Jake nodded. "He was a NASCAR driver." He never spoke of his father very often. The hurt was still too deep, still raw even after all these years.

"Is that how he died?"

"A pileup one Sunday afternoon."

"It was hard for you, growing up without a father."

It was a statement, not a question, and he knew she was thinking of Christopher.

"Sure, it was hard. We'd been best friends. I missed him. I used to go into my room and pretend he was there. I'd talk to him, tell him I hated him for dying. Then I'd end up bawling my eyes out and begging him to forgive me.

"My mom remarried about three years later to a great guy, definitely one *without* the need for speed. He was a carpenter who had custody of his only child, a daughter. Julie's the sister I mentioned last night at the gallery."

Carly hesitated, as if debating what she was about to say.

"Christopher's dad was killed in an accident. Chris never knew him."

"Maybe that's not such a bad thing."

She shook her head, stared into space. "I don't know. He wishes he had a dad." Then she shrugged, smiled a wistful smile. "Or a dog. Sometimes I'm not sure which he wants more."

"Aren't dogs allowed here?"

She looked over at him as if she'd almost forgotten she wasn't alone.

"They are, but . . . the place is too small."

He nodded. She had relaxed, kicked off her shoes, curled her legs up beneath her.

"You have any brothers or sisters?" he asked.

She paused with the coffee mug to her lips. Her eyes clouded before she blinked and looked down. "No. I was an only child."

She appeared so vulnerable, so very alone. He wished he could come right out and say what he really wanted to say, ask her why she had run from Borrego Springs. Why she had changed her name, felt compelled to stay hidden all these years.

Why hadn't she let the Saunders help her?

He was tempted to confide in her, but until he knew what she was running from, he didn't want to spook her. He hated to think he might cause her to leave the life she was establishing for Christopher and disappear again.

He couldn't take the chance of that happening. If it did, he doubted he'd be able to forgive himself.

So he chose safer ground. "You must have studied a lot of history to be able to recreate early California figures in your work."

"I grew up in libraries. They were always warm and . . . well, warm."

She stopped abruptly, leaving him to wonder—warm and what? Warm and safe?

"How's the painting coming?"

"Which painting?"

"The one on the back porch. Is that mine?"

She smiled over the lip of her coffee mug. "Let's just say I haven't started yours yet."

"What do I have to do to get one?"

Her eyes widened, as if she wondered exactly what he was hinting at. A pink blush slowly crept up her cheeks.

"What I always tell Chris when he asks for anything is that he has to be very, very good."

FOURTEEN

As soon as the words were out of her mouth, Carly wanted to crawl under the carpet. She couldn't believe she was actually flirting and had no idea where her burst of bravado had come from.

She couldn't help but notice how he seemed to take up the whole sofa as he sat sprawled with his legs out, ankles crossed, resting his empty coffee mug on his stomach. His thick, dark hair was mussed just enough for her to want to run her fingers through it. His clear blue eyes were alive, alert. And they never left her.

She'd been nervous as a cat when he first made it apparent that he wanted to stay a while. She'd offered him coffee, listened while—bless his heart—he did all the talking, as if he somehow knew how hard this was for her.

It wasn't that she was unaccustomed to being around men, she waited on them day in and day out at the diner, but having one in her living room was entirely different. She caught herself watching the way he moved his hands, the way he rubbed the back of his neck with his palm and rolled his head on his shoulders.

As the minutes passed, she'd grown more at ease. When she thought about how he had invited Chris to go along with them and then gently carried him into the house, a feeling of tranquility crept over her, one that she hadn't dared let herself enjoy in a long, long time.

That surprising warmth stirred a long-slumbering hunger, a need she rarely allowed herself to acknowledge. She remembered Joe's words of advice.

You've got to let someone in sometime.

Time eased away as she sat in silence, cradling her empty coffee mug between her hands, surreptitiously watching Jake move, listening to the deep timbre of his voice. It was as satisfying as sneaking a bite of chocolate.

His masculinity filled the room, gently wrapped itself around her. What would it be like to make physical contact? To kiss him? To have him touch her hand, her hair? To feel like a woman more than a mom for a few stolen moments?

With a start, she suddenly realized Jake had set down his coffee cup. He was ready to leave.

Any other time she would have been relieved that she would no longer have to be on guard, watching every word. Now, part of her ached with disappointment.

Jake could tell that she was tired, so he stretched and glanced at his watch. "Thanks for having dinner with me."

When Carly unfolded her long, slender legs, he realized that without her shoes she seemed even more vulnerable. The way she was smiling at him was doing things to his composure.

"Thank *you*. It was sweet of you to ask Christopher along. He had a wonderful time."

"He's a good kid."

"Thanks. I like to think so. I want to keep him that way."

She led him to the front door, tried to open it for him.

"This sticks," she explained as she began tugging on the doorknob. "It warped last year when we had all that rain, and it hasn't been right since. There's a little bit of technique to getting it op . . ."

The door gave before she expected, throwing her off balance. When she landed against his chest, his arms automatically closed around her. He heard her swift intake of breath, felt her freeze. Neither of them budged, not until he put his hands on her upper arms and moved her away.

"Sorry about that." She turned to smile up at him.

"Anytime."

He stood in the open doorway, awkward, an imposter trying

like hell to convince himself that he wasn't doing anything wrong, that he had not crossed any lines.

Having seen her face-to-face and glimpsed an inside view of the life she had made for herself and her son, knowing Rick Saunders' child was happy and well adjusted, Jake found himself reluctant to tell anyone at all that he'd found her, even Kat.

It was almost as if by guarding her secret, he could keep Carly all to himself. Given time, if he could win her trust, perhaps he could help her and Rick's son, find out why she'd changed her name, why she'd run from the Saunders.

Hell, it was a long shot, but since he knew both parties, he might even be able to bring about a reconciliation between her and Anna Saunders, but that would only happen if and when Carly trusted him enough to hear the truth.

Kat would be chewing him a new one right now if she could see him like this, or worse yet, read the pipe dreams in his mind.

"Are you still leaving town tomorrow?" Carly was blushing, holding on to the edge of the offending door as he pushed open the screen.

"I decided to head back Monday morning instead."

"But then you'll be back . . . because of the house."

He thought of the ramshackle Craftsman waiting on the hillside, and an unfamiliar tug of anticipation hit him. It had been a while since he'd had anything but work to look forward to. He'd be kidding himself if he didn't acknowledge that he wanted to see Carly again, too.

"I'll definitely be back. I've got some clients down south to deal with first. Some loose ends to wrap up."

"It's good you own your own business."

He glanced away. "Yeah." Definitely the truth, partially anyway.

Had she stepped closer? He wasn't sure, but he caught a whiff of the heady floral fragrance of her hair. It lingered, tempted. He wanted to touch her again, but didn't. Wanted to stay, but couldn't.

So he said, "I was hoping that . . . if you have some time tomorrow, that you might come see the house. If I do lease it I'll need some advice on color before I start painting." He could already envision her there, standing on the porch overlooking the sea.

"That would be great. I'd love to, but . . ."

"Chris, too, of course."

"We'll come, but only if you let me bring a picnic lunch."

"It's a deal."

The awkward silence returned. Neither of them wanting to say good-bye.

Jake tried to break the spell. "Well, it's late. I'd better get going."

Shouts of "Bunco!" and the sound of something heavy hitting the floor next door drew their attention. Carly shook her head and giggled.

"My neighbor, Mrs. Schwartz, is having Bunco night with the girls."

Jake stared over at the plaster burro and cart statuette highlighted in the glow of the amber porch light next door. Carly crossed her arms and rubbed them against the chill damp air.

Above her, the butterfly mobile gently swayed in the breeze off the ocean. The night air was moist and heavy, tinged with the sharp sting of salt. Beyond the perimeters of the cinder block wall around Seaside Village, the surf pounded against the rocky coastline and short strip of private beach.

Jake looked back, saw her framed in the doorway. The glow of lamplight from within cast her in silhouette. Backlit, her blonde hair shone like a halo, long and full around her shoulders.

In that split second of time, in one heartbeat, he found himself wishing she was someone else. Anyone else. He wished to God she was simply a woman with no past, a stranger he had met on an innocent stroll through town. He wished he was what he claimed to be—a consultant who had needed some R and R away from his ordinary world.

"Good-bye . . . Carly." His heart nearly stopped. He'd almost called her Caroline. He turned and cleared the first step.

"Jake?" The sound of his name, coming so unexpectedly and perhaps a bit desperately, stopped him cold. She quickly stepped through the door, joined him in the darkness.

He lingered at the edge of the porch, willing something to happen, afraid something might.

Maybe he was overestimating the situation, reading his own desire into the moment as Carly hesitated just above him. His position on the lower step put them eye to eye.

"Good night, Jake." She spoke so softly he barely heard her.

It wasn't until he felt her hand against the side of his neck that he even realized she had reached for him. Her fingers teased the curls above the nape of his neck with a touch as light as the gentle night breeze off the water.

With the slightest tug she invited him to kiss her. Their lips met, brushed as lightly as the waxed paper butterflies skimmed one another. His hand went to her hip, rested there as naturally as if it belonged, as if it had been waiting forever just to touch her.

As quickly as it began, the kiss ended. It had been short, yet achingly sweet. As innocent as a youth's first kiss. But he wasn't a fumbling, virginal teen. He knew *exactly* what he'd be missing tonight.

Her hand slipped from his neck, her fingers might have trailed down the front of his sweater, he was too shaken to know for sure. She stepped back, clasped her hands together.

"Thanks again for a lovely evening, Jake. Good night."

He didn't even remember to say good-bye again as he moved in a fog to the car, hit the alarm release on his key ring. Slipping into the front seat, he closed the door and tightened his hands on the top of the steering wheel.

He rested his forehead on the backs of his hands and sat there with his eyes closed for a few seconds and heard Rick Saunders' words ringing in his head—as clearly as if Rick were sitting in the passenger's seat.

Hey, Montgomery! I'm getting married. Will you be my best man?

By the time Jake started the engine and the beam from his headlights lit up her front porch, Carly was gone.

FIFTEEN

Carly closed the front door in a daze, turned off the lights and moved through the darkness to her studio in the enclosed back porch. She heard Jake's car start, listened to the sound of the motor fade as he headed back up the hill toward town.

Rubbing her arms against the chilly dampness, she looked out at the night. Above the high wall of the surrounding bluff, stars shone like glittering teardrops.

She had shocked Jake Montgomery when she kissed him good night. She'd seen the confusion in his eyes. His expression had made it perfectly clear that the kiss wasn't expected.

What he didn't know was that the spontaneous gesture had startled her as much as it had him.

Even now she had no explanation for why she'd kissed him, except that he had been so sweet all evening, asking Chris along, treating him like a grown-up, not once patronizing him. Then when they'd returned home and she'd been shy and tongue-tied, Jake had opened up, put her at ease as he talked about his family. In her vocabulary, family had always been synonymous with disaster, hurt, and loss.

When he told her that he had been eight years old when his father died, she'd had an urge to put her arms around him and tell him that she knew, she *truly* did know how much his life must have changed afterward.

But although his father, like hers, had died when Jake was young, essentially Jake's life had remained stable. Jake had a mother who deeply cared for him, and not only that, he spoke lovingly of his stepfather and stepsister. In fact, he had never once referred to her as anything other than "my sister Julie."

Over and over Carly was reminded of how different their childhood experiences had been. Jake's world growing up would have been as foreign to her as life in some far-off country. He'd been raised in a world of family, the likes of which she had only read about or seen on TV. The kind she hoped she was creating for Chris.

Wilt had once told her that real families were nothing like the ones she constantly watched on reruns of old black-and-white sit-coms. He'd assured her those kinds of families didn't exist anymore, that they never really had.

Neither did the updated versions—parents and kids merged by second marriages, step-moms and step-dads and a mixed bag of step-siblings who stood around exchanging witty banter and getting along with each other.

It was all a crock, according to Wilt.

But for Jake, at least, the concept of family meant something. After his father died, he still had a mother who had kept him from falling into a bottomless void of loneliness, not to mention the tangled web of social services and foster homes.

Listening to him earlier, she'd been reminded of all she had missed.

Lingering in the darkness of the studio, worn-out doubts and insecurities plagued her. How could she possibly pass on the concept of something as foreign as family love, loyalty, and commitment to Christopher when she never experienced them firsthand?

"When's Mommy coming home?"

She was five. Skinny legs, knobby knees and elbows, blond braids, wearing a baggy sundress. She left her bike on the sizzling sidewalk and walked into the house in Albuquerque to get a drink of water.

The sun was blistering hot, the air as dry as brittle bone.

"Daddy? When's Mommy coming home?"

"She's not." That's all he said about it the day her mom walked out on them. "She's gone and she's not coming back, so don't ask me again, you hear?"

He was lying on the couch in front of the television, just like always, as if nothing terrible or unthinkable had happened to change their lives forever. The coffee table was littered with empty beer cans, an overflowing ashtray, crumpled cigarette cartons, and prescription pill bottles.

It was Wednesday, but it didn't matter to Bobbie Nolan what day it was. He never went to work the way other dads did. He got checks from something called disability for as long as Carly could remember. Mommy made most of the money, at least that's what she always said whenever her parents argued after Mommy got home late from dancing at the Kitty Kat Club.

The day her mom left, Carly stood on a kitchen chair to get her own glass of water. Then she walked into Mommy and Daddy's room to see if her mother's things were still there, hoping maybe he was wrong, that he was just being fuzzy-headed—that's what Mom called it—the way he got sometimes. But the minute she walked over to her mom's dresser, she knew he was telling the truth.

All the makeup was gone. So was the silver-handled brush Mommy used for her blush, the one Carly didn't have permission to touch. There was no slippery silk nightie wadded up on the unmade bed, no high heels scattered around on the floor.

Carly held the water glass tight to her chest and sat down on the closet floor and pressed her back up against the wall to keep her heart from beating its way out.

She cried for what seemed like days in the dark on the closet floor, cried until Daddy came and took her for a ride.

Secretly she hoped they would go by the club to look for Mommy, but they only drove down to the liquor store.

He was worried about running out of beer.

An ache Carly didn't dare acknowledge drove her out of the studio, so she wandered down the narrow hall to look in on Christopher.

She drew his covers up. Needing to touch him, she let the palm of her hand linger on the mound of his shoulder beneath the comforter.

In her own room, she paused in front of the mirror, able to make out only a dim outline of her head and shoulders. She touched her lips with her fingertips.

It was still hard to believe she had actually kissed Jake Montgomery a few moments ago. She still felt the warmth of his mouth. Still tasted him. She closed her eyes.

Had she really kissed him out of gratitude, or from some deeper need, some longing for intimate connection?

Had she seemed desperate? A single mom looking for a meal ticket?

She had no idea how to go about establishing a new relationship. No idea of how to make one last. She'd never had a chance to find out.

God, it had been so long. When she first left Borrego, fear of discovery was never far from her mind. Time had slipped away as she moved from place to place, at first scared of her own shadow and yet forced to focus on building a stable life for Christopher. She hadn't met any man who truly interested her—not enough to take a chance on.

Not until the moment Jake Montgomery had walked into the gallery.

She pulled her sweater over her head, tossed it on the chair near the bed, fighting to convince herself she shouldn't make more of tonight than what it had been—an evening out with a really nice guy.

There was nothing wrong with giving him a very innocent good-night kiss.

But it was hard to convince herself of that when, for her, it had been much, much more.

It had been a big step toward connecting again, one that very well might be the first on a road to somewhere she'd never been before. Somewhere she'd only dreamed of going.

Only time would tell.

SIXTEEN

With a garage-sale picnic basket in hand, Carly negotiated the warped front porch and lingered on the doorstep of Jake's rental house on Lover's Lane, high above the sea.

He was waiting for her inside, standing just over the threshold, anxious to hear what she thought, as if her opinion actually mattered.

Chris nudged past her to stand beside Jake and look around the living room.

"Wow, Mom. It's big, huh?"

"Mostly it's a big mess." Jake shook his head, taking it all in.

Chris was hopping from foot to foot. "Can I walk around?"

"No." Carly shook her head.

"Sure," Jake said at the exact same time.

Chris' gaze shot back and forth between the two of them. "Which?"

"Go ahead," Carly told him, "but don't touch anything."

She glanced at Jake and smiled tentatively as she stepped inside. When he had called about picking them up this morning, he thoughtfully hadn't mentioned the kiss, nor had he on the drive up the hill. He wasn't acting any differently than he had last night. He wasn't awkward, embarrassed, or hesitant.

She wished she could say the same for herself. She had to force herself to look up at him as he held the door open for her.

Carly set down the basket and turned her attention to the wonderful house. It was easy to see the beauty of the place beneath the peeling paint and chipped plaster.

Moving along with Jake beside her, she ran her hand over the detail in the painted woodwork and paused to study the view from every window.

She walked over to the built-in sideboard, opened one of the glass-fronted doors. By some miracle, very few had broken panes.

"It's absolutely beautiful," she sighed.

"I have a feeling Tracy Potter might think differently."

Carly caught him smiling into her eyes. "I have a feeling you're right," she laughed.

Chris came bounding in from the kitchen with an empty jar in his hand. "I found this on top of the wastebasket. Can I go look for bugs?"

"No, I think you should stay right here."

"Aw, Mom. I'll stay close to the house."

"Let's go take a look." Jake walked into the kitchen. Carly followed until Chris cut between them so he could walk behind Jake.

The back door had to be forced open. As Jake stood in the center of the deck, Carly walked over to the railing and looked around. There was no ocean view, but the sound of the sea hitting the shore echoed off the hillside.

About sixty yards from the back door, a dry creek bed cut through a shallow arroyo lined with cottonwoods and mesquite.

"Mom? Can I *pleeeze* hunt for bugs?" Chris sidled close to her hip.

"I don't think that's a good idea," she told him.

"He'll be fine," Jake assured her. "We'll picnic outside so I won't be reminded of all I have to do to get this place ready to move into." He glanced down at Chris. "But the final decision's up to your mom. She's the boss, right?"

Carly shook her head and smiled. It was hard enough to tell Chris no, especially now that they were double teaming her.

"Okay." She ruffled Chris' hair. "But you stay near the house. I'll go get the basket."

Chris rushed off the porch, jar in hand, headed for a nearby bush. Jake followed her inside. She paused in the dining area.

"I'd paint the walls all white and strip the woodwork so that the detail shows." She tried not to notice how close he was standing or how his eyes hadn't left her for more than a heartbeat.

"That's what I thought, too," he agreed, his voice low and even. "Restore it to what it was originally. Of course, that'll depend on how long I'm here and what the owners allow."

Perhaps he was subtly reminding her that his stay was only temporary, that this wasn't his place, but a rental for a few weeks this season. That she shouldn't expect anything permanent.

The picnic basket was in the living room. They reached for it at the same time. When their arms and shoulders touched, Carly pulled away first. She watched Jake's fingers close around the mended handle.

When she straightened, she met his eyes, and her stomach cartwheeled. She couldn't go on pretending that nothing had happened last night. Maybe she had let hormones make a fool of her, but she had to know, one way or the other.

"Jake . . . I'm sorry if I embarrassed you last night. I certainly embarrassed myself. I've never . . ."

He set the basket down again. "Let's get one thing straight."

"What?"

"You didn't embarrass me. You surprised me, but embarrassed? You're talking to a man who once licked a margarita off a tabletop in Ensenada. I don't *get* embarrassed."

"I didn't want to give you the wrong idea." She looked down at her hands, studied her fingernails.

"You gave me some ideas, but there was nothing wrong with them." A slow, sexy smile replaced the serious expression on his face.

"Why did you do it, Carly?"

"Do what?"

"Kiss me last night."

"I suddenly wanted to . . ." *Had to.*

"I'm glad you did."

". . . to thank you for the nice dinner," she finished.

"I should feed you more often. It was a nice kiss, but it was over too fast. What do you say we try it again? Maybe get it right this time?"

He moved before she realized he wasn't kidding. His arms suddenly closed around her, brought her up against him. She shut her eyes, leaned into his solid warmth, and melted from the inside out. His lips teased hers, his embrace tightened, his kiss deepened.

He kissed her until her head swam and her knees went weak.

Colors swam and blended in her mind. Inspired light and color, scenes and vignettes came to her. Sunsets and rainbows, the shimmering surface of the sea. His heart beat against hers, an echo that eased the aching loneliness that lingered in the shadowed corners of her heart.

She took a step back, but Jake continued to hold her at arms' length. For an instant she thought she saw haunted confusion in his eyes, but in a flash the look was gone.

"What's happening here, Carly?"

"I don't know," she whispered, shaken, realizing that he didn't have any better idea of where this was going than she.

Thoughtful, Jake picked up the basket, ran a hand through his hair. Together they walked in silence through the house and this time Carly reached the back porch first. He noted the attractive blush across her cheeks before she shaded her eyes and looked for Christopher.

"He must have gone around front." She hurried down the back steps, calling the boy's name. Rounding the corner of the house, she walked out of sight.

He set down the basket and looked around. Spring rains had thickened the grass on the hillside, turned it emerald. Here and there, blooming yellow mustard stood out like splashes of gold against the vibrant green.

There was a deep peace and serenity here that the city had lost. Inside himself, he was far from peaceful.

Sleep was a luxury he'd done without last night. Around three in the morning he wished he'd checked into a real motel with room service, a television in every room, cable movies, and twenty-four-hour news. Doomed to suffer insomnia at Rose Cottage, he'd tossed and turned in the too-soft bed, haunted not only by suffocating clusters of roses, but by the memory of Carly's sweet kiss, the fragrance of her hair, the fleeting taste of her lips.

From the moment she had climbed into the car this morning, he'd been aching for another. Now he wanted more.

He shoved his hands into his back pockets, tested a loose floorboard with the toe of his shoe. He wasn't fool enough to rationalize that he was hanging around for the sake of his friendship with Rick or to honor his friend's memory.

Maybe in the very beginning, before he'd laid eyes on Carly, his quest had been altruistic, carried out because he had wanted to help bring closure to the Saunders and to assure himself that Rick's son was being well cared for.

In the beginning that's what it had been all about. But what about now? *What would Rick think of what I'm doing now?*

The answer was pure and simple.

Rick wasn't around to think anything.

It was a perfect spring day. The Southern California sun was working overtime to make up for winter.

Jake answered a knock at the door, surprised to find Rick standing on the other side.

"What's it been? Three years since we've actually seen each other?" Rick asked. He pumped Jake's hand as Jake ushered him into his sparsely furnished condo.

Marla had ended up with most of their stuff after the divorce. She wanted it a lot more than he wanted anything around to remind him of her.

"Can't be that long, but it probably is," Jake admitted. "How about a beer?"

"Sure." Rick looked tan and rested, more than Jake could say for himself, but then, Rick was a trust-fund brat who would never have to work a day in his life if he didn't want to.

Rick followed him into the kitchen and took the Pacifico Jake handed him. "Thanks, buddy. I came by to ask a favor of you."

"Shoot." There was little Jake could say no to, not since Rick had lent him some of the money he would need to start his own firm. Not only that, but Rick had made Jake promise not to think about paying him back until it wouldn't be a hardship.

"Montgomery, I'm getting married. I want you to be my best man."

"Married? You?" Rick was a consummate playboy. Jake almost laughed, until he noticed a new expression of ease and maybe even contentment in Rick's eyes, one he'd definitely never seen there before.

Some girl had finally gotten to the playboy, hook, line, and sinker.

"Can't think of anything I'd rather do," Jake told him. Inwardly he groaned at the thought of donning a tux and writing a toast worthy of a wedding that would no doubt be the social event of the season. "I have to admit though, I'm surprised," he added. "Back when I got married, you said you planned to stretch out your bachelorhood until you were sixty."

"Hang on, buddy, 'cause there's more. I'm a dad. I've got a kid! And he's great." Rick reached into his back pocket, pulled out a bright envelope of Kodak photographs. He opened it, fished around, handed one over. "You can keep it. I have a couple more of that pose."

Rick stood by beaming as Jake stared down at a very, very young looking blonde in a denim jacket holding an infant up to the lens. Her hair was cropped close, spiked, the tips dyed bright canary yellow. A row of silver studs outlined the multitude of pierces along the curve of her ear.

She had a killer smile, but there was something in her eyes besides happiness, an inner wisdom, or perhaps it was sorrow. Perhaps the kind of knowledge that only came with time or hard knocks.

"She looks great." Jake had no idea what else to say. The girl didn't look much older than twenty-one, if she was that. She was certainly attractive, even in spite of her hairstyle and makeup.

Naturally Rick had picked a beauty. Looks would have been a prerequisite—but Jake was surprised by more than her youth. He always figured Rick would settle down with someone sophisticated, someone from the Saunders' social stratum.

"She is great. I met her during my forty days and nights in the desert.

I've been in Japan for almost a year and a half, but before I left, I went down to Borrego Springs to check out some property I bought outside of town. I met her one night when she was working as a waitress at the Crosswinds Restaurant. As they say, the rest is history."

Jake could just imagine what Rick's parents must be thinking. He'd have gotten the same sermon from his own granddad if he'd proposed to someone who looked like Rick's intended bride.

"I'm on my way back out to the desert to pick up Caroline and Christopher and bring them back to Long Beach. I just broke the news to my folks. Naturally, they're having a shitfit. Especially my mom." Rick shrugged, flashed his bad-boy smile. *"Caroline's not exactly Junior League material, but she's pretty and fun and hey, the kid's definitely mine. He already looks just like me, don't you think?"*

Jake studied the photo. The baby's eyes were exactly like Rick's. Even the shape of his head was the same, but like most babies, the kid probably looked like a lot of people.

They finished their beers, and Jake walked him to the door. He waved good-bye, watched Rick put his Porsche into gear and back out of the parking stall.

He had no way of knowing Rick Saunders would never make it back to the desert to pick up his fiancée and their son.

After Rick died and Jake heard that Caroline had disappeared, Jake felt he owed it to the man who had believed in him enough to loan him a stake in the future to find her.

Jake's memories evaporated when Carly suddenly came running around the side of the house. Her face was ashen, her blue eyes wide and full of fear.

"I can't find Christopher. He's gone."

"He can't be far." *Could he?*

"I've looked all around the house." Her voice rose on every word.

Jake's heart started pounding, but he kept his cool. It wouldn't do to frighten Carly anymore than she already was. He cupped his mouth, hollered, "Chris, get over here!"

They both stopped breathing, listening for a response. The only sound was that of a high-flying jet in the distance.

Carly grabbed his hand. "Oh God, Jake. Where is he?"

He started toward a ravine overgrown with low brush and taller cottonwoods. There were huge boulders, smaller rocks and natural debris scattered along the dry creek bed. His mind raced through a list of possible dangers—rattlers, coyote, rabid squirrels, transients.

"Chris!" He shouted and whistled. Carly clung to his hand, following right behind him. He felt a tug on his hand and heard her cry out softly. He whipped around and caught her as her shoe skidded along the sandy soil. He slipped his arm around her, supporting her until she was steady on her feet. She was shaking like a leaf.

"I'm all right," she assured him, stepping back to shout, "Christopher!" Silence was the only answer.

"Stay here." Jake started down the incline toward the bottom of the creek bed. "He might come around the front of the house and won't see us."

"Christopher!" Carly's voice was high and tight.

Suddenly, Jake heard a child's voice straining against the sound of the sea.

Jake headed down the ravine dodging fallen branches and outcroppings of thick weeds. He found Christopher in a low spot a good seventy-five yards down. He was clutching the jar to his chest, standing in the middle of the dry creek bed, waiting for Jake to get to him.

"What happened, sport?" Jake knelt down, ran his hands down the boy's arms, looked him over for signs of bites or scratches.

"I kinda got mixed up, Jake." There was a quiver in his voice and his lip as he looked up into Jake's eyes. "I went the wrong way. I didn't see the house and I didn't know where I was going."

Jake let out a relieved sigh and smiled to calm Chris' fears. He got to his feet, put his hands on the boy's shoulders, and turned him to face downhill.

"This is a creek bed. Water heads downhill, to the ocean. If you ever get lost, just remember to stay calm and think about whether you want to go up or down. My house is up, away from the beach.

Your house is down, in town. Remember how we drove uphill to get here?"

Christopher nodded. "So if I walk down, I get to the beach, and if I go up, I get to your house."

"If you're in this creek bed, yes. But no matter what, they all head downhill, to the ocean. Does that help?"

"Yeah. I'll remember."

Suddenly, they heard Carly calling Chris' name.

Jake hollered, "I found him!" He put his arm around Christopher's shoulder and started leading him toward the house.

Carly came running down the creek bed, her hair flying, eyes only for her son. When she reached them, she went down on both knees, grabbed him by the shoulders and searched his face.

"What were you *thinking*?" she cried.

"I found a huge beetle, Mom. Huge! Look." Completely over his fright, he was unaware of hers as he triumphantly held up the jar and showed her his prize.

"Don't you ever, *ever* do anything like that again, do you hear me, Chris?"

"I didn't *do* anything."

"Carly . . ." Jake tried to interject but she ignored him.

"You were told to stay by the house and you didn't. You wandered off. You could have been hurt."

"Sheesh. I'm right here. Calm down, Mom." He flashed a look at Jake as if to say, *women!*

"Don't tell *me* to calm down."

Jake tried again. "Carly, he's all right."

She whirled on him, her eyes bright with unshed tears, her face the color of chalk. "I should have *never* let him wander around alone."

He put his hands on her shoulders, fighting the urge to tell her he was the last person who would want anything to happen to her boy, reminding himself that she and Chris had made it on their own all this time.

"He's *okay*, Carly."

"But he might not have been." Her gaze scanned the hill as if any number of predators might be hidden there. "He could have disappeared . . ."

"Why don't we all go back to the house and eat lunch?" Jake suggested.

"Yeah," Chris echoed. "Let's eat."

"I want you to take us home," she whispered, on the verge of tears, fighting hard not to cry. Jake moved in closer, lowered his voice as he slid his hands down to her upper arms.

"I know you were scared, but don't take it out on Chris. You'll frighten him, too. Let him walk back to the house on his own. We can see him every step of the way."

She shook her head. "*You* said he'd be all right earlier, and look what happened."

"*Nothing* happened, Carly. You're overreacting."

"No, I'm not." She lowered her voice. "You can't possibly understand. He's all I've got." She turned to her son. "Walk up to the deck and sit there. I'm right behind you."

Knowing when not to argue, Chris started walking. Before Carly could take two steps, Jake urged her to look up at him.

"Carly, you're right. Maybe I shouldn't have suggested we let him wander around alone, but I thought he'd stay close to the house. Do you think I want anything to happen to him?"

"I should have known better, that's all." She stared up at him in silence.

He should have known better, too. He was the one who had come all this way to make sure Rick's kid was all right, not to put him in jeopardy.

Now not only was Rick's memory haunting him, but he was falling for Carly—and she was pissed enough to take his head off.

He was beginning to think that maybe he should never have come to Twilight.

SEVENTEEN

When Carly reached the deck, Chris was already seated on the bottom step on the verge of tears. He rarely cried. Not that she spoiled him, but he was such a good kid that he was just never in much trouble.

Even now she was upset at herself, not him. It terrified her to think he had disappeared so quickly, that he might have fallen or been injured while she was inside kissing Jake.

Her life had consisted of a litany of bad choices she wished she could make over, things she wished she could undo. Thankfully, this time Chris was all right. She'd learned a terrifying lesson, but everything was just fine.

Carly glanced at Jake, saw him leaning against the railing, arms crossed, mouth set in a firm line as he stared out toward the arroyo. Now that her fear had subsided, she was shaken and exhausted. She sank down onto the step beside Chris.

The sky was clear, the beautiful weather an indication of the warm months to come. She hoped it wasn't too late, that her insecurity and fear hadn't ruined a perfect afternoon.

"Hey, guy," she said, slipping her arm around Christopher. "I'm sorry I was so upset, but when I couldn't find you, I got so scared."

He wiped his cheek on his sleeve. "I know, Mom, but I was *okay*."

"But *I* didn't know that."

"Can't we stay and eat lunch with Jake? Please?"

She raised her face to the sun, let the warmth seep into her skin. With a sigh, she turned to Jake. He was frowning, staring off into the distance.

"What do you think, Jake? Is it all right if we stay?" she asked him.

He shifted, met her eyes. Then his gaze cut to Christopher.

"Sure." He reached for the picnic basket. "It would be a shame to let a perfectly good lunch go to waste."

Chris jumped up. His tears dried as fast as they started.

"I'll show Jake my beetle while you get the lunch out, Mom." Then he assured Jake, "My mom makes *really* good sandwiches. She's a great cooker."

"I'm sure she does a lot of things really well."

Jake hunkered down beside Chris, took hold of the jar with the beetle in it, held it up so that they could examine the underside of the bug. He started pointing out and naming beetle body parts as Chris listened in rapt attention.

Carly got up and brushed off the seat of her jeans. Her heartbeat had slowly returned to normal, the last of her fear ebbed, but regret slipped in to take its place. Jake's pensive silence hurt her more than she could have guessed.

Jake drove them down the hill again immediately after they'd finished their picnic. He pulled up in front of the mobile home and kept the motor running. Carly had been withdrawn since their argument, lost in thought on the way back, but it was pretty hard to cheer up somebody else when you were feeling lower than the curb.

Things were moving too fast. Her spontaneous kiss last night was one thing, but he only had himself to blame for talking her into letting Chris run around alone and worse yet, for initiating a second kiss.

He should have left Twilight as soon as he'd seen that Rick's boy was doing fine, but he'd unexpectedly been drawn to Carly from the moment he'd met her, attracted in a way that was hard to fathom. And then there was the house.

He never operated on impulse, yet this whole crazy weekend he'd done nothing but. He'd left L.A. on a hunch, found Caroline

Graham, rented a summer house in a town he'd never set foot in before, and now he had taken things on all counts much further than he ever should have, especially since she had no idea that he was a P.I. or that he'd come to Twilight looking for her.

The worst part was that there was no way in hell he could explain things to her yet. Not until she knew that she could trust him never to do anything to hurt Christopher. If he told her now, he might scare her into uprooting Christopher and running for cover again.

He may have temporarily altered his own life, but he didn't have the right to irrevocably change hers and the boy's.

"Hey, Jake!" Chris was out of his seat belt, leaning between the seats, bouncing with excitement. Jake realized he wasn't looking forward to going back to the L.A. area any more than he was looking forward to the next few awkward moments.

"What, Chris?"

"Wanna come in?"

Jake met Carly's eyes. There was nothing in their clear, green depths that gave him any hint of what she might want him to do, so he played it safe.

"I wish I could, but I've gotta go pack."

"I wish you didn't have to leave," Chris said.

It never ceased to amaze Jake how children wore their hearts on their sleeves, right out in the open where they could be so easily battered.

"Yeah, I'm not looking forward to it, either." That's all he dared admit to either of them or himself.

"Go on in, Chris." Carly handed the keys over. "I'll be right there."

"Okay! Can I call Matt and tell him about my bug?"

"Sure, but don't talk too long."

"Stay as *loooong* as you want, Mom." Chris winked at Carly before he jumped out and ran up to the house.

Without Chris, the silence in the car grew deafening. When Carly finally turned to Jake, it was all he could do not to reach for her.

"I'm sorry about today." She turned away to look out the window. "I didn't mean to ruin things this afternoon. I know how excited you must be about the house." She sounded so down that he reached for her hand, not knowing what else to do to let her know that he didn't blame her for overreacting. She'd lost Rick. He knew what Christopher meant to her.

"I know you were just scared. You obviously know what's best for Chris."

"Sometimes I wonder," she said softly.

"What do you mean?"

She shrugged. "I don't have all the answers. I just try to do the best I can."

"That's all anybody can do."

"I wish kids came with a manual."

He found himself smiling. She turned to him again. Her stunning eyes moved over his face. He could easily see why Rick had fallen for her. His friend hadn't proposed solely because she'd given birth to his son.

"He's a great kid, and you're doing a fine job of raising him."

"Thanks. That means a lot to me." She looked down at her hands. His gaze followed. Her fingers were long and tapered, unadorned by any rings.

"I'd better get going," she said.

"Me too."

Chris stuck his head out the front door and hollered. "Hey, Mom. I'm okay in here. Talk as long as you want." He gave her a thumbs-up and disappeared.

Jake watched the delightful blush paint Carly's cheeks. Tempted to kiss her again, he lifted his hand to pull her close, but then unnecessarily adjusted the rearview mirror. He was already in way too deep.

"Thanks again for today," she said softly.

"You're welcome." He opened his door, walked around to open Carly's. He reached into the backseat for the picnic basket. She waited beside the car until he handed it over.

" 'Bye, Carly." The natural thing for him to say would have been, "I'll call you."

They both knew it. His conscience made him mute.

Christopher held the phone to his ear as he knelt beneath the front window sneaking peeks at his mom and Jake. Matt was on the other end of the line.

"I can see 'em," Chris told him.

"What are they doin'?"

"They're just standin' there talking."

"Are they smiling?"

"I can't see Mom's face, but Jake is just lookin' at her."

"Is he holding her hand?"

"No way."

"It'd be good if he did."

"Oh." Chris ducked down when Jake got the picnic basket out of the car. Then he popped back up.

"What's happening now?"

"They're still standing there." His heart sank. "My mom looks kinda sad."

"Uh oh."

"I gotta go," he whispered. "She's comin' in."

He hung up on Matt and scrambled to set the phone on the old trunk before Mom walked through the door. By the time she came inside, he was stretched out on the sofa, feet crossed, hands beneath his head. His heart was pounding.

"Hey, Mom."

"What's up?" She stood there hugging the picnic basket.

"Oh, nothing. Did you have a nice talk with Jake?"

"Are you sure you're all right? You're acting funny."

He jumped up to prove he was fine, then followed her into the kitchen.

"So, you think Jake will call us when he gets back?"

She set the basket on the kitchen counter, slowly turned around and looked at him for a really long time. Then she walked over to him, got down on one knee and put her arms around him.

"He might or he might not call, Chris. That's something we'll just have to wait and see. Jake's a really nice man who was kind enough to take us out for tacos and up to see his house, but that's *all* he is to us—a really nice man." She pulled away so she could look him in the eye, to make sure he was really listening. "Don't go getting your hopes up about anything happening between Jake and me, okay?"

He nodded okay, but once hopes were up, they were pretty hard things to pull back down.

EIGHTEEN

Long Beach,
California

The 710 Freeway dumped Jake into town near the Aquarium of the Pacific. He drove past the Marina and Shoreline Village with its shops and restaurants and the Queen Mary across the water.

Instead of heading straight to his condo, he turned into Naples, an area where million-dollar homes were wedged side by side onto thirty-by-ninety-foot lots fronting either Alamitos Bay or a man-made canal dredged out of marshland back in the early twenties.

His grandfather had raised Jake's dad there. It was the kind of area where kids who left home wanted to buy property and move back—if they could afford it.

Kat had said his grandfather hadn't sounded like himself, so he decided to stop by and check on the old man for himself.

Jackson Montgomery's maid ushered Jake in and quietly slipped off to her own room. Granddad was in the living room watching television, but when Jake walked in, the older man picked up the remote and punched the mute button.

"What are you doing here?" Jackson continued to slouch in an overstuffed brown leather recliner.

"Nice to see you, too, Granddad."

Jake sat down opposite his grandfather, his gaze drawn by the view beyond the two-story windows that fronted the bay. A long, sleek sailboat silently cut the black water, trailing a blue-white phosphorescent wake. As the sparkling wedge widened, the reflection of lights spilling out of the sumptuous homes across the bay danced on the water.

"Want a Scotch?" Jackson asked.

Jake shook his head. "No, thanks. I haven't eaten yet. I just stopped by to see how you're doing."

"Well, I'm not dead yet, if that's what you came to find out. Why don't you fix me another?" He picked up the tumbler that had been sitting on the table beside him, handed it over to Jake who got up and walked over to the wet bar.

Jake freshened the ice and poured a healthy dose of Scotch, knowing if he didn't, the old man would just send him back to add more.

Jackson looked unusually pale, too shrunken and frail for someone who'd always been larger than life. It was a moment or two before Jake realized that, for the first time, his grandfather not only looked his age, but also very vulnerable.

"How are you, Granddad?"

"Oh, hell, I'm all right. Nothing a long fishing trip down to Cabo and a few shots of good tequila wouldn't cure." He took a sip of Scotch, reverently cradled the glass in liver-spotted hands. "Sure you don't want a drink?"

"Positive."

"What's wrong? Are you working?"

Jake shook his head. "Not tonight."

He knew what was coming next. There wasn't room for a sigh between his answer and his grandfather's first verbal attack.

"When are you going to quit wasting your time with that Goddamn nickel-and-dime business and come work for me? You could have made some real money by now if you'd come into the company. Why in the hell you want to run around sifting through other people's dirty laundry is beyond me."

For as long as he could remember, Jake had wanted to be a detective. When he was a kid he always tried to figure out how books and movies were going to end, and he thought he was pretty good at it. As he got older he realized there was more to being a detective than solving puzzles and guessing how plots unfolded.

At thirteen, when he announced to his folks that he wanted to be a policeman, his mother had withdrawn into worried silence. She'd come to his room that night after he'd gone to bed and sat down beside him in the dark.

"I lost your father because of his racing. It was his dream, Jake, so I never stood in his way. If, in a few years, you still want to be a police officer, I'll support you, but I'm asking you now to think about it and to think of me and what I'd be going through if you were out there in harm's way."

He never forgot those quiet words she'd spoken in the dark, and when he went to college, he'd majored in criminal justice, but always with the intention of doing undercover work and never planning to go to the police academy.

From day one, he'd loved private investigating and would never trade it for a desk job, even if that meant giving up being the CEO of Montgomery Pipeline Supply.

That he became the owner of his own firm had never impressed his grandfather. The old man never asked about his work, and knowing how he felt, Jake never volunteered anything about it, either.

"Granddad, you've wasted a hell of a lot of time trying to convince me to quit being a P.I. When are you going to give it up?"

"You're as stubborn as your father. I couldn't stop him from ruining his life either. He could have had anything. He could have been running Montgomery Pipeline Supply all these years. If he had, he'd still be alive. But no, he *had* to marry that *woman*."

"That *woman* is my mother," Jake cut him off, wondering why he'd even bothered to stop by. "She wasn't the one responsible for Dad wanting to race."

"She encouraged him."

"She loved him."

Something his mother strongly believed, something his granddad never understood and never would, was that loving someone meant encouraging and supporting their choices and helping them dream big dreams. She had always been there for his dad, no matter how terrified she was when he raced. She'd never once failed to champion Jake, either, never ever trampled on his dreams.

Jackson swallowed more Scotch. "I was only trying to keep you from making the same mistake as your father."

"That's what life is all about. Living and learning." Jake thought of Carly and Christopher, of their afternoon at the house. Of Carly's fear, of Christopher's curiosity and trust. Of how they were learning from each other.

He wondered what Carly was doing now, tried to imagine her in her small studio, painting. Was she listening to the sound of the sea? Was she thinking of him at all, or was he out of sight and out of mind? He turned to hear what his grandfather was saying, tried to concentrate on something other than Carly.

Jackson shook his head. "Mistakes can kill you. Just look at your father. I never understood him. Or you." He lifted his head, pinned Jake with a watery blue stare. "Your secretary said you were up the coast."

"Kat's my partner, not my secretary. I drove up the coast to Twilight Cove."

"Never heard of it." Which, in Granddad's vernacular, meant that the place had to be worth next to nothing.

"It's a little south of San Luis Obispo. I'm thinking about spending some time up there this summer. I found a great rental house to lease for a couple of months."

That got the old man's attention. He stopped staring at the bay and put his drink down. "What *kind* of a house?"

"A fixer-upper. An old Craftsman built in the early 1900s."

"You buying it?"

Jake shook his head. "Can't afford it."

Jackson snorted. "If you'd worked for me, you could. You could have had anything you wanted. I'd have given you anything."

"If only I'd have moved out of Mom's house at fifteen and lived with you. If only I'd done everything you wanted me to do."

"You'd have been better off here than living with her and that bleeding-heart-liberal *handyman* she married."

"Manny was a skilled artisan. Why would I leave anyone like Mom and Manny to live with a belligerent drunk?"

"Touché." Jackson took another sip of Scotch, lifted the glass to the light, and swirled the ice in the amber liquid.

"You ever really loved anybody, Granddad? I mean, have you ever really, *really* loved anybody? Even Grandma?" Jake had barely known his grandmother. His only memory of her was a pale shadow hovering beside Granddad. She wore neat, tailored knit suits and pearls. Always the pearls. She said very little and kept the old man's glass full. She'd died shortly after Jake lost his dad.

Jackson mumbled something. Jake leaned forward. "I'm sorry. What did you say?"

"I said it's not worth it."

"What's not?"

"Loving anybody."

"Why the hell not?"

"Because they always leave you—one way or another."

Any notion of asking for a loan had evaporated the minute Jake had walked in. He would sooner lie down buck naked on hot coals. He'd go ahead and rent the house above Twilight for the summer, do some minimal painting, clean it up enough to make it livable for the brief amount of time he would get to use it.

Owning the Craftsman overlooking the sea had been a pipe dream. He would have probably ended up hating the commute, not to mention having to squirrel away time to get up there.

Jackson drained the Scotch and set down the empty glass. Jake had no idea how many drinks the old man had polished off before he got there, but there was no use trying to carry on a conversation now. Only a fool debated drunken logic.

Granddad stared at him, his heavy jowls hanging, almost as if his skin was beginning to slide off his face. The old man was working himself up to say something. When he finally did, it came out as a tight growl.

"Why'd you come over?"

"You left me a message."

"But why come to see me? You could have just called." The words were slurred, as if Jackson were talking around a mouthful of dimes. "D'you come by to see if I was dead yet?"

"I didn't come by to have you try to pick a fight."

Jake stood up, unwilling to waste any more time. As he walked past the old man's chair, Jackson grabbed his wrist. His grandfather hadn't the strength to keep him from walking out, but succeeded in stopping him in his tracks.

"Why, Jake? D'you come over because you think I might change my mind and that I'll put you into my will so you can get that house you want? You think I owe you something, just because you're m' grandson?"

Something inside Jake snapped as he listened to the weak, surly old man who had made his dad and mom's short time together miserable.

"You really don't get it, do you, Granddad? You never have. You cut Dad out of your life the day he chose racing over your company. You continued to make Mom miserable after he died, complaining about the way she was raising me, demanding I stay with you every summer. You honestly want to know why I still come by to see you? Why I'm still even in contact with you? Because it matters to *her*.

"Mom's the one who insisted I go on those fishing trips every damn summer. She wanted me to spend time with you because we're family. *She's* the one who insisted we stay connected because, even though Dad was gone, I was still a Montgomery.

"She taught me and Julie that the only thing worth anything in this life is family. Strip away that goddamn money you're so worried about, and what have you got left? Nothing. You've tried to use it as leverage for years, first with Dad, then me, but you never understood that neither of us cared enough about it to dance to your tune."

Jackson slowly righted himself, propped his elbow on the arm of the chair, and leaned forward. "So, you're trying to tell me that you *suffered* through those fishing trips to Baja, eh?"

Memories flashed through Jake's mind. Billfish flashing like bright iridescent slivers of rainbows against the open sky. Blazing sun on aquamarine water. Bonfires and barbeques at night. Flaky lobster served up on fresh, warm tortillas. Rocking to sleep on the open deck of the yacht. Swimming and diving for abalone with Rick and the other sons and grandsons of club members he'd eventually come to know. Laughing brown-skinned girls who taught them how to make love. Cold bottles of *Corona*.

The sun-drenched summers of his youth.

Despite the verbal abuse he'd had to take from Granddad, he had had Rick's friendship, and when he got back home, there was plenty of love and support from Mom and Manny.

"You must really hate me." Jackson slumped back into the chair.

Jake shoved his hands in his pockets and shrugged, refusing the invitation to his grandfather's private pity party.

"You know what, Granddad? I should, but I don't. You can thank Mom for that, too. But thank yourself for the fact that I feel very little for you at all." He glanced out at the bay, envied the old man's spectacular view but nothing else. The stunning view of the water was all Jackson Montgomery could enjoy anymore. The view and his Scotch.

"I've got to go." Drained, Jake longed for a shower, a cold beer, and the solitude of his own place.

Jackson acted as if he hadn't heard. "I got a call the other day. Somebody asking if you were still in business."

"Oh, yeah?" Jake was surprised his grandfather had even bothered to remember. "Who from?"

"Anna Saunders."

The name sent Jake's mind reeling.

Why me? he wondered. *Why now?*

The Saunders had hired the well-established firm of Alexander and Perry not because he'd been employed there, but because of the prestige and success associated with the firm. But Charles Saunders had told him early on that he was relieved to know that someone who had known and cared about Rick would be assisting on the case.

But Saunders hadn't been relieved enough to retain him to continue the search when Jake left Alexander and Perry.

"Did Mrs. Saunders say what she wanted?"

"She talked about how nobody ever found that woman or the boy."

"Yeah. I know."

"Maybe she wants you to give it a try. She wants you to call her."

Jake ran his hand over the back of his neck. Was this synchronicity or just bad timing?

"Why now?" Merely thinking aloud, he wasn't really expecting an answer.

"Maybe you ought to call her and find out."

NINETEEN

Carly pulled Betty Ford over to the curb in front of Twilight Cove Elementary and kept the engine running as the primary grades spilled out of the building. Chris spotted the car and ran over, opened the door, and hopped in, automatically reaching for the seat belt.

"Why the long face?" She ruffled his hair, noticing he wasn't his usual exuberant self. "Didn't you get to share your beetle?"

He shrugged and then sighed, a sure sign things hadn't gone well. "Yeah. I shared it. I even chased some of the girls with it at lunch, but then it died."

"I'm so sorry. Did you get into trouble?"

"Nah."

"So what's wrong?"

He dug in the backpack. Carly glanced down, saw a crumpled piece of yellow paper in his hand. He held it up.

"I can't read while I'm driving, honey."

"It says Friday is Grandparents' Day and I don't have any."

Carly hit the turn signal and carefully eased out onto Cabrillo Road. *Grandparents' Day.* When would these people realize not every kid came from a cookie-cutter family? That most parents were just trying to keep it together, to get by day to day without having to prop up the educational system by showing up all the time?

"We're all 'posed to bring a grandparent, but Mrs. Schack said if we don't have one, then we can bring someone who's like a . . . mentor."

"A mentor?"

He scratched his nose and sighed. "You know, Mom. Somebody who can share a skill or hobby."

Carly didn't think life should be this hard on a kindergartner. Lost in thought, she continued down the road, then turned between the tiki torches. One was lit, the other wasn't.

"Mom?"

"What?"

"What about it? I need a grandparent by *Friday*."

"How about Mrs. Schwartz?"

"Oh, sheesh, Mom. What if she came with purple hair or something? Besides, *what* is she going to share? How to yell Bunco and fall off a chair?"

Carly had to bite her lips and collect herself before she could answer. "It's not nice to make fun of Etta. She might be a little eccentric, but she loves you dearly."

She pulled into the parking space in front of their mobile home, turned the key. When the death rattle stopped, she took the flyer from Chris.

Grandparents' Day.

"What about Selma?" she suggested.

His eyes widened as he immediately shook his head. "She's nice, but . . . *not* Selma, Mom." He scrunched his brows and tapped his forehead, thinking.

"How about *Jake*?" The idea had not just come to him, she could tell because, despite his intelligence, he was a terrible actor.

"Jake isn't even in Twilight, and I'm not sure when he'll be back." *Or if he'll want to see me again when he gets here.*

"I like Jake a lot. How 'bout you, Mom?"

"I think he's very nice."

"Do you think he likes you?"

"I'm sure he likes both of us."

"What about Joe?"

Chris had changed the subject so quickly she shook her head. "What *about* Joe?"

"He could be the grandparent for the day."

"You mean Joe Caron? The cook?"

"Yeah. Joe's great."

"He has to work."

"He wouldn't have to talk long. Since everybody has to have a turn, it'll only take a few minutes." Chris reached for the door handle, ready to go inside. "Think about it, Mom," he said, sounding very much like she did whenever she tried to talk him into something. With that he opened the door and jumped out.

Carly pulled the keys, wondering if Joe might consider attending grandparents' day. She knew he had grandkids of his own. Their photos were stapled to the back door in the diner. Besides, he *was* the grandfatherly type, with his huge belly laugh and easy going nature.

"Mom! I gotta use the bathroom." Chris was hopping up and down the porch steps.

When she unlocked the front door, Chris shot around her, headed down the hall.

"I'll ask Joe tomorrow," she called after him. "Maybe he will be able to help."

Chris skidded to a stop. "Ask him to wear his bullfighter cape, too, okay? Will ya remember, Mom? I'll be the only one with a bullfighter, even if he is only a *fake* grandpa."

She never knew her own grandparents.

Mom never came back after she walked out, but she'd never been there that much anyway, so life stayed pretty much the same for six years. Dad's world narrowed to the living room couch, his bed, the liquor store where he cashed his disability checks.

She had food and a roof over her head. He signed her up for school when she was five. Teachers reported that she was a bright and capable child, quiet and serious.

They had no idea what home was like.

By December of the sixth grade she was in the middle of her best school year yet. Miss DeCoudres, her teacher, had seen the loneliness in her, recognized her need to shine, and often let her stay after school to help straighten up the room and check papers.

She liked to think that Miss DeCoudres could see deep into her heart and knew who she really was—not the little blonde who wore old, stained clothes, the girl with the tangled hair. Not the girl who went home to a mess clouded by a smoky haze, forced to get dinner together herself if she and Dad were going to eat anything at all.

She loved the way Miss DeCoudres always smelled like baby powder, the way she wore her hair long and straight. She wished just once she could get up the nerve to ask if Miss DeCoudres would teach her how to fix her own hair so it would look nicer, like the girls who had someone at home to braid and comb theirs for them.

Her teacher wore pretty clothes, mostly jumpers and pleated, plaid skirts. She had pins with rhinestones, too, one for each and every holiday.

Miss DeCoudres was wearing her special Christmas pin, a glistening emerald tree with a bright yellow rhinestone star and little multicolored stones for ornaments on the last morning that Carly ever walked into her favorite classroom and took her seat up front.

When it was time to go to the cafeteria for lunch, she was still sitting at her desk. Miss DeCoudres walked over and stood in front of her. As if her teacher's voice was being funneled to her through an empty oatmeal box, she heard her say, "Are you all right, dear? You look pale. Maybe you need to go to the nurse?"

While Miss DeCoudres reached down to feel her forehead, she stared at her teacher's plaid wool skirt because lifting her eyes would take too much effort. She wasn't exactly sick. Just numb.

She'd gotten up that morning and dressed and walked into the kitchen to make herself a bowl of Count Chocula.

It wasn't a good idea to wake Dad before school, so she usually left without even talking to him. But that morning, after she grabbed her backpack and walked through the living room, she got a creepy feeling along her spine and turned around. Dad was sprawled on the couch.

Seeing him there at that time of day wasn't all that strange. Lots of nights he never made it to bed. But that morning his mouth was hanging open and his skin was the color of a bad bruise.

She walked over, gazed down at the foam on his lips and stared into unseeing, olive-colored eyes.

No one needed to tell her that he wouldn't be walking down to the liquor store later for a case of beer and a carton of cigarettes. Cancer sticks he always called them, then he'd laugh as if he hadn't said it a hundred thousand times already.

Miss DeCoudres was waiting patiently for her to look up, so she mustered barely enough courage to finally put into words what she had tried to deny all morning.

"I think my dad's dead," she whispered, shaking all over, tasting each word, cold and hard as stones.

Her teacher dropped to her knees. Suddenly they were eye-to-eye, the intimate contact jarring and unfamiliar.

"What are you saying, honey?"

"My dad's dead on the couch at home. I'm pretty sure he is. He was kinda blue. And his skin was real cold." When she realized she was looking at Miss DeCoudres through a smeary blur, she blinked. A hot tear trailed down her cheek, and she got embarrassed and quickly wiped it off with the back of her hand.

The nightmare thickened after that. She never saw Miss DeCoudres again. Never even went back home. Child services picked her up at school, and that night she slept at a foster home, a way station where she waited four weeks until they placed her with another foster family.

She wasn't an infant. People looking to adopt never chose eleven-year-olds. She quickly learned that moving from one foster home to another wasn't any better than taking care of a drunk.

TWENTY

The next morning, Jake put on a pair of wrinkled Hawaiian-print swim trunks and a faded navy T-shirt, crossed the cold tiles in the compact kitchen of his two-bedroom condo in the Marina Pacifica complex. He referred to it more often as the office than as home.

The counter held a microwave, blender, and toaster oven, all of which he rarely used. Crumpled sacks and garish plastic cups collected from nearly every fast food restaurant in town littered the rest of the counter space. A folded pizza box protruded from the wastebasket.

He finger-combed his hair, opened the refrigerator, pulled out the crisper drawer and started tossing oranges onto the counter. Rummaging through the cupboard, he finally found an old green glass juicer he bought one Sunday morning at the Vintage Swap Meet. Nearly everything in the apartment had been left behind by the previous owner, or he'd bought it at the Veterans Stadium parking lot swap meet.

He was alternately staring out the window at the waters of Marine Stadium and cutting oranges in half when the front door opened and Kat Vargas sailed in. She headed straight for the kitchen when she saw him.

Short, athletically fit, with hair so black it glistened, Kat leaned in the doorway, arms crossed, shaking her head as she checked out his state of undress.

"Late night?" he asked, taking in the pillow creases on her cheek.

"Not really."

"I know what a wild woman you are." He cleaved another orange in half. Kat had either been sleeping with a one-night stand or home alone.

"Yeah, right."

"Let me guess, you rented two movies instead of one." He grabbed up the last orange and whacked it in half.

"You're right. And I had to see them both through to the end. You know I can't sleep until Jackie Chan saves the world from destruction." She was a sucker for martial arts movies, the cornier the better.

"You really need to get a life, Vargas." He was only half kidding. If he wanted to spend more time at Twilight this summer, she was going to have to take on more work.

"I have a life," she assured him. "And I like it just the way it is." Her eyes told him differently.

"Beer, cold pizza, and rental movies on nights you aren't doing surveillance?" Jake started smashing orange halves on the juicer and twisting them until they were dry. Then he poured the juice with pulp, ground seeds and all, into a tall plastic Slurpee cup.

A Boston whaler filled with weekend boaters motored by the window. Across the stadium, two jet ski riders looped each other in a dance of spray and ear pollution.

He held up the juice, turned to Kat. "Want some?"

"No, thanks. Did you get in late?"

Jake nodded. The Tyrannosaurus rex on the side of a mini-mart cup flashed horrendously sharp teeth. He took a long swig of juice and headed toward the door. Kat followed him to the rickety rattan dinette set that had come with the condo. The chair creaked as he sat down and shoved aside a box of plastic utensils.

Kat picked up a fork, stared at it a moment, set it down. "I have to give you credit, Montgomery. You might have been too lazy to buy silverware for eight years but you're finally popping for the heavy plastic."

Kat leaned back in her chair. "When *did* you get back?"

"Late last night. I stopped by to see my grandfather and then picked up dinner."

"How'd things go up north? You ready to tell me what's up yet?"

Kat lived for the job. He'd found that out the first week he'd agreed to take her on. Dedicated to her tae kwon do, convinced men weren't worth her time, she had very little social life. Like him, she became devoted to the job, which made her the perfect partner.

Jake finished off the juice and set down the tall cup. "How much can you handle alone?"

"What do you mean?"

"I mean, can you run things for a while around here? I'll do the paper chases, employee theft, high-dollar fraud that I can trace through accounts. Handwriting analysis. I'll have a phone and computer hookup."

He named the things he was best at, things she found tedious. Kat's taste ran more to surveillance, de-bugging rooms, find-and-serve jobs. Things that kept her out of the office and on the move.

She blinked twice, her eyes intent on his face.

"Why?"

"I rented a house in Twilight Cove for the summer. I'd like to try and spend a few days every week up there."

"Wow. This is kinda sudden, especially for you."

He tried to shrug it off. "Hey, shit happens."

All of a sudden, Kat slapped the table. "You found your mystery girl! I can't *believe* it." Her eyes widened, her mouth dropped open. Her voice came out in a whisper. "You not only found her, you've *fallen* for her!"

She was on her feet now, pacing the open living room. "I can't believe it. *I* find an article in a magazine and recognize the detail in a painting—in a photograph of it yet—one like that weird little piece hanging over your desk. *You* drive up to find the gallery and check it out, and there's Caroline Graham, sitting right there in Twilight Cove. What kind of luck is that?"

"Dumb luck." He didn't dare add that he was starting to think some things were simply meant to be. She'd laugh him out of the condo.

"It gets better," he told her.

She sat on the back of the sofa. "Go on."

"Anna Saunders called my grandfather and wants to talk to me. . . ."

"To find someone you've already found! You're kidding, right?"

Jake shook his head. "I'm not sure, but she contacted my grandfather first, to see if I was still a P.I. and to tell him to have me call her."

"She has no idea you've already found Caroline?"

"How could she?"

"Then you can name your price."

"No way."

"Why not?"

He hesitated a second too long. Kat jumped on his silence.

"You're not going to tell her you found Caroline, are you?"

"Let's just say for now, I plan to stall Mrs. Saunders."

"Why?"

"It's complicated."

"So The Obsession is real, and you're in love with her." Kat sniffed. "Or in lust anyway."

Jake walked back into the kitchen, rinsed out the juice cup, and set it in the dish drainer beside the sink. Kat Vargas was only twenty-nine, but she'd had her heart badly broken a couple of times, and what was left of it was hard as cement.

He walked back into the other room and sat down across from her, found himself thinking about Carly and all the feelings he hadn't wanted to come to grips with alone.

"There're some sparks between us. I won't deny that. She is pretty irresistible," he admitted. *Sparks? Hell, with a little bit of kindling, I'd have a wildfire on my hands.*

"You just *met* her, Jake. You don't even *know* her. Maybe you're just attracted because you've been carrying that photo of her and the kid around for years. Same thing with that painting you bought off that old guy in the desert. You've spent hours staring at that weird landscape with the ghostly Indian and Spanish explorers. A painting *she* painted. It's got to be *subliminal*."

She looked at his crotch. One of her slender brows slowly rose. "Well, maybe it's not *all* subliminal. Maybe it's due to the fact that you live like a monk."

"Oh, yeah. Next to you anyone looks celibate." He shook his

head. "She's real, Kat, and she's nothing like what I thought she'd be. She's intelligent, caring, responsible. She's a great mother to Rick's son."

"Jake, think about it. You believed you owed it to Rick Saunders to keep looking for them. Maybe you feel now that you found them, you're responsible for them."

"This started out about Rick, but it's moved to a purely personal level."

"I watch the Sci Fi channel. Next thing you know, you'll be convinced Rick led you to them from beyond the grave for a reason."

"You ever think about ending up all alone, Kat? I mean, when you're all through playing Ms. Bond?"

She sobered. "I like myself. I like my life. I'm alone because I want to be. If I ever fall in love again, it'll be against my will, believe me. I'm not naïve enough to think love lasts forever anymore. I learned that the hard way. You take what you can get when you can get it. Ride the highs and wait out the lows."

She told him she had been engaged once, but she never mentioned it again.

"So, you really never plan on getting married?"

"Hey, Jake, you're a perfect example of what happens when wedded bliss goes sour. Your one-and-only winds up screwing somebody else. Now you can't even commit to unpacking your boxes after all these years. Why would I want to end up like you?"

She didn't give him time to answer before she asked, "What'll you do about Mrs. Saunders?"

"I'm going to talk to her later this morning. See what information she might already have. Something about this whole thing doesn't click."

"What do you mean?"

"If Anna Saunders' only concern is with her grandchild, and if Caroline knows that, then why did Caroline feel she had to run in the first place? Why didn't she just accept the Saunders' help after Rick died?"

"Maybe it's not really your friend's kid, and she was afraid they'd find out. Maybe they wanted blood tests."

"I thought of that." He shook his head. "But he's the spitting image of Rick. He has some of Rick's mannerisms, too. I think there's something else going on. I'll stall Anna Saunders for a while until I can get some answers."

"So you're *definitely* not going to tell her that you found Caroline?"

"No. Not yet. Not if I can help it."

"Caroline's all right with you being a P.I.? What did she say when you told her you knew Rick?"

He turned, stared out at the boaters in the marina. When he didn't answer right away, she jumped on it.

"You haven't *told* her?"

"Not yet. I was afraid she'd disappear again."

"Damn, Montgomery. When you dig a hole, you dig it deep." Kat got up again, stretched, rolled her head around on her neck and took a deep breath. "Well, one of us ought to get to work around here. I'll check the answering machine and do call backs."

"Don't take on any more clients than you can handle alone for a while," he warned.

She paused on her way to the office they shared in what would have been a master bedroom, the one where he had hung the painting Wilt Walton sold him years ago.

He'd driven out to Borrego after Rick's death to interview Walton and find out if Caroline's former roommate knew of her whereabouts. Jake had still been an agent of Alexander and Perry then, but, as a former friend of Rick's, he'd hoped to appeal to Walton.

Walton claimed he had no idea where Caroline had gone. The guy had been a character, but instinct had Jake believing him.

Kat was watching him from the doorway. "You're serious enough about this woman to keep it from Anna Saunders, aren't you? And at the same time, you haven't told Caroline that you're on to her."

He nodded.

"I hope you know what you're doing."

"So do I."

TWENTY-ONE

Anna forced herself to stay calm when her housekeeper announced that Jake Montgomery was on his way up. When she heard Estelle open the door, her heartbeat accelerated. Smoothing her hand over her hair, Anna walked into the foyer, greeted him, and dismissed the maid.

An intense ache of sorrow uncoiled in her the moment she saw Jake again and intensified when she reached for the solid warmth of the strong hand he offered. Rick would have been the same age as this tall, handsome man. Looking at Jake was like running a knife through her heart as she was forced to recall the two boys together, sunburned teens, summer friends.

She imagined her son would have matured in much the same way, maybe without such broad shoulders or hard sculpted jaw, but Rick surely would have been as tall and just as attractive, as fair as Jake Montgomery was dark.

But there was a seriousness lurking in this young man's eyes, a gravity Rick had never shown. Her son had grown up without a worry in the world, always carefree, always joking. There wasn't much he took seriously—which totally frustrated focused, structured Charles.

As she quickly assessed Jake Montgomery, Anna found herself wishing she could look into her son's laughing eyes once more and take back every last thing she had ever said about how he ought to grow up and take on some responsibility, act like an adult.

But it was too late to say all the things she longed to say, needed to say to her boy, too late to tell him she had always loved him just the way he was.

"Come in, Jake. Please." She led the private investigator through the wide, formal foyer to the living room. Indicating the sofa with a wave of her hand, she invited, "Have a seat."

"Thanks, Mrs. Saunders."

"Please, call me Anna."

As she chose a chair opposite him, his gaze swept the wide bank of windows twice before he looked back at her again.

If he wanted the place, she'd hand him the damn key. All he had to do was find Rick's son.

"Would you like something to drink?" she offered.

"No, thank you." He pulled the hem of his tweed sport coat out from under his hip.

"I won't beat around the bush and take up too much of your valuable time, Jake," she began. "I want to hire you to search for my grandson and the woman who stole him."

He leaned forward. "What about Alexander and Perry? I have to admit I'm more than a little surprised you called me after all this time." His voice was deep and not unpleasant. Very serious.

"I know that when you left them to start your own firm, Charles opted to stay with Alexander and Perry because of their reputation."

"I completely understood. I was just getting started. The other agency had better connections and resources, but what most investigators don't often admit is that even an amateur with a computer can find almost anyone if he knows where to look."

"*Almost* anyone but the woman who has my grandson. They might have the best reputation, but that firm still has nothing but dead ends." She reached for a file folder on the glass-topped coffee table and handed it over. "This is everything they've come up with."

She watched him carefully scan the contents. He could have made a fortune playing poker for high stakes, his expression giving away nothing until he came to an eight-by-ten photo at the back of the file.

He studied it carefully, then extended it toward her.

"Who is this?"

"That's Caroline Graham."

He stared at the black-and-white head shot again.

"This isn't the same woman in the picture that Rick gave me. I've never seen this photo."

Anna swallowed, automatically reaching for the gold and diamond heart necklace at her throat. She fingered it as she spoke.

"I didn't know that Rick had ever given *anyone* a photograph of Caroline. I certainly don't have one, and there's no other photo in the file."

"He came by my place the morning of the accident on his way back to the desert and showed me a stack of photos he'd taken of Caroline and his son. Even gave me one of them. He came by that day to ask me to be his best man."

Anna felt a swift blush of anger stain her cheeks. Jake Montgomery reached into his back pocket, pulled out his wallet, flipped it open. He slipped out a small photo and handed it to her.

Anna looked down at the poorly cropped picture with frayed edges. She hadn't seen it since the day Rick had showed a stack of similar photos to her and Charles—the day that he had announced he was getting married, that he had a son.

The same day he told them that it didn't matter what they said, that his mind was made up. At first she'd been in shock and had done little more than glance at the young woman in the photo as Rick and Charles argued fiercely.

She'd tried to be the voice of reason and to convince Rick that he needn't ruin his life marrying beneath him. He said he'd known that they would react this way, that they wouldn't approve of his choice, but he didn't care. He'd told them of his month-long fling in the desert with the waitress, of how he hadn't even seen her in well over a year, but when he looked her up again, he discovered she'd given birth to his child while he was in Japan.

Charles doubted the child was Rick's, certain Rick had been trapped. That's what she had thought, too, until Rick showed her the photos of the baby. There was no doubt the boy was his. She had photos in Rick's baby book that were nearly identical. The image of that bright-eyed boy had melted her heart.

But the mother, Caroline, was another matter. She looked tacky and coarse, barely twenty-three, if not younger.

Even now it made Anna heartsick to think it was altogether possible that Rick had never even known the girl's real name.

She handed the tattered photograph back to Jake.

He pocketed it without looking at it again, then pointed to the eight-by-ten lying on top of the open file on the table.

"Obviously that's not the same woman," he reiterated.

"No. I can see that it's not."

He flipped through pages of information, some compiled since he worked for the firm. Caroline Graham's Social Security and driver's license numbers were listed along with proof that she was born in Albuquerque. The photograph was copied from her high school yearbook. She was in a foster home until she ran away a few months before her eighteenth birthday.

She had surfaced not long afterward in Borrego Springs and took a job as a waitress. She was eighteen by then and Child Services had no interest in dragging her back to New Mexico. She stayed in Borrego and met Rick almost five years later.

Jake picked up the larger photo. "When you saw this, did you have any idea that this wasn't the same woman he proposed to? That this wasn't the same woman as the one in the photos with his son?"

"I saw the stack of pictures Rick had taken only once and very quickly. He left behind the one of him holding the baby. She wasn't in it. I . . . I told him I didn't want one of the girl, so he kept all the rest. If he had them when you saw him on his way out of town, then they were all destroyed in the accident."

She sighed. Fingered the jeweled heart again. "When Charles died two years ago, I swore to him I'd keep searching, but for a while, I hadn't the heart to go on. I've contacted Alexander and Perry a few times, but they've put the case on the back burner, I'm sure. Jake, I'll be honest. I'm not getting any younger. I want to see my grandson. I promised Charles I'd go on searching."

"Why call me now?"

"Because they have no personal stake in this. You knew Rick.

You were his friend. You tried to help us once. Will you take the case again or not?"

He hesitated so long she was afraid he'd turn her down.

"Look, Jake. My husband told me that a couple of years after Rick's death, you paid Charles back some money that Rick had loaned you. We hadn't even known about it, and if you'd never paid the debt, no one would be the wiser. You're an honest man, Jake Montgomery. A man of your word. That's why I want you to take this case again. For Rick's sake. For his son's. But most of all, for an old woman with a broken heart and a promise to keep."

She thought she saw him blanch and knew she'd struck the right chord. "I don't need someone who will give me false promises and take my money."

She could tell that he was uncomfortable whenever he looked at the photo she had thought was Caroline Graham.

Finally he met her gaze. "Why did she run?"

Taken aback, Anna blinked. "What do you mean?"

"What was she so afraid of? Why run from you and your husband? I would think that anyone in her position, a young, unwed mother, a waitress, would welcome and gladly accept your help. So why did she disappear?"

Anna cleared her throat and continued to looked him straight in the eye. Her Grandpapa Riley's advice came rushing back to her.

Never let it show when you're bluffin', my girl. Never let 'em know it.

"I . . . I have no idea."

"Let me look into this before I make a firm commitment and see what I can dig up. We're fairly busy right now."

"I thought you ran a one-man firm."

"I did when I first started, but I have a partner now. Her name is Kat Vargas."

"Are you telling me you're too *busy* to take my money?" She didn't know where she would turn if he didn't agree to help.

"I'm just saying I can't make you any promises right now." He picked up the photograph. "May I have this? I'll have a copy made and get it back to you. Finding out who this really is might be a start."

"Of course. Anything."

He straightened his jacket, got to his feet.

"I'll call you," he promised.

"I can't wait long, Jake. I'm sixty-five years old, and I'm not getting any younger."

She walked with him to the edge of the thick champagne-colored carpet, watched him move across the marble floor of the foyer to the door where she bid him good-bye.

Afterward, Anna walked out onto the balcony. Her hands closed around the iron railing. She took long, deep breaths to calm herself, the way her personal yoga instructor had taught her.

She closed her eyes and replayed the entire interview. No matter how many times she went over it, she found it impossible to shake the feeling that Jake Montgomery had been holding something back.

Jake walked into the office, jerked off his tie, and hung it over the doorknob.

Kat was at her own desk working through a list of documents on the computer. She raised her hand to let him know she was aware of his entrance, but didn't speak.

He went into his bedroom across the hall and tossed the photo on the unmade bed shoved up against one wall. A pile of books made a less-than-adequate bedside table big enough for a dusty clock radio. There was a lamp on the floor, a thirteen-inch television on a low stack of boxes on the opposite wall.

All temporary arrangements that had become permanent.

Jake opened a cardboard file box and rooted through it until he found one marked C. Graham. The mattress sagged as he sat down on the foot of the bed.

When he had first started hunting for her, he expected Caroline to turn up again as soon as she registered a car, opened a credit account or applied for a new driver's license. Even if she had changed her name, experience told him that she would most likely choose the same birth date or place of birth, the same first name—something that would eventually show up in a search.

He'd tracked down a few missing persons through data entered on warranty cards sent into manufacturers, but there was nothing current on Caroline Graham anywhere.

Kat suddenly appeared in the doorway. She never walked, she bounced, and so did her straight shoulder-length hair.

"So, how'd the meeting go with Ms. Saunders?"

"I told her I'd think about it."

"Stalling."

"Yep."

"Does she suspect anything?"

"No. How could she?"

"You could have slipped up. I've never seen you this way before."

Jake stood up. The file slid off his lap, the pages fanned out across the floor. "What way?"

"Discombobulated." She glanced down at the spilled file. "Maybe in love? You know *that's* always dangerous."

"Watch it, Vargas."

"So, what next?"

"I want you to check on something. Call her high school in Albuquerque. Have them send a copy of Caroline Graham's photograph from the yearbook."

"One picture of her isn't enough anymore?"

The photo Anna had just given him was lying facedown on the bed. He picked it up and handed it to Kat. She stared at it a second, then looked up.

"Who's this?"

"*That's* Caroline Graham. At least that's a photo that Alexander and Perry came up with after I left. Everything else they've found was pretty much what I already knew, same driver's license numbers, Social, Albuquerque record of birth, high school."

She had a keen enough eye to remember the face of the girl in the photo in his wallet and knew that the young woman in the eight-by-ten wasn't the same one. His photo had come directly from Rick. It had to be of the real Caroline.

"Not the right Caroline Graham, evidently. So what's up?"

"I've got to go over to TC Motor Sports and pick up their books. While I do that, will you scan this photo and have the original sent back to Anna Saunders? And then see what you can find on a Carly Nolan." He spelled the name for her. "Check Social Security, birth and death certificates in New Mexico. Check the DMV in New Mexico, Arizona, Nevada, California. If you can't find anything, widen the search."

"If she's not Caroline Graham, then who *is* Carly Nolan?"

"That's what I'd like to know."

TWENTY-TWO

Everyone in Twilight Cove was ready for summer, but the sun wasn't cooperating. Typical of California coastal towns in May and June, the sky remained overcast until noon, plunging spring temperatures and moods.

Carly had been in a funk since she'd left for work that morning, and even when the sun finally burned through the low cloud cover, her mood didn't lighten.

"Hey, cheer up." Joe handed her an order of soup and date nut bread. "The sun's out."

"I'll try." Easier said than done. She had been trying to convince herself that Jake's two-week absence from Twilight wasn't the reason she was feeling so glum.

For all she knew he could have decided not to lease the rental house after all, but she didn't have the nerve to ask Tracy or Glenn.

When she got back to the counter, Joe waved her over to the kitchen. She made certain the handful of customers didn't need anything before she ducked into the next room.

"What's up, Joe?"

"I'm worried about you, *chica*. You don't seem like yourself."

"I'm all right."

He leaned back against the big dishwashing tub and crossed his beefy arms. "I'm Christopher's official grandpa now. If something's wrong, you can tell me. I don't gossip."

"I know, Joe." Holding tight to her feelings was something she'd done all her life. She didn't know how to open up, even if she'd wanted to.

"Really, I'm okay. By the way, Chris is still talking about the *nopales* you took to school for the kids to taste. They couldn't believe it was really cooked cactus."

"I had to come up with something. He was expecting a bull-fighter."

"At least you set the kids straight on that one, even though it meant death to a town legend."

"Selma thought it would be good for business if people believed a retired *matador* was whipping up their dinners. I let it go all these years, but I couldn't lie to Christopher's whole class. They sort of forgot I wasn't anything special when I unwrapped that prickly pear cactus I'd cooked up and then let them taste it."

"You *are* special, Joe, to Chris and me. Don't you forget it." Moved by his generosity, Carly tentatively put her hand on his shoulder. Exchanging affectionate gestures didn't come easy if you hadn't grown up with them.

Just then Selma walked in and she planted her fists on her hips. "What's going on around here? Isn't anyone interested in making money today?"

Joe winked at Carly then walked over and slipped his arm around Selma's shoulders.

"She's just jealous." He pulled Selma closer, lowered his voice and thickened his accent. "How about coming over to my place after work? We'll share a nice bottle of wine. I'll cook my special chicken mole. Candlelight dinner and pay-per-view. What do you say, *mi amor?*"

Selma lifted his arm off her shoulder, let it drop. "I'm not your *amor*. My long-standing rule is *never* date the cook. It's one hell of a way to ruin a good business." She glanced at her watch and reminded Carly, "You'd better leave if you're going to get over to Avila Beach before Chris' game ends."

Carly whipped off her denim apron and headed for the door. "Thanks, Selma. See you tomorrow. Bye Joe. And thanks again."

Jake was counting the miles on the way up the coast, calculating the hours until he would finally be back in Twilight. It was Wednesday, and he was just wondering how late Carly would be working at the diner when he glanced into the rearview mirror and noticed a nondescript, gray sedan two cars back in his same lane.

He'd first spotted the Buick in Thousand Oaks on Highway 101 when he'd turned off the 405. The driver had maintained the same distance between them, changed lanes shortly after he did, essentially dogged his tail the whole way.

Nearing an off-ramp, he exited the freeway and headed for Paseo Nuevo Mall on State Street between Canon Perdido and Ortega streets. Another quick check in the mirror told him all he needed to know. The Buick had exited, too, and was still on him, hanging back, pulling behind a red Honda. The driver was a single, white male in a sport coat. His features were hidden behind wide sunglasses, but Jake recognized the shape of his head and shoulders.

Jake circled the parking lot and finally pulled into a parking stall near Nordstrom and got out of the car. He walked straight for the entrance and didn't look back. As soon as he was inside the door, he pocketed his sunglasses and made a quick right into the men's shirt section, zigzagged around a few display tables, and then doubled back toward the door.

He paused, picked up a cotton sweater, put it down, and then walked over to a table full of men's cargo shorts. He carried a khaki pair toward the dressing rooms and stepped inside.

On the quick count of five he walked back out, cut left and came up behind the heavyset man he'd seen at the wheel of the Buick.

"Jesus, Godes, you've gotten sloppy since I left A and P. Seems like you could have done a better job of not getting spotted."

The other P.I. slowly shook his head and turned around. "Hell, Jake. I tried to tell J.A. you wouldn't be an easy mark."

"Why the tail? What are you after?" Jake hadn't seen Sam Godes since his last day at Alexander and Perry. They'd been hired in the very same month and year, but obviously, Godes was still there. The minute Jake recognized him, he knew that his former employers had put a man on his tail—and he knew why. Still, he wanted confirmation.

Godes shifted, rubbed his hand over his jaw, and looked up at Jake. "Come on, Montgomery. I can't tell you that."

"You owe me big time, Sam. I took over all your cases for three weeks when your kid was in the hospital and you'd run out of sick days. I told you then that payback was hell. The least you can do is tell me what gives."

Sam Godes sighed and shook his head. "The Saunders woman called in and talked to J.A. himself. Said she thought you were on to something, that you may have a lead on the Graham woman and her grandkid. She wanted you tailed. I told the boss I thought it was a big waste of time, but he wanted to keep her happy, so here I am. Why don't you just tell me what's up, and I'll tell them case closed."

"I'm headed up the coast to visit a long-lost aunt."

"Give me a break, Montgomery."

"How 'bout you give me one. Turn around and head back to L.A. and tell them you lost me."

"Yeah, I *really* want to tell them you gave me the slip."

"What's it gonna take, Sam? You gotta give me a break on this one. You still owe me for those three weeks. I need time."

Godes cocked an eyebrow at Jake. "I'll take my time, spend my per diem on a room up here, drive back to L.A. tomorrow and tell A and P that you wound up visiting your long-lost aunt."

Godes was giving him time to put his cards on the table and tell Carly who he really was and maybe even get her to consider meeting with Anna Saunders.

Godes pulled his sunglasses out of his breast pocket. "So, we're all settled after this one. No more payback."

"You're clear," Jake agreed.

Godes turned to walk away.

"Hey, Sam."

"Yeah?"

"Thanks."

Jake watched Sam walk away before he tossed the cargo shorts on a nearby table and headed for the door. As Godes started across the parking lot, Jake spotted the Buick parked a few rows away from his own car. His attention was drawn to a slim young African-American woman with a baby carrier in one hand and a Nordstrom's bag in the other when she reached the door at the same time he did.

She smiled up at him and said thanks as he held the door for her and let her walk out first.

Once he was back in the car, he readjusted his rearview mirror, started the car and backed out of the stall. Godes' Buick was nowhere in sight. As Jake drove up the on-ramp and headed back onto 101, he passed the woman he'd held the door for. She looked over, recognized him, gave him a smile and a nod as he passed her and headed for the fast lane.

Carly was halfway up the canyon road when Betty Ford broke down. The old gal heaved, shook, wheezed, then died, but thankfully not before Carly pulled over to the shoulder.

The two-lane road was well traveled. It wouldn't be long before someone came along, but she had told Christopher that she would make it in time to see the end of the game and pick him up. She hadn't made any arrangements for the Potters to bring him back with them.

With a groan, she pushed the emergency flasher button. There was nothing she could do but let the engine cool and try to start the car again while she waited for help—that and wish she'd budgeted for a cell phone.

Jake checked the directions again, made another left and spotted the ballpark. He parked near Glenn Potter's car, got out and hit the alarm button on his key ring. The Stingrays were playing on the nearest diamond. He couldn't help but smile at all the pint-sized players in their official blue-and-gray T-shirts.

He scanned the bleachers. Disappointed when he didn't see Carly, he sat beside Tracy Potter.

"Welcome back, Jake. We expected you last weekend."

"I got hung up with work, but I finally managed to get a couple weeks away."

Time off wasn't quite the truth. He had a file box full of accounting records from a fraud case to review. With those and a laptop he could work anywhere and express the documents back to Kat.

As far as the Potters or anyone else knew, he was a self-employed business consultant. Completing the rental application had given him pause, but he'd used the standard, "self-employed," gave them a couple of bank account numbers, and asked that they keep all information confidential.

"I have a great partner." Greater than he knew. Kat hadn't minded taking over, doing things just the way he would do, loving every minute of being in charge. He had a feeling she was just humoring him, certain that he'd come dragging back with his heart in pieces, but since he had no intention of handing his heart over to Carly or whoever she was, that wasn't even a possibility.

"Glenn said he'd heard from the owners," he told Tracy.

She nodded and dug around in her purse. "They agreed to a six-month lease and half the rent on the house as long as you're still willing to make it livable. Glenn had a locksmith up there. Here're the new keys." She handed over two shiny keys on a Potter A#1 Realty key ring. "You can move in whenever you want. They really don't seem to want much to do with the place. Glenn described what a disaster it was, but I don't think he did it justice. I can't imagine why on earth you want to stay there."

"So you've seen it?"

"Glenn drove Matt and me up there last weekend. I've never seen such a mess in my life. It's a tear down, Jake."

Tracy hadn't let him down. He'd known exactly what she'd say about the place. Just then Christopher spotted him.

"Hey, Jake! Hi! Jake, hi!"

Jake smiled and waved just as the last Stingray at bat struck out and ended the game. The kids ran off the field and Matt and Christopher walked over to the bleachers.

When Chris climbed up and sat as close as he could get, took off his cap and brushed his hair back, Jake was again reminded of how much the boy resembled Rick, not only the way he looked but the way he moved. He had no idea who Carly Nolan really was or what she was up to, but there was no doubt that Chris was Rick Saunders' son.

"I didn't know you were coming back today."

"I didn't either, until this morning. Where's your mom?"

Chris frowned. "Late, I guess. She's *never* late, though."

"We'll take you home with us," Tracy said just as her cell phone went off. "Maybe this is Carly now."

Chris and Jake listened expectantly as Tracy's eyes widened.

"Oh, no! She's what? Are you sure? Maybe she was *poisoned*. Stop crying, Paula. We'll come home right now. If it gets any worse, call the vet."

Chris suddenly grabbed hold of Jake's hand, his little face drained of color.

Tracy snapped the phone shut and shouted to Glenn.

"Vet?" Jake closed his fingers gently around Christopher's hand, but not without noting how fragile it felt. "What's up, Tracy?"

Tracy efficiently gathered up her things—camera, blanket, purse, water bottle. Glenn hurriedly lugged ball equipment to the car.

"That was my next-door neighbor. Our Pekingese, Willa, was out in the yard howling, so Paula walked over to see what was going on. Willa is violently ill, poor baby. We've got to get home. I can't tell you the money we've got tied up in that damn designer dog."

She was off the bleachers, her arms full, headed for the car. "Come on, Chris," she called over her shoulder. Matt was already trailing in her wake. "We'll take you home."

Chris still had a death grip on Jake's hand. He looked up, his eyes imploring, "I'm not s'posed to."

"You're not supposed to what?" The kid was still shaken up from Tracy's phone call. So was Jake for that matter.

"I have to wait here. Mom said not to leave till she gets here. I know she's on the way. She *never* forgets. I'm only s'posed to ride with her unless she tells me. I'm scared something's happened to her, Jake." His bottom lip started to quiver as tears filled his eyes.

"Chris, come on! Hurry." The Potters had the car loaded. Glenn was climbing into the driver's seat.

Jake took Chris by the hand and walked him over to the car. "He says Carly told him to wait here."

Tracy leaned out the window. "It's okay this time, Chris. This is an emergency. Willa's sick, and we've got to hurry. She might have eaten something poisonous."

Chris tugged on Jake's hand. "Maybe you can stay with me till my mom gets here. Please, Jake?"

It was a no-brainer. He wasn't about to refuse, but he wasn't sure the Potters would leave Chris alone with him.

"I'll wait with you, if it's okay with the Potters."

If Carly failed to show, he could always drive Chris to Twilight himself. He wasn't going to panic over what might have happened to Carly. She was probably stuck at work or already on the way.

"Would you mind, Jake?" Tracy was in the car, still hanging out of the passenger window. Glenn had the engine running. "We'll probably pass Carly on the way out of the park."

"Sure. Go ahead. Tell her we'll be waiting right here."

They drove away, the car kicking up dust as Glenn peeled out of the parking lot. Jake took Christopher by the hand and led him back to the bleachers where the boy had left his small bag of gear.

Soon all the other parents and kids had driven away, too, and they were alone. Jake had taken care of his niece and nephews before, so he wasn't uncomfortable, but he found himself thinking about how this was Rick's kid and how Rick should have been here.

"Wanna toss the ball around?" Chris looked hopeful.

Jake shrugged. "Sure, why not."

Chris's smile, another distinct echo of Rick, spread about a mile wide. "Great!"

With the first toss Jake realized Chris would do more chasing than catching so he squatted down and started to gently lob the ball.

"Know what, Jake?"

"What, Chris?"

"We had grandparents' day at school, and I didn't have any, so Mom said I could ask Joe from the diner. He brought a bullfighting sword with him. It was real sharp and pointy and the principal almost took it away from him. She said if Joe was a kid she'd have to suspend him. We can't bring anything like that to school, you know?"

"Really."

"Yeah. But Joe said he had to confess, once and for all, that he *wasn't* a bullfighter, that he was just a cook. The sword was only a souvenir. And he brought this *really* dangerous cactus with *killer* needles all over it. He *cooks* it!"

"No kidding."

"Yeah. Only the bravest kids tasted it. It was great."

"Sounds like you had fun."

"I asked Mom if I could share you at school, like a fake dad, but she said no."

"What's a fake dad?"

"You know. Some of the kids have a real dad, but their mom gets married again, and then they have a real dad *and* a fake dad at the same time. They live with one and they live with the other one sometimes, too."

"My real dad died when I was eight. Then I had a 'fake' dad, but I felt like he was another real dad," Jake volunteered.

"I don't have either kind. Hey, Jake?"

"What, Chris?"

"How do you spell your name?"

"Why?"

"I'm learning to write stuff at school. Maybe Monday I'll draw a picture and write about you playing catch with me. Can we stop now?" Chris had already chased more balls than he'd caught.

"I'm getting pretty tired myself."

They walked back to the bleachers, and Chris scrambled to the top, so Jake followed. The boy sat down, propped his elbows on his knees, his chin in his hands.

"Wonder where my mom is? I hope she's okay."

Jake was worried, too, but tried not to let on. "She'll probably be along any minute now."

"Know what, Jake?"

"No. What?"

"I hope Willa's okay. Have you ever had a dog?"

"Two. Larry and Moe, but not at the same time. They were both mutts. They never got sick."

"What's a mutt?"

"A mixture of different kinds of dogs, not one special kind like a Pekingese."

"I want a dog so bad. I'd even take a mutt, but Mom says we can't have one. We might have to move."

"Move?"

"She always says that, but we haven't moved for a long time. I don't even remember the other places we lived. She tells me that we can't have a dog or a cat because we might have to leave all of a sudden. And she thinks our place is too small for pets, but Mrs. Schwartz has one, and her place is smaller than ours."

"Does your mom ever talk about where she'd like to move to?"

Chris shrugged. "Not really. I don't want to move anyplace."

"It must be a lot of trouble to move all the time."

"We've got emergency bags all packed, just in case of an earthquake, too." The boy pulled down his sock and scratched his ankle, then pulled it back up. "She doesn't talk about moving too much anymore."

The boy's innocent comment confirmed Jake's worst fears. Carly was obviously prepared to relocate any time she believed her identity had been compromised. If he'd told Carly the truth about himself the night they first met, she most likely would have been gone the next day.

There had to be more at stake here than keeping Anna Saunders from taking part in Christopher's life.

"Hey! There she is!" Chris started waving and bolted down the bleachers. Jake watched Carly enter the parking lot and pull up next to his car. When she jumped out, the old Ford's engine continued to rattle.

Chris ran up and threw his arms around her thighs. Carly hugged him tight, though she was looking across the lot at Jake with a frown marring her expression. The breeze drew a few strands of hair across her lips. She brushed it back, then gave Christopher a quick kiss on the top of his head.

The whole time he'd been in Los Angeles, he had tried to convince himself that his initial attraction to her hadn't been that intense. The longer he was away, the more he'd convinced himself it was nothing but a brief infatuation. And why not? He'd been focused on finding her on and off for six years.

But now, seeing her again, there was no denying her allure. On an emotional level, he felt a strong, irresistible pull whenever he looked at her. A magnetic force he'd never experienced before.

But his investigative side never rested. As he watched her smile over at him, he couldn't help but wonder if she had ever trusted Rick enough to tell him her real name.

Who was she and what in the hell was Carly Nolan running from?

TWENTY-THREE

Carly brushed her hair back, licked her lips, and tried to smile. Both the delay and her concern for Christopher had shaken her, but she refused to let them see her as upset as she had been the last time they were all together.

"Mom, where were you?" Chris wriggled free and demanded an explanation.

"Betty stalled on the way up the canyon. I thought I was going to have to have her towed, but I got her started again after she cooled off. I saw the Potters on their way back. They told me you were waiting here with Jake."

She met Jake's eyes and started walking toward him with Chris tagging along beside her. Her anxiety over being late coupled with the excitement of seeing Jake again had her heart racing.

"I'm sorry, Jake. I've never, ever been late picking Chris up before."

"I didn't mind. The Potters offered to take him home, but he insisted that he wasn't supposed to ride with anyone but you."

"That's the rule unless I tell him differently. Maybe we should talk about some exceptions, though. I'm really sorry we held you up."

"It's no problem. We tossed the ball around."

"Yeah. And we talked," Chris added.

"Really? What about?" Carly hesitated a second before walking over to the bleachers. As she picked up Chris' small duffel bag, she wondered what he might have said.

"Oh, just guy stuff." Chris looked up at Jake. "Huh, Jake?"

"Yeah. Guy stuff."

She almost smiled at the two of them standing there together, but it was bad enough having Chris walking around with stars in his eyes over Jake. One of them had to keep a clear head.

Jake said, "I called Glenn to let him know I was on the way back to town, and he suggested I stop by the game and pick up the new keys to the house."

He walked them back to Betty Ford and waited while she loaded Chris up and fastened his seat belt. When she tried to start the car, the engine didn't even turn over. There was nothing but a repetitive clicking noise.

"Oh, no," she groaned, embarrassed.

"That doesn't sound good to me," Chris piped up.

"Me either," Jake added from where he stood beside the car.

"I think she's about done for." Carly grasped the top of the wheel with two hands and stared over her knuckles through the windshield. Arlo Carter down at the Twilight service station managed to keep Betty running, but he'd been predicting impending doom for a couple of years now.

Jake opened Carly's door. "I'll call Triple A and have your car towed back to Twilight and drive you two home."

"I can't let you do that, Jake." She shook her head and didn't budge. The last thing she wanted was to be dependent upon anyone, especially Jake. She was still haunted about the money she'd taken from Wilt's and fully intended to pay him back someday. But it was best not to leave a trail of debt behind.

"Yes, you can." He'd already pulled out his cell and punched the automatic dial for the Auto Club. He gave a description of the car, told the dispatcher where to find them.

"They'll be here in thirty minutes. Might as well wait in my car." He stepped back so she could get out.

Chris was already out of the car. "Come on, Mom. Jake will get us home."

Carly still hadn't budged. "I'm used to taking care of myself," she said softly.

He put both hands on the door, leaned down close to the open window. His gaze slowly searched her face thoroughly enough to make her catch her breath.

"Let me in, Carly." He put his hand beneath her chin, gently forced her to meet his eyes. "Let me help you."

• • •

Forty-five minutes later they were on the road again, this time in Jake's SUV. The back end was filled with five-gallon drums of paint, brushes, rollers, poles, drop cloths, and boxes. There was an old toolbox on the floor of the backseat.

He'd put on a classical guitar CD, and for a long while they were all content to ride along in silence, listening. Carly looked into the backseat at Chris and softly said, "He's asleep."

Jake glanced into the rearview mirror. Sure enough, Chris was slumped over, sound asleep, looking small and vulnerable. The kid's trust only intensified his guilt.

After what Chris had unwittingly told him, he knew that exposing the truth would not only mean the end of their friendship, but that Carly would most likely leave town and turn her and Chris's lives upside down.

Driving back to Twilight Cove, Jake made a silent pact with himself to tell Carly the truth the minute he had convinced her that he was there to help and not to ruin her life.

Back at the ballpark, he'd tried to start her car again, which had given him time to take a look in her glove compartment. The registration was right on top of the original owner's manual. It was current, but filed under the name Etta Schwartz. There would be no way to trace Carly through the vehicle.

They rode along in what would have been comfortable silence had his mind not been racing.

The beautiful drive through the open country, the rolling fields of flowers and vegetables lulled them into a quiet, peaceful camaraderie. There was something right about having her and the boy with him, so right it tempted him to reach for her hand. But he didn't.

Get over it, Montgomery.

The picture didn't fit anymore. A wife and kids of his own was an old, faded dream.

Best not to go there. You don't even know who she is.

"Are you staying at Rose Cottage again?" she asked.

"Not this trip. I decided to camp out at the house. Glenn had the electricity and water turned on, so I brought a sleeping bag, an air mattress, and a microwave. I hope I'll get to stick around a couple of weeks before I have to go back to L.A."

"Will it be hard working from here?"

"I've got a great partner." He couldn't say more, so he let the subject drop. As they rode along in silence again, listening to the guitar soloist, it was easy to imagine how good things might be between them, until he reminded himself that nothing about keeping a relationship going was easy. It would be even harder with all the lies between them, both his and hers.

As they came around the last bend in the canyon, the panorama of the ocean at sunset unfolded against the horizon. The setting sun stained the sky, slowly transforming the tints from blazing brilliance to muted evening hues.

"Have you started my painting yet?" he asked her.

"You'll be the first to know when I do." She smiled as she stared ahead, watched the colors collide.

"Are you seeing them right now?"

"Who?"

"People from the past. The characters that you include in your paintings."

"Sometimes I get fleeting glimpses. I can't explain how it happens. I work on the landscape first, give them a place to stand. Sometimes when I pick up the brush, they suddenly appear in my mind's eye, and then they begin to take shape on canvas."

She sounded perfectly serious, though he'd been half kidding when he asked.

"You don't think they may have actually existed once, do you?"

She shrugged, looked at him, and smiled. "Who knows? Maybe. I like the idea of believing in the magic of them suddenly coming to life again in my work."

When they pulled up in front of the mobile home, and Jake turned off the motor, Chris came instantly awake.

"Mom, can Jake stay for dinner?"

"We're just having macaroni and cheese, but you're welcome to share," Carly offered.

"It's the box kind," Chris bragged. "That's my favorite, Jake. How about you?"

"It's the only kind I ever make." Jake pictured the slick little tight macaroni with orange mystery cheese sauce. "Really, it is."

Once they were all inside, he insisted she let him set the table. Carly mixed up the mac and cheese, rustled up a hearty green salad, and toasted bread with butter and Parmesan.

The three of them sat at the small Formica dining table. He and Carly both fell silent, but Christopher chattered away.

Jake couldn't help thinking that this was the way it should be for Carly and Chris. They should be part of a family that cared about and watched over them. They deserved a host of extended family to celebrate Christmas with, to share birthdays and all of life's triumphs and tragedies. But for whatever reason, whatever it was Carly feared, they'd been denied the joy of family.

Most days what the two of them shared was probably enough.

But what about Carly's nights? Were they as long and lonely as his?

What of the dreams she surely dreamed in the desert when she thought that she and Rick and Christopher would have a future together?

When they finished dinner, Christopher cleared the table without having to be asked, showing off for Jake as he carefully carried everything across the kitchen. Carly asked Jake if he wanted coffee or decaf, but he declined both.

"Do you have any homework?" Carly asked Chris.

"Nope. I did it during free time in class."

"Then you'd better get to bed. Get ready and I'll come tuck you in."

Chris paused in the kitchen doorway, macaroni smudges on his Stingray T-shirt, one sock crumpled around his ankle. His hair was shoved to one side, matted down by his ball cap. There were crumbs at the corner of his mouth.

"Can Jake tuck me in tonight?"

"Chris . . ." Carly turned to Jake with an apology on her lips, but he gave a slight shake of his head. Chris' request was not the imposition she thought. It simply left a hole in his heart where his conscience had been hiding.

"Sure thing," Jake promised. "Call me when you're ready."

When Chris ran out of the room, Carly turned to him.

"I'm sorry," she said softly. "I never meant to impose on you like this."

"Carly, helping you, being with Christopher, these aren't impositions."

"He already thinks the world of you, Jake."

He glanced over at the empty doorway. "I know."

The trouble was, he really did know. And it was killing him.

Chris changed faster than ever, tossed his dirty clothes into the laundry basket, jumped into his 'jamas and brushed his teeth. He even wet the corner of a bath towel and scrubbed his face before he flew back to his room and hopped into bed.

"I'm ready, Jake!" he hollered. Then he scrunched down and pulled the covers up to his chin and tried to pretend he was sleepy when Jake walked in, but he ended up grinning like the Cheshire cat in the Alice video.

"You look pretty well tucked in to me," Jake teased.

Chris liked the way Jake's voice sounded. Not all soft and lovey like Mom's. It was big and deep and . . . comfortable, like the old sofa in his mom's studio. It made him feel all toasty just like when he drank a cup of hot chocolate on a cold afternoon.

"You gotta sit on the edge of the bed and talk about stuff before you tell me goodnight," he told Jake.

"What kind of stuff?"

"Important stuff. Like, you ask, 'How was your day?' And if I say it was bad, you say, 'It'll get better.' "

"How do I know that?"

"Because tomorrow's always better. It's when you get another chance to do things right."

Jake sat. Chris could tell he was trying to be real careful not to squish him. Jake kept looking at him funny, too, like he was thinking about somebody else, maybe. Chris started to worry that Jake might be thinking of some other kid.

"It's your first time, right?"

"First time for what?"

"Tucking somebody in."

"Officially, yes. I've got a niece and nephews, but they never asked me to do this."

"Since it's your first time, you don't have to tell a story."

"Thanks. I've got to get up to the house before it gets too dark anyway."

"Yeah. I know."

"You feeling tucked in yet?"

Chris wriggled a little deeper beneath the covers. "Kinda. Jake?"

"What, Chris?"

"Are you married?"

"No. I was once, though."

"You got any kids?"

"Nope."

"Do you ever want any?"

Jake got real quiet, like he was thinking really hard, then he said, "Well, that's a difficult question. I used to want some really badly when I was first married, but since I'm divorced now, I don't think about it much."

"You'd be a real good dad."

Jake looked at the wall, then he looked really funny, like somebody was pinching him.

"What makes you think so?" When Jake spoke, Chris could hardly hear him.

"You don't yell or anything. You're a good ball thrower. You've got a *killer* car."

"It takes more than that to be a good dad, Chris."

Chris didn't think so, but he was willing to listen to what Jake thought. "Like what?"

"Like patience. Do you know what that is?"

"Sure. Mom always tells me to be patient. It means you have to wait and wait for something to happen or for somebody to do something, and you can't get mad or whine if it takes too long."

"Right. You have to be a good teacher, too, so you can teach your kids what they need to know."

"Like how to play ball."

"Yeah, and other things. Like about life."

"Like a mentor."

"Right."

"*And* you have to love 'em no matter what they do," Chris added, feeling proud of himself, thinking about his mom.

Jake waited so long to say something else that Chris thought he was all done talking. Then, in a voice that sounded like he was catching a cold, Jake added, "That's probably the most important part."

Chris yawned, rolled over and smiled against the pillow. Jake pulled the covers higher around his shoulders and gave his head a pat.

"See," Chris mumbled, closing his eyes. "I know you'd be a real good dad. You already know all about it."

Carly walked Jake to the door. She'd heard him and Chris talking softly, but knowing how important it was to Christopher to have Jake to himself, she resisted the urge to join them.

The thought that her son was losing his heart to this man scared her to death, but no matter what came of her own relationship with Jake, she hoped it was better that Chris be exposed to the man's kindness and honesty than to deny her son.

When she and Jake stepped out onto the porch, he pulled on his sport coat. Before she realized what she was doing, she reached up and straightened the back of his collar.

When he instantly froze, she feared she'd overstepped some boundary she wasn't aware of and began to pull back.

He surprised her by slipping his arm around her waist and drawing her up against him.

"I want to kiss you, Carly."

Step away. Move out of his arms. You don't really know him, do you? Don't take the risk.

She closed her heart off to the warnings in her mind.

"Then do," she whispered against his lips.

His kiss came on a gentle sigh, almost as if he were trying to resist but couldn't, as if he'd fought some inner demon and lost.

His mouth lingered over hers, teased, tasted, toyed. She held onto the waistband of his slacks, kissed him back, thirsting for more. He pressed his palm against the small of her back and pulled her close, letting her know that he wanted even more intimate contact.

Her breasts flattened against the hardness of his chest. She felt his arousal through their clothing.

It was her turn to sigh. She melted against him, wrapped her arms around him, returned the deepening kiss. Their tongues explored, tasted. A soft moan escaped her. Jake tightened his hold as he slowly backed her up against the side of the mobile home.

Not until her legs turned to rubber and her insides to mush, did he lift his head. He stared into her eyes through the darkness that enveloped them.

"We need some time alone together," he whispered.

"You mean you're tired of dating Chris, too?"

"We need to talk, Carly."

His sober tone frightened her. She had no idea what he had on his mind.

"What about?"

"About things. Us. Life. About the fact that I've been fighting the urge to touch you since you drove up to the ball park."

Us. She put a finger against his lips. "Can't we just *be* for now, Jake?" It was all too new for this plunge into intimacy. She was barely off the diving board, still hadn't come up for air, and he wanted to talk about *us*.

"What about tomorrow night? Can you get the neighbor lady to sit with Christopher?"

Mentally she ran through the week's schedule and almost groaned aloud.

"Tomorrow's Thursday. I have to work."

"Friday, then?"

"Maybe."

"Call me." He squeezed her hand. "I left my cell number on the pad beside your phone in the kitchen."

She thought he'd say good-bye and walk away, but he continued to hold her close, almost as if he couldn't bear to let her go.

No one had ever held her this way, as if she were something precious, someone who deserved to be loved. Not even Rick.

Jake held her tenderly, as if she might break.

Finally, after another heated kiss, he turned her loose. He finger-combed his hair, ran his hand around his waistband to straighten his shirt.

" 'Night, Carly. You have my cell number. The next move is yours."

As she watched him walk away, she couldn't help wondering where they were headed, and then she said a silent prayer that it was someplace where hearts were never broken and promises lasted a lifetime.

If a place like that even existed at all.

TWENTY-FOUR

Friday morning was picture-postcard perfect. The sun was shining, the ocean calm with just enough onshore breeze to ruffle the geranium blossoms in two huge terra cotta urns flanking the door of The Cove Gallery.

Feeling more alive than she had in years, Carly paused to admire the bright fuchsia blooms spilling over the sides of the urns as she carried her latest finished piece inside.

"Well hel-lo stranger! Where have *you* been hiding?" Geoff spread his arms in greeting as he stepped out from behind the counter and crossed the room to meet her.

Taking the large, mounted canvas, he held it at arms' length, admiring the work with a slow, deliberate eye. It depicted the cove during a storm. Bloated gray clouds hung low over the water. Wind battered the crescent bluff. A sea captain stood alone near the edge of the land, buffeted by the elements. With one hand he anchored his hat, with the other, he clutched the lapels of a double-breasted pea coat.

"This is a real beauty."

"I named it *Weathering the Storm*."

Geoff winked at her. "Has Mr. Luscious anything to do with the inspiration behind this one?"

There was nothing she could do about the blush kindling her cheeks, so she simply smiled. "Jake's been angling for a sunset, but I guess the sea captain just had to be finished first."

Geoff carried the painting into the back room where he framed and wrote labels for the pieces to go on display.

While Carly waited for him to return, her gaze swept the room. She noticed quite a few new paintings hanging since the night she had filled in for Geoff.

He walked back into the main room carrying two steaming mugs with tea bag tags dangling over the rims. He handed her one.

"Thanks." She took care not to slosh the steaming liquid. "How's business?"

"Business is off to a great start, but let's not go there right now. I want to hear *all* about your love life." He led her over to two low retro armchairs positioned so that they offered a view of the gallery pieces as well as the front window.

He folded one leg beneath him, blew on the steaming tea. His left brow slowly arched as his lips curved into a knowing half smile.

"Well? Are you going to dish the dirt or not?"

When she drove Chris to school earlier that morning, she had a feeling that seeing Geoff might help settle her nerves. Her heart was already lighter, and she was smiling.

"There's no dirt to dish," she laughed.

"Oh, come on. Last time we talked, you were getting ready to go on a picnic at the hunk's place."

"Has it been two weeks? Let's just say things started out fine, but then Chris took off down the arroyo, and I thought he was lost. I got pretty upset."

"Well that's understandable. Is Chris all right?"

She nodded, testing to see if the heady lemon herb tea was cool enough to sip. "He's fine, and of course I eventually settled down. The next day Jake had to go back to L.A."

"Too bad."

Carly took another sip. "But he's back."

"Aha."

"Aha, what?"

"Originally he claimed to be passing through, just here to inquire about your work. Looks like he's attracted to a bit more than your talent."

"Actually, he's rented a house up on Lover's Lane because he's planning to spend a few days a week here this summer."

"Go, girl." Geoff stared down into the cup as if looking for a sign, then met her eyes again. "Or aren't you interested?"

"I'm interested. Very interested." Then she took a deep breath. "I'm just not sure how he feels about me. We've been to dinner and on a picnic, with Chris along. The last time we were together, Jake left the next move up to me."

"What's the problem? Call him."

"And then what?"

"What do you *want* to happen?"

It had been so long, she wasn't sure. She'd been so young when she fell for Rick. He'd been her first headlong infatuation, her first love. During the month they shared, she'd gone from a girl to a woman, lost her virginity, learned of sensual delight and passion.

The rest of their story had been an emotional roller coaster ride from beginning to end. She had no idea what to expect from a real relationship.

What *did* she want now?

"Yoo hoo. Carly . . ." Geoff leaned closer, waved his hand in front of her face. "Where'd you go?"

"I'm sorry." She rested the mug on her knee. "I was just trying to come up with an answer. I have no idea where to go from here."

"Has he kissed you yet?"

"Yes."

"More than once?"

"Yes."

"Well then." He tapped his chin, watched a couple walk past the gallery window, ready to greet them if they came inside, but they kept on walking. "I'd say you need to sample the goods."

"This isn't exactly like picking out a melon at the store."

"Let me be perfectly frank, honey. Right now you're dancing around each other, having little forays that verge on real intimacy. Why not find out if you two are suited for each other? Apparently you *like* being with him, right?"

"He's wonderful. Plus, he's really great with Christopher. I enjoy being with him, even though most of the time I feel nervous and awkward. I don't want him to get the feeling I'm desperate, because I'm not."

"Anybody can see that a woman like you would never have to be desperate. You're just out of practice."

"You have no idea."

"Then I'd say take it to the next level. Pump up the volume. Get intimate. Give yourself a chance to find out how you are together."

"What am I supposed to do? Just call him up and tell him I'm ready to . . . well, you know." Blushes were impossible to control.

"I'd say you're *long* overdue if you can't even *say* it." Geoff uncurled his legs, stood up and held out a hand for her empty mug. "Want a warm up?"

"No thanks, I've already stayed longer than I planned. I have the whole day off today, and Chris is going to his first sleepover at Matt's tonight."

Geoff had started across the room with the mugs but stopped in his tracks and swiveled around. "Let me see if I have this right. It's Friday. You have the night off, *and* for the first time in *forever*, you're going to be alone *all night long*?"

He gave a dramatic little shiver of delight. "This is perfect! Now listen up, Carly, and let Uncle Geoff tell you *exactly* what to do."

Jake shifted the cell phone, leaned against one of the front porch pillars, and watched the whitecaps far offshore.

"Hey, Kat. Did you come up with anything on Carly Nolan yet?" He could hear her shuffling through paperwork on her desk.

"You bet. When I called the high school in Albuquerque, I found out that when Caroline Graham was registered as a senior, a Carly Nolan was enrolled as a sophomore. Caroline never graduated. It turns out Nolan wasn't listed as a junior or a senior the following years, which means she and Caroline both left the same year. There's no record of Carly Nolan in any high school in New Mexico or Arizona *or* California after that."

Jake walked over to the steps, sat on the porch. He had on paint-spattered, faded Levi's with rips across one knee and beneath the back pocket. His worn, black high-top athletic shoes were smeared with the same white semi-gloss paint he'd been rolling on the walls.

"Did you ask them to fax us a copy of the photo of Carly Nolan?"

"Duh. And guess what? Same *exact* face you've been carrying around in your wallet." Kat began ticking off the facts as she knew them. "It seems Miss Nolan never took out a driver's license in New Mexico. There was nothing at the DMV listed for her at all until six years ago when she applied for a license in California. No car has ever been registered in her name. Phone number is unlisted. She has a Social Security number, though. Filed for it the same year she got the California license."

Jake leaned against the porch column. "So, Carly and Caroline Graham attended the same high school for a year, but Carly seems to have disappeared until six years later. Supposedly Caroline Graham was working at a restaurant in Borrego, according to the Social Security records."

"There's more." Kat was always proud of her sleuthing abilities and delighted when they paid off. "While I had the school on the line, I asked for the counselor. He gave me the name of the woman who had been there when both girls attended, but she retired a few years ago. I found her in the Albuquerque phone directory."

"Let me guess, she's elderly, retired, loves to talk."

"You got it. Luckily, she still has a mind for detail. Remembered both girls. Caroline was always in and out of trouble, always in the principal's office or on suspension. Carly was, too, even though she tested out high on the IQ charts. She didn't apply herself and as far as I can tell she never received a high school diploma from anywhere."

"Did she and Caroline know each other?" Jake watched a small dust devil whip across the drive.

"It's way better than that. They were both living in the same foster home. Caroline, Carly, and two younger boys. The two girls ran away. They took off in March of Caroline's senior year and never turned up in the foster care system again."

Jake was silent for so long that Kat finally asked, "Are you thinking what I'm thinking?"

"That Carly assumed Caroline's identity."

"Right. We *know* she was living in Borrego passing herself off as Caroline Graham when she moved in with that Walton character. Your buddy, Rick Saunders, knew her as Caroline, too, but the pictures he had were of Carly Nolan, the woman you met in Twilight Cove."

Jake got up and started to pace the front drive. "So, Carly most likely ran away with Caroline Graham. Sometime after that, assuming Caroline's identity, she shows up in California and uses Caroline's Social Security number to get a job."

Kat filled in the rest. "Then right after Carly left Borrego Springs with the kid, she started using her *own* name again. She applied for a driver's license as Carly Nolan, established her own Social Security number, and no one was the wiser. While you and the Saunders' P.I.s were searching for Caroline Graham, digging up *her* history, Carly Nolan was the one you really should have been after the whole time. It was a seamless plan. Carly had simply assumed her own identity again."

"We had no idea who she really was and would have never found her—"

"If I hadn't seen that travel magazine article about the gallery and noticed the painting."

"But that leaves another, even bigger question hanging."

"Yeah, I know," Kat said. "What happened to the real Caroline Graham?"

TWENTY-FIVE

That evening Jake showered in rubber thongs.

He wasn't the greatest housekeeper in the world by any stretch of the imagination, but he did have some standards. The old bathroom upstairs wasn't even up to those.

His shoes squished when he stepped out onto the old tile floor. He dried off, then towel dried his hair, shoved it in place with his fingers and walked into the bedroom to grab clean clothes. He'd gone through all his Hungry Man dinners already and wasn't looking forward to canned soup, so he had decided to drive down to town and have dinner at the diner.

He was so hungry that he clearly imagined the aroma of baked chicken, sure that paint fumes had finally gotten to him, convinced he was hallucinating, until he walked downstairs and discovered Carly seated on a blanket spread out on the living room floor.

She'd centered a tablecloth on the plaid blanket and laid out a romantic dinner for two complete with white ceramic dishes that he recognized from her place, long-stemmed wineglasses, and candles in crystal candleholders. White linen napkins were folded into bird of paradise blossoms.

His heart stumbled when she smiled up at him, her eyes filled with all the things he wished he couldn't recognize—expectation, a touch of fear, an underlying trust that he didn't deserve.

When he had told her the next move was hers, he hadn't expected any more than a phone call.

Now without trying, she had succeeded in making him feel like a bigger heel than he already thought he was. Silently cursing himself, it didn't help knowing that she had plenty of secrets of her own. He smiled back at her as he walked into the room.

The candlelight reflected in her deep green eyes made her

appear younger, more vulnerable than ever. She'd worn her hair loose and free, draping her shoulders. A blush pink, sleeveless sweater complemented the high color on her cheeks.

If what he and Kat suspected was true, Carly was only twenty-six, not twenty-nine.

"This is a nice surprise." He sat down on the floor at the place she'd set for him.

"You said you wanted to talk," she told him softly.

"I said the next move was yours." He motioned to the candles, the wineglasses. "Wow."

There was no way in hell he could explain his motives now, not without making her feel like a fool.

She stared up into his eyes for a second, then looked away as she reached into the basket again. "I brought some bottled water. And some wine. I didn't know if you like wine. I would have opened it, but I can't seem to make this corkscrew work."

Her hands shook as she passed him a bottle of water, then the corkscrew, a very nice bottle of Pinot Grigio, and started fidgeting with the food boxes. He set everything down.

"Carly?"

Startled, she froze with her hands on a half-opened container of chicken. "Have you eaten?"

"No. Your timing couldn't be better. I'm starving." He closed his eyes and inhaled deeply. "God, that smells great."

"It's Joe's special herb chicken. The recipe is a secret."

"Where's Chris?"

"Sleeping over at Matt's."

"Give me your hands."

"My hands?"

"Those things at the ends of your arms. Connected to your wrists." He held his own hands out across the place settings.

She extended her hands toward his. He took hold and held them gently but firmly. She was still trembling.

"Everything looks beautiful. I really appreciate all the trouble you've gone to tonight." He held onto her, forcing her to meet his eyes. "Are you all right?"

She opened her mouth, closed it again, and shook her head.

"Not really. This wasn't my idea," she confessed. "It was Geoff's. Now that I'm here, I'm afraid I've made a fool of myself."

"Never. Now, I haven't had a decent meal in two days, and I'm starved. What do you say I open the wine, and let's eat? We can pretend we're eating box macaroni and cheese in your kitchen if it makes you feel more comfortable."

Her fingers had tightened on his hands while he spoke, but he could see she was relieved.

"Okay. That sounds great."

He let go, picked up his plate and handed it to her. "You pile on the chicken, and I'll open the wine."

"It's a deal."

Carly had changed four times before she decided on the pink, sleeveless mock turtleneck and Levi's. She had groaned when she slipped into her underwear, knowing after all the trouble Geoff had gone to that if he had seen her cotton briefs and sports bra, he'd have called the Victoria's Secret hotline and placed an emergency order.

When Jake had first walked into the room and found her sitting there, she was afraid she was going to throw up right in front of him, but he'd known the exact words to say to help calm her racing heart.

She watched him eat everything that she heaped on his plate while she only managed a few bites of salad and two glasses of wine. The wine was probably the best and worst idea of the whole plan. Buttery and mellow, it helped take the edge off, but it also stirred her blood, made the night soft and fuzzy.

She found herself half listening to Jake, concentrating not on the words but on the way his lips formed them, the sound of his voice. Warm and deep, it moved over her like a comforting caress.

"Carly?"

"Hmm?" She started when she realized he was expecting her to say something. She set down her empty wine glass. He held her gaze with the intensity of his own.

"I said that was delicious. The best meal I've had in a long time." He picked up the wine bottle, filled her glass halfway, topped off his own. "Let's go out to the porch."

"Okay." She watched him stand, let him help her to her feet. He reached for the wineglasses, handed her one, and together they walked carefully across the maze of drop cloths to the front door.

Outside, darkness tinted the hillside in black and gray. She walked to the end of the porch, sat on the low wall, looking into the darkness, out toward the sound of the breakers crashing on the point.

A slight breeze was blowing. There wasn't a cloud in the star-spattered sky. She set her wineglass down, afraid to take another sip, afraid of losing control. She didn't want to forget a single detail of this night.

When Jake moved up behind her, she was certain she'd have known he was there, even if she hadn't heard the soft slap of his rubber thongs against the porch. She felt his arm on her shoulder and then a gentle nudge as he pulled her against him. Resting against his chest, feeling the beat of his heart and every breath he took, she closed her eyes.

The rhythm of his heartbeat was slow and sure. Hers was racing triple time. Staring out at the infinite patterns of stars, listening to the sound of the sea as it echoed against the black hills, she wished time could stand still.

She wished for tomorrows, not yesterdays. Wished for no more regrets, no bad memories, no disappointments. She wanted only to remember this night and hoped for new memories to come.

He stroked her arm, moved his hand upward until his thumb was at the nape of her neck, his fingers gently wrapped around her throat. He made slow, lazy little circles against the nape of her neck.

"What are you thinking about?" His voice, so close to her ear, came to her out of the silence, stirred her down to her toes.

"The night. All those stars. How I sometimes wish that there were only tomorrows."

"Why?"

"Because then everything would always be fresh and new. There'd be no past, no regrets."

"What do you have to regret, Carly?"

She shrugged. "So many things I would have done differently. Decisions I would change if I could. Everyone has regrets. Don't you?"

"You bet. But what about the past, Carly? You've never told me anything about your past."

"I didn't come here to talk about that. Not tonight."

"Why did you come tonight?"

"Have you ever . . . taken a chance, Jake? Have you ever gambled on something you really wanted, even though it might turn out to be the wrong thing?"

She felt him tense, then relax. "I took a chance starting my own firm. Not everyone in my family was happy about it. I had . . . a friend who helped me." He shifted, drew her even closer. "Renting this house for the summer in a place so far from work and home might not be the smartest thing I've ever done."

He fell silent, thoughtful, then asked, "Do you think tomorrow, when the stars fade and the sun comes out again that you're going to regret tonight?"

"I hope not."

Although neither of them had mentioned it, she suspected he was aware of her wants and needs. He knew exactly why she'd come to him alone tonight.

Carly turned in his arms, aching to touch him, needing to look into his eyes, to have him touch her. Flickering candlelight bled through the window, moving in patterns of light and shadow over his face, highlighting his handsomeness, masking his expression.

He took her in his arms and kissed her, long and deep. White fire heat pulsed through her, made her come alive.

His hand slid unerringly beneath the hem of her sweater, moved over her midriff, until he cupped her breast. Through the soft knit material of her sports bra, she felt his thumb explore her taut nipple and an instant surge of need rocked her. She pressed against him, against his arousal.

"Oh, God." She gasped as his hand closed around her breast. "Oh, God, yes, Jake."

A sob escaped her, quickly lost as his mouth covered hers. He pressed her against the cement coping atop one of the pillars that framed the porch. Kissed her long and deep. Then suddenly he was no longer there.

He stepped back. With his hands fisted at his sides, he stared at her while he took in air like a long-distance runner.

Her heart stuttered. Carly closed her eyes.

"Don't humiliate me, Jake." Her voice dropped to a whisper. "If you don't want me, just say so, and I'll leave."

Want her?

He needed her more than he needed his next breath. She was trembling, leaning against the column for support, her eyes searching his face.

He was all too aware of what it cost her to come here tonight. She'd already taken a huge risk by letting him into her life. An honest man would admit that he never in a million years thought it would go this far this fast, but so far he hadn't been completely honest with her or himself.

Seeing her backlit by starlight with everything in her heart right there in her eyes, he knew that if he told her the truth now, it would crush her.

Tonight would be for her. Tomorrow would be soon enough to tell her the truth.

He may have come here for Rick, for Christopher's sake, but he had grown to care for Carly and her son. He caught himself thinking of her every hour of every day. For the first time in years, he found himself wanting more than a temporary arrangement.

For the first time in years, he was willing to put his heart on the line, and the irony was that he was handing it over to a woman with more secrets than he could count. Yet he still wanted her, needed only her.

He held out his arms.

On a sigh, she stepped into them, let him enfold her in his embrace. He kissed her again, cupped her face in his hands, savored her sweetness.

Then he picked her up and carried her back into the house, through the newly painted rooms, across a patchwork of drop cloths, around the ladder in the middle of the hallway.

The only room in decent shape was upstairs. He'd torn out the filthy carpet, swept the distressed hardwood floors beneath.

He carried her up the stairs to the room where his comforter was spread open across a queen-sized air mattress covered with a sheet. His T-shirts and pants were piled at the edge of the room.

He carried her directly to the bed, set her on her feet beside it, held her in his arms.

"Not exactly a suite at the Hilton." He apologized against her lips.

"I don't want a suite at the Hilton."

"What do you want, Carly?"

She slid her fingers into the pocket of her jeans, pulled out a foil-wrapped condom and slipped it into his palm. Then she wrapped her arms around his neck.

"You, Jake. Right now, I want you," she whispered.

He tossed the condom on the bed, ran his hands down her arms, held her hands as he kissed her softly, gently. Then he found the hem of her sweater, slid it up, past her midriff, her cotton bra. He tossed the pink fluff of her sweater over her head, let it drop to the bed. Within another few seconds, her bra was lying beside it.

He found her body firm and toned as he unfastened her jeans, slid them down her hips. She toed off her shoes, stepped out of the denim puddled around her ankles.

He tugged his T-shirt out of his pants, tossed it away, pulled Carly back into his arms. Her skin was cool against his, dimpled with goose bumps. He laughed softly against her ear. Her hands were at his waist now. The metal buttons on his Levi's opened one by one.

He sucked in his breath when her fingers grazed his erection, quickened when his blood surged.

"Jake." She whispered his name against his chest. Her breath sent shivers along his spine.

His hands found her breasts, cupped them, kneaded them. She moaned, raised herself up on tiptoe to kiss him full on the mouth while his thumbs traced her tight nipples.

She fumbled with his jeans, pushed them down over his hips without breaking the kiss, as if he were her lifeline, the very air she breathed.

He tore his lips from hers, whispered an urgent curse as he nearly toppled over when his foot got caught in his pant leg. He skimmed off his Levi's and his briefs and went down on one knee in front of Carly. Hooking his thumbs into her panties, he slowly pulled them down her hips, to her thighs, past her knees and shapely calves, following the soft cotton fabric with a trail of kisses.

Naked at last, she stood over him. Jake tipped his head back and stared up at her in the moonlight streaming through the bare window—Carly, with the star-splashed sky as her backdrop.

He took his time kissing his way back up to her navel, tongued it, moved up to her midriff. With his hand in hers, he gently tugged her down, urged her over to the bed, lay down beside her, tore open the packet and put on the condom.

"You're trembling," he whispered when he pulled her back to him again.

"I know."

"Are you sure, Carly?" He slipped his hand between her thighs, found her slick with desire, and knew the answer before she said a word.

"Oh, yes. I'm sure."

He kissed her again, hot, quick, demanding. She wrapped her arms tight around him, arched to meet him, cupped him, stroked him, an invitation communicated far better than any words could say.

He wanted to go slow. With her hands, her hips, her sighs, she begged him not to. He touched the curve of her hip. She reached for his erection, drew him close to the warm, wet opening between her thighs.

From the instant he sheathed himself inside her, she quickened and began to contract and convulse around him. She lifted her hips, cried his name as she thrust and pulled back, carrying him with her, urging him on until there was no denying her or his own burning need.

Promising her there was more to come tonight, he drove into her, met her frantic urgency with a need of his own. He called out her name, surged high and tight inside her. She begged him not to wait. Wasted words. He couldn't have waited another heartbeat.

As the sound of the sea pulsed against the stark, bare walls of the bedroom, Jake let go, joined Carly as she rode her own release with a cry, a moan, a gentle whisper and then a satisfied sigh.

He wrapped her in his arms, held her as their heartbeats collided, as their breathing went from ragged, harsh gasps to hushed sighs while the promise of much more pleasure to share that night hung gentle on the air around them.

TWENTY-SIX

The sun was already streaming in the windows with dust motes sifting along the shafts of yellow-gold when Jake squinted against the light and reached for Carly.

He swept her side of the bed with his arm, realized he was alone, and abruptly sat up. The comforter slipped down to his hips. He rubbed his eyes.

"Carly?" When she didn't answer, he pulled on the briefs he found lying on the floor beside the bed. The bathroom door was open, but there was no sign of her, so he wandered downstairs.

Not only was she gone, but so was any evidence that she'd been there at all. He glanced out the window. Her car wasn't in the driveway, either.

It wasn't until he went back to the bedroom to dress that he noticed a note lying on the floor beside the bed. He picked it up, read the fine, even printing written by an artist's hand.

Jake,
  Wanted to be home before Christopher got back from Potters'. Thank you for last night. Call me.

  C.

He folded the note and slipped it into his back pocket with a smile. He'd do better than that. He was going straight to her house. There was no way he could keep the truth from her any longer.

He wouldn't be able to live with himself another hour if he didn't set the record straight.

Just then his cell phone rang, and he scrambled to find it. He flipped back the edge of the comforter trailing over the floor and caught the phone before his voice mail picked up.

176

He rolled back onto the bed, propped one hand beneath his head and stared up at the lines on the ceiling, a map of patched plaster still slightly visible beneath two coats of fresh paint.

"I miss you," he said softly.

"Jake? It's your mother." She sounded as if she'd been crying.

So much for a little morning-after phone sex.

"Hi, Mom. What's up?" He sat up, suddenly afraid something had happened to Julie or one of her kids.

"Oh, honey. Your Granddad died in his sleep last night. Carlotta found him in bed this morning." She stopped abruptly, out of words.

Jake sat there with the phone pressed to his ear, listening to his mother breathe, and pictured Jackson Montgomery in his recliner, staring at the bay with a glass of Scotch in his hand and a scowl on his face.

"Jake?"

"Yeah, Mom."

"You'll come home won't you?"

After all these years, after all the grief the old man had put his mom and dad through, she was still going to bat for the old codger, still prodding him to do the right thing.

"Sure. I'll be there. I guess it's too early for any services to have been planned?"

"That's the reason you need to come home. He left his last wishes with his lawyers, and their secretary called already this morning. They need to meet with you."

Jake ran his fingers through his hair. Granddad had always made it crystal clear that his lawyers would take care of everything after he was gone. He gloried in reminding Jake that he was leaving every dime to charity and warned Jake that if he was only hanging around hoping to inherit anything, he was wasting his time.

As far as Jake was concerned, the old man owed him nothing and, by the same token, he didn't owe his grandfather a damn thing either, especially something as precious as time.

"Jake?" She was waiting for an answer. "He's family. You can't turn your back on him now. You know I'll help you any way I can."

Jake sat up, awash in a slowly spreading beam of bright yellow sunlight. He climbed off the mattress and walked over to the bare window and stared out at shimmering water that mirrored the color of the sky.

Family.

Sometimes family had nothing to do with love.

There had never been any love between him and his grandfather. Only a contest of wills. Jackson Montgomery had no concept of the true meaning of the word family.

Jake thought of Carly, home alone this morning with Christopher. He thought of what he was going to have to tell her, thought of her having to face her secrets and her fears. He thought of Anna Saunders, alone with her money and her desperate desire to find her grandson.

Family. Love that came with conditions.

I'll love you if . . .

I'll love you when . . .

I'd love you if only . . .

The old man was gone. Whether or not he drove home to plan Jackson's memorial wouldn't matter to his granddad anymore.

But it did matter to his mother.

"I'll be there, Mom."

"When?"

He calculated how long it would take him to throw together his overnight bag, secure his tools, close up the house. And he couldn't go anywhere until he'd settled things with Carly.

"Sometime tonight, probably."

"I'll call the lawyers back."

She gave him his granddad's lawyers' number in case he needed it. Jake said good-bye, took one last look at the stunning view from the bedroom, and tossed the cell phone on the bed before he headed for the shower.

At nine-thirty, Carly waited on her porch as Glenn Potter helped Christopher unload his pillow and overnight bag from the back of the Toyota. Matt jumped out and helped Chris carry his things to the house. He'd only been gone overnight, but to her it seemed as if he'd grown another three inches.

She gave him a big hug, stopping him in his tracks before he shoved the pillow into her arms.

"Can Matt stay for lunch? Please tell his dad it's okay."

Everything was so right with the world this morning that she smiled at Glenn Potter. "Matt is more than welcome to stay for lunch," she told him. She hugged Christopher's pillow, knowing the euphoric high she was on was bound to fade but hoping that it wouldn't.

She was beaming like a fool but she couldn't help it.

Glenn hesitated. "We've got to pick up Willa at the vet in San Luis, so would it be all right if he stays here until we get back around two-thirty or three?"

"No problem. I don't have to leave for work until four-thirty."

"I'll pick him up long before that. Thanks, Carly." Glenn started back to his car and then stopped. "Do you think you'll be seeing Jake this weekend?"

Carly was sure she had turned beet red when he mentioned Jake's name. "Probably," she said slowly, hoping Jake would call soon.

"I need to give him the receipt for the electrical service, but we just got the call from the vet, and Tracy can't wait to go get Willa."

She had no idea when or even if she'd see Jake today. She didn't want to make any assumptions, even after last night.

Glenn walked back to his car, then brought her an envelope from the utility company. Handing it over he said, "Jake seems like a real nice guy."

"Yes. He is." *Better than nice. Fabulous. Delicious.*

"Chris told me he's taken you both out to dinner and that you had a picnic at the house."

"We did."

"Chris thinks the world of him already. Maybe with Jake here all summer, you two might have a chance to get something going."

Get something going?

She decided she needed to have a talk with her son if he was going to discuss her private life around town.

Suddenly Glenn was in no rush to leave. He glanced off in the direction of the beach path, then shook his head. "Who woulda guessed Jake's a P.I.? I always think of a private detective as somebody like that rumpled guy on the Columbo reruns."

Carly froze with her hand poised, about to brush back her hair. Too shaken to breathe, a ringing in her ears forcing her to take a deep breath.

"What did you just say?"

"Shit." Glenn cursed under his breath, but she heard him. "He listed his occupation as self-employed, but when I ran a credit check on his bank account, his business turned out to be a private investigative firm in Long Beach. I figured he'd surely told you."

"Of course." She tried to sound as if she'd known all along, even as she hoped her legs would hold her until she could get inside. "Of course he did."

"Oh, great. Then I didn't blow it."

No. I did. Jake. A private investigator.

No doubt working for the Saunders. No doubt here to prove she was a slut *and* a bad mother. Somehow he'd tracked her down, set her up in order to help Rick's parents obtain custody of Christopher.

"Are you all right?" Glenn's expression was one of concern.

The world had just shifted beneath her feet. It had to show on her face.

She shook her hair back over her shoulder and forced a smile. "I'm fine. Just . . . thinking of everything I have to do today."

"Well, I'll be back for Matt this afternoon."

As he hurried back to his car, she stood there, numb, watching him, unable to move.

Just then the phone rang, and she panicked. If it was Jake, she didn't know whether to answer and stall him, or just let it ring.

As Glenn backed out of the parking space, she stepped inside. The screen banged behind her, giving off the usual aluminum rattle.

Her hand was shaking when she finally picked up the phone.

It was Geoff.

"I want all the details. If you leave anything out, I swear I'll . . ."

She had to get him off the line. Had to think.

"Geoff, listen—"

"Start talking. I've *got* to hear how it went last night."

"It went fine, but I can't talk right now."

"Oh, come on. Don't *do* this to me."

"I'll have to call you back."

"Carly, what's up? Are you all right?"

"I'm fine. Really. I'm just in the middle of something. I'll call you back. Promise."

She hung up without letting him say another word. Tears stung her eyes and blurred her vision so badly she couldn't even see the trunk covered with magazines at her feet. The harsh reality was that she wouldn't be calling him back. More than likely, she'd never see Geoff again.

Just like the day she walked out of Wilt's life, once she and Chris left Twilight Cove, there would be no looking back.

The boys' voices echoed in the hallway.

Think, Carly. Think.

Her hands were cold, her heart pounding. She felt gutted, like one of the rabbits her dad used to hunt in the desert and clean in the garage.

Finally she gathered enough strength to walk down the hall to her room. She opened her closet and stood there staring at the duffel bag on the floor beneath her clothes.

"Hey, Mom! Jake's here."

Nowhere to run. Before she could stop him, she heard Chris say, "Come on in, Jake. Matt's staying for lunch. Have you ever had a peanut butter star?"

Blinded by panic, Carly somehow made it down the hall and stepped into the living area. Jake was already inside. Chris was staring up at him as if he'd hung the moon and every star around it.

Jake's hair was tousled, still damp. He had on a wrinkled navy-blue T-shirt and jeans. A night's growth of dark stubble outlined his jaw.

All male and enough to tempt any woman with a pulse, he was perfect, except that he was a cold-blooded liar.

When she met his eyes, she immediately saw his hesitation. His expression was shadowed with concern and something she couldn't name. When he tried to smile she saw something she didn't even want to acknowledge, something that her foolish, inexperienced heart might be tricked into thinking was love.

"Why don't you and Matt go on back to your room, Chris. Jake and I need to talk."

"Aw, Mom. Why can't we—"

"Go! Now." She could count on one hand the times she'd ever spoken sharply to her son.

She waited until the boys quickly scooted out. In seconds she heard them talking in Christopher's room.

"What's wrong, Carly?" Jake started across the room, coming at her as if he intended to hold her.

She couldn't bear to have him touch her. Not now. She held up her hand, stopped him in his tracks. "Don't! Don't come any closer."

He held out his arms, hands palms up. "What's up?"

"You know damn well what's up. You *lied* to me. You've been lying the whole time." Enraged, hot anger spilling over her caused her to tremble. "What a fool I've been. Needy. Lonely. I fell right into your trap, didn't I?"

When he didn't ask what she was talking about, she knew that he understood completely, and any hope she had that this might all be a mistake vanished.

"You're a *private investigator*, aren't you?" Suddenly she found herself praying that he'd deny it, that he'd tell her she was wrong. Surely there was some other explanation. Maybe Glenn had mixed up Jake's account numbers with someone else's.

But then Jake nodded. "That's right. I am."

"You're working for the Saunders," she whispered.

"No. Believe me, I'm not working for anyone. I had my own reasons for finding you."

"Money."

"No. For Rick. For peace of mind."

Her hand went to her heart. "Rick?"

"He was a good friend. He loaned me some start-up money for my firm."

"I don't believe you." *Rick?* He had been *Rick's* friend . . . and she'd gone to bed with him last night.

He reached for his wallet, pulled it out, started toward her again.

"Don't come near me." She backed toward the kitchen.

"Then here. Catch." He tossed her the wallet. "Look through the photos."

Shaking so hard she almost dropped it, she flipped through the plastic sleeves. Unrecognizable faces smiled back. Three children in a formal photo, two boys and a girl. A middle-aged woman sitting alone at a picnic table in someone's backyard. A couple with the same three children from the other photograph—his sister and her family.

"So?" She started to hand it back.

"Look at the next one."

She realized there was one more sleeve. She flipped it over and found herself staring at a photo of herself holding Chris. One of the shots Rick had taken of her that day in Borrego, the day he'd found out that he'd had a son.

He had insisted they burn through two disposable cameras taking photos of the baby to show his parents. Looking at the photo now, she realized how young she was then, how naïve. And yet, she'd felt so very old.

Not quite twenty—with a son of her own. Seeing the photo now, the only one left out of so many that were destroyed when Rick died, cut her like a double-edged sword.

She tossed the wallet back. "This proves nothing. The Saunders probably gave it to you."

"No, they didn't. *Rick* did. The day he asked me to be his best man."

"Oh, God." She shook her head, trying to deny feeling anything for this man even as she longed to run to his arms and beg him to tell her this was all some crazy mistake.

"Get out, Jake."

"I came over to tell you the truth, and you're going to hear me out, damn it."

"It's a little late for that, don't you think?" A cold, bitter laugh escaped her. "I *trusted* you and you lied to me."

"That's good coming from you. Did Rick even know your real name?"

"Not until he came back to Borrego, and I'd had Christopher. I was Caroline Graham to everyone in Borrego Springs. Even my roommate, Wilt, didn't know my real name. I was in too deep. Rick wasn't like anyone I'd ever dated before. He was smart, polite. He had money. But I loved him because he saw something in me. He told me I could be anything I wanted to be, that I was smart enough to make something more of myself.

"He talked about how he had always had everything handed to him on a silver platter and how he had pretty much wasted twenty-six years of his life. He was going to Japan to work for his father's company. He was excited to prove himself to his parents. He wanted to change his life.

"I thought that month was all we'd ever have together. That he'd come back from Japan, maybe stop by when he was checking on his property but that he wouldn't necessarily want to see me again. We were from two different worlds."

"Then you had Christopher."

"When Rick came back and found out about the baby, I told him about my past and my real name. I thought he would have told his parents, but when their lawyer showed up calling me Caroline, assuming my name was Caroline Graham, I didn't let on any different."

Jake stepped toward her. She stepped back.

"I didn't come here to find you for the Saunders," he said. "I came because of my obligation to Rick. I had to make certain his son was doing all right. And that's exactly what I found. You're a great mother, Carly, and he's a great kid."

"I want you out of my house, Jake."

He walked over to the couch, sat down heavily, leaned forward and rested his arms on his knees. "Or what? You'll call the cops? Go ahead, but I'm not leaving until I get some answers. I want to help you clear this mess up so that you can stop running."

"I think you've helped enough."

"Are you planning to run again, Carly? Whose name will you use next?"

"What choice do I have? They want Christopher. The Saunders want to take him away from me like they tried to before."

"There is no *they* anymore. Charles Saunders is dead. All Anna wants is to meet her grandson, to be part of his life. She can do a lot for him, and for you."

"Oh, sure. She can take him away."

"You think she'll try to influence Chris with her money? Is that it? Chris loves you, Carly. It'll take a lot more than her wealth to break that bond. I know, believe me. I had a wealthy grandfather who tried to carry on a tug-of-war with my own mother for years . . ."

"They sent a lawyer out to the desert, Jake. He offered me a fortune to hand over my baby and walk out of Christopher's life. He said that if I didn't agree, they would take me to court and sue for custody. They already knew all about my past . . . about Caroline's past, anyway. I knew I couldn't fight them, especially if the whole truth came out. I knew they'd find out about my past, and I'd lose Chris."

"I can help you straighten everything out."

"Do you actually expect me to believe anything you say?"

"What's the alternative? You can't just pick up and leave. This is your home. Chris' home."

"He'll adjust. You'd be surprised what kids can adjust to. We've moved plenty of times."

"If I found you, Anna Saunders will hire someone who'll eventually find you, too."

"Anna Saunders hired *you*."

"No, she didn't. She wanted to, but I refused."

"Am I supposed to believe you *now*? After what you've done?"

Cornered, she paused, tried to gather her wits. Dear God, she'd slept with him last night. Made love with him. Made a complete fool of herself.

He didn't look like he was going anywhere without being forced out.

Despite his betrayal, an inexplicable ache of longing for him still lingered. She had placed her trust in him, and he had lied by omission. She had taken a chance, opened her heart, left it unprotected—and now this.

His expression was closed and unreadable except for the hurt in his eyes.

She reminded herself that *he* was the one who lied. What good would it do to drag things out?

"Please, just go, Jake."

"What are you saying?" He got off the couch, walked over to where she stood and stopped two feet away. He reached out his hand, tempted her to touch him.

She balled her hands into fists. "It's over, Jake."

A frown creased his brow, his eyes suddenly hard as flint.

"What about last night? You can't deny what happened between us. That was real. That was true—on my part at least. Let that be the beginning, Carly, not the end."

"You have no idea how hard it was for me to go to you last night. I took a big chance, Jake, and for what? You *lied*. You came into our lives knowing who I was, who Christopher was, without ever admitting that you were Rick's friend—not to mention that you're a private investigator."

"If I had told you the first day I met you, you would have run, Carly. Just like you're ready to do now. I couldn't risk it. I was going to tell you the truth until you surprised me last night."

"Then why didn't you?"

"Believe it or not, I knew just how hard it was for you to come to me like that, to offer yourself. I knew how vulnerable you were because I felt the same way. It's been a long, long time since I've felt anything for anyone, Carly. I was putting myself on the line, too. It was a beautiful night. I just didn't want to ruin things, that's all."

"Pretty words. You just wanted to get me into bed. Maybe you just wanted to prove you could have something that was Rick's."

His gaze hardened, his eyes turned steel blue. "I'm not that kind of man."

"You can say anything you want now, can't you? I'll never know the truth."

TWENTY-SEVEN

Jake ached to hold her, but the last thing she wanted now was his touch. Her face had lost all color, her eyes shimmered with tears of anger and despair.

Even knowing that she had lived her own lie for years, when she had accused him of lying to her, the truth hurt.

"You want to talk about truth, Carly?" Mindful of the boys in the back room, Jake lowered his voice. "Who is Caroline Graham? What is she to you? *Where* is she?"

Her color bleached to ash. She slumped down onto a dinette chair and stared down at her trembling hands. When she finally raised her eyes to meet his again, her voice came so softly that he had to strain to hear the words.

"She's dead."

"Wake up, Carly."

Someone was shaking her, whispering into her ear. She opened her eyes to the darkened room, recognized Caroline's voice. Raising herself on an elbow, she stared into a perfect face with features beautiful enough to be a model's. They'd been living with the same foster care family for two years.

Caroline's perfume, Beautiful, was flowery, subtle, yet unmistakable. She kept the bottle hidden beneath her mattress, but Carly was welcome to use it anytime she wanted.

"What's up?" Carly rubbed at her eyes and yawned.

"This is it. Get up. We're leaving."

Carly's heart started pounding so hard she was sure Caroline could hear it. They'd talked of running away, schemed and planned, and now the adventure was about to begin.

"Get up and dress. Bring your parka. I've got some guys from Tucson waiting at the end of the block. They'll give us a ride to Phoenix."

"It's dark out." Carly sat up, groggy, disoriented. She'd been out with four friends, partying around the block with one of the kid's parents and their friends. The liquor was free—if you didn't count letting a couple of the dads feel you up.

"Come on." Caroline tugged on her arm.

Carly was determined not to be left behind, but she'd never been one to hop out of bed. She rubbed her eyes, tasted cotton mouth.

"Dennie will be home soon," Caroline warned. Dennis Jensen, their forty-five-year-old foster father had walked into the bathroom after Carly had just stepped out of the shower and molested her the night she'd moved in, his way of making sure she felt welcome.

Ashamed, degraded, and confused, she'd sat curled up in the corner of her bed with her back pressed against the wall until Caroline got home from work that night.

The older girl had held and petted her while Carly cried and told her everything.

"Hey, it's bad, but it's not the worst thing that's bound to happen to you in your life, Carly."

"How . . . how can you say that? How can you act like it's nothing? He . . . he put his hand on me, Caro. He touched me all over. He . . . he would have . . . I think he would have raped me if Nola hadn't come looking for him." She shivered, hugged herself tight. "I know he would."

Caroline shook her head. "Nah. He wouldn't. He can't get it up. He tried it on me when I first moved here, too. I was about your age. I told him I'd cut his useless little pecker off and hand it to Nola if he ever tried it again. I'm sorry I wasn't here to warn you, kid. Just steer clear of him and protect yourself."

After that night Carly made certain that she was never alone with Dennie. Caroline watched her like a hawk, and if they weren't out someplace together, Caroline made certain she was home before Dennie got back from the late shift at Walgreens so that Carly would never be alone. Hanging out with Caroline and her hard-core friends was the better of two evils.

"What about Nola? What if she catches us leaving this late?" Carly glanced at the clock. It was two-thirty in the morning.

"Nola? She'll believe anything I say. She's such an airhead. She's got a one-digit I.Q. or she'd never have married Dennie in the first place." Caroline pulled Carly up, shoved some clothes at her. "Get dressed. If there's anything else you want to take, it has to fit in your pockets. Nola's half asleep in front of the TV. I'm going down to the corner to wait with the guys and keep them interested."

Carly sat on the edge of the bed and pulled on a long-sleeved top that Caroline handed her. In the six years since her dad died, she'd been in four foster homes, and this was by far the worst of the bunch.

Nola had a thing for kittens, which of course tended to grow up too fast and breed almost as fast as rabbits. She took care of her animals with as much finesse as she took care of the revolving foster kids the county gave her.

Dennis was hardly ever home, and when he was, he was always bellowing at Nola to either shut the cats or the kids up.

Carly did okay in school, but not great. She ran with Caroline and the bullies who might have otherwise found her an easy target. Both Caroline and Carly were leggy blondes, although Caroline had a body that a lingerie model would envy, and Carly had yet to develop much of anything. Caroline was popular with a rough crowd, and she spread the word that Carly was her half sister. Carly's own reputation had grown to epic proportions by mere association with Caroline.

After Dennie had shoved his fingers up inside her and pressed her against the cold bathroom wall, Carly figured that letting one of the boys put his hands on her wouldn't be half as bad.

Carly sighed and watched Caroline slip out of the room, knowing in her heart this was a turning point in her life from which there would be no going back. She'd taken care of her dad for most of what little childhood life gave her. Taking care of herself on the streets had to be a hell of a lot easier.

With Caroline laughing in the front seat of the Firebird convertible, her arm around the driver, a nineteen-year-old parolee who went by only one name, Lucky, Carly sat in back beside Lucky's friend, Raul, warm, stoned, not a care in the world. The cloying scent of marijuana stained the air inside the car.

They were speeding down a side road off Highway 40, somewhere past Winslow, Arizona, when Caroline started licking Lucky's ear and tugging on his earlobe with her teeth. Dark wine-colored lipstick stained his neck. Carly started giggling when the lip print suddenly seemed hilarious to her.

Wind rattled the car's soft top and whistled through a gap where the back window didn't fully close. The wheels hummed against the pavement. The speedometer read seventy-five.

It was freezing. So cold that Carly was glad she'd brought along the puke-green parka that Nola had recently picked up for her at the Goodwill. She pulled the hood of her parka over her head, smoothed the backs of the acrylic knit yellow gloves on her hands, and then continued to watch Caroline make a fool of herself keeping Lucky interested enough to drive them all the way to Blythe, on the California border.

The guy was definitely a loser. Even Carly could see it. So was his friend. When she first balked at climbing into the backseat with the sullen, silent, Raul, Caroline had whispered to her that the guys were only a ticket out of Albuquerque. In a couple of days they'd be gone.

Caroline glanced over her shoulder at her audience and winked. Carly slid her gaze over to Raul, who was getting hot and bothered by the show in the front seat. She'd let him slide his hand under her shirt, but only after he gave her another hit off the joint.

When a thick rain that bordered on sleet began to smear the front windshield, Carly shivered, wishing Lucky would slow down. Her dad never ran out of stories about all the fatalities caused by black ice and idiots, and Carly was certain an idiot was driving, even if she wasn't sure they were on black ice.

"Hey, flash your tits at those guys in the motor home up there." Lucky pushed on Caroline's shoulder until she was no longer leaning on the console, but back in her own bucket seat.

"Where?" She rubbed her warm palm in a circle on the fogged passenger side window. "I don't see them."

"Up ahead. They passed me a few minutes ago while you were jacking around with my ear. Get ready, and when I go by, lift your sweater."

She pursed her full lips, leaned toward him, pretending to be miffed.

"And if I don't want to?"

He looked over his shoulder at Carly. "Then maybe I'll have your little sister do it."

"She's not flashing anybody." Caroline glared a silent threat at Raul. "And you keep your hands off her."

"Hey, back off." Lucky shifted gears and started to pass the motor home. "I guess you two girls could walk to California. Come on. What's the big fucking deal? Do it."

Caroline got to her knees. "The fucking deal is it's fucking cold out there."

"Press 'em up against the window. You owe me."

"Shit. This is probably the stupidest thing I've ever done," Caroline mumbled as she shrugged out of her plum-colored parka. Her fuzzy-pink, fake angora sweater showed off her full breasts to perfection. Leashing them in a bra was something she would never have considered. A knit tank top was all she ever wore beneath her clothes.

Carly was butt cold, watching the scene unfold through a haze of smoke and a clouded mind. She started to laugh when Caroline got to her knees in the front seat and turned to face the window.

Lucky made his move as soon as Caroline grabbed the hem of her sweater in both hands. With the windshield wipers slapping at the slush, it was hard for Carly to see the road ahead. Lucky whipped the wheel to the right. Carly slid away from Raul and slammed up against the side of the car. Her seat belt prevented her from rocking forward.

In the split second before impact, she was aware of a sharp bend in the yellow line down the middle of the highway, of Caroline kneeling in the passenger seat, her high, ivory breasts bouncing as she whipped up her sweater and pressed against the foggy glass.

"Shit!" Lucky cursed and jerked the wheel in the opposite direction.

Metal scraped and tore against metal. The motor home swiped the front half of the Firebird, sent it careening across the road. Then the car started to roll.

Caroline's vinyl purse flew back and hit Carly in the face as the horrific sound of breaking glass and Raul's oddly high-pitched scream filled her ears. The never-ending roll after roll as the car tumbled down the steep embankment, shook her insides and rattled her bones. Her seat belt tore into her ribs and shoulder.

Finally the Firebird partially righted itself as it came to rest in a gully yards below the highway.

For a few moments there was only deathly silence. Carly blinked, tried to move. She shook her head, thinking that they must have smoked some really great shit, until she felt an ache in her left shoulder. She sat up. All her limbs moved.

As the fog in her mind slowly cleared, her thoughts drifted, until she realized Caroline was no longer in the front seat. Most of the windshield was missing—all that was left was a crystal mosaic of shattered glass.

Beside her, Raul moaned. He was wedged between the seat and the floor, his left leg twisted out from his hip. His eyes were closed, his lips curved in a tight grimace of pain. Blood smeared the corner of his mouth.

Lucky was slumped over the steering wheel. Carly unfastened her seat belt, hooked the long strap from Caroline's purse over her shoulder. For a second she panicked, thinking she was trapped when the door wouldn't budge, but then she managed to shove it open far enough to crawl out.

Her teeth chattered and her knees shook as she wandered over frozen ground. Watery snow had stopped falling. The sky was ashen with the gray light of dawn.

A blotch of hot pink against the scarred earth on the embankment above her drew her gaze to Caroline's inert form. Carly stumbled, knelt down. Shaking her head, she tried to clear it. Slowly she reached out, touched the hem of Caroline's sweater, pulled it down to cover her friend's breasts. Caroline's bloodied hair was tangled over her face, her neck twisted at an impossible angle.

Carly knew without having touched her friend that Caroline was gone. Still, unable to stop herself, she pulled off a glove and laid her palm against Caroline's neck, feeling for a pulse, just to be sure. Nothing but cold stillness lay beneath her hand.

Taking hold of Caroline's hand, she cradled it in her lap, and she knelt there in the dirt, waiting to hear the scream of an ambulance. Surely the men in the motor home had phoned 911. Surely they'd seen Lucky swerve and the car plunge off the road.

She sat there as Caroline grew cold, her own throat raw and burning, until she was so cold she couldn't feel her fingers anymore. Finally she let go and pushed herself to her feet and stared down at Caroline. Her beautiful friend was lying against the sandy soil of the Arizona high desert Indian country like a broken, discarded Barbie doll.

As the sun rose higher over the mountains, staining the sky a bright orange-pink, Carly blinked, fumbled with her glove, then adjusted the strap of Caroline's purse. Dazed, confused, she climbed up the embankment until she reached the highway and started walking. Her shoulder ached, her mind refused to work.

She'd gone blissfully numb inside, cold and silent as Caroline.

She walked for two miles or more before a big rig pulled over and stopped at the side of the road up ahead of her. The driver, five-foot-ten with a thick mustache and kind eyes the color of black coffee, asked where she was headed.

"Someplace warm," she mumbled.

"I'm going to California," he told her. "Get in if you want a ride."

He had to help her into the cab of the truck, let her sit in silence for miles and miles as the endless desert rolled away from them like a parched seascape.

When he pulled over for a lunch stop around noon, he finally spoke to her again.

"M' name's Wilt Walton. I'm sixty years old, and I'm gonna retire in ninety-three days. Not that I'm counting."

She listened but couldn't seem to form a complete sentence.

"You got a name, honey?"

Her hand tightened on the purse resting on her lap.

"Look, it's none of my damn business why you're out on the road alone. You don't have to worry. I'm not sending you back. If things were so great at home, you wouldn't be out here by yourself, right?"

She stared through the windshield at all the big rigs lined up in the parking lot alongside a diesel station and diner. There was a twenty-foot-tall bright red plaster teepee in front. Yum-Yum Pie was painted on two sides of the teepee.

"You high, honey? You smell like the inside of a joint."

She tried moving her head, finally nodded ever so slightly.

"Yeah," she whispered. "A little. I guess."

As he leaned on the wheel, waiting for her to tell him her name, her mind sluggishly started working.

The foster care people in New Mexico were surely looking for her by now. Her and Caroline both.

She was only fifteen. She'd be hauled in to explain Caroline's death. Maybe Lucky and Raul were dead, too. If she were older, if she were eighteen, she could stay on her own, but she was only fifteen. They'd test her. Find out she'd been smoking pot. Throw her in juvie. Worse yet, send her back to Dennie and Nola's. There was no way out.

Unless . . .

She ran her fingers over the scarred surface of Caroline's vinyl purse and tried to speak, but her throat was stuffed with tears she'd yet to shed.

She cleared her throat, turned to Wilt.

"Caroline. My name is Caroline Graham."

TWENTY-EIGHT

"So you became Caroline."

Jake had sat down again, listened while staring at the top of the trunk where all her magazines were neatly arranged, as if life could be as perfect, easily altered by moving the furniture or choosing the right paint for the walls.

"If she'd lived, Caroline would have been eighteen a month after we ran away. I figured I could fend for myself using her identification. Wilt offered me a room at his place." She shrugged. "At first I thought he felt sorry for me, but when I got to know him better, I realized he'd been looking out for me. He told me more than once how lucky I was that he'd stopped to pick me up before somebody else did."

"Did you ever tell him the truth about Caroline and the accident? About who you really were and what you'd done?"

"No. When it all started, I never wanted to be Carly Nolan again. My own life hadn't been worth finishing. I tried to be like her. I *wanted* to be her. Caroline was as wild as she was beautiful. When she walked into a room, everyone turned to look at her. To think that she was gone . . . well, it was too much. Maybe, maybe somehow she'd live on, if I took her name.

"She already had her Social Security card and she'd gotten a driver's license after one of her boyfriends taught her to drive. She'd been working at Lotta Burger close to Dennie and Nola's after school and on weekends. I figured I could get a job right away if I just pretended to be her."

Jake began to pace, unwilling, unable to remain still any longer. Carly crossed her arms protectively, watching him almost warily whenever he moved close.

196

He paused a few feet away, stared down at her, wishing he hadn't heard any of it. Not wanting to know she'd been through so much in such a short life. Amazed at how she must have had to work to become the woman she was now. She'd done it all on her own.

"So, by simply becoming yourself again when you left Borrego Springs, you were able to start over with a clean slate." He shook his head. "It was ingenious, really. No one ever put two and two together."

"You did. You found me."

"Only because my partner, Kat, was reading a travel article about Geoff Wilson's gallery and saw the painting that reminded her of one I have in my office. One that I bought from Wilt Walton."

"*What?*"

"Right after Rick died, I went out to Borrego to find you. The Saunders' story had run in all the local papers, claimed they were despondent, not only over the loss of their son, but their grandson. They accused you of being on drugs. You had disappeared with the baby. They feared for his life."

"I've never had anything harder than pot and not even that after Caroline died. I'd never, ever let anything happen to Chris, and you know it."

"I do now. Back then, I worked for the investigative firm they'd hired. I'd gone out to see if Wilt could or would tell me where you'd gone. He wouldn't talk about you much at all, but he did show me your paintings. He was pretty proud of them. I badgered him into selling me one."

"Which . . . which one?"

"Sunset over the desert, the ghost of a lone Spanish conquistador staring toward a mirage oasis. A Native American is crouched not far away, watching him from the rocks."

She nodded. "I remember. I remember them all. It was like leaving a part of myself behind when I left my paintings."

"When Kat showed me the article, I followed a long shot and drove up to The Cove Gallery. The rest you know."

Drained and exhausted, she felt like someone three times her age.

"Wilt has no idea where I am. He never knew my real name, either."

She ran her fingers through her hair, sweeping it back out of her eyes. He knew what her hand felt like moving against his skin now. Knew the taste of her lips, her scent.

Just as he knew she was hurting and that he was responsible.

"Why did you really run, Carly?"

Tensing, she shoved away from the counter. "I *told* you. I didn't want to sell my baby to the Saunders. I knew that no matter what I said or did, I couldn't fight them, and they would eventually get custody of Christopher. I knew that if they found out about my past, if they found out what happened to Caroline, that they'd learn about the accident and how I had assumed her identity—and *that's* against the law. Even if I *hadn't* done anything illegal, I was barely twenty. I didn't have the money to fight them. I was still in shock over Rick's death and terrified of losing Christopher."

"No court in the state would take Christopher away from his natural mother unless she were on drugs and totally indigent."

"How was I supposed to know that? Besides, how can you be sure? The Saunders have money and power. Judges can be influenced, can't they?"

"Carly, let me help you straighten this mess out. Trust me."

"Trust you? I *did* trust you. For the first time in years I trusted someone completely. I let you walk into our lives, into our home, our hearts. Dear God, Jake, I trusted you enough to let you get close to my son. I *slept* with you last night. Look where trusting you got me."

"I came over here this morning to tell you the truth."

A small, brittle laugh escaped her. "Now I'll never know that for certain, will I?"

"You have to believe me."

"Why should I, Jake? After what you've done, why should I believe anything you say?"

"Because." He shoved his hand through his hair. Shook his

head, hoping he wasn't making the most fatal mistake of all. "Because I'm in love with you."

Not now. Not like this.

Carly fought her tears. She'd waited so long to let love into her life that to have it come like this, clouded by doubt and betrayal, was unbearable.

"I know what you must be thinking . . ."

Jake's voice moved over her, through her. She knew that as long as she lived, she would never forget the way it made her feel all mellow and warm, even now. She wanted to believe so very badly.

". . . I don't fall in love lightly, Carly."

"And you think I do? Until last night, I hadn't been with anyone since Rick."

"I know that. I know what it meant for you to come to me. You gave me a very precious gift last night. This morning I realized that I would have never touched you unless I loved you. When you showed up ready to lay your heart on the line, I couldn't ruin that moment for either of us by telling you the truth last night."

"So you made love to me anyway, knowing everything I believed about you was a lie."

"Only because I was afraid you'd walk out the door and I'd never see you again." He stepped closer, so close she could feel the warmth radiating from him. She wanted him to touch her, hated herself for needing him at all after what he'd done.

"What makes you think that's not going to happen now?"

"You don't give yourself easily." He held her gaze. She hadn't the will or the desire to look away. "Or your heart."

"Oh, Jake."

He reached for her, closed his hands around her upper arms. She didn't have the will to move. Not now. In so many ways the burden of a lifetime of secrets had been lifted now that she'd told him everything. Someone else knew. He knew all about Caroline, her death, the truth of her own identity. All of it was out. Though she felt as bleak as before, there was still a sense of release, if not freedom.

"Please, for God's sake, Carly, let me help you."

After all this time, all these years of looking over her shoulder, of running from the Saunders and carrying the burden of fear of losing Christopher, after all her years of loneliness, she was too afraid to hope that Jake might actually be able to help.

"How?" she whispered.

She watched him slightly relax. He ran his hands up and down her arms, gently held her wrists.

"Let me talk to Anna Saunders. I was Rick's friend. Hopefully she'll hear me out. I'll tell her what a wonderful mother you are. I'm not saying I can change her mind, but it's the only way this might be settled amicably. Would you consent to meeting her? Would you let her meet Chris?"

The idea of coming face-to-face with the woman who had wanted her son desperately enough to buy him scared her to death.

"I'm afraid to take that chance."

"What if I were by your side?"

"You can't make me any guarantees, Jake." She wished he would say that he could, that his word would be enough to stop Anna Saunders from fighting for Christopher.

"Life doesn't come with guarantees, but I can tell you this, Anna has no grounds whatsoever to prove that you're an unfit mother."

An infinitesimal glimmer of hope sparked inside her. She *had* changed her life. She'd turned off the reckless path of self-destruction she'd been on as a teen. She'd done her best to give Christopher all the love and devotion she had. She'd made a home out of nothing. That had to count for something, didn't it? Surely that had to be enough.

Her initial anger had cooled to a low simmer. She longed to believe Jake was telling the truth as much as she wished she could believe he loved her. If he could help her now, she'd be a fool to turn him away.

Besides, it would be idiotic to pretend that she didn't love him. The terrible-wonderful feeling she carried in her heart had to be love, it had to be the reason that the thought of running away and never seeing him again hurt more than the fear of staying.

She stepped back and he let go of her. Walking over to the front door, she opened it and held on, grounding herself with the solid feel of wood, as if it were a lifeline. She wanted things to be different—more than anything she'd ever wanted in her life. She wanted to let Jake take her in his arms and make the hurt go away, but it was too late for that.

Any minute now Chris and Matt would come running back into the room, and Christopher would beg Jake to stay.

"Please, Jake," she whispered. "If you care at all, please go. I need time. I . . . things have changed. Don't make this any harder than it already is."

She expected an argument, but none came. He ran his hands through his hair, shoved them into his pockets.

"I have to leave for Long Beach as soon as I can get things straightened up at the house. My grandfather died last night."

"I'm sorry." There was nothing more she could say to him right now. She was so numb, words of consolation wouldn't come.

He took her hand again. She stared down at his fingers as they enfolded hers. Still numb, the hands might have belonged to two other people, not them. To lovers. What were they now, she wondered. What were they now that the truth was out in the open?

"I've got to meet with his lawyers and make arrangements for his memorial. You have my cell number. If you need anything at all, call me. While I'm in Long Beach, I'm going to see Anna Saunders . . ."

With her free hand, she grabbed the neckline of her blouse. Her heart began to pound beneath her fist. "Are you going to tell her you've found us?"

"Nothing she's said ever led me to believe she wanted to take Christopher from you, but I also know you're not lying. Once I get through my grandfather's memorial, I'll meet with Anna. She'll never learn where you are from me."

"How can I believe you?"

"Trust me, Carly. All I've ever wanted to do is help you and Chris. I'll call you as soon as I know something." His hand tightened on hers.

"Jake . . ."

"This isn't over between us by a long shot. You're not the only one hurting here. I put my own heart on the line, too, Carly, and I'm not letting you out of my life that easily. I'm expecting . . . no, I'm *trusting* you to be here when I get back, so trust me. Let me try to help you."

TWENTY-NINE

Chris knew something really weird was going on.

Maybe Mom thought just because he was a little kid that he wouldn't notice, but he did. She'd been acting grumpy since Jake came by. Grumpy and sad at the same time.

Another weird thing was that Jake had left without telling him good-bye, and then Mom made plain old sandwiches for him and Matt, tuna with mayonnaise, and he couldn't even talk her into cutting them into stars.

After lunch, she said that he and Matt could watch cartoons until Matt's dad came to pick him up, which was *really* strange, because she never let him watch longer than half an hour at a time. While they flopped on the living room floor in front of the television, Mom went into her studio and sat there staring out the window instead of painting.

By the time Matt's dad picked Matt up, Chris was not just worried, he was getting scared.

"Hey, Mom, let's take a walk down to the beach and look for shells." Their beach wasn't very big, but there were always birds to chase and shells and sand dollars that washed up. And there were lots of nature trails that wound up the face of the bluff, too.

"Not today, Chris."

"Why?"

"Because I said no."

"But why?"

Mom let out a big sigh. "I don't feel like it, honey."

"When I feel bad, you always tell me it would do me good to get out and get some fresh air. Maybe it will do you good."

"I don't think so. Not today."

He watched Mom's shoulders sag the way they did when she

was sad. They'd been drooping since Jake left. Seeing her like this made his stomach hurt.

"I don't feel so good, either," he said softly.

Suddenly she looked over at him as if she were finally paying attention. "You just said you wanted to go for a walk."

"My tummy hurts."

"Where?"

He pointed to his belly button.

She left the kitchen and came over to where he was sitting on the couch, sat down next to him, and put her arm around his shoulders.

He wanted to ask her what was wrong, but things were all jumbled up inside him, and he didn't really want to know if it was something really bad.

When Mom tightened her arm around him, he let her hug him. Even though he was afraid he'd start crying like a baby, he still wanted her to hold him. He buried his face against her and smelled her good Mom smell.

She pulled back and brushed his hair off his forehead.

"What's really wrong, honey?"

"I heard you talking to Jake before. You both sounded mad, and now you're acting sad. What's wrong? Did somebody do something bad?"

"No. No one's done anything." She didn't exactly sound real sure.

"Who's Annasaunder?"

Mom got very still and didn't answer for a minute. Then she cleared her throat. "Anna Saunders is . . . a lady who lives far away."

"Is she trying to hurt you or Jake?"

She pulled him onto her lap and held him the way she liked to, as if he were still a baby. Lately he'd pretended he was too big for that, but this time he didn't laugh and try to wriggle off. If she wanted to cuddle, that was okay with him.

Mom spoke with her lips close to his hair. "She's not trying to hurt us. She . . . she wants to get to know you, that's all."

"Why?"

"She was your dad's mom."

"My dad's mom? My *dead* dad's *mom*?"

"Yes. She's your grandmother." Mom brushed his hair off his forehead again, and this time she kissed it.

"I have a *grandma*?" He tried not to get too excited. A grandmother was supposed to bake cookies and tell you how great you were, no matter what you did. At least that's what Matt told him. And they gave you presents, too. He nestled against Mom, still wondering why he hadn't known about Anna Saunders before.

"Why isn't her name Anna Nolan like ours?"

"Well, because your dad's name wasn't Nolan."

"Why?"

"That's hard to explain. Sometimes people don't have the same last names."

"Where does she live?"

"She lives in Long Beach."

"How come we never see her?"

"She . . . didn't know where we lived."

"Hey," he said, suddenly remembering. "Jake lives in Long Beach, too."

"Yes, he does."

"You think he'll come back soon?"

"I don't know."

"I wish he would. I miss him when he's not here. Why don't we call him and ask him over for dinner?"

"He's very busy." Mom got very quiet and held him tight.

"I like things just the way they are. With just the two of us. That's enough, isn't it? Just us?"

"Jake's a nice guy. Why don't you like him?"

Mom swallowed hard. He could feel it as he lay against her chest. Her heart was beating really fast.

"Jake is a busy man. He had to drive back to Long Beach this afternoon. You can't expect him to be here all the time."

"Why don't we call up my grandma and tell her to come see us?"

"She's very busy, too."

"Like Jake?"

"Maybe we should put on some sweatshirts and go for that walk on the beach. How about that?"

"Do you think my grandma has any pictures of my dad?"

"I'm sure she does."

"Maybe she'll show them to me if I ever get to meet her."

It was a few minutes before Mom whispered, "I'm sure she will."

On the drive down the coast, Jake imagined himself sitting in the somber office of some funeral director with Jackson Montgomery's ghost hovering beside him. The Ghost of Summers Past, laughing in his ear.

When he walked into his condo that evening, stressed from battling the tangle of rush hour on the 405 Freeway, preoccupied with the blowup with Carly, Kat was still there.

As he closed the door behind him, she walked out of the office with a stack of phone messages in her hand.

"Sorry about your grandfather."

"Thanks."

"Here." She shoved the notes at him, reached for the purse and sweater hanging on an oak coatrack near the door. "Those are all from Anna Saunders."

His hand tightened on the slips of paper. "Thanks."

Anna Saunders had been calling him since the day after he'd returned to Twilight, but he'd put off calling her back and had told Kat to try to stall her.

"She had a tail put on me. One of Alexander and Perry's guys, but I made him."

"Then what?" Suddenly she no longer appeared interested in leaving. "Did you shake him?"

"No, I confronted him. He owed me one, so I got him to stall A and P."

"And you took his word for it?"

"Yeah. And I made sure he was gone before I got on the road again. If he followed me, he somehow turned invisible."

"Would you have done it? Let somebody off the hook like that?"

"In this case, yeah. I'd have done the same thing."

"I know everything's not all right, but is there anything I can do?"

"No. Thanks, but it'll all work out."

"What about The Obsession?"

He ran his hand over the stubble on his jaw. "She's been better, too."

"From the look on your face I gather you finally told her you are really Jake Montgomery, P.I.?"

"Actually, somebody else told her before I could, at the worst possible time."

"Ouch. And she's still pissed."

He shrugged. "How'd you guess?"

"The look on your face says it all."

He was more than ready for Kat to leave. He didn't need to have her launch into a I-thought-you-knew-better-than-to-fall-in-love lecture. He wasn't about to explain that Carly was more than pissed, that she was scared and upset and rightly so if the Saunders had really tried to take Chris from her. What he wanted right now was to be left alone to think and talk to Anna Saunders before it was too late.

"Hey, drive carefully." He opened the front door for Kat.

"I can take a hint. I won't be in until around noon tomorrow. I've got to go up to the courthouse in L.A. first thing in the morning."

"Fine. I may or may not be here. I have an appointment with my grandfather's lawyers."

He watched Kat run down the steps, admiring her trim figure. She was graceful and athletic while feminine and sexy at the same time. Any man would be lucky to have her, but she had protectively encased her heart in bulletproof Kevlar.

He thought he had, too, but loneliness made for weak defenses, and thinking back, once he'd laid eyes on Carly, the fight against feeling had pretty much been over. He'd lowered his defenses, and now he was definitely feeling the pain.

Kicking off his shoes, he wandered toward the kitchen. On the way, he laid the stack of memos on the wicker table, picked up the portable phone and dialed his mother to let her know he was back in town and that he'd contacted Jackson's lawyers. They were ready to go over the old man's last wishes in the morning.

That done, he rummaged through the freezer until he found two bean-and-chicken burritos in a plastic sack on the back of a shelf. He pulled them out, opened one end of each wrapper, and set them on the microwave turntable.

An old jar of salsa was hiding in the fridge, but it was a science project with a layer of green fur floating on top. He tossed it and grabbed a package of hot sauce out of a collection of leftover fast-food packets of ketchup, mayo, relish, and mustard.

While he waited for the burritos to heat, he walked back to the table, picked up a pink phone memo, and stared at Anna's number. He punched it into the phone.

One short ring later he heard Anna say hello. Her voice was laced with ice.

"This is Jake Montgomery."

"Oh. Jake. Yes."

"Sorry I couldn't get back to you right away. I was out of the area."

"You know, Jake, after we spoke last, I started wondering why you didn't jump at the chance to take the case, and that got me thinking that you might already know where Caroline was, or at least you had a strong lead and didn't want to get my hopes up. Have you continued searching for her pro bono all these years?"

"Rick was my friend. I wanted to make sure his son was being taken care of."

"When did you plan to tell me? Or were you?"

"Why didn't you call and ask me that instead of having someone from Alexander and Perry tail me?"

There was a slight pause.

"You know?"

"Yeah. I saw him. He was easy enough to spot." Suddenly it hit

Jake that Sam Godes had been very easy to make. Maybe too easy. As his thoughts churned, Anna went on to explain.

"It was Art Litton's idea. I called to get his advice and tell him what I suspected. He suggested I contact Alexander and Perry and have you followed."

Jake knew Litton. A high-dollar lawyer with the scruples of a python.

"You told me that all you ever wanted was to play a role in Christopher's life. What's going on, Anna?"

There was dead silence on the other end of the line. Lights from the shopping center across the footbridge from his condo building shimmered on the water.

He could hear her voice break when she finally answered. "I promised Charles I would find Christopher, Jake. If you had taken the case, I wouldn't have had to have you followed. You were Rick's friend, or claim to have been. Help me make certain his son has everything he needs."

Jake thought of the tug-of-war on his own emotions that his grandfather had put him through. If just once Jackson Montgomery had said please. Please come for the summer. Please let me in. Accept my love. Instead, he'd made demands.

Outside of his immediate family, Jake wasn't used to trusting in the goodness of man. He'd seen enough of the other side of life, and knew just how devious people could be. But this was his best friend's mother. Fate had taken her son early on and then her husband when she needed him most. If he could convince her that she and Carly both wanted what was best for Christopher, if the two of them would just sit and talk things out, maybe they could make peace.

"Would you like to meet her, Anna? If I could take you to where they live . . ."

"Twilight Cove?"

He froze, stiffer than the freezer-burned burritos, certain he'd never mentioned exactly where he was going. There was only one way she'd know where Carly and Chris were. Sam Godes had gone back on his word.

Jake searched his memory. He had been sure Godes hadn't trailed him. He'd have never gone on to Twilight if he'd thought any differently.

"How'd you find out?"

"Alexander and Perry had two investigators following you. I suppose it's a compliment to you that they thought it necessary. One was a man, one a woman posing as a young mother. I have photos of you and my grandson in a park, playing catch. Another of you and Caroline, who we know now calls herself Carly, getting into your car."

"If you already know where Christopher is, why call me at all?" He was so pissed at her, more so at himself, that all he wanted to do was hang up. Acid was etching out the lining of his stomach.

"I wanted to let you know that I'm suing for legal guardianship of Christopher. She'll be served with papers right away."

"Is that what you really want, Anna? To tear them apart? Do you think Chris will love you for it?"

She sounded less than certain when she said, "He needs a good mother."

"He *has* a good mother."

"A mother who misrepresented herself to my son. A mother who assumed an alias and used it for years. Why all the running and hiding if she's so innocent?"

"Carly's a wonderful mother."

"She's a gold digger. A slut."

Charles Saunders had been one of the good old boys at the yacht club. Jake imagined the man couldn't stand the idea of losing to someone like Carly. "You sound like your husband, Anna. Are you sure this is what *you* want?"

He was certain Anna didn't stand a chance in hell of getting guardianship of Christopher—he'd bet money on it—but she could make Carly's life miserable for a very, very long time. Social Services would interview friends and neighbors. They'd nose around at Christopher's school. There would be psych evaluations.

Carly's past would be dragged out in the open. She'd been a fifteen-year-old runaway, a discipline problem headed for juvenile hall when she assumed Caroline Graham's identity. Rick wasn't around to prove she had ever been completely honest with him about her real name and what she'd done.

"Have you or your lawyer given a thought to Christopher's welfare while Charles planned all of this, Anna? Let's say that by some long shot, you succeed. It won't matter that you're his grandmother or how much money you have. You won't be able to force him to love you." Jake leaned against the wall, stared up at the ceiling, and tried not to think about what the threat of losing her son would do to Carly. "He'll wind up hating you. Is that what you really want?"

Silence echoed over the line before Anna said, "I promised Charles."

Screw Charles, Jake thought as he strangled his anger.

"Forget Charles. What do *you* want?"

"I want to keep my promise to him. I *have* to keep my word. I'm hanging up now, Jake. I believe we've nothing more to say."

He couldn't let her hang up, not knowing whether she'd ever take another call from him.

"Is this what Rick would want?"

For a second or two there was no answer. Then her voice broke. "Rick's not here, is he? My son's not here to say."

Jake closed his eyes. Her determination reminded him again of his grandfather. It had been so important for Jackson to try to "salvage" him after his dad died. Jackson couldn't stand the notion that he had failed to control his own son's life, so he'd tried to meddle in Jake's.

"If you cared about Christopher at all, you wouldn't want to turn his whole world upside down. What you really want is Rick back."

There was no answer, but he could hear her ragged breathing on the other end of the line.

"You can't do this, Anna. It's only going to bring heartache to everyone, and when it's all said and done, you're the one that's going to be hurt the most. Why don't I come by tomorrow? We can sit down and talk this over rationally."

"My mind is made up," she said, though she sounded less than certain. "Everything's already in motion. I'd thank you not to bother me again."

The line went dead and Jake put down the phone. The room smelled like cheap burritos. He wasn't even hungry anymore. He hoped to God that Carly's worst nightmare wasn't about to become a reality.

He punched in Carly's number, waited as he let it ring and ring, but she never picked up.

THIRTY

It had been less than twenty-four hours since all hell broke loose in her life.

Somehow Carly had made it through the night by unplugging her phone and working in her studio. Sleep wasn't an option.

It was nine in the morning. Chris was happily eating Fruit Loops on the living-room floor in front of the television watching "Shark Week Day One" on the Discovery Channel. Carly was still in her terry-cloth robe, barely finished with half-a-cup of coffee when the doorbell rang.

Jake. It was her first thought, until she remembered that he'd gone back to Long Beach.

Mesmerized by the great white, Chris hadn't budged. Tightening the sash on her robe, she opened the front door. A county sheriff was standing on the porch, hat in hand along with a legal-sized envelope.

"Ms. Carly Nolan? A.k.a. Caroline Graham?"

When she heard Caroline's name, all she could do was nod.

He handed her the envelope. "You've been served." Then he turned to walk away.

"Wait!"

"Ma'am?"

"What . . . what is this?"

"Could be any number of things. I'm just a disinterested party, ma'am." He put his hat back on and walked down the steps toward the gleaming black-and-white patrol car parked beside Betty Ford.

Clutching the document, she glanced around to see if anyone was on the street. None of her neighbors was out and about yet, but she glimpsed movement behind Etta's drapes.

Somehow she made it to the table before her legs gave out. She ripped open the envelope, scanned the documents. She was to appear at the Superior Court of Los Angeles County on June 29th at two o'clock.

Four weeks.

Four weeks.

Anna Saunders had filed a petition for guardianship of Christopher.

Anna Saunders knew where she was and knew her name was Carly Nolan.

She stared down at the pages. Jake hadn't wasted any time.

Chris was still on the floor, watching a diver in a mesh suit protected by a steel cage as he tossed hunks of fish out to a school of frenzied sharks.

Carly easily related to the bait.

When the phone rang a few minutes later, her first impulse was to rip the cord out of the wall, but acting on autopilot, she answered it. If it was Jake . . .

If it was Jake, she honestly didn't know what she was going to say or do. She was too numb to think.

"Carly?"

"Yes?"

"It's me, Geoff. You never called back yesterday, and I mean to tell you, I'm miffed."

"Geoff?" Thankfully it wasn't Jake, but she still couldn't form a coherent sentence.

"What's wrong?"

She struggled to get the words past the lump in her throat. "Can you . . . can you come over?"

"I'll be right there."

She was still at the table twenty minutes later when Geoff gave a quick knock, opened the door, and strolled in with his arms full of grocery bags.

He called out a greeting to Chris as he breezed past Carly and on into the kitchen.

Chris waved, still stretched out on the floor with his head

propped up on one hand. The diver on television was out of the cage and back on the deck of a boat trolling beach-ball-sized chunks of bloody chum.

Geoff started unpacking the bags, piling fresh veggies all over the countertop along with a carton of eggs, a pint of heavy cream, a half-gallon of fresh-squeezed orange juice, a bottle of champagne and two champagne glasses.

"First I cook, and then we talk." He paused, crossed his arms and looked her up and down. "You look like something the cat dragged in."

"I feel worse than that."

He tipped his head. "I take it my little plan backfired. I figured I owed you one of my special veggie omelettes as an apology."

She didn't object or explain as he unerringly found a skillet and began to chop and sauté onions along with red and green bell peppers. While they simmered, he opened the bottle of champagne.

Carly cupped her chin in her hand, watching Geoff break half a dozen eggs into a bowl. He whisked them together before he added heavy cream.

It was easier to let him have his way than protest that she wasn't hungry. She hadn't really eaten since dinner with Jake on Friday night.

Geoff brought her a mimosa he'd made with champagne and orange juice.

"So . . ." He took the sautéed veggies out of the pan, left them in a bowl, and poured in the eggs. As the edges of the omelette started to set, he turned around, leaned against the kitchen counter, and folded his arms. "So, how are *you* doing?"

Her hand shook as she forced herself to take a sip of the mimosa. "I've been better."

"God, Carly. I'm so sorry. This is all my fault."

Carly lowered her voice so that Chris wouldn't hear. "Actually, Friday night was . . . unforgettable. Everything went according to plan. Dinner was a huge success."

More than a success. His hands, his lips, the very way he spoke her name on every sigh had moved her to new heights. For as long as she lived, she would never, ever forget that night in his arms.

"And afterward?"

"I'll never forget it. But it's over."

"I thought you two had something going."

"We did. Until I got home yesterday and heard from Glenn Potter that Jake isn't the owner of a consulting firm. He's a private investigator."

Geoff went back to the stove, lifted the edge of the omelette so that the creamy egg mixture would cook evenly.

"And that's a bad thing?" he asked.

She took a deep breath, shuddered. "Jake didn't come to Twilight just to buy a painting. He came specifically looking for me."

Geoff paused with a spatula in the air and waved it like a wand. "Why?"

"He knew Chris's father."

"Ohmygod. There's *way* more to this than meets the eye, isn't there?"

She fought a sudden wash of tears and nodded.

"Just let me get this dished up, and then you can start at the very beginning."

Twenty minutes later, Geoff's omelette was gone. Carly's was still on her plate, untouched. She'd given him the *Reader's Digest* version of her life right up until yesterday when she'd learned about Jake's duplicity. There wasn't the relief she'd experienced after telling Jake, but at least baring her past had been a little easier this time.

"This morning right before you called, a sheriff knocked at the door and asked if I was Carly Nolan, a.k.a. Caroline Graham, then he shoved an envelope at me and left."

Geoff's right brow slowly rose. He pulled the papers toward him and glanced over them with a look of pure disdain. "Let me guess . . ."

"Anna Saunders is petitioning the court for guardianship of Christopher."

"Jake told her where to find you."

"I don't know how else she'd know."

Trust me, Carly. All I've ever wanted is to help you and Chris.

She closed her eyes. Tried to shake off the notion that Jake had betrayed her. There was nothing else to believe.

Geoff grabbed his empty plate and pushed away from the table. "What in the hell is the woman thinking? There's no way she can prove you're negligent or abusive. This is just a waste of time and money. It's ridiculous."

She clasped her hands in her lap, her fingers cold as ice. She stared out into the studio. "I should pack up Christopher and leave . . ."

"Running away isn't the answer anymore, Carly. It won't solve anything. You'll just have to keep on running. It's time you fought back."

"But what if she wins?"

"How can you lose?"

"Geoff, I passed myself off as someone else for years. That's against the law."

"Did you commit fraud while using your friend's name? No? Then it's not like you ran up debts in her name or stole her credit cards and bank accounts."

"Of course I didn't do any such thing."

"For heaven's sake, you're a great mother." He slipped his plate into the soapy water in the sink then made a fist in the air. "Just bring the old bitch on. As soon as I get home, I'm calling you with the name of a good lawyer. He's a friend of a friend of mine in San Luis Obispo. You're calling him first thing in the morning."

Tears began to slide down Carly's cheeks. With a quick glance at Chris, she wiped her face on the sleeves of her terry robe, damning and missing Jake at the same time.

"All I've ever done is make one stupid decision after another, Geoff. I thought that somehow everything I was doing was for the best, but a lot of wrongs never add up to a right."

"Running away again certainly isn't going to help you now. Besides, you're not fighting alone this time. You're not a nineteen-year-old unwed mother, either. You've built a home here. You have friends who consider you family. Do you think any of us will let anyone take Christopher away from you?"

Family.

A dream that had died when she was a child, blossomed for a brief time in Borrego, but perished again with Rick on a treacherous mountain grade.

Geoff sat down across from her again and pointed to her plate.

"I'm not going anywhere until you've eaten half of that omelette. I know thin is in, but *you* can't afford to lose any weight." He glanced down at his watch, a slim rectangle on a black leather band. "I've got to open the gallery in forty minutes, so you eat up, missy. Don't make me have to get butch about it."

Carly found herself smiling through her fear. She picked up her fork, forced herself to take a bite.

Maybe he was right. Maybe this time, if she fought back, she'd finally be able to put the past behind her and stop looking over her shoulder.

Maybe from now on, things would be different.

Half an hour after Geoff left, Carly was in the shower rinsing her hair when Chris called out from the other side of the shower curtain.

"Mom! It's Jake! He's on the phone!"

She stuck her head and shoulders around the edge of the shower curtain, and there was Christopher, holding the portable phone toward her.

"Tell him I can't talk."

He held the phone to his ear. "She can't talk right now. She's all wet and she's *naked*. Yeah. She's in the shower." He looked at Carly, the phone still pressed to his ear. "He says it's important."

"Tell him I don't want to talk to him."

"She doesn't want to talk to you. Water's dripping all over the floor."

Knowing Chris would stand there and give Jake a blow-by-blow description of everything she was doing, Carly shut off the water, grabbed a towel before she stepped out of the tub, and took the phone.

"Thanks, now go on." When he flashed her a bright smile and gave her a thumbs-up, she waved Chris out of the bathroom and locked the door behind him.

"Hello?"

"Carly, it's Jake."

At the sound of his voice she closed her eyes against an unexpected rush of longing. "What do you want?"

"I spoke to Anna Saunders late last night. She . . . she called in her own investigators after she talked with me, and there's no other way to say this—she had me followed. She knows about you, Carly. She knows where you live, and she knows your name."

"You're way behind, Jake. She's petitioned for guardianship of Christopher. A sheriff knocked on my door at nine this morning and handed me papers."

She heard him mumble a curse.

"So, if you called to warn me, you're a little too late. I do like the part about a detective following you around." She sat down on the toilet seat cover and pulled the towel closer. Water was streaming down her back, dripping off her soaking-wet hair and onto the floor.

"Jake, I really don't have time for this. Good- . . ."

"Carly, don't hang up! Listen to me."

"Look where that's gotten me."

"I'm not giving up. I'm going to talk to Anna again."

"Oh, really? Have a nice chat." She punched the talk button off and sat there staring at the phone while the puddle on the floor widened.

THIRTY-ONE

Thirty minutes after stepping off his grandfather's sixty-foot Hatteras Sportfisher, Jake was sitting in his mother's kitchen surrounded by the scent of home and childhood memories.

The air in the room was close and warm, as were the intense feelings that filled him whenever he walked in the back door.

This house had been home to him until he'd married Marla. Like many Long Beach natives, he'd gone to Cal State Long Beach right out of high school, worked part time, and commuted from home. It was a simple house, with three bedrooms and a den in the quiet, historically designated California Heights area with streets lined with magnolia and jacaranda trees.

This was what he'd wanted before he'd married Marla. A house on a quiet street, three kids. A dog. A car without payments. But he'd wanted his own firm, too. Wanted more than to work in a cubicle at A and P or be their errand boy. He wanted to build his own client list, set his own hours, turn down the more mundane cases, and take on the challenging ones.

But what he'd wanted hadn't meshed with what Marla wanted. Once they were married, she'd started needing other men, and unfortunately, he hadn't been willing to look the other way.

He watched his mother bend over the open oven with a red-and-white checkerboard oven mitt on each hand as she reached for a golden-brown loaf of banana bread.

In her mid-sixties, Sheila Olson was still trim, though she'd be the first to admit she had to work hard to stay that way. She played golf two days a week, walked a mile and a half every morning, and still found time to watch Julie's terrible trio.

Her family was and always had been both her passion and her inspiration.

She had been widowed the first time at twenty-four, but even then she had the courage to stand up to Jackson Montgomery when Granddad, overflowing with grief of his own and embittered by sorrow, blamed and deluged her with "I-told-you-so" and "What-else-did-you-expect?"

She stood her ground when Jackson insisted that he knew what was better for young Jake than she. He even swore not to let her ruin his grandson's life the way she had his son's, but as stubborn as she was gentle and loving, Sheila had easily won using love, something Jackson never understood.

Sheila turned the loaf pan upside down over a wire rack and the bread came out clean. She flipped the loaf right side up and walked over to sit beside Jake at the oak breakfast nook Manny had painstakingly built her.

"This will be cool enough to cut in a few minutes. I think you should take it to Kat, fatten that girl up a bit." She took a deep breath and finally asked, "How'd it go this morning? Did you have any trouble?"

"No trouble at all."

The ocean was blessedly calm that morning, the slight offshore breeze glassed the waters between Long Beach and Catalina. A pod of dolphins had escorted him, a fitting tribute to his grandfather, who had loved cruising open water more than anything or anyone.

"I would have come with you, you know." She watched him closely, perhaps worried that he might be taking his grandfather's death harder than he let show.

"I know how seasick you get, Mom."

She shrugged. "Still, I would have come."

She would do anything for him. Anything at all. As a kid he'd taken her love for granted, assumed that was the way things were supposed to be. As an adult, he knew better. He knew how lucky he was to have her.

"I know, Mom. Thanks."

Granddad had left specific instructions that Jake be the one to spread his ashes at sea between Long Beach and Catalina. Jake had taken the yacht out alone.

"Can you stay for lunch?" Sheila asked.

"Sorry. I've got to get back to the office. Kat picked up a client, a fraud case that needs a little more expertise than she has at running numbers at this point. What would take her a couple of days will only take me a few hours to untangle. I've got to go over the accounts they sent us, look for evidence of embezzlement."

"Is everything else going all right? You've been away so much."

"It runs just as smoothly without me. Kat's great. Besides, I've needed some time off for a long time. All I want to do right now is convince Anna Saunders to meet with me. I'm going by to try to talk to her tonight, see if she won't agree to settle this thing out of court, but I probably don't stand a chance in hell. She thinks she had to keep this thing going because her husband, Charles, wanted it that way."

"You could always make a scene outside her door."

He laughed. "If I get arrested, I'll call you."

He'd told his mom why he'd gone to Twilight Cove and shared his excitement about renting the house. Last night over dinner, he'd described Carly and how the search for the mother of Rick's child had led him to her. He'd talked about Christopher and of Anna Saunders' determination to have her grandson.

Sheila could relate to Carly's situation. "Don't blame yourself for all this, Jake. From what you've said, Anna Saunders has had people searching for that child for years. Eventually she would have succeeded, don't you think?"

He doubted it, but he didn't bother to explain why.

"How does a woman my age think she's going to cope with a six-year-old boy?"

Sheila shook her head and paired up the salt and pepper shakers, funny wooden figures in mushroom-shaped chef's hats that he'd given her for Mother's Day when he was around Christopher's age. Their painted faces had worn off a long time ago but she still insisted on using them.

She sighed. "People waste so much time butting heads while life slips through their fingers. When I think of all the good times your grandfather could have shared with us if he'd hadn't drawn a line in the sand. He could have joined us for the holidays, seen you graduate from high school and college. He didn't have to miss your wedding."

Jake had forgotten Jackson had refused to attend his and Marla's wedding simply because Sheila would be there. Time tended to smooth away the rough edges of life the way water rounded river rock.

He tried to imagine his grandfather sitting at the crowded dining-room table with the rest of them, but couldn't quite see Jackson joining hands as Manny gave the blessing or suffering through Julie's kids' antics. They loved to show off mouthfuls of mashed potatoes.

Not in a million years would Jackson Montgomery have ever fit in here.

Unfortunately, it was all too easy to see Chris and Carly surrounded by the circle of his family.

"You know, it's funny." He ran his fingers over the glossy oak table as the image of Manny using his sander in the garage workshop flashed through his mind. "This morning, out on the water with no one around, nothing but the sound of the gulls and the dolphin and the smell of salt air, I held the urn with Granddad's ashes, and a kind of peace came over me, the kind I never experienced when the two of us were together. It was as if every argument we'd ever had didn't matter anymore."

He recalled watching the ashes drift on the water as he sprinkled them over the rail. The spreading stain widened, the ashes disappeared from sight. In that moment, he wondered if it wasn't his inner peace he experienced, but that maybe Granddad had found his own contentment.

"I think maybe Granddad's finally happy," he told her.

"I hope so." Sheila reached across the table for Jake's hand. "I really do. Now what are we going to do about you now that you've found this woman? You've never said all that much about it over the years, but I know how it's bothered you that you couldn't find her for Rick."

"Me? I'm fine."

"Fine isn't good enough. You're falling in love, Jake. I hear it in your voice and see it plain as day on your face when you talk about Carly Nolan. I haven't seen you like this for a long time. How do you feel about her boy?"

"He's a great kid."

"I know you've always wanted a family of your own and how devastated you were when you and Marla split up. Honey, just don't let old wounds keep you from having what you really want." She let go of his hand but continued to hold his eyes with the intensity of her gaze.

"When I lost your dad, I thought that I'd never love anyone that way again. I didn't trust God anymore. He'd not only taken Jack from me but left you fatherless. What kind of a God could be so cruel? Then Manny came into my life, bringing Julie with him. Suddenly I had a loving husband and a daughter I'd never have known had your father lived." She leaned closer, her voice full of emotion. "We never know what's in store for us, Jake. We just have to make it through the storms and wait for rainbows to appear."

He thought of Carly back in Twilight, of the storm she was weathering. The rainbows in her life had been few and far between.

But this time, he'd be damned if he let her go through the storm alone. He was going to be right there beside her whether she wanted him or not.

Jake rang the security buzzer outside Anna Saunders' condo with little hope of her actually letting him in, but somehow she'd agreed to give him a few moments of her time.

Standing in the gilt and marble foyer with his hands casually shoved into his pockets, he told her, "Thanks for seeing me."

She kept her distance, obviously nervous, as she stood beside a glass and wrought iron table, her softening profile reflected in the mirror on the wall beside her. She was a handsome woman with eyes very much like Rick's. The gray in her hair was dyed blonde. She wore it short and stylishly.

It was clear she had no intention of inviting him in to sit down as she had the last time. Her posture was wooden, as if she were afraid to show any emotion, which made him wonder if she wasn't as certain of herself as she wanted him to believe.

"I'm leaving for Twilight Cove soon, and I came to invite you to ride up there with me, to meet Carly and Christopher face-to-face. See for yourself how happy and well-adjusted he is. Get to know them. That's what you really want, isn't it? To be part of their lives?"

A light flared in her eyes, then quickly faded. "I want to see my grandson, but . . . I don't care to meet that woman. She tricked my son into proposing. She knew what he was worth and knew the only way she could have him was by getting herself pregnant."

Jake refused to believe it. "I saw Rick the day he died. He couldn't hide his excitement, although he did mention you weren't happy with his choice. He wanted to be a father to Christopher. He couldn't wait to marry Carly."

"All I care about is Christopher's future happiness."

"Whether you win or lose, you'll ruin his life if you put him through this."

"I don't see how giving him all of the opportunities and the education he deserves will ruin his life. Do you? Someday he'll inherit everything the Saunders family has built for over a hundred years. Do you think she can prepare him for that?"

"Do you think you can?"

She appeared uncertain.

Jake went on. "You can give him all that without taking him away from Carly. There are some things that money just can't buy, Anna, and believe me, love is one of them. I know that much from experience."

"Christopher is still very young. There is an infinite number of things he probably wants that his mother can't dream of ever giving him," she argued.

"My grandfather died last week. You know how he died? Alone. There was no memorial, no tribute from family, no one to shed a tear when I spread his ashes over the water, and I did it, not as a tribute to him, but out of obligation. I did it because my mother wanted me to grant his final request. Even though he'd treated her like shit for years, she expected me to do what she thought was right. Is that how you want to end up? An obligation? As the woman Christopher thinks of as someone who took him away from his mother?"

He glanced around the penthouse, made a point to let her watch him take it all in. "All the money you have, all these things, are cold comfort when you're all alone, aren't they?"

He was getting to her, though he hated that she was close to tears, but he was determined to do whatever it took to save Carly and Christopher the agony of a guardianship hearing.

"Come with me to Twilight Cove, Anna. I'll pick you up on Saturday. If you don't want to drive up with me, you can get a commuter flight. Go meet them."

Her hand gripped the edge of the table beside her until her knuckles whitened. She closed her eyes as if she didn't want to see her reflection in the mirror and whispered one of her husband's favorite phrases, "When hell freezes over."

THIRTY-TWO

Tuesday afternoon, Carly drove into San Luis Obispo to meet with Tom Edwards in his law office downtown.

In his early forties, Edwards specialized in family law. She found the stocky, balding professional easy to talk to, although the worry of having to come up with money for his fee was never out of her mind.

Wearing a dark suit with a stark white, heavily starched shirt and yellow silk tie, he ushered her into his upscale office, offered her a seat, a low, black leather and chrome chair, and then sat down behind his desk. Formal photographs of a dark-haired woman and two children adorned the bookshelves behind him.

She handed him the papers she had been served and, careful not to leave anything out, related her story. She liked that he leaned back in his chair and gave her his complete attention.

When she finished, he straightened. "From everything you've told me, Ms. Nolan, I don't believe we have much to worry about. As long as D.P.S.S., the Department of Public Social Services, interviews don't turn up anything that would go against you, and the psych evaluations turn out fine, your son will be staying right where he belongs."

She mentally went back over the argument she'd had with Jake, and all the questions he'd put to her.

"What if they claim I lied to Rick? That he didn't know who I was? I did explain everything after he proposed and he . . . he still wanted to marry me anyway."

"That was the day of his accident?"

"No. I told him the day he proposed. Then he drove back to Long Beach to tell his parents about Christopher and our engagement. He died on the way back to us."

Edwards looked down at his notes. "Do you know if he told his parents about your having assumed the name Caroline Graham?"

"I . . . I have to assume that he didn't, or they would have found me as soon as I applied for a Social Security card or a driver's license. Even Jake Montgomery was searching for me under Caroline's name. So were the investigators the Saunders initially hired. So, no, I don't believe Rick told them."

The memory of the accident was still raw as the day it happened, and she realized it always would be, no matter how much time passed.

She shifted in the chair, straightened her skirt, pressed her feet together. "I wasn't exactly the kind of woman they would have wanted Rick to marry. In fact, that's why he went home to break the news to them alone."

Throughout the interview, Edwards' expression showed no emotion, which gave her confidence. A good poker face was probably an asset in a lawyer.

"So, we've no way to prove that you ever told Rick Saunders the truth, only your word. Weighed against positive statements we'll have regarding your ability to care for Christopher, the impact of your having assumed another name shouldn't be that great. You were still a minor then."

"But it *could* matter?"

"Of course. Anything can happen in a courtroom."

She knew that without him having to put it into words.

He glanced down at the papers she'd given him.

"I'll call Mrs. Saunders' lawyer to let him know I'm representing you."

Her stomach churned. She hadn't been able to eat anything at breakfast, and now she felt lightheaded. She had arranged for Tracy to pick up Christopher after school, and still had to go by the Potter's to get him.

Edwards rested his forearms on the desk and smiled. "Would you like my secretary to bring you some coffee?"

Coffee was the last thing she needed on an empty stomach. She shook her head and gathered up her purse to leave.

"No, thank you. What I'd really like is for you to tell me that I have nothing to worry about and that this is an open-and-shut case. I need to know that Anna Saunders will never, ever be able to take Christopher from me."

He came around the desk to help her stand.

"I'd do that if I could, Ms. Nolan. But unfortunately, as I said before, anything can happen."

By the time she picked up Chris from the Potters' and got home, Carly was mentally drained but physically wired.

Chris sat at the table to do his homework and went into his room to play. Carly walked into her studio. The turmoil of the past few days had sapped all the enjoyment from her painting. It was usually a welcome outlet for all her pent-up heartache and desire.

As she stood in the cool addition with its partial view of the hills, she was plagued with doubt. Had she done the right thing in telling Christopher about Anna Saunders? He'd been full of questions ever since, bugging her with requests to call or write to Anna and invite her to visit.

She'd never lied to him and never would, yet she longed to protect him from what was happening. She couldn't bear to have him as confused and terrified as she. Most hours of the day she walked around feeling as if her very life hung in the balance of the outcome—for Christopher was her life.

With a sigh, she stood back and studied the painting she'd begun for Jake earlier in the month—Twilight Cove at sunset. Still in its early stages, the ghostly characters that were her trademark had yet to materialize.

The painting had completely stalled, perhaps because whenever she picked up a brush to work on it, she thought of Jake.

I miss Jake.

Chris had waged a one-man campaign, asking about Jake more than he asked about Anna Saunders. She missed him, too, and had given up being so stupid as not to admit to herself how much she ached for him.

In the short time they'd been together, she'd come to believe it was going to be possible to let someone else inside her circle of two. She'd glimpsed what it would be like to be loved, *if* indeed he did love her at all. How could she believe him now, no matter how badly her heart wanted her to?

"If you need anything, Carly, if you need anything at all, call me."

She'd been tempted to call more than once, until she remembered that he couldn't give her what she really needed.

She wanted things back the way they were the night they made love. She wanted her innocence back. She wished she had never found out about him and why he'd really come to Twilight.

How quickly he'd become part of their lives. How easily he'd slipped into her heart, into her thoughts. He'd brought her back to life.

She wanted so badly to believe that he meant what he'd said, to believe that he truly did care about her and Chris, but by not admitting his connection to the Saunders, he'd betrayed her.

A small voice inside wouldn't let her forget that she'd lived a lie, too, convinced that was the only way to survive.

Closing her eyes, she shut out the painting and wrapped her arms protectively around herself before she scrutinized the canvas again. She studied the deserted bluff, the fountain with its slow, sparkling cascade of water, the younger version of the fig tree off to one side of the grassy area that was now the park.

She experienced the stillness of the wind at sunset, the hour when the water was often calm and glassy and mirrored the sunset sky.

Gradually, as she stared into the shadows and highlights of the oils, she almost felt the warmth of the sun on her face and caught the scent and tang of the salt spray hitting the rocks in the cove.

She listened to her heart as it whispered that this was not meant to be Jake's painting after all. Her palms began to itch as inspiration flooded her and she knew exactly what she wanted to do. She picked up a tube of black paint, opened it and then a few more tubes.

Quickly she began to squeeze colors onto her palette. Choosing a brush, she warned herself to slow down, but she didn't want to waste the few hours she had left before she was due at the diner.

There was just enough time to try to channel the creative energy pulsing through her.

On Saturday Jake stopped in San Luis Obispo with one final errand to run before he drove into Twilight. Once he'd gotten off the highway, he'd dialed Carly again, but got no answer and found himself automatically dialing Alexander and Perry. It wasn't his first try, but this time the receptionist put him through to Sam Godes.

"Godes."

"It's Jake Montgomery."

There was a telling silence on the other end of the line.

"Thanks for nothing," Jake said.

"Hey, look, I'm just doing my job here."

"How'd you do it?"

"What'da ya mean?"

"Who was on me?"

"A female agent. She's new but she's good. African American."

Sam went on but Jake only half listened. He knew exactly who'd been following him. Hell, he'd held the door for her, the well-dressed woman with Nordstrom packages and a baby carrier. Probably hadn't even had a real baby in it. She'd even passed him a time or two on the open highway. He'd seen her, hadn't thought a thing of it when he turned off at Avila and she kept going, but she must have quickly doubled back, followed him to the park. It would have been easy to take photos of him and Chris and Carly with a telephoto lense.

He'd been watching for Godes. Not another investigator.

Shit.

"Hey, for what it's worth, Jake, I didn't think it would work, but your radar must have been scrambled."

A lot had been scrambled lately, Jake thought. With his mind on Carly, he'd made it easy for Godes and the woman to double-team him.

"If she's looking for another job, have her call me," Jake told him.

"What about me?"

Jake hung up. He hoped he hadn't pushed Anna so hard yesterday that she'd be more vengeful than ever, but there was no telling. He'd given up on trying to guess what people were going to do a long time ago. So few ever did the right thing. Most people he'd run across, like Godes, looked out for number one.

"Watch it, Montgomery," he told himself as he got out of the car, "or you'll end up as hard-hearted as Kat."

Two hours later, Carly put down the palette and cleaned her brushes, occasionally glancing over at the painting, certain now that it was right, perhaps not exactly the way she had wanted it to be, but the figures in her paintings were always inspired, as if they were in control. The final product would never be right until she listened to them.

It was time to think about getting Christopher fed and over to Etta's, but as she started into the kitchen to make him a bowl of noodle soup and a toasted-cheese sandwich, the phone rang.

With the days getting longer and more tourists coming to town, the crowd at the diner was picking up. She expected it to be Selma asking her to hurry and come in early.

"Carly? It's Jake."

She recognized his voice the moment he'd said her name and the world stopped turning. Her heart jumped into her throat.

"Jake—"

"I'm in town and I'm coming over."

"I have to work tonight."

"I won't stay long."

"I really don't think—"

"I'll be there in fifteen minutes."

Before she could protest, he hung up. She wrapped her hand around the receiver, stared at the burners on the stove while her heart raced.

Slowly she put down the phone, then opened the cupboard, took down a can of chicken-noodle soup, and tried to carry on as if her life hadn't just spun completely out of control again.

• • •

Calm determination settled over Jake long before he'd pulled up in front of Carly's mobile home. He sat there listening to the end of an old R and B classic as four mellow singers crooned, "Come on, girl. Reach out. Reach out for me."

He gripped the steering wheel, cut the motor and pulled the key. Then he looked over his shoulder into the backseat where a homely, black-and-gray spotted dog lay with her muzzle on her paws. Her expressive brows shifted when she looked up at him with one brown and one blue eye.

The volunteer at the animal shelter wasn't certain, but the vet later agreed that she had to be part Australian shepherd. The mixed-breed mutt was about three years old, calm and housebroken, which was why Jake chose her, despite unknown origins. Maybe her eyes didn't match, and she was a bit on the scrawny side, but there was only one more day before she was going to be put down, and the dog seemed so desperate for love that he couldn't leave her behind.

"This might just turn out to be the second stupidest thing I've ever done." He'd been talking to the dog since he'd picked her up in San Luis Obispo earlier that afternoon.

The front door of the house opened before he was out of the car, and he was arrested by the sight of Carly in her jeans and midriff-skimming T-shirt. With her long hair and slim figure, she might have been mistaken for an eighteen-year-old, but he knew too well that she was all woman.

He ached to take her in his arms, but could see by the determined set of her lips and the way she was clinging to the edge of the screen, that was impossible.

"Stay here," he told the dog before he opened the door and stepped out of the car with his insides twisted into a knot.

Carly came down the steps to meet him. Obviously she didn't want him to set foot on the porch, but he didn't let that deter him, not with his heart at stake.

"Joe called me," he told her.

"Joe? Called *you*?"

Jake nodded. He couldn't take his eyes off of hers and wished he hadn't been the one to put the disillusionment in them.

"He said that you told him Christopher has been down in the dumps."

"Chris is confused. Frightened. His grandmother is fighting me for guardianship, Jake. Chris realizes something's going on."

"What have you told him?"

"I've never lied to him and I won't start now. I explained that Anna Saunders was his grandmother, but I didn't tell him about how she's trying to . . . take him away."

"There's always hope that she'll change her mind." Maybe slim to none, he wouldn't even bet on it, but Carly needed to believe.

"It's a little late, Jake. The petition hearing date is set." She shifted impatiently. "This isn't getting us anywhere."

He reached for her hand, sensed her hesitation when she tried to pull away. He wouldn't let go.

"Walk with me to the car."

"Please—"

"Come on. I've got something to show you." He'd already started for the SUV, thankful when she went along. He opened the back door. The dog sat up and began to sniff the air.

"I got her at the pound. I thought that if Chris had a dog, it might keep his mind off what's going on. It's totally up to you, though. If you don't want him to have her, I'll take her up to my place."

Carly hadn't moved, but the dog had walked to the edge of the seat and was staring up at her with mismatched marble eyes. Slowly Carly reached out, let the dog sniff the palm of her hand. Jake saw traces of paint on her fingertips, ochre, gold, black.

"I brought along bags of food. She's had her shots. Her former owner died, and no one else wanted her. She's not a puppy. She won't need to be house trained."

The dog was licking Carly's hand, pressing her head against her palm.

Jake waited, careful not to push any harder. Finally when Carly looked up at him, her hand was still in his—more than he'd hoped for. He figured the dog had distracted her.

Just then the screen door banged. Together they turned to see Chris come barreling down the porch steps.

"Jake! Jake! You're back."

Carly tugged on his hand, silently pleaded with him to let go. He did so with reluctance. She stepped aside when Chris charged into Jake and then spotted the dog.

"Is that *your* dog, Jake? Way cool!" Without hesitation Chris started petting the hound and scratching behind her ears. "Matt's dog likes this the best. When did you get him? What's his name?"

"He's really a she." Jake couldn't help but laugh, delighted as the dog started wagging her tail and showing more life than she had since Jake had laid eyes on her at the pound.

"She doesn't have a name yet." Jake looked to Carly, waiting for a decision. She stepped up beside her son and smoothed Christopher's hair.

"She doesn't have a name because Jake just got her. He brought her for you."

Chris slowly turned, his eyes wide with disbelief.

"For *me*?" he asked softly.

"For you," Jake said.

"To keep?"

"To keep." Jake reached into the back of the car for the leash he'd picked up at the pet supply outlet along with bowls and a fleece dog bed. He clipped the leash to the dog's new collar and handed it to Chris. "I got her at the pound in San Luis Obispo, so until she's used to living here, you should keep her on the leash, okay?"

"I know." Chris was so excited his words ran over each other. "Matt has to walk Willa every day, and he always uses the leash. It's not good to let dogs run around without a leash, is it, Jake? Maybe that's how she got lost in the first place." He paused and his smile instantly faded. "You don't think somebody's looking for her, do you?" His voice lowered to a near whisper. "You don't think somebody will come and want her back. If I keep her, I can't let anybody take her away again."

Carly quickly turned away and started toward the house. Chris was still waiting for an answer, staring up at Jake with his even little brows puckered into a deep frown. More than ever he reminded Jake of Rick.

"Nobody's looking for her. She was in the pound for a week, and no one showed up to claim her."

Like the sun bursting through the clouds after a rain, Chris's face brightened. "I'm gonna walk her around a minute in case she has to go, okay?"

"Good idea. I'll unload her stuff. Stay right here in front of the house." He made short work of carrying the huge bags of dog food up to the porch and came back for the bowls, bed, and rawhide chews, not once letting Christopher out of his sight.

Together they went inside. Carly was at the stove grilling a cheese sandwich. Jake unfastened the dog's leash so that Chris could lead her to his room. Although it was nearly as big as he, Chris still insisted on carrying the fleece dog bed down the hall himself.

"Come on, girl. Come with me." Chris waited in the doorway to the hall, but not for long. The spotted dog jumped up and followed him.

Jake watched boy and dog disappear into Chris's room before he walked into the kitchen and stood behind Carly. He stepped close enough to smell the heady floral scent of her shining hair and was tempted to slip his arms around her waist, to enjoy the way she fit against him, but he was treading on thin ice, and he knew it.

"I didn't just come by to bring Chris the dog," he admitted. "I came to ask you up to the house tomorrow."

Her hand that held the spatula stilled. The utensil hovered over the cheese sandwich on the griddle. She'd yet to turn and meet his eyes.

"Are you working?"

Tomorrow was Sunday. Her day off. "No. I just can't."

"Can't or won't?"

Finally she turned around. "Won't."

"I'd like to see you without Christopher."

"You told me that once before and I was stupid enough to put on a dinner for two. Whatever has to be said, say it right here, right now."

"You're burning that sandwich."

She whipped around, flipped the toasted cheese over. It was on the edge of dark brown but not ruined. Again she faced him, her green eyes wide with distrust but void of contempt.

"Tomorrow. Up at the house. Come for lunch."

She shook her head, wary. "No."

He held up both hands. "Broad daylight. I won't touch you. Carly, trust me."

"Trust you?"

"I never meant to bring this down on you, Carly." He glanced toward the hall and lowered his voice. He shoved his hands in his back pockets in an effort to keep from reaching for her. "See me tomorrow. It won't take more than an hour of your time."

Just then Christopher came running out of his room.

"Come see, Jake. She likes her bed. She's lying there with a chewy. Come see." Chris took hold of his hand and tugged. Jake followed him down the hall.

Sure enough, the shepherd was curled up on the dog bed Chris had placed on the floor beside his own bed. She was gnawing on a rawhide bone. Chris dropped to his knees beside her and kissed her on the nose.

Chris' voice was full of reverence and awe. "I was gonna call her Belle, but I decided on Beauty. Because she's so beautiful." He looped his arm around the mutt with mismatched eyes and stretched out beside her. Then he looked up at Jake with such gratitude and admiration that Jake's heart hurt.

"You know what, Jake?"

"What Chris?" He had a hard time getting the words out with a boulder weighing on his chest.

"This is about the best day of my whole life."

Carly took the bowl of soup out of the microwave and set it on the table alongside Christopher's sandwich. Jake walked back into the living room. She thought he'd come to her, try to take her in his arms even, but instead, he headed for the door.

She clung to the back of one of the dinette chairs, watched him open the front door before he turned to face her.

She reminded herself not to forget what he'd done to them. She'd be a fool to go to his place tomorrow, crazy to meet him there alone.

"Noon tomorrow, Carly."

Before her weakness was put to the test, he walked out the door.

THIRTY-THREE

Chocolate. Jake and chocolate. Both irresistible.

In spite of a multitude of misgivings, Carly found herself driving up to his place the next day, finding it impossible to turn down a shred of hope, no matter how slight, wanting, against her better judgment, to see him again.

It was another picture-perfect morning, the kind coastal-dwelling Californians cherished before the overcast days dubbed "June gloom" rolled in.

Her anticipation mounted as the car wound up Lover's Lane. Before she was ready, she spotted the house perched high above the sea. No one could deny the setting was perfect. The view from nearly every window was breathtaking.

As soon as she turned onto the gravel drive, Jake stepped out onto the porch. Hands in his pockets, dressed in a black polo shirt and khakis, he looked fit and far too handsome. The shade of the porch hid his features, yet she'd memorized his face, his cerulean eyes, the smile lines etched at their corners. His full lips, the cut of his jaw.

He was almost too much to resist, yet she had her mind made up. She'd come to hear him out, that was all—then she was leaving.

She parked beside his SUV and left her purse and keys in the car. The yellow mustard blooming on the hillsides rippled beneath a strong breeze off the water. She paused to watch the mustard sway, let her gaze travel to the hilltop, and squinted against the noon sun.

When she looked away from the pastoral scene, she realized Jake was standing beside her.

"You came." He sounded relieved as he reached for her hand.

She hadn't the will to pull away. The simple touch rocked her, and she swayed toward him, caught herself, and finally withdrew her hand for the same reason she never let herself keep chocolate around. One taste was never enough.

"I'm here against my better judgment. I hope I won't be sorry."

"Me too."

He took her by the arm, walked her across the drive. It wasn't until they were on the porch that she noticed the woman standing in the house.

Of medium height with short, stylishly cut blonde hair, she was dressed in rich brown slacks and a matching sweater and was staring down into the empty fireplace with her back to the door. As if she sensed their arrival, she slowly turned.

At first Carly thought the woman might have been Jake's mother, but as soon as she met the woman's eyes across the empty living room, she realized they were the same shape and color as Christopher's—and Rick's—except that these eyes were tinted with a cool, judgmental stare and now and again a hint of uncertainty.

Carly's step faltered. She stopped halfway across the porch.

Trust me.

She should have known better than to trust him. She shouldn't have come.

"What's going on, Jake? How could you?"

"Hell froze over," he mumbled and then added, "Would you have come if I'd told you?"

"No."

He caught her arm above the elbow, with gentle force, he made her look up at him and ignore the older woman waiting in the other room.

He lowered his voice but it was full of urgency. "It took me hours to convince Anna to meet you. This is a chance to set things right, Carly, to clear things up between you without lawyers and courtrooms."

She could feel the chill in Anna Saunders' stare from across the porch and shivered. The woman had already judged her and found her wanting.

"I can't do this, Jake. What if it backfires?"

He slid his hand down her arm until he clasped her fingers. "I can't make you," he said softly, his gaze wandering over her features, her hair, her lips. "But life doesn't hand out many second chances. Take this one, Carly. Talk to her. You've got everything to lose and nothing to gain if you turn away now. Didn't you teach Chris to believe that tomorrow is always better? And that's when you get another chance to do things right?"

"I taught Chris about Santa and the Tooth Fairy, too."

Torn, she wavered, conscious of the warmth of the hand dwarfing hers. Slowly she faced the woman across the room. Anna Saunders hadn't moved, except to place one hand above her heart.

Jake leaned closer. His breath stroked Carly's hair when he spoke. "She's a mother, too, Carly. Give her a chance. Let her give *you* a chance. Ask yourself what Rick would want."

She's a mother, too.

A mother who lost a son. Maybe, just maybe, Anna Saunders *would* understand. It was worth a try. Anything was worth a try with Christopher's future at stake.

A tightness gathered around Carly's heart. She took a deep breath, tried to ignore it, but failed. Anna Saunders had buried her son. She couldn't even imagine Anna's pain, the fathomless, enduring heartache that no mother should ever have to bear.

She's a mother, too.

Carly squared her shoulders, looked over, and nodded to Jake. He let go of her hand. She pictured Chris as she'd last seen him, safe at home, entertaining Etta, introducing Beauty to Napoleon Bonaparte, trying to teach Beauty to lift her paw and shake.

"I'll be right beside you," Jake whispered.

"No." She gave a slight, determined shake of her head. "This is something I have to do alone. Something between two mothers."

In those fleeting seconds while Anna watched Carly Nolan debate meeting her, she had also studied Jake Montgomery's expressions.

Clearly he was in love with the woman, but she wondered if he even knew it yet.

As much as she hated to admit it, Carly Nolan was lovely, far from what she'd expected. Only hazy remembrance of the photo Jake had pulled out of his wallet had lingered. She'd thought she would be meeting an older version of the girl with poorly dyed hair and too many earrings. Someone ragged around the edges and unsophisticated.

Instead she found herself face-to-face with a lithe, attractive blonde modestly outfitted in black slacks and a knit sports shirt lingering uncomfortably in the open doorway. Her makeup was minimal, applied so that it enhanced her natural beauty rather than exaggerated it. The changes in the woman who Anna had come to think of as Caroline Graham gave her a moment's hesitation.

Anna could tell by the set of Carly Nolan's shoulders as she walked into the room that it was she, Anna, who had the advantage of surprise, which put her a little more at ease.

Anna stepped away from the fireplace. Jake had brought two lawn chairs in from the sundeck, the only furniture in the room. She walked over to one, hesitated.

"Why don't you have a seat?" Anna offered Carly.

Carly waited until Anna sat down, then crossed the floor and took the other chair. Carly didn't relax but rather, perched on the edge of the chair.

"Why did you come?" Carly Nolan asked her.

"Jake badgered me into it. I'm sure he hopes that I'll see something in you that will lead me to believe you love my grandson and are taking excellent care of him."

"Of course I love him. If I've made mistakes along the way, they were made out of love."

"You lied to my son."

"No. I told him the truth. I couldn't have married him with a lie between us."

Anna shifted on the hard chair. The odor of fresh paint filled the house even though the doors and windows were open. She leaned forward, surprised that Carly had not once flinched under her intense stare.

"Why were you posing as someone else?"

"I was fifteen when it started. I was scared. I had to support myself. Pretending I was eighteen was the only thing I could do."

"You ran away with Christopher. Kept us away from him—"

Carly cut her off before she finished. "Because of your lawyer, of all the things he said."

"You were afraid there was just cause for us to become Christopher's guardians."

"Listen, Mrs. Saunders, I was nineteen. I couldn't fight you in court."

Anna gave her credit for not bursting into a maudlin display of tears. "Yet you intend to fight me now. You might very well lose everything you own."

"Everything I own? What else matters? I could lose my son." Carly's voice dropped to a whisper but her gaze never wavered. "You know the heartache of losing a child, Mrs. Saunders. I don't see how you could wish that on me or anyone, for that matter."

Anna felt the color drain from her face, recalled the stunning spring afternoon when her whole world was shattered by a phone call.

She'd existed for weeks in a cocoon of numbness, carried on conversations, accepted condolences from friends whose expressions had told her they were truly sorry, yet at the same time relieved that they'd been spared such heartache.

"How could you say that to me?" Anna had underestimated the other woman's strength of will.

"I'm desperate, Mrs. Saunders. If I wasn't I wouldn't have set foot in this house today."

I don't see how you could wish that on anyone.

Anna couldn't get the words out of her head.

"I want to meet my grandson," she blurted, fighting tears. Deep down, that was the only reason she'd ever let Jake Montgomery talk her into flying up here, the reason she hadn't told Art Litton that she was coming. He'd always been loyal to Charles, so much so that after Charles's death, he hadn't wanted to give up the hunt for Christopher. She knew without a doubt that Art would advise against any kind of withdrawal of the petition. He would never advise her to back down.

But Art Litton be damned, she *had* to see Christopher for herself, wanted so desperately to meet him that she'd taken Jake up on his offer, flown up and hired a driver to bring her to Twilight.

When she saw that something akin to hope had flared in Carly Nolan's eyes, she thought of Charles and of Art Litton and warned herself to remain resolute.

"Will you drop the suit?" Carly asked.

The last time Anna spoke to Arthur Litton, he hadn't gotten his hands on any information from the court-ordered investigation. He advised her that at this point things looked very promising, but that there were no guarantees.

"You're asking me to take your word for it that Christopher is a well-adjusted child, that you are a perfect mother without letting me see him for myself? Without letting me talk to him?"

"I never said I was perfect. I'm certainly doing the best I can. How do I know you won't frighten him? Or threaten him? He knows nothing about your petition." For the first time Carly looked away. Staring down at her hands she admitted, "Chris overheard me mention your name and asked about you. I told him that you were his grandmother."

"What did he say?" The desperation in her own voice disgusted her.

"He was excited. His friends talk about their aunts and uncles, grandmothers and grandfathers, all the time. It hasn't been easy trying to explain why there's no one in our lives. There's just been the two of us, and as much as I've tried to do for him, the one thing he doesn't have is family."

Family.

How would have things worked out if Rick had had his way and married this woman? Would she have ever fit into their world? All Rick talked about the day before he died was his son, so much so that she suspected he was only marrying Carly because of the baby.

The girl was just part of the package. A child certainly wasn't enough of a foundation to cement a lasting relationship.

Most likely, Rick would have been married and divorced by now, but even so, Christopher would have grown up as one of the family, sharing holiday traditions. By now he'd be learning to sail boats on the bay, the way Rick had as a child.

There would have been father-son outings. Birthdays.

But all these years, she and Charles had been denied time with their grandson. Time she would never, ever recover. And poor Charles. He never got the chance even to see the boy.

"Put yourself in my place, Ms. Nolan. Christopher is my son's only child. My only grandchild. I want to know he's in the best possible situation. I can't make that decision until I meet him, until I see him for myself. You can either cooperate or not. At least I've made an attempt by coming here. What are you prepared to do?"

THIRTY-FOUR

Blindly Carly walked out of Jake's house, away from Anna Saunders and her perfectly matched outfit, her gold earrings, diamond rings, gold bracelets—reminders of wealth and power in a world where money has the last word.

Jake was waiting on the far end of the porch. He turned the minute Carly cleared the front door, searched her face with unspoken questions in his eyes.

They exchanged a look. His eyes were full of concern, apology, an underlying, smoldering heat that couldn't be denied. She started for the stairs, so intent upon getting home to the safety of the familiar, to Chris, that she nearly stumbled.

Jake unfolded his long legs, stepped away from the low wall that surrounded the porch, reached her as she cleared the last step. Tempering his strides, he fell into the cadence of her step as she headed for the car.

"How did it go?"

She thought he might have heard every word, but the sound of the sea wrapped around the hills, birds sang spring songs in the cottonwoods along the arroyo. Perhaps he hadn't heard a thing.

They stopped beside the Ford. He looked down into her eyes, reached for her hand.

"Tell me," he urged.

"Did you expect her to meet me and simply withdraw the petition? That would be the perfect ending to a sappy movie of the week, but this is real life, Jake. Wake up and smell the coffee. She wants to meet Christopher."

His eyes hardened, his mouth tensed. He let go of her hand and took a step back.

"Don't tell me about real life. I wanted you and Anna to get to know each other outside of a courtroom, and that's happened. What's wrong with my hoping the two of you would stop and think about Christopher? He has you, Carly, but it would be great if he had extended family, too."

"He has plenty of family. He has Etta and Selma, Joe and Geoff. And the Potters."

"You're right. But have you ever thought of what would become of him if something happened to you? If Anna had never found you, he might have ended up in foster care, in the kind of place you ran away from. He'd never know he had family who cared about him."

His logic frightened her. She'd often thought that she should have made provisions for Chris in the event something happened to her, but that would have meant letting someone in, explaining everything, filling out legal documents.

"She doesn't care about him. She doesn't even know him," she argued.

"She knows he's Rick's." Impatiently, he ran his fingers through his hair. "I probably shouldn't have wasted either of your time. I thought I could help."

"Did you think you were helping when you walked into our lives and treated us as if you *cared*? You moved into my son's heart, and you expect me to forgive you for pretending to be a decent, caring guy. Now you want me to try and *understand* the woman who wants to take my son away from me?"

"If I didn't care, I wouldn't be here, Carly. I'd have called Anna Saunders the first day I laid eyes on you, told her where you were, and taken her money on the spot. I wouldn't have turned down her offer when she asked me to take the case. I wasn't working for her when I met you, and I'm not now. I'm blue in the face trying to convince you that I would have *never* told her where you are."

"No, but you led her right to us."

"Damn it, Carly. I love you. That ought to count for something." He looked as if he'd startled himself with another raw declaration of his love for her.

He turned and stalked away, wide shoulders rigid, his hands at his sides. As she watched him go, she remembered the night he'd first walked into the gallery, how she'd seen him as a man who didn't waste movements, a man who walked with a purpose. That purpose had been to track her down.

Let him go.

Her heart was deaf to her mind's advice. She raised her hand, reached out for him.

"Jake, wait."

At the sound of her voice, he stopped and turned, but didn't walk back. His stance telegraphed impatience, his expression closed—that of a man who had defended himself for the last time and had nothing more to say.

On the second try, she found the words, though they bore the metallic taste of fear.

"I've agreed to take Chris to Plaza Park in an hour. I've agreed to let her meet him."

Cool and distant, Jake said nothing at all, simply looked at her.

Carly turned away, reminding herself this was *his* fault, not hers. She opened the door, started Betty Ford. Something between embarrassment and downright shame hit her when she realized she would have to drive tired old Betty Ford past the window. Anna Saunders would see her beat-up car.

She kept her hands steady on the wheel, her chin high. By the time she headed back down the drive, Jake had already gone inside.

An hour later, Carly fought to quell the small riot going on in her stomach as she tried to get Chris ready to go. In the end she had agreed to the meeting, not because Anna requested it, but for Rick—certain it was what he would have wanted.

At least there was still a glimmer of hope. Maybe when Anna met Christopher, the woman would be reminded of her own son and remember what losing him had done to her.

Chris was excited when he heard they were going to the park, but Carly couldn't bring herself to tell him why. She simply couldn't find the words. Trying to make it seem like any ordinary Sunday afternoon outing, she let him choose what he wanted to wear and reminded him to bring along a sweatshirt.

She changed her clothes, took off her good slacks and slipped on her jeans. No use pretending to be something she wasn't. Besides, Anna had already given her a once-over.

"Can we take Beauty?" Chris was standing by the door with the leash in his hand. The dog sat at his feet, already used to following him all around the house.

"I think we should let her get used to being here alone."

His little brow furrowed as he stared down at the dog that stared back in adoration.

"She'll be all right. Etta leaves Napoleon alone when she comes over here to sit with you," Carly reminded him.

"But Etta's had Napoleon a long time. He's used to being left all alone."

"Not today, Chris. Please."

With a long-suffering sigh, he went to put the leash in his room. Beauty padded along after him.

Carly looked into the studio at the painting she'd originally started for Jake. The one-and-only figure in the piece was finally taking shape. The deserted bluff, the vastness of the Pacific backlit by a vibrant orange and yellow sunset, dramatized a stark loneliness.

She wished she could undo the sadness rendered on canvas, but if she altered it now, it would never, ever be right.

When they got to the plaza, she and Chris walked past the fountain, across the expansive grass-covered bluff to the sidewalk promenade that bordered the cove.

She had to trust her intuition, to do what was right, not for Anna Saunders or herself, but for Chris.

"Look, Mom! Over there!" He pointed out to sea. "I saw a dolphin jump out of the water."

She scanned the brilliant sparkling ocean reflecting the afternoon sun. A few surfers bobbed in the current, waiting for waves, but she saw no sign of a dolphin.

Chris tugged on her sleeve. "Can we get an ice cream later?"

She reached down, straightened the shoulder seam of his navy sweatshirt. When had he grown from a toddler to a boy?

Someday would she look at him and suddenly realize he'd gone from a boy to a man? Would they share the years between?

"I don't want you to spoil your dinner."

"Maybe we should ask Jake to dinner."

"No. Not tonight. Matt's coming over, remember? We have to pick him up later." Both boys had Monday off because of a teacher inservice. Tracy had asked if Matt could sleep over so that she and Glenn could register early for a motivational seminar they were attending.

Carly hoped having Matt around would keep her mind off of whatever happened this afternoon.

Together she and Chris leaned against the iron safety rail overlooking the view that had enticed so many tourists and locals. Chris tried to hook his legs through the lower rail and dangle them over the edge, but as always, she pulled him back, admonishing him to be careful. Then she looked around, hoping that maybe Anna wouldn't show. Her heart stumbled when she noticed the woman watching them from a few yards away.

I'm not ready.

At first Carly thought Anna was alone, but then she saw Jake at the far end of the bluff leaning on the guardrail, staring at the ocean.

Her palms grew clammy. Her throat tightened, making it hard to swallow. She had an urge to grab Chris by the hand and sprint across the park.

Anna had almost reached them. Carly glanced over at Jake. This time their eyes met.

Life doesn't hand out a lot of second chances.

He had sounded so sure—as if he'd found out the hard way.

Anna hadn't changed clothes, but she was wearing sunglasses that covered her eyes, masking her expression. Walking along the edge of the bluff, she looked out of place and uncomfortable. The steady breeze off the water battered her hair.

Chris was still trying to sight dolphins when Anna reached them. The woman nodded to Carly, then turned to face the water, standing a foot from Christopher.

Both women flanked him, neither willing to say a word, neither knowing exactly what to say.

Carly snuck a glance at Anna and saw her wipe away a tear that had slipped from beneath her glasses. The mother inside Carly wondered what it would be like to stand beside the son of her son for the first time.

"What are you looking for?" Anna drew Christopher's attention.

Before he answered, he looked to Carly for permission. She'd preached to him never to talk to strangers, and he took the warning seriously. Carly nodded, but her lips trembled when she tried to smile.

"I saw a dolphin jump out of the water. They kinda curve up and dive back in. Like this." He demonstrated by arcing his hand through the air. "I saw it right by the surfers."

"Do you like the ocean?" Anna was gripping the rail so hard her knuckles were white.

"Sure. We have a beach of our own where we live. Huh, Mom?"

"We do," Carly agreed.

"Where do you live?"

"Seaside Village. It's around those rocks." He pointed to the end of Twilight Cove. "It's the next cove over, but you can't see it from here." Then he smiled. "I'm Chris. This is my mom."

"I already knew your name."

"You know my mom from the diner?"

"No. Your mother and I met earlier today. My name is Anna."

"Hey!" He whipped his head around to Carly. "Her name's Anna, like my grandma."

When Carly saw Anna cover her mouth, she suspected the woman was having difficulty swallowing.

"This *is* your grandmother, Chris."

Anna dropped her hand and cleared her throat. "I've waited a very long time to meet you," she told him.

Christopher, in all his sweet innocence, took Carly's hand and squeezed. "Really, Mom? Is she *really* my grandma?"

"I wanted to surprise you. She came a long way to meet you."
When an overwhelming protectiveness swept her, Carly rested her
hand on Christopher's head.

She so ached for him. It hurt that he'd never known Rick, that
he hadn't ever known a father's love.

Seeing Anna's emotional reaction to Chris, Carly ached for
her, too.

"Wow." Hands at his sides, dolphin forgotten, Chris tipped his
head back and stared at Anna in amazement.

"You don't look like a grandma."

The corner of Anna's mouth twitched. "What do you think a
grandmother looks like?"

Chris shrugged. "Kinda chubby with fluffy white hair, not gold
like yours. Grandmas wear glasses and aprons and bake trays of
gingerbread men."

Carly bit her lips. Christopher had just described the Little Old
Woman illustrated in his Gingerbread Man picture book.

"I've never made a gingerbread man in my life," Anna admitted
honestly.

"My mom makes them, and I get to help. We use the recipe in
the back of my book, and she lets me put the raisins on for eyes and
buttons."

The colors of the ocean and the sky suddenly flooded into a
watercolor wash as tears swam in Carly's eyes. She turned away—
damned if she'd let Anna see her cry—pretending to watch the
surfers.

The woman trying to insinuate herself into Christopher's life
didn't know what he liked to eat or the names of his favorite books.
She couldn't know that he got quiet when he was scared or that he
got sullen if he stayed up past his bedtime. She didn't know that
he wore Batman underwear, that he liked to brag he had his own
private box of Band-Aids. She had no idea what treasures he kept
hidden in his collection of empty Altoids boxes under his bed.

She had no right to him at all. DNA was their only connection.

"Do you have any pictures of my dad? Mom said you'd show
me some when I come visit."

"When you come to visit?"

Carly quickly explained. "I told Christopher about how you wanted him to . . . come to *visit* at your house." She was certain her heart was going to break into so many pieces it would be impossible to collect them all again.

"Would you *really* come visit me?" Anna asked.

"If I can bring my dog, Beauty."

"I'll have to think about that."

"Maybe I better not come then."

"I'm sure we can work something out."

"Can I see the pictures now?" Chris stepped closer, staring at her leather handbag.

Anna tried to smooth down her flyaway hair, but without any luck. She glanced around the park before turning to Carly.

"Would it be all right if we sit on that bench under the tree?"

"That's a fig tree," Chris piped up, pleased with himself for remembering. "There's a big, huge, giagantor one in Santa Barbara. I never saw it, but my teacher said so."

"Then it must be true," Anna told him.

No matter what she was feeling, Carly couldn't deny him this chance to fill in the missing pieces of his life.

"Go ahead. I'll be right here."

Waiting to take you home.

THIRTY-FIVE

"Come on, Grandma! See how fast I can run."

Anna watched this boy, this miracle of Rick's, feeling as if time had reversed itself. In Christopher she saw her own son at six, his sturdy legs, the tilt of his head when he concentrated, the flash of a dimple in his cheek when he smiled. Meeting this child was more wonderful than she could have imagined, and yet, at the same time, more than bittersweet, knowing Rick would never, ever see his wonderful son.

As she carefully picked her way across the uneven, grassy lawn toward a wooden bench, she was reminded that she was not here for her own sake, but for Rick. She prayed that on some level her son's spirit was beside her, watching Christopher through her eyes.

"Sit here, Grandma." Chris slid over on the bench, warm and welcoming. She hadn't expected this. She'd convinced herself that Carly would have turned the boy against her, but a wide grin split his face as he patted the seat next to him.

She sat down, leaving a space between them, less than a foot that he quickly scooted to fill.

"Can I see the pictures now?"

"Of course." She opened her purse, found her matching wallet. She hadn't been without the photographs for years. Sometimes the plastic sleeves would flip open, and when she was totally unprepared, there was Rick smiling up at her, his image unraveling another piece of her heart.

Christopher leaned closer to peer over Anna Saunders' arm. He didn't know which was more exciting, meeting his real live grandma or finally seeing a picture of his dad.

She sure wasn't like anything he imagined, but if she was anything like Matt's Grandma Potter, then things were going to be *great* from now on.

He noticed her hands shook as she pulled a wallet out of her purse.

"Are you cold, Grandma?"

"No. Why?"

"Your hands are shakin'."

He could tell that bothered her and wished he hadn't said anything because she suddenly laid her hands and the wallet in her lap and took a deep breath.

Then she said, "I'm not cold. I'm a little nervous, meeting you for the first time."

He reached over and patted her hands gently.

"It's okay, Grandma. I'm right here."

She made a funny sound in her throat while she fumbled with the wallet, opened it, and flipped to some color pictures, then handed it to him.

He centered the wallet on his lap, brought it closer to see through the plastic sleeve.

"That's your father when he was about your age," she said.

"He's wearing a baseball uniform."

"He loved baseball."

"Me, too! I play T-ball but I'm gonna play baseball when I get bigger. My best friend, Matt, is on the team." He flipped to the next photo. There was his dad, older, all dressed up, with a girl tucked in his arms.

"Who's that *girl* in the shiny blue dress?" he asked.

"I can't recall. Someone he took to the Winter Formal in high school. There were so many girls in his life I lost track of their names."

He couldn't imagine why his dad had wanted to hang around with girls. Slowly, he looked through all the photos. Another was just like the Winter Formal picture, but his dad had his arms around a different girl. Another showed him in a funny, flat hat. His grandma told him it was worn for graduation.

"Where's Mom? Don't you have any pictures of him with Mom?"

He suddenly found himself wondering how old Anna Saunders was.

"No, I don't have any photos of him with your mother," she said very quietly.

Chris was starting to worry too much to think about that right now.

"Grandma? Are you real old?"

"Not that old. Why?"

" 'Cause I don't want you to die."

She pulled back. "I have no intention of dying anytime soon. Why on *earth* would you say a thing like that?"

"Well, I've been waiting a really long time to get a grandma and I don't want you to die now that I have you."

Jake had kept his distance when Anna first walked up to Carly and Christopher. After a few minutes, Chris ran across the park and Anna followed slowly behind.

Carly was left standing alone, valiant, but terrified.

As much as he'd tried to convince himself to butt out of her life, he still couldn't bear to let her go through what had to be one of the hardest moments of her life alone.

She didn't notice him drawing near until he was almost beside her. "Carly?"

"Oh, Jake. I had no idea this would be so hard."

Tears shimmered in her eyes. She looked so abandoned, so uncertain, that without thinking, he slipped his arm around her shoulders, expecting her to shrug him off, but her attention was completely focused on Anna and Christopher, and she ended up leaning against him.

"He's so *happy*," she whispered.

Christopher was looking at photos in Anna's wallet.

"I don't have one single picture of Rick." Carly drew in a long breath, shuddered. "When Chris was a toddler, I thought of framing a photo from a magazine and telling him it was his daddy, but then I realized that when he grew up, I'd have to tell him the truth. He is forever asking me what his dad looked like, if he was strong, what kind of a car he drove."

As if she only just realized she was leaning against him, she straightened, but didn't move away. "I used to tell him to go look in the mirror and he'd see just what Rick looked like." Then she let go a melancholy sound that might have been a laugh. "Chris said, 'Mom, did my dad really look like a little kid?' "

Jake reached into his back pocket, pulled out his own wallet, and handed her the photo he'd carried for so long. He watched her study the picture of her and Christopher taken in Borrego. The color faded from her cheeks when she realized the picture wasn't trimmed, but folded. She lifted the edge and looked down at the complete picture. It was of Chris, Rick, and her. One of the shots Wilt had taken for them.

"I've carried that around ever since Rick died and I started searching for you."

She ran her fingers around the frayed edges. "I was so young." She shook her head. "So long ago. A lifetime."

"Chris should be able to see a picture of his dad whenever he wants to. I'll have it copied so that you'll have a photo of the three of you, but I'd like to keep this one."

"Why, now that the search is over?"

"Because I'm afraid I've lost you again."

Anna discovered her grandson's endearing charm. He was bright. Intuitive. All boy.

Being with him made her want to stop time in its tracks, but she was anxious to get back to Long Beach and consult with Art Litton, her lawyer.

She walked hand in hand with Christopher, back to the edge of the bluff where his mother waited beside Jake Montgomery. Seeing the couple together, the man's arm draped over Carly's shoulder, infuriated her. She didn't need to be reminded that the P.I. had known of Christopher's whereabouts and had kept her in the dark for weeks. The fact that he'd been Rick's friend made it even worse.

Carly was obviously very upset and failing dismally at hiding her feelings. Anna tried to convince herself that she didn't care. Carly Nolan's hurt would never make up for all the years she'd suffered the loss of both Rick and his son.

Jake must have sensed that she wanted to speak to Carly alone for he immediately distracted Christopher and the two of them wandered over to where a vendor was selling popcorn from an old-fashioned wagon.

She watched through a mist of tears. "He's a wonderful boy. So much like his father." She spoke aloud, without thinking.

"Thank you."

Anna had meant it as an observation, not a compliment, but she let Carly's response go and focused on the tense, vulnerable young woman beside her as an awkward silence lengthened.

Distracted, Anna listened as Jake laughed at something Christopher had said.

"Will you withdraw the petition?"

It was a moment before Anna realized Carly had actually said something to her. She shifted her purse to her other hand.

"Excuse me?"

"I asked if you'll withdraw the petition for guardianship now that you've met Christopher and you've seen for yourself how well he's doing."

Anna's gaze darted back to Christopher. He was tugging on Jake's hand, leading the big man over to a drinking fountain, chattering all the way.

His room was ready and waiting for him in Long Beach. The court date was all set. How could she back out now when they were so close?

It was a second before she realized that there was no *they* anymore. Charles was gone. He'd pushed Arthur to go see the girl in the desert, to offer her money for the baby. He was the one who had thought having custody of Rick's son was for the best.

Charles had taken care of everything, given her everything. She owed him so very, very much.

The hospital room was cool and quiet. Always so cold that Anna never went inside without a heavy sweater. She'd been there for weeks, sitting beside Charles's bed, making certain he was comfortable, pestering the nurses to come in more often, seeing that the doctor stopped by every morning and evening, even though there was no hope.

There were monitors and wires, tubes and rolling equipment crowded around the bed in the private room. It wasn't a bad room. The walls were even papered, not like the old days when everything was white and industrial. But the floors were still cold and hard and the air pungent with an antiseptic smell that never quite masked the sour scent of urine and feces. Death lurked in the corners, patrolled the hallway.

She hated every minute of her time there, hated that Charles had to be confined, wired, tubed, barely able to speak. He'd been in and out of a coma for days now. The nurses had assured her that it wouldn't be long.

As much as she hated to say good-bye, even one more second was too long to see him suffer.

The morphine drip was nearly empty. The heart monitor slow but steady. Anna was half asleep when she heard him whisper her name. She opened her eyes to find Charles watching her from the hollows of what had once been the most handsome face in the world.

"Not . . . not long now," he rasped. "You have to promise . . . me . . ."

She left the chair, took his bony hand and held it as tight as she dared, leaned close so that she could hear every word.

"What, darling? What do you want?"

"Promise."

"Anything."

"Promise you . . . won't give up. That . . . you . . . find the boy. Christopher. Bring him . . . 'ome. Please, Anna."

She had no idea where he found the strength. He'd been out of his head before, but tonight his eyes were clear, as if even the drug could not keep him from begging her to make the promise.

"For . . . Rick." He slowly smiled, and she wondered if what she'd heard of death was true. Was Rick there now? Was their son beside Charles, ready to accompany him to the other side?

She glanced around the room as a chill passed through her, clinging to Charles' hand, knowing there was no time left.

"I promise, darling. I promise I'll do everything I can to save Christopher. To bring him home."

Satisfied, Charles quieted again, smiled into her eyes before he closed his own and let go a heavy, rattling sigh.

The monitor shrilled when his heart stopped beating. Two businesslike nurses came bustling in. One checked the monitors, felt for Charles' pulse.

He was gone, but the promise had been made.

If only he'd give Anna some sign, tell her what to do now. He'd always taken care of everything. Given her everything.

Nothing was the way they'd imagined. Christopher was six years old now. The girl, Carly, was a strong young woman, obviously not wealthy, but keeping her head above water and raising Christopher right, as far as Anna could tell.

She was tempted to call Art Litton when she got home, but she knew he'd only parrot Charles' wishes and remind her of how foolish she'd been to come to Twilight on her own.

But it wasn't Art who would have an active six-year-old on his hands when this was all over. He wouldn't spend a second worrying about the possible consequences of what they were doing to Christopher.

Anna realized Carly Nolan was still waiting for an answer.

Just then Christopher called out, "Hey, Mom! Grandma! Look at me!"

She looked over in time to see him turn a crooked somersault and come up laughing. Jake bent down to brush grass cuttings off Chris' shirt.

Anna clutched her purse tighter and shook her head. Her heart was pounding like an out-of-control jackhammer.

Bring him . . . home. Please, Anna.

There was so much to consider. Carly was so different than she had imagined. Christopher so loving, so beautiful.

She put her hand over her heart, afraid it would seize up and stop beating altogether. The wind was battering her hair into a lop-sided haystack, the sun no doubt damaging her skin.

She had to get home, to think this through.

She needed time. She took a deep breath, refused to cower or look away from Carly.

"Will I withdraw the petition? Actually, now that I've seen Christopher, I . . . I want to be with him more than ever."

THIRTY-SIX

Carly was running on adrenaline fueled by fear when she stopped by the Potters' to pick up Matt, then drove both boys home.

They weren't back five minutes before Etta knocked at the door. Not even the sight of Etta's apple-dumpling shape covered in lemon-yellow spandex and a gypsy-black Cleopatra wig lightened Carly's mood.

Etta cradled a casserole dish against her sagging breasts.

"I made extra spaghetti and meatballs because I noticed you weren't home all day, not that I was spying, mind you, but I thought you might be hungry."

Carly didn't know whether to laugh or to cry.

"Thanks, Etta." She reached for the covered Pyrex dish. "It smells great. Chris and Matt will love it."

It didn't look like Etta was going anywhere fast as she lingered on the porch with Napoleon sniffing around her feet. Beauty whined and nosed against the screen.

"Is everything all right?" Etta was perfectly aware that things weren't all right. She'd gotten to know Carly's moods when they lived together.

"About the same." There was no going into detail with Chris in the house. Worry lines replaced Etta's smile.

Just then the phone rang, saving further explanation. "I'd better get that," Carly said.

"You go right ahead, honey."

"I'll walk over tomorrow after work, and we'll catch up, Etta. All right?"

Etta smoothed her hand over the ebony nylon wig. "I'll make some muffins and put the coffee on."

Carly carried the casserole dish into the kitchen and caught the phone on the fourth ring.

It was Jake.

"Anna's gone."

Carly cradled the phone, turned her back on the living room, and lowered her voice.

"Next time I see her, it will be in court."

"Carly, don't."

"Don't what? Don't be defensive? Don't get mad? I'm through cowering, Jake. I've got to look out for myself and my son now."

"She may change her mind."

"Do you really believe that?"

"I have to."

"I wish you wouldn't call here anymore, Jake."

"You don't mean that."

She wished she didn't, but as long as he was around, touching her, offering her a shoulder to lean on, she'd only be reminded of how he'd made a fool of her, how he'd broken her heart.

"Let me take you and Chris and Matt out for dinner."

"No, Jake."

"I can bring you a pizza."

"Please, no."

"Carly—"

"Bye, Jake."

She hung up, stared down at the portable phone in her hand. It rang again. She let it ring five times, pushed the talk button, heard Jake say her name and hung up again. He called three more times before giving up.

It's over.

She knew better than to kid herself. What she felt for him wasn't going to go away overnight, despite everything he'd done.

She closed her eyes, remembered the taste of his lips, the strength and gentleness of his touch. Making love with him had been so much more than she ever dreamed. . . .

Stop it.

One night. One night was all they'd shared. She tried to convince herself that what they had was no different than a one-night stand, but failed miserably. She'd put her heart on the block. There had only been two men in her life, Rick and Jake.

Best friends.

She walked into her studio. Too jumpy to concentrate, she called Geoff. He drove into San Luis nearly every Monday morning to shop, so she asked him to pick up an inexpensive answering machine if he went in tomorrow.

"Congratulations!" He laughed.

"What for? What's so funny?" If he'd known what the last few hours had been like for her, he wouldn't be laughing.

"For joining the twenty-first century. Hang on one sec, I'm ringing up a sale."

She listened to Geoff as he spoke softly and politely to a customer.

"Guess what?" he said a minute later.

"What?"

"Someone put down a deposit on *Weathering the Storm*."

He'd priced it higher than any other of her paintings. The news would have made her ecstatic a month ago.

"That's nice."

"I hate to say it, but you sound like hell. What's going on now?"

"To make a long story short, Jake talked Anna Saunders into coming to town, and then he persuaded me to meet her. I let her meet Chris."

"I take it she didn't change her mind."

"No. Now she's more determined than ever to have Chris." She had to press her lips together to keep them from trembling.

"What was Jake *thinking*?"

"He was trying to force a happy ending." Her heart was so heavy that simply breathing was an effort. "He doesn't know that they don't exist."

"Of course they do. When you stop believing in happy endings, you'll be in *real* trouble."

"I *am* in real trouble." She began to pace from the kitchen to the living room and back. "I don't want to talk to Jake, which is why I need the answering machine."

"I've never heard you sound this angry before."

"No? I've never felt like this before. I'm so mad I could spit nickels."

He laughed. "I haven't heard *that* in years."

"Will you pick one up for me?"

"Of course. And it's on me. Call it a contribution to the legal aid fund."

"Absolutely not. I'm not exactly a charity case yet."

"You know this isn't going to stop him, don't you?"

"Who? Jake?" She massaged her temple.

"Yes. Jake. I have a feeling he's not going to let a little thing like an answering machine keep him from talking to you. Listen, Carly, I'm here for you, you know that. You need to keep your spirits up, and don't let this ruin everything that's good in your life."

She looked out the huge front windows. Long afternoon shadows stretched across the quiet street out front. Spring was finally here and the weather was warming up. It was odd, she thought, how life went on even though she was caught up in a vortex of pain.

"Don't make me cry, Geoff."

"I can't help but worry about you."

"I'm through falling apart. I refuse to lose Chris."

"What about Jake?"

"What about him?"

"From everything you've told me, I still can't help but think he's on your side, whether you want to believe it or not."

She tensed. "Has he spoken to you?"

"No. But it sounds like he tried to help you work things out with Mrs. Saunders. It's not his fault that it backfired. He must feel like shit."

She'd been so upset she hadn't given much thought to what Jake might or might not be feeling. She tried to tell herself she didn't care.

Those last few moments at the park had been a nightmare.

Anna had calmly called Chris over and told him that she was going back to Long Beach.

He asked her to stay, to go home with them, but Anna had hugged him tight and though choked with tears, had told him not to worry, that she promised she would see him soon.

Carly had taken Christopher's hand and walked away from Jake and Anna with barely a good-bye.

He must feel like shit.

She pictured Geoff sitting on a bar stool behind the counter at the gallery.

"I can't help the way Jake feels. He brought this on himself the day he chose to pretend he was just another tourist." She held the phone so tight her hand started to cramp.

"Remind me never to get on your bad side, would you? I'll bring the answering machine over as soon as I get back. Let me know when you hear anything new from Tom Edwards. Promise?"

"I promise."

"And Carly?"

"What?"

"Try visualizing that happy ending."

She hung up.

Geoff was big on visualization. He liked to light candles, play New Age music—Native American flutes and singing whales—but the only thing Carly could visualize right now was the determined look on Anna Saunders' face when Chris hugged her good-bye.

She set the phone down and stared around the living room. No one was going to take her son from her. Nor was she about to stand around feeling helpless. Not anymore.

There was nothing here she couldn't leave behind except a photo of Chris in his T-ball outfit. She picked it up, looked in on the boys, who were playing with Matt's Game Boy, and carried the photo down the hall to her room.

She laid the picture on the bed, flipped on the closet light and then pulled out her long black duffel bag lying on the floor behind her shoes.

With Matt staying over, they couldn't leave until tomorrow, but the delay would give her more time to plan. Betty Ford would get them out of state, then she'd sell the wagon and buy bus tickets to somewhere far away. Maybe Canada. Definitely not Mexico. She could pack the car in the middle of the night, when the boys were asleep and Etta wasn't on patrol.

She sat down on the edge of the bed and stared at the sagging duffel, thinking about what Geoff just said.

Don't let this ruin everything that's good in your life.

The life she'd made out of nothing. The home she'd established for Chris. She'd done her best. She was a good . . .

"Mom?"

Both boys and Beauty were framed in the doorway. Chris stared at her duffel. "Are we going someplace?"

The corner of her mouth quivered when she tried to smile.

"I thought it would be fun for us to go on vacation."

"Can Matt go?"

"No, he can't, honey. It's just going to be the two of us. Just you and me."

The way it had always been. The way she should have left it when Jake Montgomery came along. She'd been an idiot to think she could let someone into her life without paying a terrible price.

"We won't be leaving until we drop Matt off at home tomorrow," she explained.

"How long are we gonna be gone?" Chris crossed his arms over his chest and frowned as he looked from her to the duffel and back.

"Oh, I don't know. Maybe two weeks." She tried to keep her voice light, her smile pasted on, but the words left a bad taste in her mouth.

"Wednesday's hot dog day in the cafeteria."

"We'll buy hot dogs on the road." Mentally she tallied the emergency money she had hidden in a zip lock bag in the toilet tank. It would have to last until she found another town, another job.

"But, Mom I'll miss T-ball . . ."

"Yeah, T-ball," Matt echoed, looking glum.

Christopher's eyes were huge with disbelief. He'd never seen her like this, and she could tell she was frightening him. Gently she put her hands on his shoulders.

"Maybe we should drive to the Grand Canyon before school is out. There won't be very many tourists there yet. Don't you think that would be fun?"

Chris shrugged, unconvinced. "Maybe. What about Beauty?"

Beauty. They don't sell bus tickets to dogs.

"Oh, we'll take her along, of course." She was amazed at how steady her voice sounded. Beauty was a complication, but having her along might help Christopher adjust. She'd find a way to work things out. She always did.

"Shouldn't we tell Jake good-bye? And Grandma?"

"We'll leave them both a nice note. Now, why don't you two go back and play with Matt's Game Boy and I'll warm up dinner, okay?"

"Okay." Chris dragged his feet. Matt and Beauty took off ahead of him down the hall.

She closed her eyes.

This won't work.

Not again.

She sat down on the bed, suddenly deflated, empty as a popped party balloon.

She wasn't fifteen anymore. She wasn't nineteen with an infant who only needed a full diaper bag and regular feedings. She had a home and a job and a life here in Twilight, and most of all, she had Christopher, who had a life of his own.

She took a deep breath and stood up. No matter what the outcome might be, she would stay and fight for what was hers, what was right. The running was over.

Before she could put the duffel back in the closet, someone knocked on the front door. She wondered if she'd ever have a moment's peace as she headed down the hall.

Halfway to the living room she heard Chris say, "Hey, Jake. Come on in. Guess what? We're going on a vacation, but I'd rather stay home for hot dog day."

Carly stepped into the room. "Chris, you and Matt go back to your room and take Beauty with you."

She waited until they were gone before she turned on Jake.

"I thought I made it clear that I don't want to talk to you."

"A vacation?" He leaned back against the door, crossed his arms, and shook his head.

She watched his gaze dart around the living room.

"What's wrong with making vacation plans? The petition hearing isn't going to drag out forever, you know. When it's over, Chris and I will need some time away." Her insides were fluttering as she walked into the kitchen and filled the tea kettle with water. Anything to keep moving, to distract him, to keep Jake from reading her mind.

"How do you plan on disappearing this time? You haven't got any aliases left, or have you?"

She slammed the kettle on the burner harder than she intended. "What I've got is none of your concern. Besides, if I want to move, that's my business, not yours."

"What about Chris? Will he thank you for it when he grows up?"

She lowered her voice. "You saw Anna today. Now that she's met Christopher, do you really think she'll change her mind? I can't wait around and just roll over and play dead."

She lifted a plastic canister of assorted flavored teas out of the cupboard, pulled one out without even looking at the packet.

"What if I won't let you go?" He followed her into the kitchen, backed her up against the stove, though the only thing he really threatened was her composure.

"I'd like to see you stop me."

"If you're so bound and determined, I *can't* stop you, but I can sure as hell give you something else to think about."

Before she knew it she was in his arms, and he was kissing her. Putting up a weak resistance, she moaned against his lips but she was defenseless against the magic of his kiss, his tongue, his mouth.

Carly closed her eyes, felt his large, warm hands against her back as he pressed her closer. Lost, she kissed him back until reason kicked in, and she remembered everything.

She pushed against his chest until he lifted his head and let her go.

•   •   •

Christopher pressed his back against the wall in the hallway, arms spread like an airplane, the way the cops on TV always did when they were sneaking up on someone. With Matt plastered to the wall beside him, they clung like two starfish to the fake wood paneling.

"Did you hear *that*? Your mom said something about *moving*!" Matt whispered.

The anger in his mom and Jake's voices already had Chris's stomach tied in a big knot. Mom said something about Anna, too, but he couldn't hear it. Then she told Jake that he couldn't stop her.

Stop her from moving?

He blinked hard, tried to imagine living in another house, going to another school. Having another best friend.

"I don't want to move."

"What are you gonna do?" Matt whispered with his lips against Chris's ear.

Chris thought of the backpack in his room with a change of underwear, a sweatshirt, an old parka, some cheese and cracker snack packs. He thought there might even be some canned pudding in there, too. Mom called it the emergency pack, and right now, he was pretty sure this was the biggest emergency ever.

"I'm gonna run away."

"By *yourself*?"

Chris slowly turned to Matt. His friend's blue eyes were huge, and he was standing so close that Chris could see little specks of white in them.

"You wanna come with me?" He mouthed the words, afraid his mom might hear—but she was still arguing with Jake.

"I dunno." Matt shrugged. "Where you going?"

"To hide someplace where she can't find me and make me move."

"Then what?"

"I dunno that either. Maybe she'll change her mind before I come back."

"Why don't you just *tell* her you don't want to move?"

How could he explain that he'd never heard his mom talk like this before? That she never, ever sounded this mean or this scared before. So he shook his head, pretty sure after all the crazy things she had said earlier that her mind was made up.

Matt was quiet for so long that Chris was afraid his friend would turn him down. He hoped with all his heart that Matt would go along, because the idea of running off by himself was pretty scary, especially since it was already late afternoon.

"Well? You wanna come with me?" Chris couldn't wait any longer.

"What about Beauty?"

He almost started bawling when he looked down at his beautiful dog. Beauty's nose was resting on his leg.

"I'll put her in the closet. If we take her, she might bark, and somebody will find us. Are you coming?"

Matt shrugged and then slowly nodded. "Okay. Let's go."

They slid along the wall all the way back to his room where Chris wrote a note and then grabbed his backpack and coaxed Beauty into the closet. He knelt down and whispered in her ear that he'd come back for her soon, then he kissed her on the nose and shut the closet door.

Matt started out the door toward the hall. Chris had to grab the collar of his shirt and drag him back into the room.

With his lips against Matt's ear, Chris whispered, "We can't just walk out the door! We gotta sneak out the window."

It took some doing to get the warped window open without making any noise. Standing on his desk, Chris used one of his marker pens to pry up the hook on the screen before they pushed it out. After Matt climbed through, Chris handed out the backpack and followed close behind.

When they reached the far end of the porch opposite the front door, Matt hesitated.

"Are you comin' or not?" Chris shouldered the pack, ready to go.

Matt looked like he wanted to say no, but then Chris pointed to his knee, a reminder that they were blood brothers to the end.

Matt sighed, but when Chris turned to jump off the end of the porch, Matt was right behind him.

• • •

Shaken by Jake's kiss, Carly sidestepped him and reached for one of the thick pottery mugs she'd splurged on at the Summer Crafts Fair last year. When she turned around, he was still so close that she bumped into him. For a second she was almost too startled to say anything. He was so solid, so close, so tempting, that it was easy to forget that he was the enemy now.

"Would it be too much to ask for you to give me some space in my own house?"

"Is that what you really want, Carly?"

She gripped the mug with both hands. "Yes."

He reached for her again, slipped his hand through her hair to cup the back of her neck. "Are you sure?"

She closed her eyes, resisted temptation, and whispered, "Yes. I'm sure. Please, Jake. Don't do this."

Not until she sensed he'd stepped back did she open her eyes and automatically ask, "Do you want some tea?"

"What I want is for you to stop and think. Think about the rest of your life. The rest of Chris' life."

"He's all I ever think about."

He gave a slight shake of his head. "Then promise me you won't do anything so foolish as to run away."

She set the mug down. "I don't owe you anything, especially any promises, Jake."

A deep sadness crept into his eyes. "No. You don't. You don't owe me anything."

She was tempted to reach for him, to trace his full lips with her fingertip, to cup his strong jaw with the palm of her hand. It would be so easy to give in to desire and ignore the fact that her mind was screaming no.

I love you, Carly. She'd never forget hearing him say it.

She crossed her arms, sighed. "I thought about leaving," she confessed. "I was tempted, but I have to do what's best for Chris. I have to believe in myself, too, and in what I've done. I *am* a good mother. I know that in my heart. It's just so terrifying to believe that for the first time in my life, everything will turn out all right."

Jake said, "I wish I'd done things differently. I wish I deserved to be a part of your life, but as you said, you don't owe me any-thing." He turned, as if about to leave, then suddenly stopped. "I thought that having you and Anna meet would help, Carly. That there was no way she'd continue with this once she met Chris. I guess I should have known better than think things would work out that easily."

"Did you *really* think it would?"

He shrugged. "I guess after all I've seen in my line of work, I shouldn't have. In this case, I guess I wanted it for you so badly that I'd convinced myself I could help."

She didn't know what to say that hadn't already been said.

"You'll need a good lawyer . . ." he began.

"I already have one. Geoff recommended Tom Edwards in San Luis Obispo." She dropped her hands, amazed at how much better she felt now that she'd made a commitment to stay and make a stand—-and said it out loud.

"Well, then." He looked around the kitchen, his gaze ultimately resting on her again, touching her eyes, her lips, before he said, "I'll let myself out."

Wishing wouldn't make things different or turn back the clock. They couldn't start over.

"I'd better go and check on the boys." She couldn't bear to see him walk out the door so she started for the hall.

She glanced into Chris's room and not seeing the boys any-where, walked into her own room. Her duffel was right where she'd left it, so she tossed it back into the closet before she went back down the hall.

"Hey, where are you guys?" She walked into the bathroom, snapped on the light, looked behind the shower curtain.

"Chris?" In his room once more, she looked under the bed. "Matt?"

A piece of notebook paper was lying on the floor near the desk.

She picked it up, intending to put it back on the desk when she noticed the screen was unhooked and hanging open at the bottom.

Headlines flashed through her mind, sordid, nightmarish tales of children stolen out from under their parents' noses, taken from their own rooms.

She scanned the words on the page in her hand, then ran to Christopher's closet and whipped the door open. Beauty lay on the floor, muzzle on her paws, staring forlornly up at her. The dog's tail thumped against the carpet. Beauty began to whimper.

Christopher's emergency backpack was gone.

Her son was gone, and it was all her fault.

Hers and Jake's and Anna Saunders'.

THIRTY-SEVEN

"Jake!"

Hearing the panic in Carly's voice, Jake froze with his hand on the door handle of his car. She pushed the dog back inside and ran across the porch, her face ashen, the bleakness in her expression communicating stark fear.

"They're gone." She handed him a piece of lined paper. He glanced down at huge letters scrawled in crayon, suddenly finding it hard to swallow.

BY MOM

I DONUT WANTTO MUVE.

WE RUND AWAEE.

♥   CHRIS

Jake stared at the cryptic note, his gut tightening as he pictured Chris trying to catch the ball in the park in Avila.

"Hey, Jake, how do you spell your name?"

"We'll find them." He knew it would take more than his assurance to strip the fear from her eyes.

He started to walk the perimeter of the mobile home while Carly ran straight to her neighbor's, rapped on the front door, hurriedly spoke to Etta, and then met him at the end of the walk beside the plaster donkey wearing the chipped sombrero.

Carly shook her head. "She hasn't seen them."

Calling the boys' names, they quickly walked Seaside Village, covering winding avenues that curved out like the spokes of a wheel and that had a small grassy park in the center. Jake noticed hundreds of places to hide between the mobile homes, behind aluminum storage sheds and landscaping, in boats on trailers stored in driveways.

There were as many seasonal visitors as full-time residents at the place, so many of the homes were closed up tight. Jake doubted the boys would break into one even if they could.

A few times Jake walked up long driveways to peer into the small backyard spaces of the vacant mobile homes, but the boys weren't there. From the grassy area, they followed a winding path down to the beach.

Standing at the end of the path they could see the entire beach, smaller but broader than Twilight Cove. There wasn't a soul in sight, but there were countless footprints. Spotted sandpipers danced along the glistening sand at the water's edge.

Jake checked his watch. It was almost four.

"Are the Potters home?"

"No, they went to stay in San Luis overnight. To . . . to a real estate seminar. Oh, Jake. What am I going to tell them?"

"By the time they get back, we'll have found the boys. Maybe Matt just wanted to go home."

"No, he would have asked me to drive him. I . . . I talked about going on a trip and taking Chris out of school. If he heard us arguing, then he could be thinking anything."

Jake scanned the beach again. The tide was out, the sun catching on bits of mica in the wet sand, flecks of glittering fool's gold. Narrow hiking paths led up the gradual sloping hillside away from the strand.

"They could have taken any one of those trails." Jake pointed to where the path veered off in different directions across the bluff. Taller grasses could easily shield two small boys from sight.

"What if they make it to the highway?" The wind off the water blew her hair across her eyes. She pulled it back and anchored it with one hand against her neck. "What if someone picked them up already?"

"They may have gone to the highway, but Chris wouldn't willingly get into a car with a stranger."

"How do you know that?"

"He wouldn't leave the baseball park with the Potters because you told him to wait for you. I'm sure he knows not to get into a strange car. He's a smart kid."

"A second ago you said he wouldn't *willingly* get into a car with someone he didn't know. They could be abducted."

Anything was possible, but he wasn't willing to frighten her any more than she already was.

"Oh, God, Jake."

Wanting to absorb her fear and pain, he slipped his arm around her shoulders. She was so shaken she didn't even notice.

"We should split up," he said, planning out loud. "You drive up the highway in both directions and see if you can spot them. I'll follow the main nature trail at a jog. If they are on the way to Matt's, you'll spot them on the road."

Gently, he withdrew his arm and then pulled his car keys out of his pocket and started to hand them over. "Do you feel all right to drive?"

"I can do anything I have to."

"Take my car. I don't trust Betty." He tried to smile, failed miserably.

She grabbed the keys without argument, turned to leave. He grabbed her elbow and she looked back at him again.

"Carly, we'll find them." The desperation in her eyes was killing him. He let go and watched her run back down the beach path alone.

An hour later Carly parked in front of her own place again and found Jake pacing the narrow porch, talking on his cell phone. She climbed out of his SUV, hurried up the walk, and handed him his keys with a silent shake of her head.

Tears were streaming down her face, warm and wet. She could feel them, but was barely aware of anything. For the past hour she felt as if she'd been looking at the world through the distorted glass of a fish bowl, submerged, unable to breathe.

Jake snapped his phone off. "You didn't find them."

She wiped her cheek with the hem of her sleeve. "No."

"I got a hold of the Potters. I called Glenn's office and got his cell number off the machine. They're on the way back." Jake glanced at his watch. "I told them I called the police."

Carly bit her lips and closed her eyes, afraid the nightmare was only beginning. On the run at fifteen, she'd been terrified, but she'd been old enough to know what dangers she faced. Chris and Matthew had no idea what could be waiting for them. They were so young, so innocent and defenseless.

If anyone wanted to grab them, force them into a van or a car . . .

She wanted to scream, to tear her hair, and to rail at God to give her baby back, but she was helpless, stuck in a damn fishbowl, fighting for every breath.

Jake was on the phone again briefly. Then he turned to her, took her by the shoulder, and led her inside. Once she was seated in her old rocking chair, he went into the kitchen. She heard water running, heard the kettle hit the burner.

Familiar sounds. Everyday sounds that were suddenly foreign. Nothing seemed normal anymore.

He walked back into the living room and stood beside her, hands in his back pockets. She hated the undisguised worry in his eyes.

"I put the kettle on." He paced over to the open front door and looked through the screen. "It's getting dark. I'm betting they'll be home in a few minutes. They'll get hungry and come out from wherever it is they're hiding. Chris eats like he has a hollow leg."

A tear plopped on the front of Carly's sweatshirt. Mesmerized, she watched the dampness spread, as if that were all she had to concentrate on.

She heard a car and looked through the screen door as a black-and-white police cruiser pulled into a parking stall out front.

A young, heavyset officer stepped out, adjusted the thick gun belt around his even thicker waist, and then picked up a clipboard. The sun flashed on the bright gold badge pinned to his crisp, navy shirtfront. He looked like a boy. Too young to be a cop.

He didn't even know Christopher.

He had no idea how much her son meant to her, how very special Chris was. The young officer couldn't know that her heart was breaking or how hard it was for her to breathe or even think straight.

She watched as he took his time walking up the steps clutching a little spiral notebook in his hand.

Her first reaction to the sight of the official car in Wilt's driveway that day was one of panic, until she remembered that she was nineteen, and no one could make her go back to New Mexico now, not if she didn't want to.

It had been close to five years since that horrible morning Caroline had died. She had no idea if anyone had ever looked for Caroline or even identified her friend's body.

Haunted by the image of Caroline lying cold and alone in that gully off the highway, Carly had made one call to New Mexico the morning after she reached California. She phoned the Highway Patrol, made up a story about how she was looking for her brother, and inquired about accidents along Highway 40.

They confirmed three teenagers had been involved in a crash two days before and that one of the men in the car, Raul Herrera, had been admitted to emergency in Winslow, where he remained in critical condition. Lucky Marvin had been D.O.A. along with an unidentified female.

A Jane Doe. No one would mourn Caroline. No one would identify her, claim her body, see her buried. Hundreds of miles away, Carly had closed her eyes and hung up, conscious of the silence in Wilt's empty house.

Forgive me, Caroline. Forgive me for leaving you there all alone.

She never called back with a tip to identify the Jane Doe. Of all the people in the world, Caroline would understand her decision and would have done exactly the same thing in her place. Caroline would have been proud that she'd had the guts to walk away in the first place. It had been her only way out.

For the next few years, she had tried to put Caroline's death, the accident, her own duplicity behind her, but on that hot, sunny afternoon, the sight of a Borrego Springs patrol car outside Wilt's door had brought it all back.

She walked to the door with Christopher in her arms and recognized Jerry Holmes. She served Sergeant Holmes a cinnamon roll and coffee almost every morning at the Crosswinds.

"Hi, Caroline." Like everyone in Borrego, he knew her as Caroline Graham.

Jerry usually smiled, but that afternoon as he rested his hands on his gun belt and looked everywhere but at her, she realized he hadn't stopped by to say hello.

"Wilt's not here," she told him.

"I came to see you, actually. You were dating Rick Saunders last year . . ."

Like everyone else who knew her from the Crosswinds, he'd seen them around town together and asked her about Rick.

"Yeah?"

He looked at Christopher in her arms. Frowned.

"There's no easy way to say this, Caroline. There's been an accident up on the grade. Rick's car went off the road. I got the call over the radio and wanted to tell you before you heard it someplace else."

"Is he . . . is he hurt bad?" Flashes of the accident in New Mexico came back to her. Caroline on the ground. Lucky twisted over the steering wheel.

Jerry scratched his neck with a beefy hand. His gun belt creaked whenever he shifted his weight. Fear heightened her senses so that she became aware of everything at once, of the smell of bacon Wilt had fried for a BLT at lunch, the way Jerry towered over her. She was usually standing over him while he ate.

"He's dead, Caroline. Rick didn't make it."

Jake let the young officer into Carly's mobile home. When the uniformed policeman halted just inside the door, his gaze fanned the room like a minesweeper and stopped on Carly.

"We got your call about some runaways. How long have the boys been gone, ma'am?"

Her eyes found Jake's. "I . . . I'm not sure. I don't know."

"Just over an hour," Jake said. "We've looked everywhere."

"Ages?"

"Six." Carly found the strength to push out of the rocker. "They're both six. We've looked up and down the highway, checked the beach." She turned to Jake. "And the nature hikes along the bluff to the south." Jake nodded.

"You're sure they're not still in the house? Kids hide right under your nose sometimes and then get too scared to come out."

Carly stepped up to the spit-shined young man, tempted to grab and shake him. "They aren't here. If they were, I'd have found them."

Jake walked to the dinette set, picked up the note, and handed it to the officer.

"Christopher left this."

The young cop read it, folded it, jotted something on the tablet, and asked Jake, "The boy's your son?"

You'd be a real good dad.

"No, I'm . . ." Jake looked to Carly. Her arms were wrapped around her midriff, her intense pain physical now. Beauty lay on the floor pressed up against her ankles.

"No. I'm . . . just a friend."

THIRTY-EIGHT

"You thirsty?" Chris handed Matt his bottle of water. "Don't take it all. Just sip it. We gotta make it last."

He'd heard that line in a movie once, a jungle movie about a plane crash. Right now he wished they *were* lost in a jungle. At least it would be warm.

They'd been walking forever, and it was getting darker. Chris was sure Matt was gonna wuss out and start crying about how much he wanted to go home. Chris wanted to go home too, but not until Mom changed her mind about moving.

If she didn't, he figured that he was old enough to take care of himself. Heck, he'd been taking care of Matt since they left the house. He'd given him the parka instead of the sweatshirt and never even made Matt carry the backpack.

They'd raced out of Seaside Village and ran down the beach. The tide was out and all the big black rocks were showing at the point. He'd led the way as they climbed and jumped from rock to rock until they rounded the end and were at Twilight Cove. The waves weren't very big, so they easily made it across the rocks all the way to the beach.

They sneaked up the long stairs to the park, then stopped to watch some older kids play soccer. Leading the way, Chris walked Matt through the alleys instead of the streets until they got to the side of the highway.

They waited behind some high bushes that were covered with stickers until the coast was clear, then they darted over to the other side and started up a dry creek bed.

"I'm hungry," Matt whined.

"I'm hungry, too, but I'm not crying about it."

Chris wished they'd left earlier. Being out alone in the dark was scarier than he thought it would be, even with Matt along.

"You're just not crying 'cause this was your idea."

"So?"

"So you're only acting like you're not hungry. You know this was a dumb idea, but you won't go back."

"It's *not* a dumb idea."

Matt suddenly sat down on a rock in the middle of the creek bed and pressed his eyes against his knees. He'd slipped, ripped his jeans, and skinned his knee when they climbed around the point.

"Come on, Matt. We gotta keep going. Look up. There's the first star. Make a wish."

Matt's head jerked up and he looked around. "I don't wanna be out here in the dark. What about coyotes? What about rattlers? I wanna go home!"

Chris tugged on Matt's sleeve until he got him to his feet. "We can't go home. Everybody's probably *really* mad at us by now."

"When are we gonna eat the crackers and cheese?"

"You gotta be patient. Keep walking. We're almost there."

"Where?"

Chris stared up the creek bed, but it was getting harder to see. He didn't tell Matt where they were going because he wasn't real sure he knew the way.

The Potters pulled into Seaside Village while another officer was still questioning Carly and Jake. Tracy was far cooler and calmer than Glenn as they answered every question the policeman put to them. She could remember in detail what both Matt and Christopher had been wearing when Carly picked Matt up. She calmed Glenn and reassured Carly that they didn't hold her responsible.

"What I don't understand is why they ran off. You say Chris talked about not wanting to move? You're not moving, are you?" Tracy's already large eyes were huge as she looked to Carly for answers.

Carly glanced at Jake and then away. "I . . . I'd thought about it, you know, maybe someday. I talked about going on vacation, but . . ." she couldn't seem to control the infinite amount of tears that came suddenly and out of nowhere, ". . . Wednesday's hot dog day."

She knew she wasn't making any sense, knew that she was the only reason her son had run away. If she and Jake hadn't been arguing, if Jake had never come to Twilight in the first place, Christopher and Matt would still be right here where they belonged, eating Etta's warmed-over spaghetti and meatballs.

Etta had changed into a platinum wig and pink stretch pants, and along with a contingent of neighbors, spent the last twenty minutes milling around out front. Eventually she separated from the group, marched up to the door, and insisted on coming in to sit with Carly until they heard something.

Tracy made and served tea, puttering like a Stepford wife, assuring everyone that Matt and Chris would be just fine—until she accidentally let go of a mug, and it crashed to the floor. She dissolved into an hysterical heap on the kitchen floor.

Selma and Joe arrived in time to take over. Selma guided Tracy to the bathroom to rinse her face while Joe mopped up the floor and started heating a huge pot of chili that he'd lugged over from the diner. They had closed down as soon as they heard about the search.

Glenn spent most of his time on his cell phone organizing a door-to-door search and then decided to take Tracy home so that he could coordinate the volunteers.

Carly couldn't do anything but sit balled up in the corner of the couch and quietly go insane.

Jake knew that the longer the boys were missing, the more danger they were in. He checked in with the officer in charge of the search, discovered that someone had seen the kids in the park, but apparently no one paid much attention to them with so many other kids around.

The local search-and-rescue volunteers had been called out. The Laura Recovery Center Foundation sent in a local volunteer assistant with their hundred-page guide to mobilizing large groups of volunteers.

Even with all the help, the more time passed, the more helpless Jake felt. He wanted to join them, but every time he looked at Carly, he couldn't leave her.

He turned on another lamp in the living room, watched as she struggled to her feet and left the room. He hoped she'd gone to lie down, but she was back in five minutes wearing a heavier sweatshirt.

She had washed her face though, and her hairline around her temples was still damp. Her skin was so pale it was nearly translucent.

"Are you hungry?" Jake had forgotten about dinner. He didn't have a conscious desire to eat, but his stomach was rumbling.

Selma and Joe were in the kitchen arguing over whether or not people liked chili better over rice or without. Etta, her wig askew, was sound asleep in Carly's rocking chair emitting window-rattling snores.

As soon as Jake mentioned food, Joe dished up a huge bowl of chili and rice.

"How about something lighter for Carly?" Jake suggested and Joe whipped up half a peanut butter and honey sandwich.

Jake carried it over to her, but she took one look, shook her head and wrapped her arms around herself again.

Suddenly there was a knock at the door, and everyone was on their feet at once. Jake opened it with Carly and Beauty flanking him. A searing light hit them both in the eyes.

A woman's voice came from behind the intense glare, insistent and professionally insensitive.

"I'm Abbigail Klasa from the local network affiliate, KBCH 7, Eyewitness News. How are you holding up with your son missing, Ms. Nolan?" The reporter shoved the microphone closer to Carly's face.

Carly blinked into the light. "What?"

"What went through your mind when you realized your only child was missing? Do you suspect foul play?"

Jake pulled Carly out of the blazing light and slammed the door.

She was trembling so violently that he was afraid she was going to collapse. Blindly, she reached for his hand and he took it without hesitation. She'd needed to hold onto something warm, something real in the midst of chaos.

He led her back to the sofa. She sank into it, rested her hands on her knees. He reached for her hands, found them cold as ice, even though the room was warm. He chafed them, held on tight. Finally she looked into his eyes, but no words came.

"I feel like hell. I'd give anything to make this all go away," he said.

She shook her head, bit her lips to keep them from trembling.

When she could finally form the words, she said, "It's not your fault. *I'm* the one who set this all in motion years ago. I never thought about how the older Christopher got, the harder it would be to move. I wasn't thinking of his feelings, just that I couldn't let them take him from me."

He tightened his hand on hers. She swallowed a sob.

"I couldn't bear to let anyone take my baby away, but right now, if it would save his life, I'd give him up, Jake. If that's what it takes to keep him safe, I'd give him to Anna in a heartbeat."

He held her tight, let her cry herself out on his shoulder. When she finally pulled out of his arms, he brushed her hair back off her damp face. Waiting was torture for them both, but the police had asked her to stay put, to wait for word.

"Would you mind if I left you long enough to see how the search is going? Selma and Joe will stay, and I'll call you from the command post."

Carly nodded. "Yes, go. I wish I could go with you. Anything would be better than sitting here in limbo."

He knew that in a while the shock would wear off, and she would no longer be content to sit and do nothing, as sure as he knew she would never give up looking for Chris. She would wait a lifetime if she had to for her boy to walk through the door again, whole and unharmed, just the way he'd left.

THIRTY-NINE

Anna walked into the penthouse, closed and double-locked the door behind her, set the security alarm.

The click of her beige pumps echoed as she crossed the marble floor. Without quite stopping, she slowed down to glance at her reflection in the oversized gilt-framed mirror above the table in the foyer. Tonight every one of her sixty-two years was showing. She walked into the master suite, anxious to get out of her knit suit and panty hose and into bed.

She'd pushed herself to the limit today, talking Carly into letting her meet Christopher in the park. On the way home aboard the commuter plane to LAX, she'd begun to question what she was doing.

If only Charles were alive, he would be the one in charge. Everything would be out of her hands.

After Rick died, she'd been angry and helpless. Like Charles, she had wanted to strike back at the girl who'd taken her son from them. If it hadn't been for Caroline or Carly or whoever she really was, Rick would have never been racing back to Borrego.

Charles had put everything in motion. After Rick's memorial, he contacted Art Litton, sat down with him, and came up with the plan to offer the girl money, more than enough money to make most people's heads spin—but Carly had refused.

She's been a good mother.

All day, try as she might, Anna couldn't keep that thought from popping into her mind. Christopher was a delightful child, the kind of child any parent would be proud of. Though she'd like to deny it, she knew that he hadn't gotten that way by himself.

And seeing him in the flesh brought home the truth—he was a living, breathing, energetic little boy, and she was a sixty-two-year-old woman.

When he's fourteen, I'll be seventy!

Even though his room was ready and waiting for him, she was now faced with the reality of the situation. This was no place for an active child, let alone a dog. When she won guardianship, she would have to move again, find a house with a yard or a place on the beach.

She'd pushed herself too hard today. After the limo dropped her off from the airport, she'd quickly changed clothes and attended the Nineteenth Annual Benefit and Silent Auction for the Children's League.

As physically and mentally exhausted as she was, the event seemed to go on forever. On the heels of her flight back, three hours of small talk with a table full of divorcées and widows had nearly done her in.

Once in her room she automatically picked up the television remote, jabbed the on button and tossed the remote on the bed before she walked into the dressing room.

Peeling off her panty hose and then her beige St. John knit, she listened to the teaser for the eleven o'clock news. Something about a hijacked bus on the 91 Freeway. She mentally tuned it out until her attention was captured by the anchorwoman's next words.

"... *we'll go to a small town up the coast where a Long Beach private investigator is involved in a search for two missing six-year-old boys.*"

Her heavy gold earrings clattered when she dropped them on the marble countertop. She grabbed a thick terry cloth robe off a hook near the dressing room door and hurried back into the bedroom. A series of inane commercials blasted from the television, so she hit the mute button until they ended.

Perched on the edge of the bed, she turned on the sound again and waited through breaking news with live film coverage of yet another bus hijacker being taken into custody.

When will these idiots realize car chases are getting old?

After highlights of the national news there was yet another teaser before a few thirty-second commercials. Finally the female anchor was back. Thin, Hispanic, still beautiful despite too much stage makeup, she stared at the Teleprompter.

"Now we'll take you up the coast to Twilight Cove, a small tourist town just off of Highway One near San Luis Obispo where it seems a private investigator from Long Beach has found himself involved in the search for two missing six-year-olds. Let's go to reporter Abbigail Klasa with our affiliate station KBCH in San Luis Obispo. Abbigail, what can you tell us about the search for the missing boys?"

"Well, Tamra, let's just say things are tense here in the usually quiet seaside town of Twilight Cove where local sheriffs and volunteers have been combing dangerous hillsides as well as the treacherous coastline for the two missing youngsters, who are best friends and T-ball teammates."

Anna clutched the remote, her attention riveted on the screen. A photograph suddenly replaced the image of the reporter, a shot of a T-ball team, all of the boys lined up in matching uniforms and baseball caps. Slowly the camera focused in on two of them and the image widened until it filled the screen. They stood side by side with their arms around each other's shoulders, their sweet smiles showing missing teeth.

Anna gasped and covered her mouth.

"We've learned the two are best friends, but no one has yet to explain why Matthew Potter and Christopher Nolan have run away. Matthew's parents remain positive that the two boys will be found safe and sound. No Amber Alert has been issued as there is no indication the boys were abducted."

An odd, strangled noise escaped Anna as she stared at the screen filled with the image of Christopher and his friend. It was uncanny how much Chris looked like Rick at the same age. The same sun-streaked hair. The same dimple in his right cheek. His eyes even crinkled when he smiled, just like Rick's.

The camera moved from the photo to Jake Montgomery standing beside the reporter. Patrol car strobe lights knifed through the darkness around them.

Anna covered her mouth with her fist, leaned toward the television. The reporter held the microphone in front of Jake.

"How did a private investigator from Long Beach become involved in the search, Mr. Montgomery?"

"Ms. Nolan and her son are friends of mine." Jake Montgomery clammed up, reticent to say more, frustrating the reporter with his silence.

Anna watched, aware of the agitated beat of her heart, fearing it was going to burst. She took a deep breath, held it, let it out.

Dear Lord, you've only just let me see Christopher, talk to him, hold him.

Do you truly give only to take away?

I've already lost so much.

Anna sat in dazed silence as the young reporter wrapped up the interview. The anchor promised the L.A. audience they would learn the outcome of the search as soon as it happened. Then the news broke for another spate of commercials.

The phone rang almost immediately after, and she jumped up, stumbling as she made a grab for it, half hoping it might be Carly Nolan with news that Christopher had been found. But after what Anna had said today, she doubted Carly would call her at all.

It was Art Litton.

Before Anna could say a word, he was crowing into the phone.

"Have you seen the news? We've got her now."

She shivered, thought she might retch.

"My grandson is missing, Art, and that's all you can think about? What if he's been kidnapped? What if he's hurt?"

"And if he is hurt, whose fault is it? Hers."

"I . . . actually, I've been thinking of reconsidering, of dropping the petition or whatever it takes to stop this thing from—"

"You can't, Anna. Not now. Look what's happened. What kind of mother lets her kid run off like that? Surely you don't think she has any right to Christopher after this, do you?"

He sounded so certain, so persuasive. Just like Charles. He was always telling her what to do, what was expected of a Saunders. She pictured Jake Montgomery standing with his arm around Carly this afternoon. Perhaps they'd gotten together later, maybe they'd wanted Christopher out of the way. She'd heard of people locking their kids outside. Maybe Carly had wanted an hour or two alone with Jake, maybe she'd left him outside with instructions not to disturb her, and he'd wandered off.

Surely the woman she'd met earlier wouldn't have done any such thing . . .

"You can't leave him in that kind of a situation, Anna."

"He's . . . he seems happy, Art. And well adjusted."

"How would you know? You can't tell anything from a photo on television."

"I've seen him. I was up there today, in Twilight Cove. Jake Montgomery convinced me to go up and meet Carly Nolan . . ."

"I would *never* have advised something like that, and you know it. You could jeopardize our case."

"Which is why I went on my own. I can't help but wonder if my visit had something to do with Christopher's running away."

"And you think he's well adjusted?"

"I did. He's darling. Polite, intelligent. She's done a good job, Art."

"You listen to me, Anna. Charles wasn't just a client for thirty years. He was one of my closest friends. I know what he wanted. You can't let him down now. Besides, you aren't doing this solely for Charles, you know. You have a responsibility to Saunders Shipping. Christopher will take his rightful place at the helm."

"What if that's not what he wants?"

"You'll never know what he wants if he grows up under her roof."

"I don't think she'd object to me seeing him. I—"

"You don't know *what* she's likely to do. I'm going to hang up and call you first thing in the morning unless there's some word on the boys before then. Don't even think about backing down now, Anna. Christopher needs you. He obviously needs a more stable situation. Don't you agree?"

"Well, yes, I—"

"You try to get some sleep."

"Are you *kidding*?"

"Then at least lie down and rest. I'll call you in the morning."

He hung up, but Anna cradled the phone in her lap. Unable to move, she stared blindly at all the lawyers on a rerun of "The Practice" on television.

FORTY

Jake let go a silent curse as he walked away from Abbigail Klasa and her damn cameraman and headed for his car.

He was still pissed at the officer in charge of the search who had introduced him to the reporter just to get her off his own back. When Jake heard that the L.A. network affiliate was picking up the story, he knew chances were good that Anna Saunders would find out that Christopher was missing.

As soon as he had left Carly's, he checked in with the officer in charge of the search, demanding to know why in the hell they hadn't brought in search dogs. He was told all available animals in the area had been transported to the Los Padres National Forest where three teenage hikers had been missing for two days.

The man thought there would be more dogs flown in by morning. Jake refused to give in to a fear of statistics. This wasn't L.A. The kids had run off, and as yet there was no reason to believe they'd been kidnapped. But out here there were an infinite number of places where they could be hiding and just as many ways they could get hurt.

Climbing back into his SUV, he scanned the dark hillside directly above the town where the volunteer search-and-rescue team had fanned out, trying to cover too much open ground without enough manpower.

Flashlight streams bobbed along, briefly illuminating the grassy slope as well as rocks, crevices, and low-growing brush.

You'd be a real good dad, Jake.

I'm learning to write stuff at school.

Maybe I'll draw a picture of you playing ball with me.

We rund awaee.

Jake leaned against the car window, watching search lights crawl

293

over the hillside. Once darkness had settled in, rescue helicopters no longer swept the open terrain. Now it was up to exhausted, cold volunteers. Geoff Wilson was heading up a group combing the beaches. Glenn Potter had organized neighborhood watch captains into door-to-door searches.

Restless, frustrated, Jake thought of all the people he'd been hired to locate, and it made him sick at heart to think he couldn't find two little boys.

He started the car, headed back toward Cabrillo Road. While crossing a two-lane bridge that spanned the dry creek bed, he remembered the day Chris had gotten turned around in the arroyo behind the rental house.

What happened, Sport?

I got mixed up, Jake.

If you ever get lost again, just remember to stay calm and think about whether you want to go up or down.

My house is up, away from the beach.

My house.

The one place they hadn't thought to look. If Chris happened on the right stream bed, they just might have made it.

Jake whipped the car into a U-turn, sped along Twilight's deserted main thoroughfare. The area around his house hadn't been thoroughly searched because it was farther from town and expert consensus was that two little boys couldn't make it that far, especially in the dark. But if they followed the stream bed . . .

He reached for his cell phone and started to hit the automatic dial for Carly's number, then stopped. He wasn't about to get her hopes up for no reason, so he snapped the phone off and tossed it on the seat beside him.

When he reached the gravel driveway, he slowed down, parked, grabbed his phone before he got out, jogged up the front steps and across the porch.

The house was dark and empty, just the way he'd left it. His footsteps echoed off the hollow walls as he walked past the cans of paint, rollers and pans stacked off to one side of the dining room.

He turned on the overhead light in the living room and searched the first floor.

There was no sign of the boys anywhere, so he went upstairs. His bedroom door was still closed. After taking a deep breath, he pushed it open, but the room was empty.

He paced to the window, stared out at the night. Damn, but he'd wanted them to be there.

Where in the hell are you?

With a ragged sigh, he turned, shoved his fingers through his hair, and started out of the room, then stopped just short of the door when he realized the comforter on the inflatable mattress was missing.

"Chris?" He walked over to the closet, opened the door, pulled the light chain. Empty.

He pounded down the stairs, trying to think like a kid.

"Chris? Matt?" Rounding the corner between the hall and the kitchen, he checked the pantry near the service porch again, then flipped on the light over the back door and stepped outside onto the deck.

There, snuggled together close to the wall, hugging the comforter, Chris and Matt lay sound asleep. A crumpled Doritos bag and two empty Snapple bottles had been abandoned nearby.

Jake knew he was smiling from ear to ear in the dark but didn't care. He hunkered down beside the boys.

Matt had fallen asleep with his thumb in his mouth. Muddy tear streaks stained his cheeks. Chris lay on his stomach, his head resting on his backpack, the comforter pulled up around his ears. Jake watched his own hand shake as he reached out to stroke the boy's blond hair.

Getting to his feet, Jake walked to the edge of the deck, leaned one hip against the railing, punched 911, and gave the local dispatcher his name, address, and the news that he'd found the boys.

Then he called Carly.

When he heard her voice, he imagined her in her living room surrounded by Selma, Joe, and Etta.

"Jake? What, Jake?" She sounded too terrified to hope.

"I found them, Carly. They're fine."

There was silence on the other end, hollow, endless silence until he heard her sobbing. The next voice he heard was Joe Caron's.

"Where are they, Jake? We'll bring Carly over."

"They're asleep on the deck behind my house. I just called the police to let them know I've got them. They're coming to pick up the boys and take them to the station. Bring Carly and meet us there."

"Want me to call the Potters?"

"I imagine the police are on that right now, but double check. No one can ever have too much good news. I'll see you at the station."

He hung up and pocketed his phone, then crossed the deck and sat down beside the sleeping boys. Gently, he laid his hand on Christopher's shoulder and slowly shook him awake.

Chris pushed up off the deck, rubbed his eyes and looked around. "Hey, Jake."

"Hi, Chris. You gave us all a pretty big scare."

The sound of their voices woke up Matt, who took one look at Jake and started bawling.

"I didn't want to do it. It was all his fau . . . fault." Matt pointed at Chris as he continued to wail.

"Baby." Chris mumbled and rolled his eyes. "We were okay the whole time, Jake. I remembered what you said about following the creek." Then he whispered, "Am I in trouble?"

"I'm just glad you're all right."

"What about Mom?"

"She's going to meet us at the police station."

"Police station?" Matt started howling.

"She's mad, huh?" Chris ducked his head sheepishly.

"I think sad is a better word for it. You scared her, Chris. You two scared everybody in town."

Chris' lower lip began to tremble, but he stubbornly threw back his shoulders. His chin jutted in defiance, reminding Jake of Carly.

"Well, she scared me, too. I don't want to move, Jake. I heard you and her talking about moving."

"You didn't stick around to hear the part where she said that she would never make you move if you didn't want to. Running away doesn't solve anything." Jake thought of how Carly had been running half her life. "It only makes things worse. I'm sure she'll explain when you get home. Right now, let's get you cleaned up and see if we can't get Matt to stop crying."

He carried the comforter and backpack as he followed the runaways into the kitchen. It took half a roll of paper towels to make them somewhat presentable again. Matt didn't stop crying until Jake promised to tell his parents not to put him on restriction forever.

Jake was about to pour them both a glass of milk when the whine of sirens split the air. Matt started sniffing. Chris took Jake's hand and pressed close to his leg.

"You're going to get to ride in a police car." As he shouldered the small backpack Jake wished he could take Chris straight home to Carly's arms.

Then he reached down for Matt's hand, and leading both boys through the house, he met the officers waiting on his front porch.

FORTY-ONE

Chris sat belted in the backseat of the police car wishing he could enjoy the ride, but he was too worried about what his mom and the Potters were going to do when they saw him.

Scared as he was, he was going to tell everybody this was all his idea. He snuck a peek at Matt, who hadn't said a word to him since Jake woke them up, and he wondered what he would do if Matt never, ever spoke to him again.

"You boys know what kind of trouble you caused around here?"

Chris jumped when the officer riding on the passenger's side turned around and started talking to them.

"Well?"

"Yes, sir," he mumbled.

"Want to tell me why you took off and worried your folks like that?" The man was watching him closely. Chris promised himself he would never, ever do anything that would mean having to ride in a police car again.

"I was scared my mom was gonna make me move away." He was too frightened not to tell the whole truth. "She talked about going on a vacation, and I didn't want to miss hot dog day."

The officer looked over at the man driving the car. "Makes perfect sense to me."

Chris thought he saw the first officer's mouth twitch, but it wasn't light enough to tell for sure.

"What about your friend there. How come he went with you?"

Chris looked at Matt again. His friend was wiping his snot on the sleeve of the borrowed parka.

"We're blood brothers."

The officer who did all the talking asked the one driving, "Think we need to call in Child Protective Services?"

Chris listened intently, not sure what Child Protective Services was, but he thought maybe it had to do with kids going to military academy. He held his breath.

The taller of the two men turned the wheel and shook his head. "No cause. They aren't habitual runaways, not yet anyway. Besides being a little dirty, they don't fit the profile for being abused. Let's just turn Tom Sawyer and Huck Finn here over to their parents, and maybe we can all go home and get some sleep."

Chris elbowed Matt who turned sorry eyes in his direction.

"They're takin' us to our moms," he whispered.

Matt threw up.

Carly and the others were at the station by the time the cruiser pulled up. Christopher's head was barely visible above the window. Jake's SUV was right behind.

He parked, jumped out of the car, and rushed over to where she was standing beside Etta, who was sobbing into the hem of her sequined sweatshirt. Selma and Joe were there, too.

Tracy and Glenn Potter and their friends and neighbors were all gathered on the curb as well, all of them highlighted in the glare from the lights on the mobile television van.

All Carly saw was her boy when the patrolman opened the back door of the car and Chris stepped out.

His face lit up with relief when he spotted her. She could barely see through her tears as he came barreling toward her yelling, "Mom! Mom!"

She fell to her knees on the asphalt, wrapped Christopher in her arms and held him tight, desperately fighting to hold herself together. He felt so small, so vulnerable—and never as precious.

"Mom." Chris tried to wriggle away. "You're crushin' me."

She pulled back slowly, wiping her eyes with the back of her hand. Running her hands up and down his arms, she finally took hold of his hands and looked him over.

"Are you all right?" She still couldn't believe he could be fine. It seemed he'd been gone a lifetime.

"Yeah." He glanced around suddenly aware of all the others. "Hey! There's Joe and Selma. Hi, Joe! Hey, Selma. And there's Mrs. Schwartz, too." Then he whispered to Carly, "What's everybody doing here?"

"Everyone's been so scared. They waited at home with me while the police looked for you."

He threw his arms around her neck and hugged her again. Her heart nearly broke when she heard him whisper, "It's okay, Mom. I'm okay now."

When she could finally let him go, Joe gave him a bear hug and passed him to Selma, then he went to Etta, and finally Geoff, who had just arrived and was still soaked from sea spray and covered in sand from the knees down.

"Are you sure you're all right?" Carly asked when he was at her side again.

Chris fell sober and took her hand. "Yeah. I'm okay. Kinda hungry, though." He looked around at the reporters and cameramen, the police, and rescue workers gathered around.

"Can we go home?" he whispered.

Glenn and Tracy, with Matt sandwiched between them, walked over to Carly.

"I told you that they'd be just fine." Tracy was beaming her perpetual smile again, but her mascara had smeared into a distinct racoon mask, and her pageboy cut was a disaster. Beside her, Glenn was whey faced and looked ready to drop.

Glenn reached over to ruffle Chris' hair and told Carly, "We'll call you in the morning. Right now, we're going to get Matt home to bed." He glanced over his shoulder at the officer standing close by and then told her, "If you need anything, Carly, just call us, all right? I'm sure everything will be fine."

Before she had time to wonder why everything *wouldn't* be fine now, the officer stepped up to her and smiled down at Chris before he said, "We're going to have to detain you all for a few minutes, Ms. Nolan. Just a routine interview, nothing that will take very long."

"But . . . he's worn out. I'd like to take him home and get him cleaned up and fed and into bed."

She was aware of Jake moving in close beside her. So did the infernal minicam.

"Ms. Nolan? Ms. Nolan! Do you have any comment regarding the petition for guardianship that's been filed by your son's grandmother?" Abbigail Klasa stepped up to Jake and made the mistake of trying to elbow her way in next to Carly and Chris.

When Carly looked back, the young woman was on the ground searching for her microphone.

"Sorry," Jake mumbled. "I must have slipped."

Carly quickly hugged Selma, Joe, and Geoff and thanked them all before she and Jake hurried Christopher inside the station.

She hadn't asked Jake to stay, but she was thankful that he was there as they were all led into a small private office. He appeared to be cool, calm, and in control.

He had found Christopher. She would never be able to thank him enough.

"Sit down, please, Ms. Nolan. Mr. Montgomery. Christopher, would you come with me for a minute? There's a lady down the hall who wants to ask you some questions."

"Is she from the military school?"

The man shot Carly a quizzical glance.

"I have no idea what he's talking about." She looked to Jake, who crouched in front of Chris.

"She just wants to make sure you're all right."

The young officer held out his hand. Chris looked so small and frightened, yet he put up such a brave front that Carly was seconds from falling completely apart. Once he was out of earshot, she turned to Jake.

"What's going on?" Panicked, she refused to sit when he gestured to a chair. "Matt got to leave with his parents. Why can't I take Chris home?"

"It's probably just routine, like the man said."

She wished he sounded more reassuring.

"How could that reporter have known about the petition for guardianship? Who would give her that kind of information?"

"I have a feeling I know," he said softly.

"Anna."

"Or her lawyer."

As the world folded in on her, Carly sank into an empty institutional-green vinyl chair and stared at the door Chris had just walked through. In no more than two minutes, the police officer came back in.

"Ms. Nolan, this should just take a couple of minutes. My partner and I were going to turn both boys over directly to you, but we had directives to hold your son until he could be interviewed."

The sterile office was more like a hospital waiting room. It reminded her of the day her dad died, the day Miss DeCoudres had walked her down the hall to the counselor's office, and social services had come to take her away.

If the interview didn't go well, Chris might fall into Child Protective Services' hands on the spot, and she wouldn't be able to see him again without supervision until the guardianship petition was heard.

"Carly?"

"What?" She jumped and turned to Jake, suddenly aware that he'd been talking to her. He was still holding her hand. She looked down at their entwined fingers, aware of what was going on, yet not quite willing to believe this was really happening to her.

Jake's calm did more to unnerve her than if he'd been ranting and raving. He was angry. Angrier than she'd ever seen him. His fury showed in the ice-blue depths of his eyes.

Suddenly his cell phone went off, the low ring barely audible, shrilly cutting the silence. He pulled it out of his back pocket, glanced at the screen, frowned and powered off.

"Do you need to answer that?"

"I'll take care of it tomorrow."

Exactly eight minutes later—Carly knew because she hadn't taken her eyes off the big black industrial clock on the wall—Chris was escorted back into the room by a female officer. A shiny replica of the official police badge had been pinned to his sweatshirt. He ran across the room and threw himself into Carly's arms.

The officer thanked Carly and added, "You can go home now, ma'am."

Carly didn't let go of Chris until Jake took her gently by the elbow and said, "Come on, you two. I think Beauty is probably at home wondering what happened to everybody."

Jake pulled his car around to the back door so that they could avoid the relentless television crew. Within minutes Carly and Chris were home again.

"Mom?" Chris tugged on her arm the minute they were out of the car, as if it weren't three in the morning. As if she hadn't spent the last twelve hours in hell. "Mom, I'm hungry."

She started for the kitchen, running on automatic pilot, her mind blissfully numb to everything except Chris. While he hugged Beauty and rolled on the floor with the dog, Carly warmed up a bowl of chili. She knew Chris was starved when he didn't even complain about the beans.

After pouring Chris a second glass of milk, she finally turned to Jake.

"Thank you." She shivered. Cold had been seeping through her for hours, the bone-chilling cold of fear.

Chris was home. Everything was still uncertain, but at least he was safe.

Jake was watching her from across the living room where he'd remained by the front door. As always, he looked too big for the small space, too rugged for the small love seat, the worn-out wicker chair.

He didn't fit here. Not since he'd lost her trust. She shouldn't have ever let him into their circle of two, and yet her body still ached for him to hold her. She needed his strength, his calm, his smiles and touches.

But as she watched him watch her, she reminded herself that even though Jake was the one who had found Chris tonight, none of this would have happened if he hadn't come dragging the past to town with him, upsetting their lives, showing Anna Saunders the way.

He finally took a step away from the door.

She started to wrap her arms protectively around herself but then stopped. "Thank you for your help and for finding the boys." She looked down at her hands, then back up at him. "Thank you for being there when I needed someone earlier."

"I want to be there for you all the time, Carly. For both of you."

"I think you should go home now, Jake. I need to get Chris cleaned up and into bed."

"I don't mind sleeping on the sofa, just to make sure the reporters don't bother you again."

Tempted to give in, she quickly shook her head. It wouldn't do to have him so close, not while she was still so raw, so vulnerable.

"We'll be fine." She glanced over her shoulder at Chris, shoved her hands into the back pockets of her jeans.

"Just the two of you. Just like before."

"We were fine on our own."

"Were you, Carly?"

She thought of the years before Jake. She'd been going through the motions, reading homemaking magazines, trying to make life picture perfect without having to feel anything except her love for Christopher. Before Jake had turned their lives upside down, she never knew how much she and Chris had been loved by so many, or how very lucky she was to live in Twilight.

Without a word, Jake stepped around her and headed for the table. He stood behind Christopher, put his hand on her son's head for a second, just until Chris looked up at him.

"Hey, pal. I gotta take off. You be good, all right? Listen to your Mom, and don't even think of pulling a stunt like that again, all right?"

Chris ducked his head again and stared down into the empty chili bowl. "Okay, I won't."

When Jake started to walk away, Chris reached for his arm.

"Are you comin' over tomorrow?"

Jake looked at Carly for the answer, but she forced herself to turn away from the question in his eyes.

"I don't know," Jake said. "I've still got a lot of work to do up at the house."

"Oh." Chris sounded as forlorn as Carly felt.

"But I'll give you a call tomorrow," Jake promised him, "no matter what."

"Okay. Night, Jake."

"Night, buddy."

Carly heard Jake's steps as he crossed the room, felt him when he moved up behind her. She didn't dare face him, not while she was fighting so hard to hang on to every shred of self-respect.

"Good night, Carly." He was so close that she could feel the warmth of his breath on the back of her neck.

She took a deep breath.

"Good-bye, Jake."

He stepped around her and let himself out.

Christopher struggled to keep his eyes open while he waited for Mom to tuck him in. It wasn't long before she walked back into his room and tossed his dirty clothes into the hamper in his closet and then sat down beside him.

She looked sad and tired and he knew that was because of what he'd done.

"Mom? I'm really sorry." He slipped his arms out from under the comforter and reached for her hand.

"I know you are."

When she looked down at him her eyes were all sparkly like she was going to cry again, and his stomach started to hurt.

"I won't run away ever again."

"I know. Were you scared?" She pushed his hair back off his forehead and kissed him.

"Not in the daytime. But when it got dark and Matt kept cryin' for his mom, I got kinda scared, too, but I couldn't tell him."

"Tomorrow you'll have to call and tell Matt you're sorry."

Chris sighed. It was going to be hard to say he was sorry out loud, but he couldn't imagine life without his best friend, either.

"You know why I ran away, Mom?"

"I think so, but why don't you tell me?"

"I heard you and Jake arguing. I heard you tell him that we were moving, and I didn't want to go."

"Sometimes we have to do things we don't want to do, Christopher, no matter how much it hurts . . ."

"But this is my house. This is where I've always lived. And Matt is my friend. He's my blood brother, Mom. I don't want to move away from him."

He watched a tear fall off the end of Mom's lashes. She tried to wipe it away real quick, but he saw it just the same.

"We're not moving, honey. Don't worry about it. This is our home."

"Then why were you so mad at Jake? What are you scared of?"

"I'm not scared," she said. But she didn't look at him when she said it. She pulled his covers up to his chin and kissed him one more time. "You need to get some sleep. We've both had a pretty rough day. Even poor Beauty is already sound asleep." She glanced down at the dog sleeping next to the bed and then reached for the bedside lamp on a table she had painted the color of a fire engine for him.

"Mom? Will you leave the light on?"

She did better than that. She crawled under the covers, drew him close, and he fell asleep with her arms around him good and tight.

Carly slipped out of Chris' bed, stepped over Beauty, who was asleep in her dog bed, and left the door to the room open as she wandered down the hallway to the kitchen. The small living room seemed immense tonight, the shadows outside the uncovered studio windows had taken on a dark, ominous quality. Wide awake, too keyed up to sleep, she almost admitted to herself that she wished she'd taken Jake up on his offer to sleep on the couch.

She poured herself a glass of milk, physically tired enough to sleep for a week but mentally keyed up. Recalling what Jake had said about reporters, she turned off the kitchen light and all but one small light in the living room. Then she walked over to the front window and slightly pulled aside the curtain.

Jake's car was still in the parking space in front of the house.

She leaned toward the window, squinted against the glare of Etta's porch light and saw Jake, sound asleep, in the passenger's seat. With a shake of her head, Carly cracked the front door open half expecting a reporter to leap out of the bushes, but everything was quiet out front, so she walked up to the window on Jake's car. Before she could tap and awaken him, he sat bolt upright, recognized her, and slowly smiled.

He rubbed his eyes and yawned as he opened the door.

She whispered, "Jake, what are you doing out here?"

"Watching the house."

"With your eyes closed? Are you crazy?"

"I'm beginning to think so."

"Go home."

"I've slept in the car lots of times."

"I didn't think private investigators were supposed to fall asleep when they were on surveillance." Despite everything that had happened, she found a smile slowly spreading across her face and a warmth replacing the lingering chill of fear she thought she'd never lose.

"Nope. Not leaving. Go on in and go to bed. Lock up and just forget about me out here in the cold car. Don't give me a second thought." It appeared he meant what he said. He wasn't going anywhere.

She let go a long, drawn-out sigh, mostly for his benefit.

"Okay, you can sleep on the couch. But don't make me regret this."

With a triumphant if not sleepy smile, he climbed out of the car, locked it, and followed her inside. Carly left him in the living room pulling off his shoes, and when she came back carrying a pillow and a blanket, he was trying to wedge himself into the cramped space on the couch.

She dropped the pillow and blanket on his stomach, turned out the light, and headed for her own room.

"Don't worry about me here folded into this little space. Don't give me a second thought."

"Don't worry, I won't." She couldn't help but smile, thankful that he couldn't see her face.

"Wanna bet?"

By the time she turned out her light and wearily crawled into bed, she was thankful she hadn't taken him up on his bet. More than anything, she ached to be held the way she'd held Christopher, cuddled and comforted. She longed to hear that everything would be all right, that the worst was over, but a nagging little voice deep down inside wouldn't let her believe anything of the sort.

She could hear Jake tossing and turning in the other room as he tried to make himself comfortable on the too-small sofa, and she was tempted to go to him, to invite him into her bed. Not because she'd forgotten what he'd done or how he'd lied, but because she longed for him to hold her, to pretend that things were the way they'd been before.

He'd stood by her all day and long into the night. He'd been there to keep her from falling apart at the seams while Chris was missing. The boys might still be missing if he hadn't thought to look for them at his place.

Tossing back the covers, she climbed out of bed and headed back down the hall. Every nerve in her body was thrumming as she padded barefoot down the hall wearing nothing but a long T-shirt that covered her to her thighs. By the time she reached the hall door and could see Jake on the couch, she realized that he had fallen sound asleep.

She tiptoed close to the sofa. His dark lashes brushed his cheeks, his hands rested atop one another on his broad chest. She reached down and pulled up the blanket that had half fallen to the floor and then tucked it around his feet. Then, without thinking, before she went back to bed, she kissed him on the forehead, so gently that he didn't even stir.

FORTY-TWO

Jake slept until seven the next morning when Beauty nudged his hand with her cold nose. Groggy, he staggered to the door to let her out, walked out on the porch to make sure she didn't run off, and waited while she did her business. When the dog ran back up on the porch, he thanked her for not taking a dump and then let her back inside.

He walked down the hall, looked in on Carly first. She was sound asleep, her eyelids puffy and showing the ravages of all the crying she'd done the day before. Tempted to crawl in beside her and hold her while she slept, he made do with walking over to her bedside, reaching down to run his fingers down her long hair and gently pulling it away from her cheek.

Beneath his fingertips, her skin was warm and tantalizing, but he forced himself to walk away. He left her door partially open and went to look in on Chris.

Like his mother, the boy was sound asleep, stretched out on his stomach, snoring softly. Jake refused to think of how last night might have ended, or how they might still be searching today and tomorrow and beyond.

He went back into the living room, put on his shoes, and left the house, headed for Sweetie's and a very tall, very dark cup of coffee.

Outside at a café table, he called Kat.

"It's about time," she groused when she heard his voice.

"You sound pretty pissed off for so early in the morning."

"I gave up calling you last night. Is your phone broken?"

"We were sort of in the middle of something up here . . ."

"I know. You look great on television, by the way."

He groaned. "You saw it?"

"I always watch the eleven o'clock edition of Eyewitness News. They save the goriest, most titillating stories for late night. Anna Saunders tuned in, too. She called about a dozen times, *demanding* Carly's phone number."

"You didn't give it to her, did you?"

"What do you take me for? Of course not. She gave up after a couple of hours. Everything all right with the kids?"

"They're fine."

"Thank God. What about The Obsession?"

He ran his hand over the stubble on his jaw.

"Her name is Carly. She's been better." He heard the office call waiting cut in. "You want to get that?"

"They'll call back. Our phone's been ringing off the hook. Your little thirty-second interview made one hell of a commercial. Quite a few suspicious wives want you to personally handle their . . . cases."

"Very funny."

"I'm not joking. You looked *very* good on television. Better than in real life."

"Someone, either Anna Saunders' lawyer or Anna herself notified the Twilight Police about the guardianship petition. Child Protective Services interviewed Christopher."

"I heard that on the early morning news when they did a follow-up to last night's story. I noticed they didn't get another interview out of you or Carly, though. Is it true that you found the boys?"

Jake groaned. "The kids ended up at my place. If I'd been thinking straight I would have figured it out sooner and saved a lot of time and misery."

"You haven't been thinking straight for a few weeks now. That's what happens when your heart gets in the way. Your head stops working. The good news is the kids are safe."

"The bad news is, Anna's lawyer has more ammo to use against Carly."

"Such as?"

"Neglect. Child endangerment. They're bound to argue Chris must have been unsupervised in order for him to run off."

"Child Protective Services didn't hold him last night," she reminded him.

"No, but I can't see a lawyer dropping something like this." He fell silent for a few seconds.

"I hear you thinking," she said.

"I am. As long as I've got my computer with me, I'm going to see what I can dig up on Anna Saunders."

"Bingo." Kat's chuckle sounded downright evil.

"What's so funny?"

"I've been wondering when you were going to think of it. I'm already one step ahead of you."

Anna's cell phone rang while she was seated in her beautician's chair about to have a color treatment rinsed.

She hadn't slept all night, but she never canceled if she could help it. It was almost impossible to get another appointment.

"Would you hand me that, Trina?" Anna pointed to her purse, hoping the girl moved fast enough to grab the phone before the voice mail went on.

"Hello?" Anna signaled the beautician to turn down the stereo. She never knew why the shop played such hideous rock music anyway when half of the clientele was over fifty.

"Anna, this is Art Litton. Do you have a few minutes?"

"A few, Art, but—"

When she heard his voice, she wished she hadn't picked up. The lawyer had been calling her every two hours with updates since last night. His excitement, combined with the perverse amount of pleasure he was getting from gaining the upper hand irritated her as much as her own conscience.

"I contacted a friend in Child Protective Services and pulled some strings to see if we could get our hands on any information before the preliminary hearing. It wasn't easy."

"But you got it." She knew it wouldn't be cheap, either. Her heart started pounding the way it had done off and on since she'd seen the first news report last night.

Thank you, God, for keeping Christopher safe.

"Anna?"

"I'm sorry, what were you saying?"

"I said I don't want you worrying, but we're up against a small-town mentality here. As of noon today nearly everyone but the mayor of Twilight Cove called Child Protective Services *volunteering* interviews on Carly Nolan's behalf. She may come off looking like Mother Teresa."

Even after her initial shock began to wane once Christopher was safe, her hands still shook whenever she thought about how close she'd come to losing him for good, the way she'd lost Rick. Anxiety caused her heart to pound.

On the other end of the line, Litton was going on and on. Anna tried to focus.

". . . they have a statement from Jake Montgomery on record that attests to Ms. Nolan's conscientious care and deep concern for the boy. Montgomery has an outstanding reputation. He's been an expert witness in countless cases, from forgery to embezzlement. It won't be easy to discount his interview. Nor will it look good to have him on the other side since he was a friend of your son's."

"Of course he's on her side. He's slept with her."

"No kidding!" His glee was almost tangible.

A pang of guilt hit Anna. "I really don't know that for certain. It's just a hunch."

"If they have been intimate, that would certainly color his testimony, and we could get it thrown out."

She heard him scribbling away. "I really have to go, Art."

"I'm more confident than ever that things are going to go our way. We're going to have that boy in Long Beach where he belongs before you know it."

She went perfectly still as an image came to mind of Christopher hanging on the railing above Twilight Cove.

I just saw a dolphin jump. They go like this . . .

We have a beach by our house.

"With all of the support she's getting, Carly Nolan is going to come off as hardworking, devoted single mother, isn't she?" It wasn't as far from the truth as what Anna once thought. She pictured the shaken but determined young woman she'd met on Sunday. The mother Christopher obviously adored.

"Maybe not after I get to the bottom of the boy's running away. Don't you get discouraged," he urged. "Think of Charles."

She had been thinking of Charles, which was the reason Anna thought that she was having such a hard time meeting her own eyes in the beautician's mirror. She saw Trina hovering behind her, anxious to rinse out her hair.

"You didn't by any chance learn *why* Christopher ran away did you?"

"The official report said there was a misunderstanding over something his mother said about them having to move. The idea upset him so much he took off, and his best friend went with him. If we can prove she was going to flee again and skip out on the petition hearing, we've got her."

Another knot tied itself off in Anna's stomach. If Christopher had been so upset by the prospect of moving somewhere *with* Carly, what would happen if he were forced to move to Long Beach without her?

As if he sensed doubt in her silence, Art Litton said, "We all knew this wouldn't be pretty or easy, Anna. You have to stay strong."

"It's all a lot more complicated than I thought it would be."

"It's what Charles wanted."

What about what I want?

She wished she knew exactly what it was that she *did* want.

Dealing with the reality of Carly and Christopher, having met them, actually having held her grandson, had put things on an emotional level, one that left her with more doubt than certainty. Jake Montgomery had known exactly what he was doing when he had talked her into going to Twilight Cove.

"Let me take you out to dinner tonight. We can talk this over at length. I'm confident that we can still win. Hey, what *happy* child runs away from home?"

Dinner with Art Litton hammering case points over and over

was the *last* thing she needed after getting virtually no sleep last night.

"I'm sorry. I'm tied up this evening." She rubbed her forehead between her brows and sighed, wished she'd stayed home and tried to nap. "Art, what happens if we lose?"

"What do you mean?"

"If the judge doesn't grant the petition for guardianship. What will happen then?"

"We'll take some time to regroup, wait for her to trip up, gather more information, file all over again."

The only one who would win in that case would be Art Litton himself. How eager would Carly Nolan be to let her see Christopher once the hearing was over? She knew exactly how she would feel if she was in the young woman's place.

"Anna? Anna are you there?"

"I'm here, Arthur." She waved Trina back over to the chair. The girl wrapped a fresh towel above the black smock over her clothes. "I'll have to call you back. I'm at the hairdressers, and if I don't get the color rinsed out of my hair, I'll be sitting in the courtroom bald."

Carly took Monday and Tuesday off and kept Chris home from school Tuesday. Wednesday morning she woke up to a rainy day that started off bad and threatened to spiral into awful.

Chris started whining that he didn't want to go to school and took thirty minutes to dress. After coercing him into his clothes, she had to stand over him to be certain he ate a bowl of cereal and a piece of toast, then handed him lunch money and prodded him out the front door.

Betty Ford's right front tire was flat as a pancake, so Carly hauled Christopher back into the house before he found every puddle on the street, and she called Selma to say she'd be late. She then dialed up Arlo Carter to see if he could come up and help her change her tire.

By the time Arlo got there, she was soaked, but she had the tire off the car. He jumped out of the high cab of a tow truck covered with surfboard logo stickers. I Live to Surf was emblazoned on his license plate holder. She decided that he had gone to bed covered in grease. It was only eight in the morning, and there wasn't a spot on his hands, arms, or face that wasn't already smeared.

"Hi, Carly. Cool. You got the tire off. Step aside, and I'll finish this up for you." Oblivious of the rain, he walked to the back of the wagon and pulled out her spare and then examined the flat.

"Looks like you ran over a nail." He pointed to it with a greasy finger. "When you called, I was kinda worried you were gonna tell me that new alternator went out."

"What new alternator?"

"Aw, man."

"What's the matter?"

He shook his head. "I just went and opened my big mouth, and I promised him I wouldn't say nothing."

"Promised who?"

"That dude from down south. Montgomery. Last month when he had your car towed in? He stopped by to see what was wrong with it. I, like, told him you needed a new alternator, and he had me charge all but twenty-five to him. He told me to tell you that the car only needed a spark plug." He laughed through his nose.

Feeling about as lusterless as the faded white finish on Betty Ford, she shoved her wet hair back and glared at the hood of the car.

Jake had paid for a new alternator for her and hadn't said a word about it.

"Well, hey, that's done." Arlo spun the last lug nut into place, stood up and hefted the old tire. "I'll take this one into the shop and plug it for you. I'll call and let you know when you can come in, and I'll switch them."

Still shaken by what Jake had done, she managed, "Great, thanks, Arlo."

She towel-dried her hair, changed clothes, and loaded Chris back into the car, but not without another argument.

"What's wrong, Chris? I thought you were looking forward to

hot dog day, and besides, the mobile science lab is here, and you always like that."

He shrugged, stared out over the lower edge of the window.

"Come on. Talk to me, kiddo."

"I'm afraid Matt's not gonna be there, and all the kids will be looking at me weird because . . . of what happened."

"Matt will be there. I talked to his mother yesterday to make sure. If anybody teases you, just ignore them."

"Aw, Mom. That's impossible. I'll still hear them, and it will make me sick at my stomach."

She knew that better than he did, but was short on any better advice this morning. When they drove up in front of Twilight Elementary, she kept the engine running. Reaching across him, she lifted his door handle and let the door swing wide.

"Have a good day, honey." She kept it light, as if things were fine. "And *run* to the door so you won't get all wet. I'll be right here to pick you up."

If they were handing out Golden Globes in Twilight for Best Actress in a Drama performance, she certainly deserved a nomination.

When she finally walked into the diner at nine, Geoff was in hushed conversation with Selma in a window booth. When they saw her they stopped talking. Selma waved her over.

"What's up?" She glanced between them.

Geoff reached for her with both hands and pulled her into the booth beside him. "Selma's got some news for you."

"Me?"

The place was blessedly empty because of the rain. Only one man was still there, seated near the front door, sipping coffee and reading the newspaper. Ignoring him, Selma got up and flipped the CLOSED sign face out. Then she slid into the booth opposite Carly and Geoff and called out, "Joe, get out here. We need you."

"Geoff told us all about what's going on, and naturally, we're ready to support you in any way we can. Geoff said that his lawyer friend in San Luis is the best around. We all got to thinking, and we don't want you to have to worry about the money you'll need for your legal expenses on top of everything else."

Carly stared at Selma and Joe, then turned to Geoff.

"But . . ."

Selma held up a hand to silence her.

"According to Glenn Potter, I've got plenty of equity in this building, not to mention the business, so I've applied for a loan."

Carly didn't stop to think twice. "I can't let you do that, Selma. Absolutely not."

"I'm staking my bets on you winning this thing. Let me put my money where my mouth is."

"I think we should have some fund-raisers, too," Joe added. "Car washes, bake sales. Get everybody in town involved, like they were during the search the other night. Everybody's talking about the way the town turned out to help with the search. Gave 'em a chance to feel good about themselves, eh?"

Carly bit her lips, unable to come up with words to express her thanks, but Selma's loan and nickels and dimes from car washes and bake sales couldn't compete with Anna Saunders' resources. She could never live with herself if she let Selma risk her business.

Selma leaned across the table and took her hand.

"Let us help you, Carly. You've worked here for almost four years and waited on almost everyone in town. I'm sure everyone will want to help when they hear what's happening—if they haven't already."

Their faces blurred and wavered when Carly's eyes filled with tears. "Things I did when I was young will come out in court. I was a runaway. I used another girl's identity."

"You never lied to us, Carly Nolan. And we all know that you're the best mother a kid could ever have. When was thinking with your heart ever wrong?"

Geoff slipped an arm around Carly's shoulder as Selma squeezed her hand. And Joe, dear gentle Joe, had tears of his own in his huge, dark eyes.

The fullness in Carly's throat made it hard to swallow, impossible to speak. As she looked at each of her friends, friends willing to risk everything to help her, she realized that the family she had always dreamed of, the family that she was certain she would never have, had been right beside her all along.

She'd just been too afraid to open her heart wide enough to let them in.

FORTY-THREE

Except for the kitchen cupboards, Jake finished painting the inside of the house and then, taking his frustration out on the place, he tore out the worn, stained carpet and had it hauled away.

Without area rugs or furniture, the place echoed the sound of the sea like a hollow seashell.

After leaving Carly a few messages, he started to feel like a stalker, so he decided to give her some space and stop calling, trying instead to concentrate on the preliminary background information on Anna Saunders that Kat faxed him.

Days passed quickly. Nights were another matter altogether. Lying on his makeshift bed, he imagined he caught whiffs of the citrus scent of Carly's shampoo and would mistake the music of the waves for the soft hush of her sighs.

He would prowl the big empty place, the bare wood floor cool beneath his feet as he padded out to the deck to stare up at the stars.

By Friday afternoon he was all set to drive into Twilight to pick up sandpaper at the small hardware store on Cabrillo when a FedEx truck pulled into his driveway. He signed for the flat envelope, recognized his grandfather's lawyers' return address.

He grabbed a bottle of apple juice out of his cooler and carried the papers onto the deck to sit in the sun.

True to his word, his granddad had left almost all of his estate to various charities, among them Rancho Los Cerritos, one of the historic sites dating back to the early settlement of California.

As he scanned the pages, Jake suddenly realized that despite everything the man had always said, his Granddad had left him a very generous inheritance. There was also a sealed envelope addressed to him by his grandfather's hand.

Dear Jake,

By now what's left of me is floating beneath the waves between here and Catalina. I can't say I ever did anything to deserve your love, but I always believed that love was for children and fools anyway.

Looking back, I can see I was never an easy man to get along with. Maybe if I'd have been a better father, my son wouldn't have felt the need to turn his back on me and get himself killed. If I'd have been a better grandfather, maybe you wouldn't look back on those summers spent with me as an obligation you endured for your mother's sake.

Regret is a waste of time. I was what I was. You, being who you are, always realized that.

Consider the sum I've left you unexpected income. Like your father before you, you're one of those men who believes in dreams.

Maybe you can use the money to make one of them come true.

His grandfather's initials were scrawled at the bottom of the page.

Jake reread the letter before he let it drop to the redwood deck with the rest of the document. He leaned back, eyes closed, turned his face to the sun hoping he would never become so embittered that he lost sight of his dreams and realizing he'd come perilously close before he'd met Carly.

Now he had enough money to buy this house, if he could get it for under market value.

If he still wanted it.

He'd rented the place because of Manny, but also to be close to Christopher and Carly for a few weeks in order to get to know them. He hadn't realized how easy that would be, or how quickly he would come to care for her and Rick's son.

Back then he had no real intention of making a permanent move, but now that the possibility of doing just that had been given to him, Carly wouldn't even pick up the phone.

Damn it, Carly. You've refused to run from Anna Saunders anymore. When will you stop running from what's in your heart?

An hour later he walked out of the hardware store just as Carly stepped out of the diner across the street. Their eyes met, and for an instant she froze, then she turned and walked toward the corner.

He stepped off the curb without looking, forced a passing motorist to slam on the brakes and honk. He smiled and mouthed, "Sorry," before he jaywalked to the other side of the street.

Carly was already out of sight. He jogged past the diner. By the time he turned the corner and saw the old Ford wagon parked at the curb, Carly had started the car.

He opened the passenger door and slipped inside.

"What are you doing?" She pulled back, leaning against the driver's side window and staring at him as if he'd lost his mind.

"You really should learn to lock your doors."

"No one else is trying to get in."

"All I want is a minute of your time."

"I know what you want, Jake, and time has nothing to do with it."

He tried smiling. "I don't give up easily. If I did I'd have never found you in the first place."

She sighed. "Is this pigheadedness the reason your wife divorced you?"

"I divorced *her*—shortly after I came home earlier than I'd planned one night and found her in bed with the doctor she worked for. He was married, too."

"Jake, I'm sorry . . ."

"Don't be. Marla was literally the girl next door. I'd loved her since I was five, but she never even noticed me until we were juniors in high school." He could shrug off the hurt now. "We went off to college together, she became a nurse. I got a degree in criminal justice. The day after graduation, we were married."

Carly had fallen silent, intent on every word.

"I was young and naïve back then," he admitted. "Marla was the only girl I'd ever loved, and I took my wedding vows seriously. I wanted to start a family and have kids right away, but the time never seemed to be right for her. I was earning my hours of experience working for Alexander and Perry, a top P.I. firm, so that I could eventually take the licensing test. We were saving money, trying to scrape together enough for a house and for me to start my own business someday."

He paused, looked down at the bag of sandpaper he'd forgotten was in his hand.

"I was away a lot, especially weekend nights when I was assigned to marital surveillance—busting cheating spouses. While I was out snapping photos of other people's trysts, I never had a clue my own wife was balling her boss—until I finished up early one Saturday and thought I'd surprise her and take her to a movie.

"I walked in and found them on the butcher block in the kitchen." He laughed. "He was inventive, I'll give him that."

"What did you do?" Carly was gripping the steering wheel as if she half expected him to tell her that he'd killed the bastard.

"I turned around and walked out. Never went back. Know where I slept that first week? At Rick's place. He was a real partyer back then. The envy of all his married friends. He had a bachelor pad on the beach in Newport. We called him a trust-fund brat Hugh Hefner."

"Jake, I'm sorry," she whispered.

"Hey, don't be. It's ancient history." It was a relief to realize his old heartache was completely gone. He hadn't been looking to replace it with a new one, but he was afraid it was already too late.

It had taken him eight years to forgive Marla. It might very well be forever before Carly forgave him for lying to her.

He longed to take her in his arms, ready to make love to her right there on the street.

"Listen, Carly. If things aren't going to work out between us, I know I've only got myself to blame."

She reached up, pushed her hair back off her face before she closed her eyes and sighed.

"My life is so complicated right now, Jake. I . . . I don't know what I'm doing or saying half the time anymore."

"Kiss me, Carly. Just once. Just so I can prove a point."

"No."

"What are you scared of? Finding out I'm right? You kissed me that first time, Carly. Kiss me again."

He leaned across the seat, slipped his hand beneath her hair and pulled her close. Her eyes widened, her lips parted, but instead of protesting, she reached for him, pulled his head down until their lips met.

He covered her mouth with his, kissed her deep, cherishing the taste of her lips, the feel of her silken hair draped over the back of his hand, her warm skin beneath his palms.

He ended the kiss before she could. In the hushed stillness broken only by the sound of their ragged, uneven breathing, their eyes met. Dazed, she stared back.

Before she could say anything, before he could do anything to ruin the moment, he got out of the car and closed the door behind him.

FORTY-FOUR

Jake's kiss left her more confused than ever. Carly tried to shake it off as she drove to the school where Chris waited with a knot of children on the edge of the playground. When his teacher saw her, she waved, and Chris came running to the car.

"How'd it go today?"

"Great! Matt and me are probably the most famous kids in the whole world." His concerns had been short lived when he and Matt found themselves Twilight Elementary celebrities.

She almost wished the other kids had "looked at them weird" instead.

"Don't go getting any ideas for an encore, all right?"

"Huh?"

"Don't even think about running away again just to get attention."

"Oh, Mom." He rolled his eyes. "Don't worry."

Don't worry. As if she could turn it off and on.

After dinner and an endless round of Monopoly, Chris was finally tucked in and fast asleep, and she was alone with her thoughts.

There was no way she was going to be able to sleep, so she forced herself to pick up a brush and work on the painting that she hadn't touched since Chris and Matt ran off.

Hours flew by as she lost herself in the piece. The sunset sky that Jake had requested was one of her best, the colors so vibrant and alive that it could have been a photograph.

The ghostly image of a woman had taken shape. Dressed in the style of a Spanish don's widow, she was seated on an ornately carved wooden bench near the edge of the bluff. A long lace mantilla draped her from the crown of her head to the hem of her gown. The cascading lace appeared to drink in the fading sunlight,

325

bringing the image to life. An open fan lay on the bench beside the woman.

Her shoulders were bowed, her hands rested limp in her lap. There was such a mournful hopelessness in her posture that the scene almost made Carly weep.

The woman's features were in profile, her face barely visible because of the lace mantilla. The final touches on her eyes, nose, and mouth would complete the work.

Carly stepped back and knew without Geoff having to tell her that the piece was good. She had poured all of her frustration and turmoil, her fear and her hopes into it. Everything that she had translated onto the canvas had come from the heart.

She felt the lone woman's loss and dejection and had positioned her to look as if she were staring into the setting sun for answers.

There was a haunting stillness about the painting that spoke not only of the end of a day, but of the end of everything the woman had ever cherished.

Not until she had cleaned her brushes and covered the painting did her mind finally let Jake in.

The memory of his spontaneous parting kiss still burned. She reached up, absently touched her lips. The scent of turpentine still lingered on her hands, so she walked to the counter where she kept a bowl of fruit.

She washed her hands in lemon and soap and rubbed lotion into them. Again and again she tasted Jake's kiss until she was filled with sweet longing.

Before she knew what she was doing, the phone was in her hand. She punched in his number, waited, praying he wouldn't answer. On the second ring, she heard his voice.

"Montgomery."

He sounded groggy, as if she'd awakened him. She glanced at the clock on the stove. Twelve forty-five. She had no idea it was so late and was tempted to hang up but couldn't bring herself to. She could hear him breathing.

"Carly?"

"Jake, I . . ."

"What's wrong? Is Chris all right?"

Naturally he would think it was an emergency. It was almost one in the morning.

"I'm sorry, Jake. I shouldn't have called."

"Is everything all right?"

She started to say yes, that everything was fine, but the words stuck in her throat.

"Carly?"

"Oh Jake," she whispered. "You hurt me. I was angry and scared. I wanted to hurt you back."

She heard the floor creak on the other end of the line, then the rustle of fabric. The phone hit the floor. He cursed, scrambled to pick it up.

"I'll be right over," he said. A promise? A warning?

She imagined him shrugging into his jeans, struggling with buttons, tearing through a pile of clothes for a shirt.

"It's one in the morning, Jake."

"It wasn't too late for you to call. It's not too late for me to come over."

Before he drove into Seaside Village, he made a U-turn and backtracked. Once inside the mobile home park, he cruised the circular loop three times looking for a surveillance car. Alexander and Perry already had what they wanted. No one was tailing him now.

So as not to awaken Etta, he killed the engine and the lights and coasted into the parking space in front of Carly's.

Soft, muted light shone behind the drawn curtains.

Clearing the porch steps, he raised his hand to tap on the door, but she opened it before he could make a sound.

A small lamp on the table beside her rocker and a scented candle on the trunk in front of the sofa drenched the room in a soft, yellow glow and a heady citrus scent. He stepped inside and without taking his eyes off her, closed the door and flipped the lock.

Then he took her in his arms. She came willingly, fell into his embrace, lifted her lips for his kiss. The need in him was overwhelming. Carly answered his kiss with one as charged as his own.

When the kiss ended, Jake looked down into her eyes and then her sweet mouth that tempted him to kiss her forever.

"Christopher?" His voice sounded ragged, torn, even to him.

"Asleep."

"Is he a heavy sleeper?" He glanced toward the hallway.

"Always."

He held her tight, ran his hand down the front of her jeans, cupped her, pulled her up against him. She moaned, lifted her hips, encouraged him to knead her with his hand until she was writhing against him.

"Oh, Jake," she whispered against his mouth. "I need you so much. I tried to tell myself it was over. I tried to forget that night, to forget what might have been, but I can't. I just can't." She shuddered, clung to him.

He tasted her tears, kissed them away. He trailed kisses down her throat, to her shoulder, nipped her through her thin knit shirt. He brushed her tangled hair back off her face, his senses alive to the silken feel of her long blonde hair against his palm.

"I want you," he whispered. "But I have to hear you say that you believe me. I never, ever wanted to hurt you."

Her glorious eyes widened. Deep and green as the ocean, he thought he might drown in their depths.

She went very still. His heart sank.

Gently he tried to pull away.

"No! Don't." Carly tightened her arms around his neck. Her nipples tingled against his chest. Her breasts flattened as he pulled her closer. Her heartbeat matched the slow, steady pounding of the waves against the shoreline.

He wanted forgiveness, assurance that she believed he never meant to harm her or Chris. She wanted to believe. She needed for it to be true as much as she wanted him.

She took a deep breath. A collage of all the things he had done to show that he cared came back to her.

Life doesn't hand out a lot of second chances.

"I believe you," she whispered. Not only did her heart want to believe him—her body gave her no alternative.

He picked her up, carried her out to the studio, the only place in the house that was totally hers, the place she claimed for herself, for her work.

Gently he lowered her to the deep, cushioned sofa covered in yards of tropical fabrics in all the colors of the rainbow.

Her senses came alive as he raised her shirt over her head and tossed it aside. She reached for him, tugged his T-shirt out of the waistband of his Levi's, skimmed it up past his taught abdomen and ribs, threw it on the floor beside her own.

His hands were all over her, urgent, hot, needy.

Tonight was nothing like the first time. Tonight their need was inflamed by the memory of what they had already tasted, what they had already shared.

Carly's hands worked frantically to open his Levi's. He had already unzipped her jeans, hooked his thumbs into the waistband along with her panties and was pushing them down over the swell of her hips. She raised her hips, aiding him. The cool night air slipping in through the open window teased her skin into gooseflesh. She shivered. Jake drew her into his embrace.

Her nipples brushed the crisp mat of hair on his chest. She traced her hand down to the open fly of his pants. Her fingers strayed into the heat and warmth hidden there. His erection was hot, pulsing. She wrapped him in her hand.

He groaned into her ear, rasped. "Careful . . ."

He let go of her long enough to finish slipping off his pants, sat on the sofa beside her. In the chill of the enclosed porch, the warmth of his body drew her like a magnet. Jake enfolded her in his arms, kissed her, worshiping her with his lips, his tongue, as if he would never get enough.

In one swift move he pulled her over him, drawing her up until she straddled his hips, then lowering her onto his erection. She was slick with need and took him inside greedily, settling her hips against his thighs.

The heavy moon dusted chalk-white light over their bodies as Jake tightened his hands on her bare hips, gently urging her to glide up and down, to rock with him. Slowly, slowly at first, pulsing with the beat of the sea, in time with a steady rhythm as old as the seas, the heartbeat of the universe.

Jake grabbed her face, pulled her down for a long, sweet kiss as she rode him. Her hair swayed, matched the tempo of the rise and fall of her hips. He whispered her name, rubbed her nipples with his heated palms, then he cupped her breasts in his hands, drew them to his lips, suckled until she gasped and threw her head back.

Frantic to reach a climax, she rode him higher, faster, until he was deep inside, so deep that she had to stifle a scream of pleasure. Her hands tightened on his shoulders until she felt his flesh beneath her fingernails.

"Jake!" The cry escaped her. She had reached the edge. As she teetered on the brink of climax, he thrust again, held her hips fast in his strong hands.

"Now," he growled low in his throat. "Now."

He surged hot and pulsing inside her. She shuddered, contracted around him in wave after wave of pleasure, the release so great that she wept with the miracle of it.

The throbbing slowly ebbed, slipped into a haunting memory. A cloud slipped over the face of the moon, deepened the night shadows.

Carly collapsed against his chest, lay her head on his shoulder, and pressed her lips to his neck. Jake's arms twined around her in a gentle, protective embrace.

She lay in his arms, listened to his ragged breathing, the erratic beat of his heart, until it slowed and settled into a gentle rhythm.

Until the cloud moved on and moonlight swept the studio.

• • •

"I wish I could stay and wake up in your arms." Jake's seductive whisper sent a shiver down her spine. She opened her eyes.

"Me too. But . . ."

Together they laughed softly and both said, "Chris."

"It wouldn't be right. Him waking up and finding me in bed with you."

"You're an old-fashioned guy."

"Is that a problem for you?"

"No. It's another gift. Thank you for that, Jake." She didn't know her heart could get any fuller. How many other men would put her son before their own needs and wants?

They untangled. Carly laughed, softly, shyly, when her knee slipped between the sofa cushions and she nearly toppled off him. Jake grabbed her around the waist, held on, unable to resist another kiss.

She sorted through their clothing. Handed him hers instead of his. Jake laughed and dressed her slowly, drawing out his movements, lingering over each touch, each brush of his hand across her skin.

I wish you could stay.

I don't want to go.

Jake smoothed Carly's hair back off her forehead, kissed her tenderly on her lips, her cheek, her temple, then took her hand and led her to the door.

"I'll call you in the morning," he whispered.

"Okay." She smiled up into his eyes as he unlocked the door and let in the damp night air.

"Carly?"

"Yes?"

He touched her lips, light as the mist hovering above the waves. "Thank you."

Then he was gone.

FORTY-FIVE

The next morning Carly learned it was possible to wait tables on three hours of sleep.

Not that she'd want to do it every day, but by the time her shift was over, she still had energy to spare. Jake had called the house before she left for work just to say good morning. His voice teased her like a seductive caress, made her long to invite him over, tempted her to call in sick.

But there was breakfast to make, Chris to drive to school. Just because she was in danger of losing her heart didn't mean she could lose her mind. Life had taught her to be more practical than that.

Besides, Jake said he had work of his own to catch up on and that he'd likely be busy all day, but he promised to call her before dinner.

After her shift she was energized rather than exhausted, and since the Potters had invited Chris to go along with them to an early movie and dinner in San Luis Obispo, she headed home to take advantage of a couple hours alone to paint.

With her radio tuned to her favorite jazz station, she walked into the studio with Beauty on her heels, opened the windows to let in the afternoon breeze, thankful that the heavy overcast had burned off before noon. The sky was a flawless blue backdrop for a gull that winged its way over the rooftops, headed for the ocean.

Her senses were buzzing. She felt more alive and aware than she'd been in a long time. Not only did the sky seem bluer, but the air fresher and the deep greens and golds on the hills brighter. When she realized she was smiling for no reason, she shook her head.

Happiness frightened her, maybe because she'd been such a stranger to it as a child, maybe because it tended to come in such temporary bursts. She likened it to the sand dollars she sometimes found on the beach, pretty but fragile and rare.

As she moved through the familiar motions of uncovering her painting, squeezing paint onto the palette, choosing a brush, she couldn't help but be reminded that if it weren't for the pending petition hearing, life would be perfect.

Yesterday, the very thought of facing Anna at the hearing would have terrified her, but after opening up to Jake last night, after giving him her trust again, she had gained a new level of confidence in herself and the future.

Viewing the painting of the Spanish widow sitting alone on the bluff, Carly's heart filled with empathy, as if she knew the woman's thoughts and feelings. She always painted the figures in her oils the way they appeared in her mind. She gave the images control of her imagination as she let her creativity and inspiration flow.

But with this particular piece she wondered if perhaps she had let fear alone dictate her subject. The woman sat isolated, staring out to sea, dejected, abandoned. Perhaps punished by fate.

Was it a self-portrait?

Did the woman draped in the mantilla really represent her, alone without Christopher? Without Jake?

Perhaps, she thought, as she dipped her brush into the paint, it was time she took control of her work the way she had decided to take control of her life.

Minutes melted into hours. When Carly finally looked up it was almost five. She wiped her brushes with linseed oil, set them aside and stepped back to look at the painting again. She smiled and nodded, finally satisfied with what she'd added.

She refilled her glass of ice water and walked into the living room in time to see a black Lincoln Town Car pull up out front. She locked Beauty in Christopher's room and went immediately to the door. Her hand tightened on the knob. Staring through the screen, she watched a man she hadn't seen for almost six years step out of the long, sleek black automobile. Dressed in a dark suit and highly polished shoes, he paused long enough to straighten his cuffs and smooth his crimson tie before he started toward the door.

"Ms. Nolan." He nodded in her direction, waited expectantly, as if he thought she would actually open the door. "I'm Arthur Litton. We met in Borrego Springs a few years ago."

"What . . . what are you doing here?"

"I see we're going to dismiss with the formalities. Of course, I'm here on behalf of Anna Saunders. I'd like to come in and talk to you, if I may?"

Carly glanced outside. His Lincoln glistened in the sunlight with tinted windows all around, a dark, threatening presence intruding on what had been an otherwise perfect day.

"I have a lawyer. Call him." She started to close the door.

"When your son ran away last weekend, it made the news in Los Angeles and cast disparaging light on your credibility as a mother and your ability to care for Christopher."

"I don't see the point of your visit, Mr. Litton."

"Oh, I think you do. This shouldn't take long." He stood perfectly still, as if determined to remain long after she closed the door in his face.

Steeling herself, she took a deep breath and opened the door. "You have exactly five minutes."

When Litton strode confidently inside, Carly felt like she'd just let in the Trojan horse. She didn't invite him to sit, but he did anyway, right in the middle of the sofa. He opened his briefcase.

"The case we've built in favor of our petition is very strong. In fact—"

Just then there was another knock at the door, insistent and repetitive.

"Excuse me." Carly opened the door. It was Etta in a red wig reminiscent of Lucille Ball. A gold satin robe covered with embroidered Chinese dragons dipped off one of her thin shoulders. Standing there clutching a glass measuring pitcher, she looked like something out of an old film noir movie.

Etta lowered her voice to a whisper. "Is everything all right?"

Carly hesitated. Just when everything seemed so right for a change, just when the fragile idea of hope had begun to bloom, fate had delivered Anna Saunders' lawyer in a Lincoln Town Car.

"I'm a little busy right now, Etta. Maybe you could come back later?"

Etta tried to see through the screen. Her eyes were huge. She held up the measuring cup.

"I *really* hate to bother you, but I need two cups of flour. It'll just take a second. If you don't mind, dear?"

Carly glanced over her shoulder at Litton, who looked perturbed. She doubted he'd ever seen anyone like Etta, let alone considered someone so eccentric worth his time.

Carly smiled. There wasn't an unkind or selfish bone in Etta's body.

"Come on in, Etta." She swung the door wide and let her neighbor in. "This is Mr. Litton. Mr. Litton, this is my dear friend and neighbor, Etta Schwartz. Why don't you two chat while I get Etta some flour?"

Arthur Litton stood and stared at the diminutive lady in uncomfortable silence. Etta, on the other hand, had no trouble launching into conversation with him.

Carly took her time taking a tin canister off the shelf and scooping out two cups of white flour. When she walked back into the living room, Etta was in the middle of debating the use of butter over Crisco in chocolate chip cookies.

"Here you go, Etta." Carly handed her the measuring pitcher. "What are you making?"

"Scones. The little ones with the currants. People think currants and raisins are the same thing, but I use currants. Then I'm doing a batch of brownies. From a box." She lingered, looked over at Litton as if about to say something more, then she smiled at Carly.

"Don't worry about a thing, dear." Etta reached over to pat Carly's hand and rolled her eyes in Litton's direction.

Carly wondered what was up with Etta, who usually only baked when she was nervous. She took her time ushering her neighbor out and closed the door.

Litton was on the sofa again, reaching into the briefcase when the phone rang. He pursed his lips and frowned at the phone across the room.

"I'll let the machine pick up." She wanted him out of here and the sooner she heard what he had to say, the sooner he'd leave.

When the phone stopped ringing, they both listened to her own outgoing message. Then the recorder clicked on.

"Carly, this is Geoff. I know you're in there. Pick up."

She shrugged at Litton, waiting for Geoff to give up and hang up.

"Carly? I'm *not* hanging up. Pick up the phone. *Pick up the phone!*"

Litton had his hands on a file folder. Carly jumped up and walked over to the phone, clicked it on.

"Hi, Geoff. What is it?"

"Are you all right?"

"Things have been better." She lowered her voice and whispered, "Anna Saunders' lawyer is sitting about ten feet away right now."

"I can be over in twenty minutes."

"It's all right, really."

"No it's not. I'm stuck here. A tour bus of Germans just drove up and parked right out front. Don't worry, okay?"

"Easy for you to say," she mumbled.

"I've got to go. They're lined up to buy note cards."

"Okay."

When he hung up, she clicked off and frowned at the portable in her hand. Weird.

She walked back to where Litton was holding a manila file on his knees.

He straightened his already straight tie. "Do you think there'll be any *more* interruptions?"

She shrugged, tempted to smile. *Welcome to my world.*

"You never can tell," she said.

Let him wait. He'd invaded her home and her fragile peace of mind. She sat down in the rocker and studied him. He looked older, his face fuller. Far less intimidating than he had seemed to her six years ago. Maybe because she was older and not as easily intimidated. Maybe she was stronger, knowing she had the support of a host of friends who cared, confident because she had put her heart on the line when she let Jake into her life, and though her heart was a bit battered, it was still intact.

"What exactly do you want, Mr. Litton?"

He opened the folder.

Suddenly there was a quick knock, and the door opened. Jake walked in and tossed a manila envelope on the Formica dining table and crossed the small living room space in three strides. He glanced down at Litton before his gaze touched her.

"Are you all right, Carly?"

"What are you doing here?"

"Etta called Geoff. He called Selma. She called the Potters, and they called my cell and told me there was an emergency." He looked at Litton. "Luckily I was in the car and already on my way over. What's going on?"

"Mr. Litton was telling me that he has built a very strong case in Mrs. Saunders' favor."

Jake's gaze hardened as it shifted to Litton. His mouth flattened into a taut line. "Mr. Litton shouldn't even be here at all, and he knows it. He could be disbarred for contacting you personally." Then he told Litton, "Carly has a lawyer. Call and threaten him."

"I'm here at the *specific* request of my client."

"Then maybe you should have told your client to go to hell and gone through the proper channels."

Seeing the look on his face, Carly was afraid Jake was going to lose it altogether. She jumped to her feet.

"Jake—"

"You don't have to put up with this harassment, Carly. Call your lawyer. He'll tell you how unethical this is."

Anger emanated from Jake in waves. Even if she hadn't been able to feel it, it was etched on his features. He was holding his temper by a slender thread. He glanced down at her, then walked over to the table where he'd left a nine-by-twelve manila envelope and picked it up.

Outside, a car door slammed. Jake walked back to her side just as there came another knock at the door. Expecting Etta again, Carly was dumbstruck when she saw Anna Saunders standing on the porch.

For a second, no one moved, not Litton, not Jake. Carly smoothed her hands down her jeans and walked over to the door.

"May I come in?" Anna was conservatively dressed in a tailored black suit that showed off her trim figure and stylish hair.

Carly held the door open as the woman stepped inside, paused to look at Litton and then Jake. The lawyer was on his feet, a florid red stain slowly creeping up his neck and face.

Anna ignored both men, focusing solely on Carly.

"How is Christopher?"

Carly read genuine concern in Anna's eyes.

"He's fine. The Potters took him to an early movie and dinner." She glanced at her watch. "He should be home any minute."

There was a second or two of awkward silence between them before Anna turned to Litton.

"When you insisted I wait out there in the car, you promised this was only going to take five minutes."

Carly had never actually seen a man squirm before, but Arthur Litton appeared to do just that.

Jake stepped closer, silently supporting her with his nearness.

He told Litton, "Carly isn't about to give in."

"Arthur!" Anna's hands tightened on her purse. "Why haven't you done what I sent you in here to do?"

"Are you sure you want to continue in this vein, Anna?" Jake held up the manila folder in his hand. "If you are, I'll be forced to turn the information I have here over to Carly's lawyer."

"Jake, what's going on?" Carly couldn't tell if he was bluffing, nor did she have a clue what might be in the envelope.

Anna's eyes widened. "What is that?"

"Before you married Charles Saunders your name was Anna Riley, am I right? You were born in Delano, in the San Joaquin Valley?"

"Yes," she whispered. "Yes, I was." Anna stared at the envelope as if Jake were holding a live grenade.

"If you don't drop the petition for guardianship, if you plan on dragging Carly's reputation through the mud, then the information I have on your own background gets presented as well."

"I was only a teenager . . ." Her eyes were bleak. All color had drained from her face leaving behind two spots of rose blush.

Jake glanced Carly's way before his gaze hit Anna.

"Sometimes teenagers make mistakes, don't they?"

Visibly shaken, Anna ignored both Jake and the envelope. Her hand went to the diamond heart at her throat as she turned to Carly.

"I didn't send Arthur in to threaten you. I sent him in to tell you that I want him to file for a dismissal. After what I went through those terrible hours while Christopher was missing and long afterward, I thought things through and I want this over and done with before my grandson gets hurt."

Anna turned to Jake. "Don't think whatever you've got in that envelope is what changed my mind, either. If Arthur had done what I asked him to do, this would all be over by now."

Briefcase in hand, Litton fought to salvage his position, although his gaze kept cutting to the envelope in Jake's hand.

"We may be filing for dismissal of the guardianship petition, but Mrs. Saunders will definitely want visitation rights. We are prepared to file a new petition."

"Arthur Litton, you've no idea *what* I definitely want. As soon as you file for a dismissal, you're fired. In fact, you can leave right now. I'd rather call a cab than ride all the way back to the airport with you."

Litton stormed past them all. The screen door rattled and slammed behind him. Carly was suddenly all alone with Jake and Anna, the three of them enveloped in a chilly, awkward silence.

Carly tried to grasp what just happened. She looked at Jake.

"It's over?"

He smiled and took her hand. "It's really over. The past is finally behind you where it belongs." He turned to Anna and handed her the envelope. "I'm glad I didn't have to use this."

Ignoring Jake, Anna requested of Carly, "I'd like to speak to you alone, if I may."

With the realization that the threat of losing Christopher was finally over, the world slowly began to right itself again.

"Fine," Carly told her. "Anything you have to say can be said in front of Jake."

She could see in his eyes how much the gesture meant to him, but he gave her hand a squeeze and said, "I'll go outside and keep an eye out for Chris. Will you be all right?"

"Of course."

Anna glanced around the small living space not much larger than her kitchen.

The odor of linseed oil and paint lightly tinted the air. There were a few toys here and there on the floor, little boy things made of plastic and movable parts. The kitchen counter was clear except for a few glasses and a bright ceramic mug. An enclosed porch was visible through an open door on the back wall. She saw a lopsided sofa covered with garish prints.

Tense, silent, Anna waited for Jake Montgomery to leave, but he hovered beside Carly Nolan like a rottweiler. Anna was still shaken, the envelope he'd given her heavy in her hand. She didn't have to look inside to know what it contained, just as she was sure that he wouldn't have hesitated to use the information against her at the hearing.

The brief but telling exchange between Montgomery and the young woman was so touching that Anna felt a twinge of jealousy and wondered if the two of them even recognized the deep intensity of the feelings they shared for one another.

"I'll be fine," Carly assured him. She gave him a tremulous smile. "Everything will be fine now."

Anna could see how badly he wanted to stay, but he confined his touch to her arm and gave it a reassuring squeeze before he let himself out.

Carly didn't take her eyes off of him until Jake had cleared the porch, then she indicated the sofa with a wave of her hand.

"Please, have a seat."

"Thank you."

Anna made herself comfortable on the small love seat and set her purse down beside her. When she realized she had given into an old habit of rolling her rings around her fingers with her thumbs, she clasped her hands in her lap.

Carly sat on the edge of the wicker rocking chair not far away. Anna had thought that the young woman would be jubilant upon hearing that the guardianship petition would be dropped, but thus far Carly had shown very little emotion at all.

"This meeting certainly didn't start out the way I planned," Anna sighed. "I'm just thankful Christopher wasn't here."

"So am I," Carly agreed. "I . . . I must say I'm in shock. What made you change your mind?"

Anna thought back to the evening when she'd turned on the news. "The night Christopher ran away I was beside myself with worry. I didn't have your number and couldn't get it. I left calls with Montgomery's partner, but she didn't return them, nor did Jake.

"I should have changed my mind the moment I met Christopher that day in the park, but you see, Carly, I had made my husband a promise, and I didn't want to betray it. I loved Charles most of my life. He took me out of a situation that was almost too horrible to bear, and for that I am forever grateful, but Charles is gone now and life is for the living.

"I already love Christopher, even though I don't know him well. I've imagined what it would be like to have a grandchild for so long that I don't think I could bear it if you refuse to let me see him again. Trust me when I say that I would never want that precious child to suffer because of something I did." Shame sluiced through her, shame that brought tears to her eyes.

"If anything had happened to Christopher because of me, I would never have forgiven myself," she whispered.

She rarely if ever gave into sentimental emotion, but the tears had been building since the moment Chris had slipped his little hand so trustingly into hers.

Anna felt the sofa sag, then a tentative touch on her shoulder. She realized Carly was seated beside her, trying to explain.

"Christopher ran away because I told him we were moving out of Twilight Cove. After we met you in the park, I was tempted to leave town, to disappear again—until I realized running wasn't the answer anymore. I didn't have a chance to tell Christopher that I'd changed my mind before he got it in his head to take off. If anyone is to blame, it's me."

"But if it hadn't been for *me* pursuing you, hounding you with the guardianship petition, you wouldn't have felt threatened. I wouldn't blame you if you refused to ever let me see Christopher again."

Carly took a deep breath, struggling to find the right words. She took courage from the fact that she was free, but it was hard to believe that Anna would leave the decision about visitations up to her.

"Your lawyer said he was filing for visitation rights."

"My lawyer, my *former* lawyer, is an idiot." Anna's lips curled into a half smile. "There will be no more filing petitions, no more threats from me. All I ask is that you allow me to see my grandson. That you let me give him the things he needs while I'm around to see him enjoy them."

Carly noticed Anna's gaze had fallen on Christopher's team photo on a shelf across the room. She stood up, crossed the room, brought the photo back and handed it to Anna.

"Would you like to have this?"

Anna's sun-spotted hands closed around the frame and held on tight. "May I?"

Carly nodded. "Back when I ordered the package of photos, I was under the false belief that we didn't have any family to give the extras to, but since this whole thing started, I've come to realize that's not true."

She thought of Selma and Joe, Geoff and Etta and the Potters. Family had nothing to do with DNA, or marriage licenses, or court decrees. It had everything to do with love.

Tears blurred her vision, but not so badly that she couldn't see that Anna's lower lip was trembling.

"You were Rick's mother. You're part of Christopher's family and always will be. You don't need a paper to tell you that, Anna, or me to give you permission to see Christopher anytime you want. All you need to do is love him for who and what he is, to be there for him when he needs you, and to respect the fact that I'm his mother."

Carly reached out to lay her hand atop Anna's on the photograph. "I know Christopher would like nothing better than to have his grandmother in his life. It's the greatest gift you could give him."

FORTY-SIX

As soon as Jake had stepped outside to give Carly and Anna their privacy, he saw Litton in the driver's seat of the Lincoln, stripping off his tie.

The lawyer reached for the ignition key but Jake was faster. He rested both hands on the lower rim of the open car window, daring Litton to close it.

"If you don't mind, I was just leaving." The man glared up at Jake, making a pretense at politeness.

"I do mind.

"What you did today could very well lead to your being disbarred should Carly's lawyer make an issue of it. What possessed you to try to railroad Carly into giving up rather than to follow Anna's wishes?"

Litton sneered. "We were so *fucking* close. I knew we stood a chance of winning, even more after the kid took off. Then I got a phone call from Anna asking me to drive her up here to call the whole thing off." He shook his head. "Charles must be rolling in his grave. I don't know what the hell she was thinking or why she changed her mind."

"You have any kids, Litton?"

"Hell, no."

"Then you'll never know why."

Jake straightened and stepped away from the car. Litton started the motor and pulled out, squealing his tires as he rounded the corner.

Shoving his hands in his pockets, Jake stared at the pockmarked asphalt of the parking space.

"Woo hoo! Mr. Mont-gom-ery!"

Jake rolled his eyes before he turned around. Etta Schwartz was standing on her front porch, a wrinkled diva in a silk Chinese robe holding a plate covered with glistening plastic wrap.

"I made some brownies. Would you like one?" Her voice had a sing-song quality that made her sound like a retired pre-school teacher stuck on fast forward.

He glanced toward Carly's, but there was no sign of her or Anna yet, so he gave up and decided to commit suicide by chocolate.

"Is the coast clear over there?" Etta wanted to know.

"Pretty much."

"I didn't see that woman come out."

He sat down on the edge of her porch and took the plate from her hand, slipped off the plastic wrap. His mouth watered when the scent of chocolate hit him.

"She's still in there talking to Carly."

"Oh, my. Should I go knock on the door? I could bring out more brownies. Or scones. With currants."

He shook his head. "No. Anna's decided to file a dismissal. There'll be no hearing."

"Oh! My prayers have been answered." She lowered herself to the porch. Her poodle slipped through a tear in the bottom of the screen door and bounded onto her lap. It made a lunge for the plate.

Jake smoothly pulled it out of reach.

"Thank you, dear." Etta smiled up at him and actually batted her false eyelashes. "One bite of chocolate can kill a dog, you know."

As the poodle wriggled around and started panting dog breath in his face, Jake was tempted to see if that was true. Just then the Potters pulled into the parking space that Litton had just vacated. When Chris and Matt's faces appeared in the window of the backseat, Jake knew he wouldn't be eating the remaining two brownies.

Chris decided that this was just about the second best day in his whole life when he saw Jake waiting on Etta's porch. When Mr. Potter turned off the car engine, he opened the door and hopped out with Matt close on his heels as he ran over to Etta's.

"Hey! Jake! What are you doing here? Hi, Mrs. Schwartz."

"Hello, boys. Want some brownies?"

The Potters walked up behind them. Just as Chris would have predicted, Matt's mom said, "They just ate Happy Meals. They probably don't have room for brownies."

"Aw, Mom." Matt started whining on cue, and two seconds later, Mrs. Potter changed her mind. He had told Chris he had been getting his way ever since they ran off. Lately at school, Matt had been taking credit for the whole thing.

They sat beside Jake eating two brownies. Mrs. Schwartz went back inside to get some more. Chris stuffed half a brownie in his mouth and watched Jake get up to talk to the Potters.

The three grownups looked over at his house, then Jake walked a little ways away and started talking really softly to Matt's mom and dad. Chris started to worry until he heard Mr. Potter say, "That's great! That's absolutely wonderful!"

Then he knew that whatever Jake was talking about was okay.

Suddenly it hit him that maybe Jake was telling the Potters that he was going to marry Mom, but he didn't let himself get all excited. Jake hadn't been coming over much lately. He decided they were probably talking about the house that Jake was fixing up. The Potters were always talking about houses.

Chris finished his brownie and looked at Matt and started laughing at the crumbs all over his blood brother's face. He didn't think it was possible that this day could get any better.

Mr. Potter came to stand at the edge of the porch.

"Come on, Matt. We've got to go. Tell your mom hello, Chris."

Chris jumped up, too full to eat another brownie, but he took an extra to carry home with him.

"Thanks, Mr. Potter, for taking me to the movie and for the Happy Meal. Thanks, Mrs. Potter." He knew if he thanked them, he was more likely to get invited again. At least that's what Mom had taught him, and so far it was working.

He stood beside Jake and watched them drive away.

"D'you have fun?" Jake kept looking over at the house like

something was wrong, but Chris didn't think things could be wonderful and wrong at the same time.

"Yeah. The movie was way cool. It was about some kids who ended up stranded on a faraway planet. Where's Mom?"

"She's inside. Your grandma dropped by."

"My *grandma*? You mean Grandma Anna? From Long Beach?"

"That's the one."

"Oh, wow! Did you bring her?"

"No. She came on her own."

"Where's her car?"

"She got a ride. He left."

"Is she spending the night?"

Jake messed up his hair. "Why don't we go see?"

By the time they got to the front door, Beauty was there with her nose pressed to the screen whining and wagging her tail about a hundred miles a minute. Chris opened the door and let her kiss his face, forced to hand Jake his brownie so she wouldn't gobble it down. Etta warned him never, ever let Beauty eat chocolate.

Sure enough, his grandma was sitting on the sofa with Mom.

"Grandma Anna!" He raced over to her, not sure whether she'd like him to hug her or not, especially since he had crumbs on his hands.

"Hi, Mom." He hugged his mom because he knew no matter how dirty he was, she still loved hugs.

"Hi, Chris. Did you have a good time?"

"Yep." He was staring at his grandma, waiting for her to say something, but she looked like she was going to cry or throw up, he couldn't tell exactly which.

"Are you okay, Grandma?"

"I am now." Her lips wiggled like she was trying to smile.

He didn't wait for her to ask, he just leaned over and gave her a big hug and then a kiss on the cheek. She smelled really good, like flowers.

"Are you spending the night?" he asked.

That made her laugh. She looked at Mom who was smiling,

too. Grandma shook her head no. "Not tonight. I hadn't planned on it."

"You can sleep in my room with Beauty. I'll sleep on the sofa," he offered.

"No, thank you, sweetheart. I think I'll go back to Long Beach and get my guest room ready for you and your mother. She's promised to bring you down for a visit very soon."

He looked at Mom, not quite ready to believe it.

"Really?"

"Really," she assured him.

"Wow. Way cool."

Carly left Chris on the sofa with Anna. The two of them had their heads together discussing the advantages of having a dog while Carly walked Jake to his car.

Her whole life had just turned on a dime, and instead of being elated, she felt no different than she had an hour ago when Litton had knocked on the door.

"Shouldn't I feel really happy right now?" She mused aloud. "I think I should be jumping for joy, but I just feel sort of numb."

She closed her eyes for a second and shook her head.

Jake was at his car door now, his hand on the handle. "Does Anna need a ride to San Luis?"

Carly shook her head. "No. She's called for an airport limo. It'll be here in awhile."

He hesitated, as if awkward, at a loss for words. Then he said, "You're free now."

The words still didn't quite register. Maybe if they celebrated . . . she decided to take Christopher over to the Plaza Diner. He'd eaten, but he wouldn't turn down dessert. She couldn't wait to share the news with Selma and Joe. She'd call Geoff and tell him to join them.

"Would you like to go to dinner with us?" she asked Jake. "I think maybe a little celebration is in order."

He shook his head.

"I'm happy for you, Carly, but I've got some soul searching to do." He reached out and cupped her face.

"Jake, what is it? What's wrong?"

"Go celebrate with your friends. I'll call you later."

Despite the fact Jake wasn't there, joy began to bubble up inside her. So much so that by the time Anna's limo arrived and she and Chris took off for the Diner, she couldn't stop smiling.

Carly invited Etta and Geoff to dinner. Etta changed into an orange spandex cat suit that she draped with a calf-length purple vest. Geoff actually closed the gallery for an hour, and Joe promised to have his order ready when he arrived.

It was a quiet celebration since they couldn't openly talk about everything in front of Chris, but she had an opportunity to take Selma aside long enough to explain how she and Anna had made peace with one another.

The only one missing was Jake and Carly wondered why he had turned down the invitation to be with them.

After dinner she put Chris to bed, checked the cafeteria menu posted on the refrigerator, and packed him a lunch because he refused to eat mystery meat on mashed potatoes.

She was on her way into the studio when she saw the flash of headlights on the cinder block wall outside the window. When she heard a car pull up in front, she went to the door. Beauty came padding out of the bedroom but Carly gave her a gentle pat on the head and sent her back, thinking Jake couldn't have picked a better dog.

She opened the front door and watched him walking up to the porch. Without a word, she let him in, then reached up and looped her arms around his neck to let him know how glad she was to have him there.

He kissed her without hesitation. She kissed him back hoping that he could tell how much he meant to her, that he would know she didn't blame him for what happened.

The kiss ended all too soon when he pulled away. He ran his

fingers through her long hair, held it back off her face and stared down into her eyes.

"I love you, Carly."

She closed her eyes, savored those precious words.

"I love you, too." She had never said them to anyone in her life except Christopher. Never had an occasion to say them to anyone else. When she let go a ragged breath, her heart was full.

"Come on, I want to show you something." She grabbed his hand and led him toward the studio where she uncovered the painting she had finished that afternoon before Litton and Anna had arrived.

She let go of his hand while he studied the painting.

"Do you think Anna will like it? I have a few more touches to add before I give it to her."

He nodded slowly. "I think she would feel privileged to own it."

She crossed her arms and tried to be objective. The woman in the mantilla was still seated alone on the ornately carved bench on the bluff, but now a little boy in a short-waisted jacket, a wide brimmed hat, and pants with silver conchos up the side seam stood before her, holding her hands.

Not far away, a young woman in a gown with a flowing skirt with layers of flounces was setting out a picnic on a bright woven blanket.

Like the woman in the mantilla, the young woman's face was not completely visible, but there was a hint of a self-portrait there.

"I had just finished working on it before Anna arrived. It wasn't exactly the vision I had to begin with. I'd painted the older woman sitting alone, but the longer I worked, the more I became tempted to add the other two." She shrugged. "I'm not sure why. All I know is that something inside me refused to leave the woman mourning on the bluff alone."

"Do you know why?"

"My life has changed. Maybe my outlook has, too. I want my work to reflect that from now on." She reached for his hand.

"That's exactly what I've been thinking about, too. My work reflecting my life. Right now I don't much like what I do."

"What do you mean?"

"I almost ruined everything for you. And for Christopher."

"Jake, you know that if it hadn't been for you, if you hadn't come to Twilight to find me, to find us, then I'd still be living in fear of Anna, never knowing how or when she might track me down. You've given Chris and me a future that I can look forward to. You've given me more than I can ever thank you for."

"I don't deserve your thanks, Carly. After what I did, I don't deserve you."

"That's all behind us now, Jake."

He shook his head. "You're starting over, Carly. That's what I want, too. I want to start over with you." He pulled her into his arms, held her tight as he stared into her upturned face.

"Marry me, Carly."

"*What* did you just say?"

"Marry me. My world turned upside down the day I laid eyes on you. You were wearing an old pink sweatshirt and you'd just walked out of Potters' real estate office. I was having coffee at Sweetie's wondering if I'd been crazy to drive up here on a hunch."

"So you were *looking* at me that day. I couldn't tell."

He nodded. "Will you marry me?"

She put her hands on his shoulders, stared deep into his eyes, hoping he could gage the sincerity of her words.

"I can't, Jake. Not yet."

His face fell. "Why not? A minute ago you said you loved me."

"I do, but it's too soon to think about getting married."

He started to protest. "It wasn't too soon for last night . . ."

She placed her fingertips against his lips. "I need time, Jake. Time to adjust to being free. Time to learn to live with this newfound sense of freedom. It's been a struggle finding the strength within myself to stand up to Anna and *you* made that happen when you opened up my heart and my world again."

He tried to pull away, but she held him tight.

"I love you, Jake, but I need to live without the shadow of the past hanging over me. I need to call Wilt—maybe even go see him. Anna and I have things to work out, too. I need time to find out who *I* am, on my own, before I can make you any promises."

She didn't add that deep down she was afraid he was proposing out of a sense of obligation—perhaps to make up for the fact that he'd lied to her in the beginning. Maybe even because of his friendship with Rick.

As much as she needed time for herself, she wanted to give him time to step back, to change his mind if he needed to.

"How long?" he asked.

She wished she could tell him how much time she needed.

"I have no idea."

"Promise you'll let me know one way or the other. Don't leave me hanging forever."

As he brought his head down for another kiss, she doubted very much that a man like Jake Montgomery would wait for any woman forever.

FORTY-SEVEN

Late August hit Southern California with all the drama of a scripted Hollywood disaster. There was the usual round of dry heat and brush fires that set the stage for winter flooding along concrete riverbeds and mud slides on bare, parched hillsides. A magnitude four earthquake shook up all the tourists, but no one else seemed to notice.

The streets and freeways were more crowded than Carly remembered, but she had no trouble negotiating them when she and Christopher drove to Long Beach for their first official visit to Anna's.

Though Carly had intended to stay at a motel in nearby Surfside, Anna wouldn't hear of it and insisted they stay with her.

The penthouse high above the bay was overwhelming in and of itself, but when Carly saw the room Anna had decorated for Chris, a room complete with photos of Rick at all ages, a collection of his favorite childhood picture books, some old toys and sailing trophies, she found herself touched—even though she realized that Anna might have put the room together back when she had planned to win guardianship of Christopher.

Early in the morning on the fifth day of their stay, Anna suggested they visit the nearby Aquarium of the Pacific while it was still cool outside and not as crowded as it would be later in the day. Chris was wild with the excitement of seeing all types of colorful and exotic sea life up close.

They entered the lobby of the cavernous building housing enormous two-story tanks filled with various sea life. Sound echoed as visitors streamed inside.

"Come on, Grandma Anna," he cried, taking her by the hand and dragging her toward one of the winding staircases in the lobby.

"The man just announced there's a sea lion show starting up on the second level!"

Just then the cell phone that Jake had given Carly to use while she was on the road started ringing inside her straw bag. She smiled when she heard it, knowing it had to be Jake, because only he and Anna had the number.

"I'll catch up to you," she told Anna with a wave and found herself breathless as she pulled out the phone and flipped it open.

"Hello?"

"Miss me?" He sounded happy, confident, even though she'd not yet given him an answer to his proposal.

She smiled at the sound of his voice, walked over to where she could stand before a window displaying a tank full of salt water tropical fish.

"Who *is* this?" she teased.

"Very funny. You know damn well who this is."

"How can I miss you yet? We've only been gone five days."

"That's four too many."

"What are you doing? Are you at home?" She liked to picture him sitting on the wide porch of the old house slowly rocking in one of his new rockers.

"I was just going out for lunch."

"Tell Selma hi for me."

"I'm not going to the diner."

"Oh."

"Want to join me?"

"Sounds good, but I don't think I could get there in time."

"Look up, Carly."

"What?" She craned her neck, stared up at the huge, life-sized whale sculpture hanging above the lobby.

"Not *that* far up. Look over at the window in front of the gift shop, just inside the entrance turnstiles."

Her breath caught when she turned completely around and saw him standing there holding his cell phone to his ear. In a blue polo shirt and a pair of khaki cargo shorts, he stood head and shoulders above most of the tourists. A shaft of light from the overhead windows highlighted his dark hair.

When he waved and started toward her, her heart skipped a beat.

Flipping her phone shut, she dropped it into her bag and hurried to meet him, threading her way through a small huddle of students being herded through the lobby by a docent.

Unexpected joy welled up inside her and spilled over. She stood on tiptoe as he gave her a quick kiss hello.

"What are you doing in town? How did you know we were here?"

"I'm back because I have a court date tomorrow morning on a forgery case, and I tracked you down because I'm still a hell of a P.I."

"Oh, really?"

"Actually, I called this morning, and Anna said you were in the shower. She told me you were all coming down here this morning, so I decided to surprise you. I've got time to see the aquarium and then have a quick bite with all of you." He looked around. "Where are they?"

"Up on the second level watching the sea lions."

"Great. Anna said that she wouldn't mind sitting with Chris tonight. I'd like to take you out for dinner on my home turf."

"You mean, as in a *real* date?"

"Yeah. Since I've already proposed, I figured I ought to take you out officially once." He had been giving her all the space and time she'd asked for, so much that she found that she missed seeing him. If that was part of his strategy, it was working.

It wasn't in her nature to play games. He wanted to take her out. She wanted to go.

"How can I say no?"

He'd chosen Lashers, one of his favorite Long Beach restaurants. Not because it was located in an old Craftsman bungalow on Broadway, but because they served a tender, juicy cut of prime rib and Yukon gold mashed potatoes.

Nervous as a kid on prom night, Jake wanted the evening to be perfect, and so far, so good. They were seated at a table for two in the corner near the window where they could look out over the small patio/garden area on the street. White twinkle lights showered the trees, giving the whole place a magical glow.

Carly looked stunning in a simple black summer sheath and low-heeled sandals, her cheeks aglow with color she'd picked up sunning and swimming on the beach. Her hair was streaked with sunshine, her lips so tempting not even mashed Yukons could take his mind off them.

The waiter cleared their plates at the end of the meal. Carly turned down dessert, and so did he, preferring to finish the last of the wine.

They spoke of friends in Twilight. He talked about how he had been looking into opening another branch of his firm in San Luis Obispo.

"From now on I don't intend to do anything but background checks, handwriting analyses, and embezzlement investigations. Maybe I'll try to prove an insurance scam now and again, but no more marital surveillance, no more domestic abuse or custody cases. No more cashing in on other peoples' misery."

Carly leaned forward. Candlelight played over her cheekbones. "Is that what you meant by changing the focus of your work?"

"Exactly," he said. "I don't want to have to cope with the way I feel when I sit someone down and tell them exactly when and how their spouse has been cheating on them. I want to believe in the other fifty percent of marriages. Not only that, but I want to believe in all the things I used to believe in before life and my job stole them away."

He reached across the table for her hands. Rubbing his thumb over her knuckles, he looked into the depths of her eyes and could tell she was searching his for sincerity.

He hoped he didn't come up lacking.

"What do *you* want out of a marriage, Carly?"

She took a deep breath, looked thoughtful. "To be a part of

something bigger than myself and yet have the freedom to be myself, too. I want someone who will accept Christopher as his son."

To Marla, freedom meant the right to be with other men, but he knew exactly the kind of freedom Carly wanted and he was more than willing to guard her right to have it.

"You already know how I feel about Christopher," he said.

"I do."

"I'd never try to change you, Carly."

"I know."

"Although I *might* try to persuade you to quit working at the diner and concentrate on your career full time." He pictured her in the Craftsman house, painting in the extra room downstairs, out on the deck, or the front porch. Anywhere her heart desired.

"That would be a dream come true."

"I think you know what I'm offering you. A lifetime of love. Commitment. Friendship. I'd be a father to Christopher. You deserve happiness tied up with a great big bow, and that's what I want to give you, if you'll have me."

They had just cleared the front steps at Lashers and were headed for the low gate in the white picket fence surrounding the restaurant when a shapely young woman walked up, opened the gate for them, and waited as they exited.

She was wearing a short, white knit sleeveless dress that fit like a second skin and accentuated her deep golden tan and coal black hair.

Carly couldn't help but envy the woman's stunning legs. They were sensuously shaped by weight training, not in the least masculine, but definitely worthy of a second look.

There was an attractive tilt to her almond-shaped eyes and an unexpected smattering of freckles across the bridge of her nose.

She gave Carly a quick once-over before she handed Jake a manila folder and asked, "Is this her?"

"Mind your manners, Kat."

"So you're Carly. I have to hand it to you. I never thought any-one would ever tie this guy up in knots, but you managed."

"Thank you." Carly smiled, trying not to let her amazement show. "I take it you're Kat Vargas?" She extended her hand. Kat's grip was firm, secure. The young woman never once looked away.

"Carly, this is my partner, Kat Vargas. Kat, Carly."

"Thought I'd just drop off the file you'll need for your court appointment in the morning," Kat told Jake.

"Thanks. I could have picked it up when I got back to the office."

"I thought you might be late, or maybe not in at all." Again she eyed Carly carefully. "Jake, why don't you go get your car? I'll wait with Carly. That way we'll have a moment alone, for some girl talk."

"Do you think I've lost my mind?" He was smiling but com-pletely serious about not leaving them.

"Most of the time, actually. Go."

Curious about what Kat Vargas had to say, Carly encouraged him to leave. "Go ahead, Jake. I'll wait here until you pull up to the corner."

Once Jake was out of earshot, Kat wasted no time. The private investigator wasn't at all the way Carly had pictured her.

"Listen," Kat began, flipping her hair back over her shoulder, "I'll make this short and sweet. That guy is crazy for you. I just wanted to let you know that if you hurt him, you'll have to answer to me. Is that clear?"

"Perfectly, but you know something, Kat?"

"What?"

"I think Jake's very capable of taking care of himself."

Kat sniffed. "Not where you're concerned. I think he had a thing for you before he ever laid eyes on you. Just make sure you don't leave him dangling too long if the answer to his proposal is no. And give me a call if you turn him down so I can pick up the pieces."

Before Carly could respond, Jake's car rolled up to the curb. When she turned around, the young woman was already walk-ing away.

Jake got out, came around and opened the car door for Carly.

"So that was your partner." She watched Kat jaywalk across the street and head for a small, red SUV. Her hair bounced with every step.

"Yeah. Pain in the ass." Jake put the car in drive and pulled away from the curb, heading down Broadway.

Carly could tell by his tone he was only kidding. It was easy to see that he thought the world of Kat Vargas.

"She's *gorgeous*. You never told me she was gorgeous, Jake."

"Is she?" His gaze flicked to the rearview mirror and back to the road ahead. "I never noticed."

"You must be kidding."

"I'm not. Besides, I know her too well. She's like a kid sister or something."

"I think she's in love with you." She'd never been jealous of anyone in her life, but she realized with a shock that if the streak of possessiveness rearing its ugly head was any indication, then she was jealous of Kat.

She had never loved anyone enough to be jealous before.

"Kat doesn't love anybody." Jake sounded offhanded but certain.

Carly very seriously doubted it.

They drove straight back to Anna's, and Jake pulled up to the curb and parked. It was a little after ten-thirty. The temperature had dropped to a comfortable level, the air was scented with the sea. As they drove over the bridge at Second and Bayshore, Jake pointed out the phosphorescence caused by red tide glowing in the boat wakes.

Carly was touched that Jake had driven her back to Anna's right after dinner—as if they really were on a first date—and yet she was disappointed that their evening together was already over.

Jake didn't make any move to hurry and sat back, rested his arm on the driver's side door, and appeared content to sit and look at her.

"When will you be going back to Twilight?" she asked.

"I hope my testimony will be over in a day, and I can head up before the weekend. Are you still planning to drive out to Borrego first?"

"We're leaving day after tomorrow really early in the morning, so that we'll be there before it's too hot."

It was over 115 degrees in the shade in the desert. Most of the shops and stores were either closed for the season, or they'd be closed all afternoon. She'd called Wilt's old number, found him still there, still painting, and excited to see her and Chris.

"We're only going to stay three days. If Wilt has any of my paintings left, I thought I'd take them back to Twilight with me."

"Will you put them up for sale in the gallery?"

She shook her head, thought back to those years and all she'd learned experimenting with style and color. "No, I don't think so. Some people keep journals. I have those paintings to remind me of the years I spent in the desert."

The silence lengthened, full of words unspoken, Jake's proposal almost a viable entity between them. More than anything, Carly wished she could give him an answer tonight, that she could, in all good conscience, say that she would marry him, but the two biggest decisions she'd ever made in her life had resulted in terrible consequences—she'd witnessed Caroline's death and ended up running from the Saunders for years. Although Jake was convinced that he loved her, and she was certain that she loved him, she wanted to believe that if their love was true, it would still be there when she was ready to tell him yes.

He took her hand. "Thanks for tonight, Carly. I needed to see you again. I'm not going to deny that I've missed you."

"I've missed you, too." She leaned over the armrest to touch his face, and he took it as a sign that she wanted more. He slipped his arm around her, drew her close, and kissed her long and deep, kissed her until they were both breathless and clinging to each other for support.

She moaned against his lips when his hand cupped her breast.

Frustrated by the console between the bucket seats, Jake groaned aloud and ended the kiss, leaned back and ran his hand through his hair with a sigh.

"Either you go inside now, or I'm taking you over to my condo. It's two minutes away." His deep voice sounded thick with desire.

More than tempted to tell him to start the car, she reached for him again, framed his face between her palms and kissed him good-bye with a kiss that was chaste but full of longing.

"I'll see you in Twilight," she promised.

"I'll be waiting."

Carly found Anna waiting, although she tried to convince her that she'd only stayed up to watch the news. She invited Carly to join her where they could see the lights of the city from the lush white couches near the bank of windows. The sliding doors were open to the cool night, the scent of the salt air, and the sounds of the city.

A siren sounded as a fire truck pulled out of the station a block away. The shrill whine faded into the distance. Anna turned off the television.

"Do you love him, Carly?"

"I do, Anna. No question. He's asked me to marry him."

"What do you want?"

What do I want? "I want to be sure. More than that, I want Jake to be sure. He had a bad experience the first time he married. I don't want him marrying me out of some mixed-up sense of obligation to Rick or to me."

Anna shifted and tightened the sash on her silk robe. "The expression I've seen in his eyes when he looks at you isn't that of a man who's with you out of obligation." She paused as if debating what she was about to say. "Do you mind if I give you a piece of advice, Carly?"

"Not at all, though I can't guarantee I'll take it."

"Life is short. If he's the man you want to spend the rest of your life with, don't wait. There were things that happened to me in my childhood that were . . . bleak, things I thought would cloud my whole life. But I found out that it's all right to be happy, Carly. Don't ever forget that sometimes you have to grab all the happiness you can with both hands."

"Thank you, Anna. And thank you for letting me spend this time here in your beautiful home. I know you love Christopher, just as I know now what I must have put you through when I disappeared. All I can say is that I'm sincerely sorry."

"So am I, Carly, but the past is behind us now."

They sat in easy silence, content with the night, the company, and perhaps for the first time in a long, long while, their lives.

Anna's voice broke the stillness again. "Did Jake ever tell you what was in the envelope that he gave me that day at your house?"

"No, and I never asked. Besides, as you just said, the past is behind us. Both of us. Now we both have the future to look forward to with Christopher."

FORTY-EIGHT

Anna spent most of late summer moving from one air-conditioned environment to the other, thankful to be living at the beach where the temperature usually became bearable in the evenings. After dark, she liked to turn off the air, open the bank of windows and enjoy her balcony.

The penthouse echoed with emptiness now that Carly and Christopher were gone. The week they had spent with her had been one of the best times she'd had in years. So much so that when they drove away in the old rattletrap station wagon, she had to fight crying like a baby.

Now, two weeks later, she was adding her own touch to a floral arrangement that had just been delivered when the call buzzer rang and she answered it, thinking it was probably the floral delivery boy again.

It turned out to be the UPS courier.

When the sturdy young woman who made all the deliveries had no trouble hefting the unwieldy package into the foyer, Anna promised her an extra tip if she would pry open the huge, elongated yet slender box with Carly's return address neatly printed on the outside.

The moment the painting was unwrapped, both Anna and the courier stepped back to take it in.

The courier crossed her arms and shook her head. "That frame doesn't match anything you've got."

Anna ignored the plain white wooden frame. That could be replaced. She only had eyes for the artwork itself. The longer she studied the painting, the more it moved her.

She recognized the bluff at Twilight Cove and the panoramic

view beyond, but it was the older woman seated on the bench and the child holding her hands as he stared adoringly into her face that constantly drew her eye.

The figures appeared quite ghostly, executed in a white overlay that was somehow transparent and otherworldly, yet at the same time, substantial and full of life. The scene depicted life in the early eighteen-hundreds at a time when the Californios lived like royalty.

She was not much given to flights of fancy and would never have chosen a painting peopled with ethereal figures such as these, and yet she couldn't take her eyes off of the work.

"Ma'am?" The courier was growing impatient.

Anna walked around behind the painting. A label on the back listed the date, Carly's name, and the simple title, *Familia*.

She appreciated the stranger in her foyer seeing her sudden rush of tears.

"That's a portrait of me," she said when she found her voice at last. Anna pointed to the child in the painting. "And that's my grandson."

Finally she pointed to the young woman seated on the ground near the wide roots of the tree.

"And that," she said softly, "is my daughter."

A few days ago, Carly had shipped Anna's painting to Long Beach, wondering if Anna would find it suitable—until a huge bouquet of roses arrived this morning along with a card that read, "Words cannot express my thanks. Love, Grandma Anna."

Now Carly was delivering another completed piece, one she wanted to present in person. She glanced in the rearview mirror and then adjusted the air conditioning. It was still hard to believe that Anna had bought them a new car.

Carly had refused the offer when she was in Long Beach, but at the beginning of their first week back in Twilight, the dealer from San Luis Obispo had left the keys on her porch and the new black Volvo wagon parked in front of the house.

She called Anna and insisted she would make the car payments, only to be told that the car was already paid for. Besides, Anna had added, it was really for Christopher. She wanted him riding around in a safe, dependable car. Carly finally gave up and graciously accepted.

As the car easily wound up the hillside along Lover's Lane toward Jake's drive, Carly turned up the radio and sang along with Trisha Yearwood, hoping to drown out her mounting anticipation.

She hadn't seen Jake in more than passing since she and Chris returned. Twilight was overrun with tourists. The Diner was crowded most of the time and Geoff had begged her to work for him on Sunday afternoons, so she agreed.

Jake had taken her and Christopher out for tacos once, but the conversation had been strained. Jake was still waiting for an answer from the owners of the house as well as from her.

She kept busy, taking on extra work hours at the diner, but with August half over, she wasn't sure if or when Jake would be leaving to return to Long Beach, and the more she thought about his being so far away, the worse she felt.

When she pulled into the drive, she was disappointed that his car wasn't there. She parked anyway, anxiety mounting as she lifted the painting wrapped in brown paper out of the car and walked up to the front door.

Jake had painted the porch floor a high gloss eggshell. Two tall rockers sat side by side facing the view.

She rang the bell twice, but no one answered. She tried the knob and found it unlocked so she opened it, called out hello a few times and walked in.

She hadn't been there in weeks, so when she looked around the living room, she was amazed at the transformation. The hardwood oak floors gleamed golden beneath streams of sunlight. Two white love seats flanked the fireplace. Between them Jake had placed a distressed plank coffee table, and in front of the window there was a deep, overstuffed chair with a small reading table piled high with books beside a kerosene lamp.

When she saw it, a chill ran down her spine.

Letting her gaze roam over the rest of the room, she noticed that the space above the fireplace mantel was empty.

She glanced at her watch before she set the painting down on the floor in front of the empty fireplace and wished she had time to wait for him, but Selma needed her at the diner in forty minutes.

With a last look around, she walked out and closed the door behind her.

Frustrated by not finding Carly at home, Jake walked through his front door and tossed his keys on the coffee table. Then he spotted the package wrapped in brown paper tied with twine resting in front of the fireplace. He guessed by its shape and size that it had to be a painting from Carly and wondered why she hadn't waited until she could give it to him in person.

A wave of disappointment swept him as he picked it up, carried it to the dining table and carefully unwrapped it, afraid that it was meant as a gesture of consolation, that she'd finally created a sunset painting for him as a fitting ending to their relationship.

The frame was dark oak, done in simple Craftsman style to match the house. First he carefully studied the sunset sky, vibrant with streaks of color from bright gold to deep indigo before he carried the painting over to the mantel and stepped back to take in the whole piece.

At first he was surprised that she hadn't chosen the setting of the bluff in town. Instead, she'd captured the exact view of the sunsets that he enjoyed from his front porch. She had also included the house in the painting, the rolling hillside and deep arroyos surrounding it.

Rendered in her near-transparent technique, a Model A Ford from the 1920s was parked in front of the house. There were two tall rockers on the porch, a lamp with a glass chimney burning bright on a table in the window. He'd just bought an identical lamp last week, and he knew for certain that there was no way Carly could have known about it.

Every detail of the painting was perfect. He was deeply moved by the care she'd taken to depict the house exactly the way it must have looked when first built.

It was a wonderful painting, a very personal one with such special meaning that it almost hurt to see it. If indeed she was turning down his proposal, he doubted he could ever hang the painting at all, for it would stir up too many memories.

He didn't know what to think as he continued to stare between the house and the Model A, and then he finally let his gaze sweep the entire canvas.

What he saw next nearly brought him to his knees.

A couple clothed in 1920's style stood together on the hillside, staring out to sea. The woman's head rested on the man's shoulder. Their arms were draped around each others' waists in a tender pose that spoke of time-forged affection.

Beyond them, highlighted by the sunset, a boy and a spotted dog chased a ball across the grassy hillside.

Jake stared intently at the painting just to be certain he wasn't seeing what he wanted to see, but the three ghostly figures were really there.

The house echoed with the sound of his hurried footsteps as he grabbed his car keys and headed for the door.

There was a line for lunch at Plaza Diner.

Tourists wearing all manner of shorts, tank tops, swimsuit cover-ups, and straw hats milled around in front, waiting for a table. Others were crammed inside the front door, taking advantage of the air conditioning.

Carly was balancing a tray with four orders of hamburger combos and two small salads, heading across the room to a booth by the window when she noticed a tall man in a dark gray felt hat, sunglasses and a rumpled khaki trench coat with the collar turned up. He had just stepped through the front door into the crowded waiting area.

She looked away as she balanced the tray on the edge of the table and started handing out plates of food, but something compelled her to glance over her shoulder and take a second look at the man. His back was to her now, and he appeared to be talking to a stocky woman beside him.

Carly thought it odd that he hadn't removed his sunglasses once he stepped inside, but she figured he was up from L.A., and there was no telling what people from down there were into.

Once all the meals had been delivered, and she was certain the family at the table was satisfied for the moment, she started to inquire at the next booth down the line if anyone needed anything else, when Selma walked up to her.

"Who's the weirdo in line?" she asked Carly.

"How would I know? Do you think we should have Joe call the police and have them check him out?"

The guy was really starting to creep her out. He had a spiral notebook in his hand and he appeared to be scribbling notes as he moved through the tight knot of customers waiting to be seated.

"I'm just going to go over and ask him right out who he is and what he's doing. He reminds me of somebody."

"Me too," Carly admitted.

"I'm thinking the guy looks like Tom Selleck on the old *Magnum P.I.* reruns, but his outfit is more like *Columbo*."

"Who?"

"You're too young. Never mind." Selma started across the room and Carly tried to concentrate on the customers at her tables. When she glanced over at Selma again, she noticed her boss had her arms crossed beneath her ample breasts. She was rolling her eyes and shaking her head as she spoke to the tall man standing directly in front of her. He was, indeed, jotting something down on a small tablet.

It wasn't until he turned Carly's way that she realized with a jolt it was Jake and that Selma was laughing.

Before Carly could move, he shoved the notebook into one of the baggy pockets of his trench coat and came striding toward her.

"What are you doing?" She glanced around and noticed that a lot more customers were staring at him now. He made a tall, imposing figure in the long coat, hat, and glasses, especially on such a warm day.

"I'm working a case."

"What are you talking about? What case?"

"I'm looking for a beautiful blonde. Twenty-six, goes by the name Carly Nolan. She's got a six-year-old boy and she's quite an accomplished artist. She just left one of her paintings up at my house, and I'd like to talk to her about it."

Carly realized the customers at the table beside her were all listening intently, so she lowered her voice, hoping he'd do the same.

"Jake, take off that ridiculous outfit."

"Can't. I'm on the job. Private Investigator Montgomery. Tracking down the woman he loves."

She closed her eyes and shook her head, then opened her eyes and reached for his sunglasses, slipped them off and handed them to him.

He dropped them into the gaping pocket of his overcoat.

"So, do you know where I can find her?"

"That depends on what you want her for." She folded her arms and bit the insides of her cheeks to keep from laughing.

"Watch it, there are kids at this table," he said softly.

By now Selma had walked over to stand beside Jake. Some of the people waiting by the door had eased closer, too. The whole restaurant had gone silent, the clatter of utensils, the hum of conversation, the ringing of Joe's order bell, had all faded away.

"I need to find out if I got the message straight," he told Carly.

"The message?"

"I think that she was trying to give me a message in her painting. I think that it means she'll marry me."

"I think you're right."

He took off his hat and coat and handed them over to Selma, who was now beaming at them. Joe had walked out of the kitchen and was standing there watching the exchange in his grease-spattered white apron with a spatula in his hand.

"And how would you know for certain unless you *are* Carly

Nolan?" He put both hands at the small of her back and pulled her close.

Carly glanced around, her cheeks blazing. Everyone in the room was intent upon their conversation.

"Jake, not here," she whispered.

She had no idea he'd been untying her apron until he pulled it off and handed that to Selma, too. Then he picked her up, kissed her long and slow and sweet right in front of a diner full of people before he turned to Selma again.

"Can you call in someone to cover her shift?"

"Jake, put me down." Carly made a half-hearted attempt to get out of his arms.

He ignored her.

"I've got a girl on standby," Selma assured him over Carly's protest.

"Great. Thanks, Selma." He gave Selma a quick kiss on the cheek and then with Carly in his arms, headed for the front door.

The pudgy woman in powder-blue shorts and a matching over-sized T-shirt grabbed hold of his sleeve. Jake turned with Carly still in his arms.

"Hey, aren't you that private investigator who was on the television news a while back? I'd like to talk to you about finding my husband. He's behind on his child support and—"

"Sorry, ma'am. We've got a couple of pressing appointments."

He moved past the woman, through the rest of the crowd, and opened the wide glass door to the street. Late summer's heat hit them as they left the air-conditioned diner. Carly had given up trying to get him to put her down and wrapped her arms around his neck.

As they stood there beneath the shade of the Plaza Diner's crisp, blue canvas awning, with the gulls calling out across the street at the park and a steady stream of tourists strolling by, she ignored everyone and everything but Jake as she smiled into his eyes.

"Pressing appointments?" she asked.

"Right. First we've got to head over to Etta's to pick up our boy, and then we're due over to the Potters' office to sign some escrow papers. I made a ridiculously low offer on the house, and the owners accepted it. I was hoping you'd give me an answer before I went ahead with the deal, but you were running out of time."

"How much time did I have left?"

"Actually, only a few hours."

"What if I hadn't left the painting for you today?"

He tightened his hold.

"Hey, I'm a P.I. I'd have gotten an answer out of you before time ran out."

EPILOGUE

Late October

A bitterly cold wind swept down off the mountains in the distance as Carly stood beside Jake in a deserted cemetery on the outskirts of Albuquerque. She slipped one hand through the crook of his arm and with the other, pulled her coat tighter, trying to ward off the long-forgotten chill of the high desert plains.

A field of grave sites stretched before them, ninety percent of them were marked with small, nondescript white crosses, but the grave at their feet had a newly laid granite headstone.

They stood side by side in silence. There was no need for words.

Jake stared out towards the Sangre de Cristo Mountains while Carly studied the stone, reading the inscription over and over.

CAROLINE GRAHAM

1974–1993

FRIEND AND SISTER

"Do you like it?" Jake asked softly. "I wasn't certain what you would have chosen, but I wanted to surprise you with this, so I tried to pick a design I thought you'd like."

"It's perfect. How did you find her?"

"Same way I found you. Persistence." He gave her a few more moments and then asked, "Are you ready to go?"

She nodded, tightened her hold on his arm, finally able to look away from the headstone.

"You're so quiet. What are you thinking?" he asked as they started walking slowly toward the rental car he'd parked nearby.

"That I'd love to be able to stay here for a while and paint, maybe walk around Santa Fe, take in the colors, the sights and sounds. The landscape is so raw. It's bleak; it's beautiful. Look at the way the passing clouds change the colors of the desert floor as they move over the land."

"We'll come back," he promised. "We'll bring Christopher and stay a while. How about over Christmas vacation?"

She shook her head. "It's our first Christmas together. Our first with Anna, and with your family, too. I want to be home."

"Somehow I knew you'd say that. Do you think she'll be ready to hand Chris over when we get back to California tomorrow?"

He'd only taken the weekend off. Starting up another office in San Luis Obispo took a lot of his time, but he was no longer as driven as he'd been when he started out before. Now he had Carly and Christopher, and he was bound and determined to give as much time to his marriage as needed to keep them both happy.

And he had the house overlooking the water to look forward to after the drive home through the canyon.

The house. Carly. And Chris.

Carly was smiling as he opened her car door. "Did you see the look on Anna's face when we dropped off Beauty, too? I'd say she probably has Chris' things already packed."

"I think you're right."

He waited when she paused to look back over the field of graves one final time, then she got into the car and he closed the door.

As he started the engine and slowly pulled away from the curb, he looked over at his wife and thought he heard her whisper, "Good-bye, Caroline. Thank you."